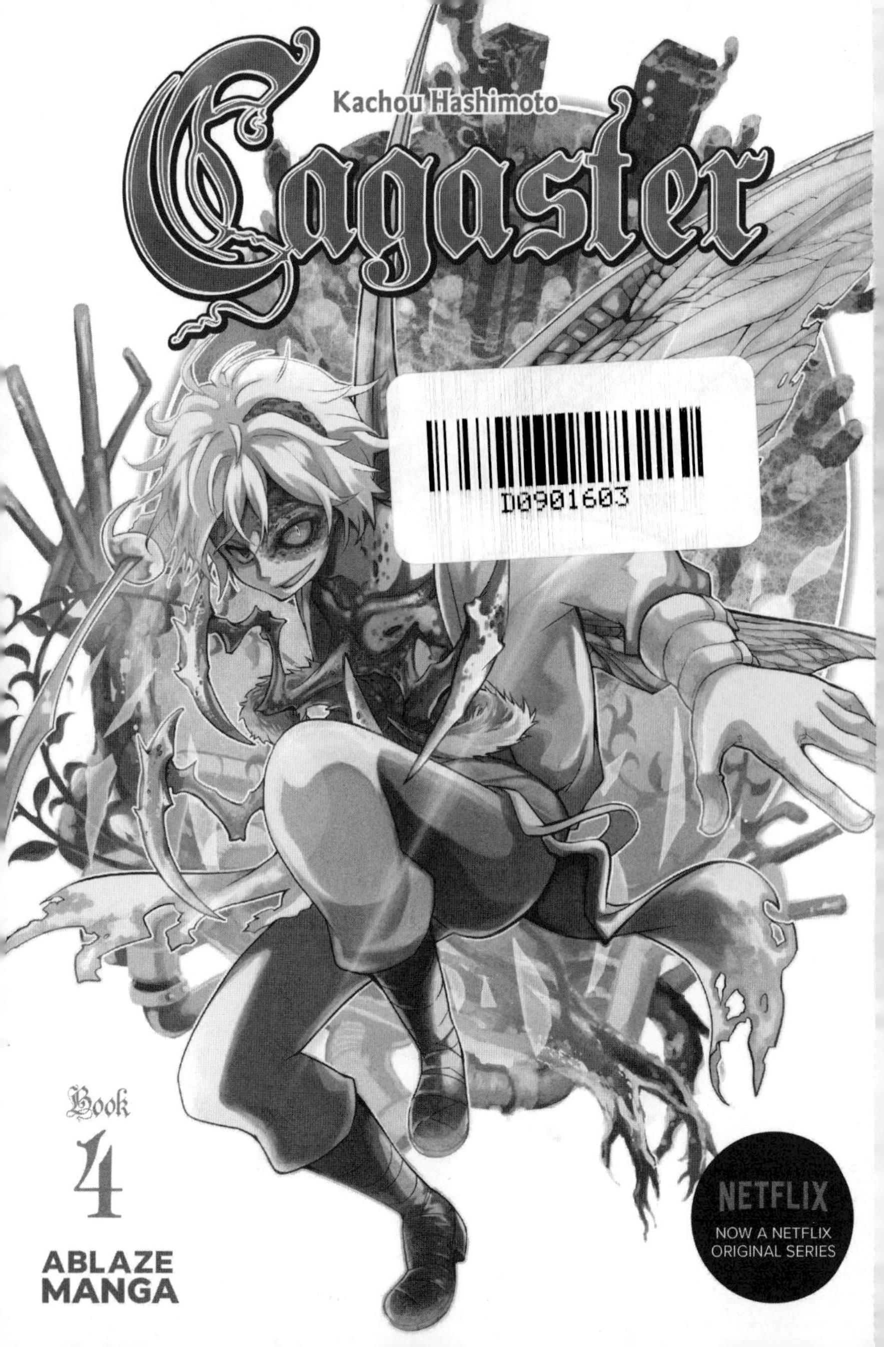
Kachou Hashimoto
Cagaster
Book
4
ABLAZE
MANGA
NETFLIX
NOW A NETFLIX
ORIGINAL SERIES

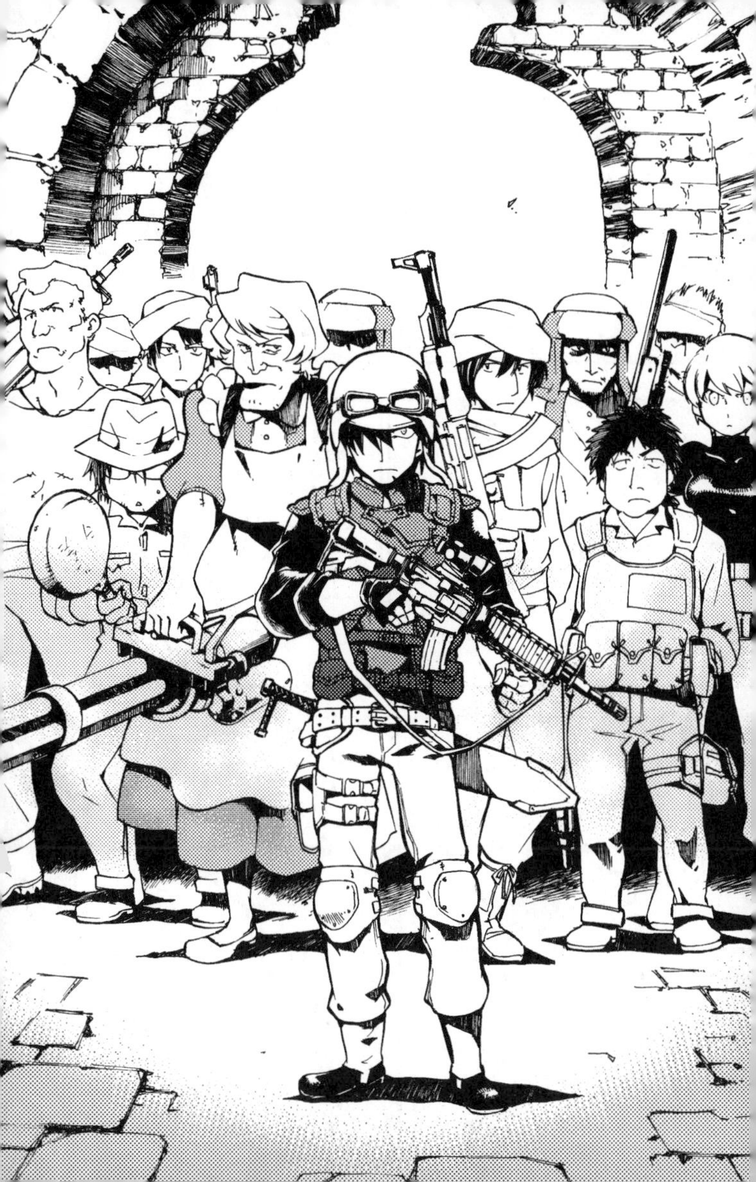

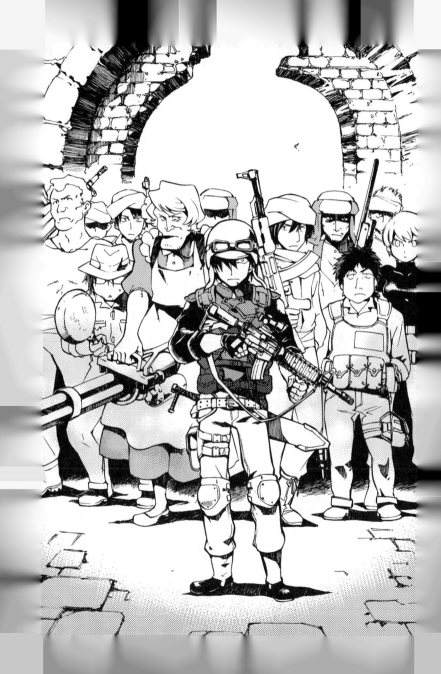

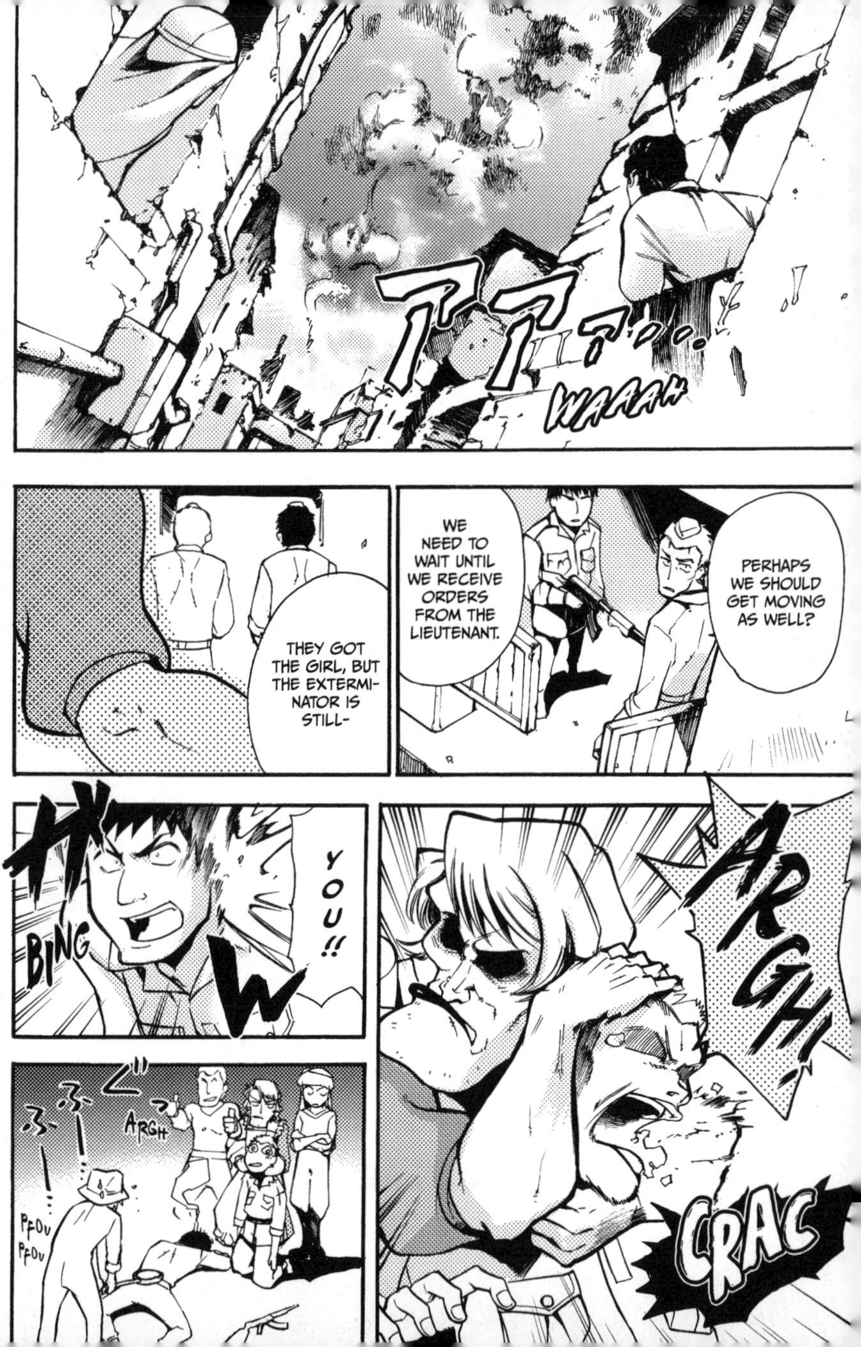
WAAAH
PERHAPS WE SHOULD GET MOVING AS WELL?
WE NEED TO WAIT UNTIL WE RECEIVE ORDERS FROM THE LIEUTENANT.
THEY GOT THE GIRL, BUT THE EXTERMINATOR IS STILL-
ARGH!
CRAC
YOU!!
BING
ARGH
PFOU
PFOU

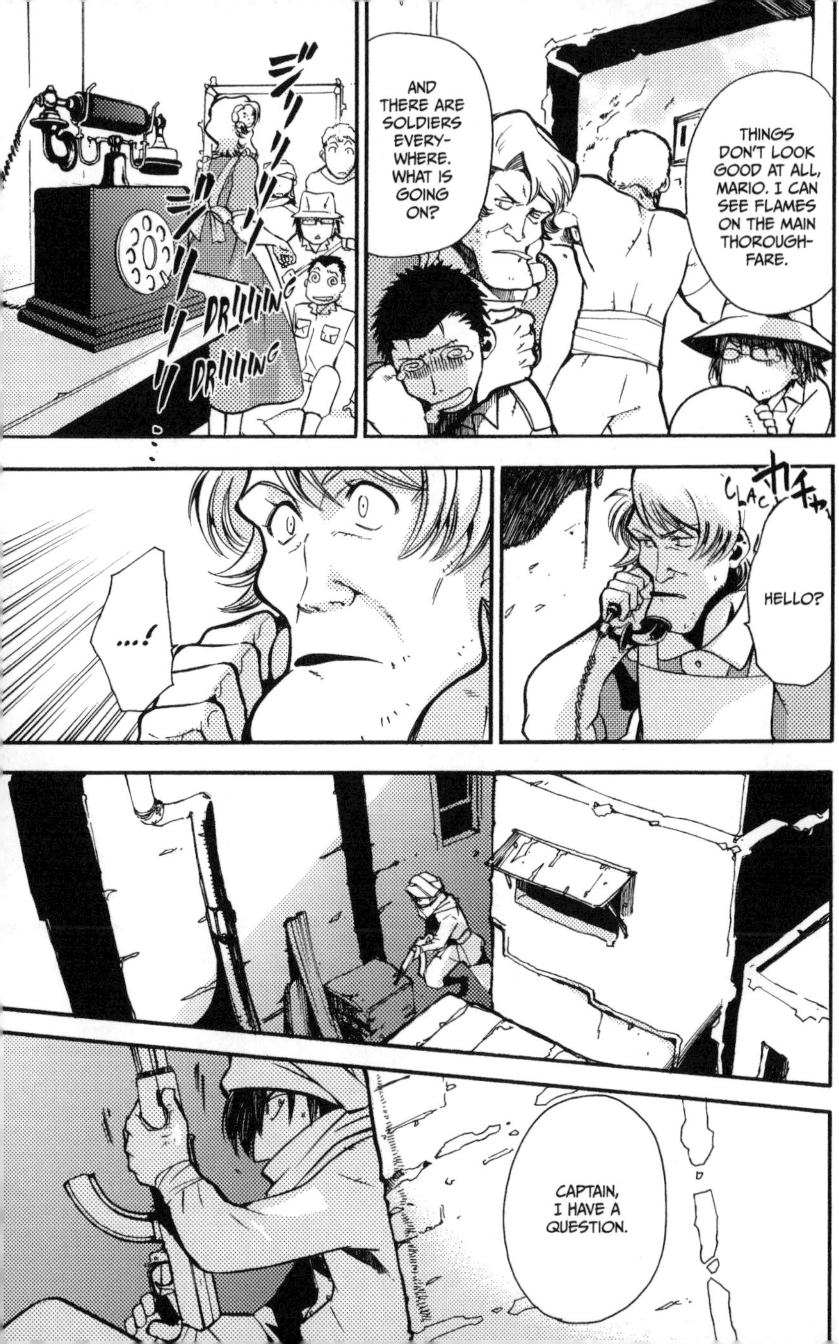
THINGS DON'T LOOK GOOD AT ALL, MARIO. I CAN SEE FLAMES ON THE MAIN THOROUGH-FARE.
AND THERE ARE SOLDIERS EVERY-WHERE. WHAT IS GOING ON?
DRIIIING
DRIIIING
CLACK
HELLO?
...!
CAPTAIN, I HAVE A QUESTION.

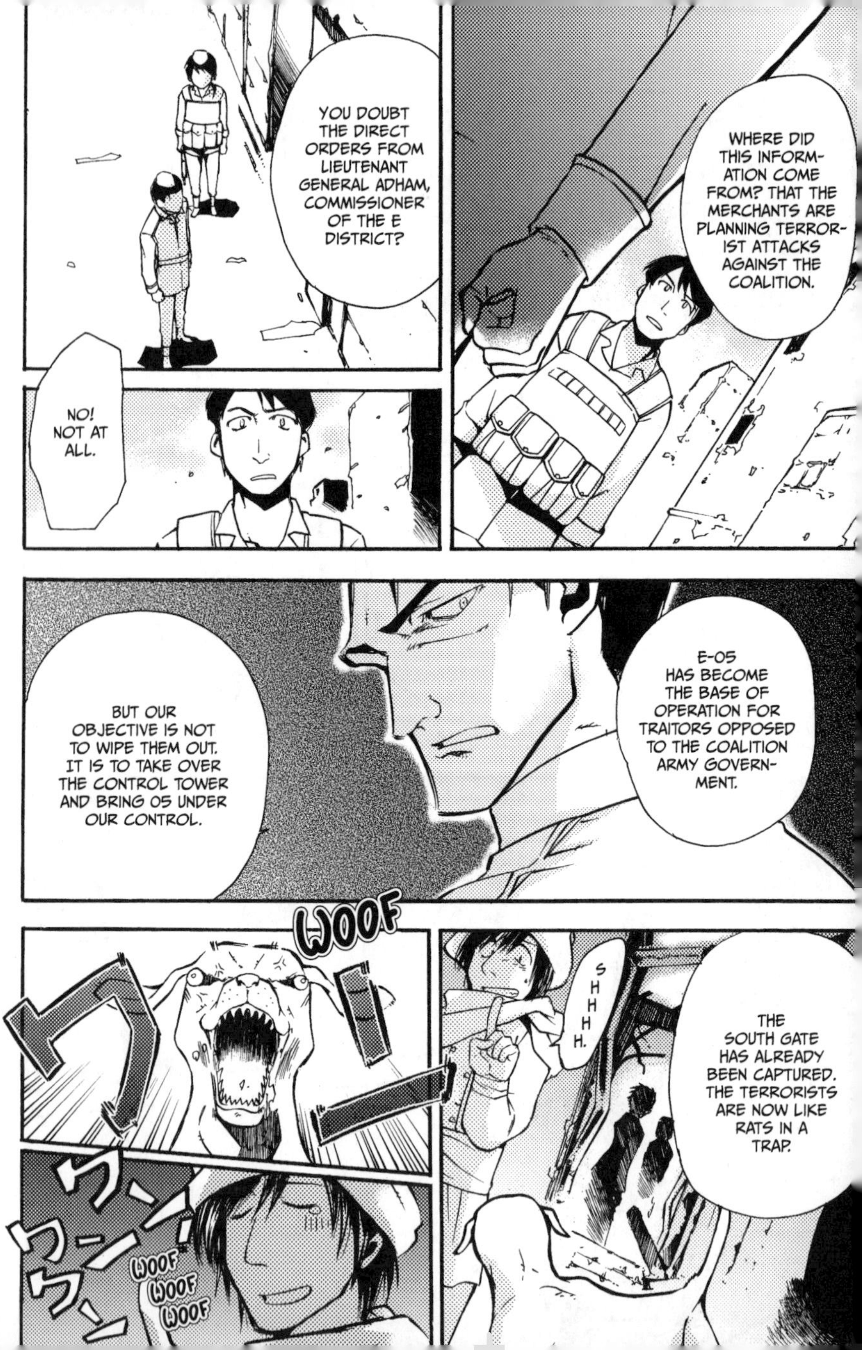
WHERE DID THIS INFORMATION COME FROM? THAT THE MERCHANTS ARE PLANNING TERRORIST ATTACKS AGAINST THE COALITION.
YOU DOUBT THE DIRECT ORDERS FROM LIEUTENANT GENERAL ADHAM, COMMISSIONER OF THE E DISTRICT?
NO! NOT AT ALL.
E-05 HAS BECOME THE BASE OF OPERATION FOR TRAITORS OPPOSED TO THE COALITION ARMY GOVERNMENT.
BUT OUR OBJECTIVE IS NOT TO WIPE THEM OUT. IT IS TO TAKE OVER THE CONTROL TOWER AND BRING 05 UNDER OUR CONTROL.
THE SOUTH GATE HAS ALREADY BEEN CAPTURED. THE TERRORISTS ARE NOW LIKE RATS IN A TRAP.
SHHHH.
WOOF
WOOF WOOF WOOF

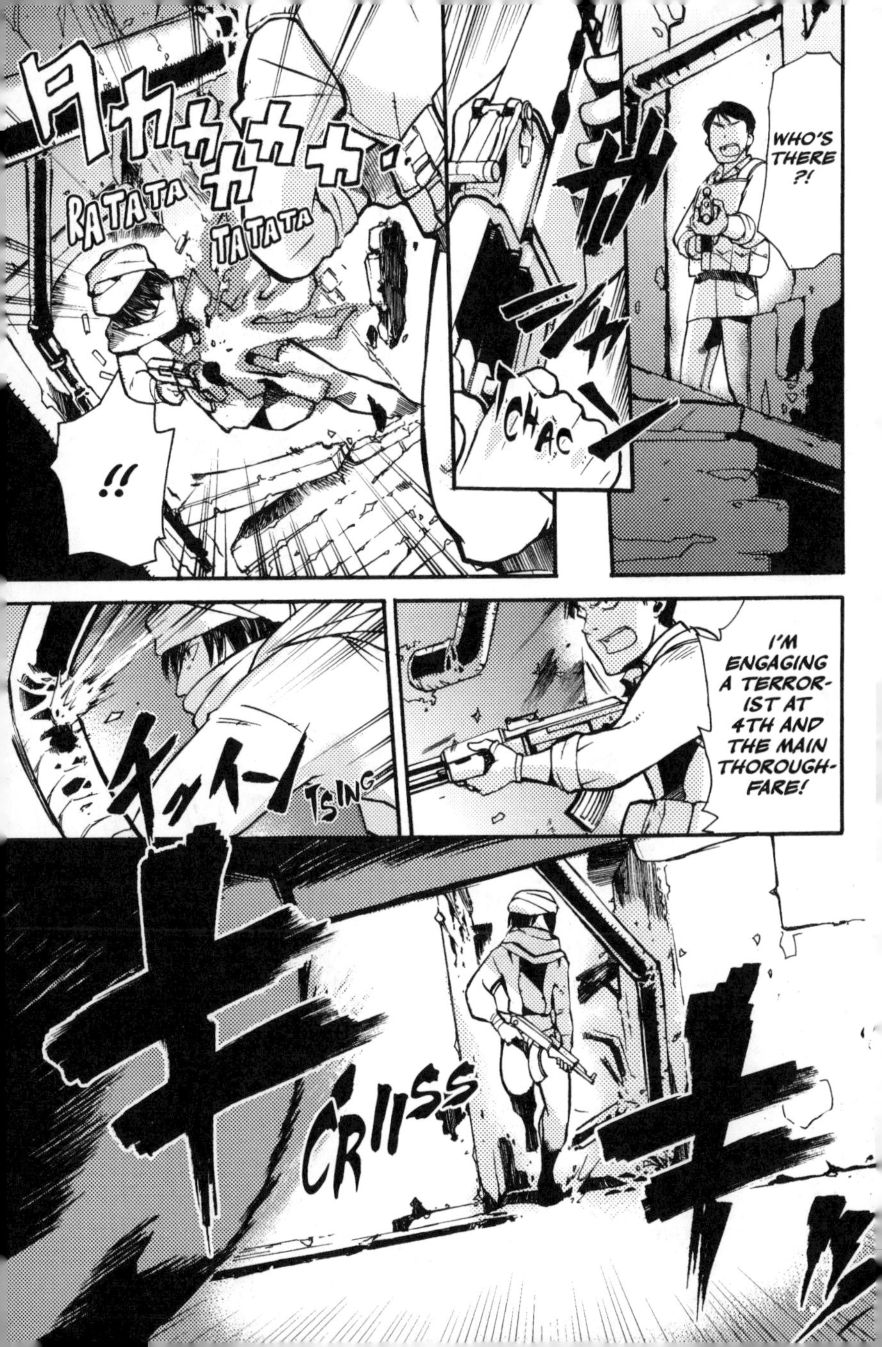

WHO'S THERE ?!
TCHAC
RATATA
TATATA
!!
I'M ENGAGING A TERRORIST AT 4TH AND THE MAIN THOROUGHFARE!
TSING
CRIISS

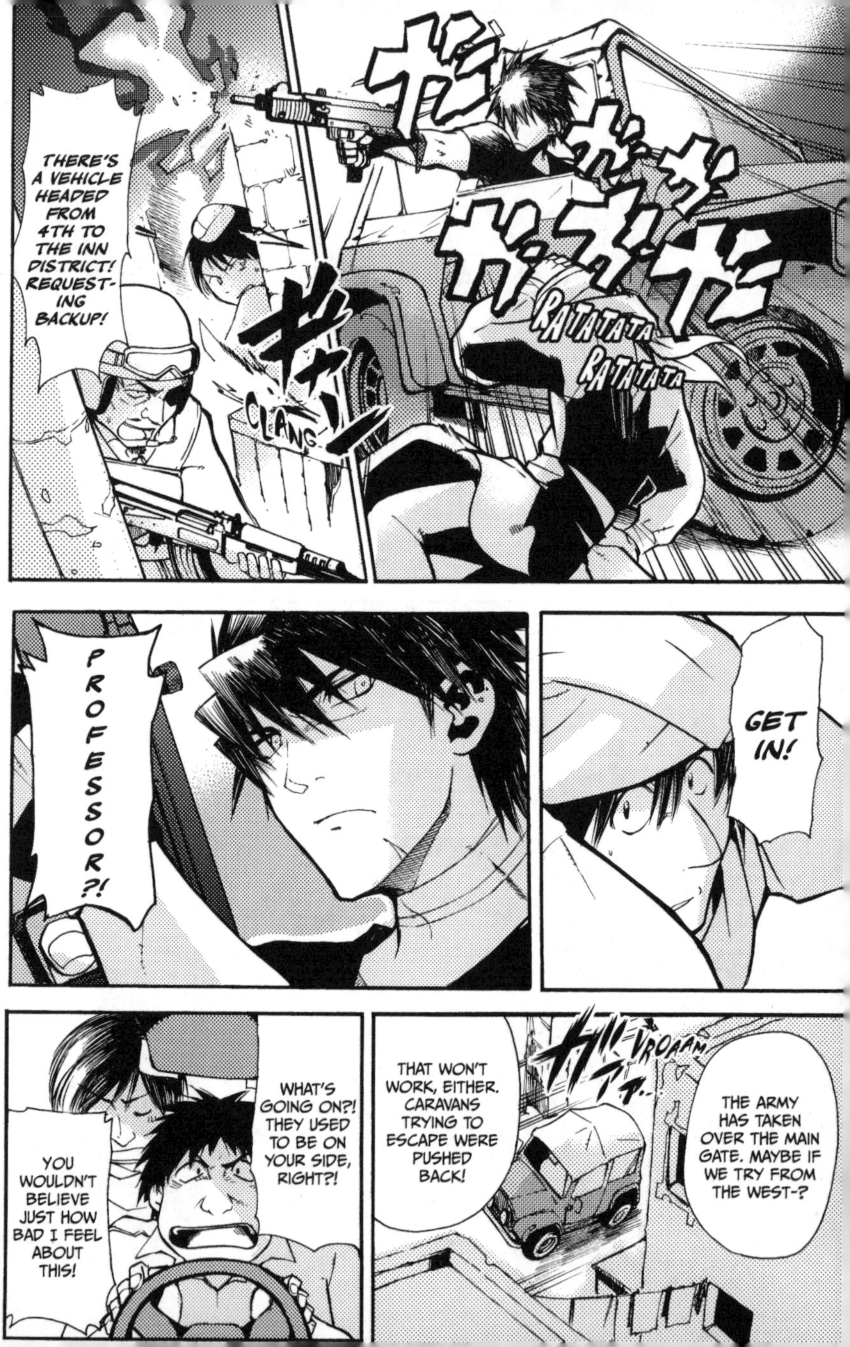
RATATATA
RATATATA
THERE'S A VEHICLE HEADED FROM 4TH TO THE INN DISTRICT! REQUESTING BACKUP!
CLANG
GET IN!
PROFESSOR?!
THE ARMY HAS TAKEN OVER THE MAIN GATE. MAYBE IF WE TRY FROM THE WEST-?
VROAAM
THAT WON'T WORK, EITHER. CARAVANS TRYING TO ESCAPE WERE PUSHED BACK!
WHAT'S GOING ON?! THEY USED TO BE ON YOUR SIDE, RIGHT?!
YOU WOULDN'T BELIEVE JUST HOW BAD I FEEL ABOUT THIS!

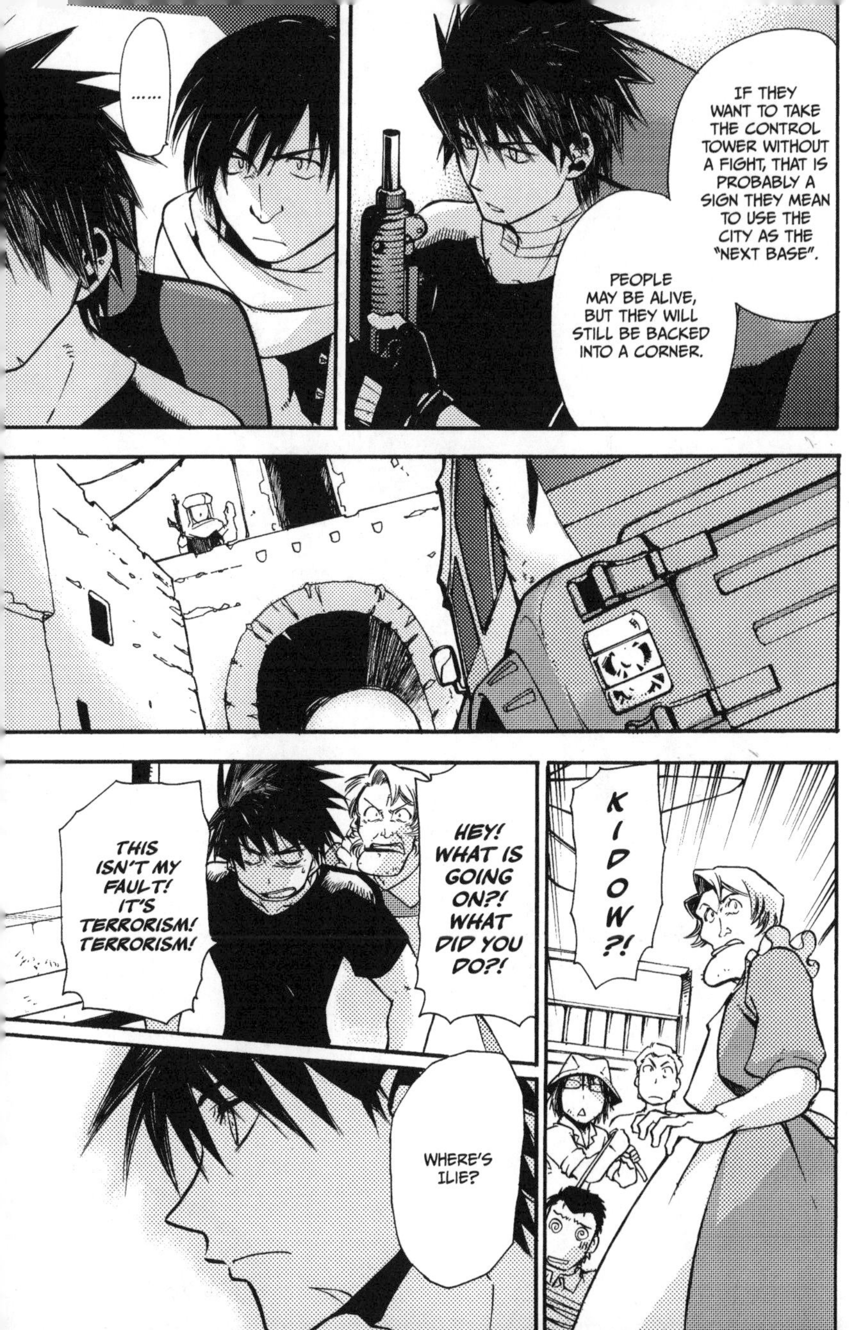
IF THEY WANT TO TAKE THE CONTROL TOWER WITHOUT A FIGHT, THAT IS PROBABLY A SIGN THEY MEAN TO USE THE CITY AS THE "NEXT BASE".
PEOPLE MAY BE ALIVE, BUT THEY WILL STILL BE BACKED INTO A CORNER.
......
KIDOW?!
HEY! WHAT IS GOING ON?! WHAT DID YOU DO?!
THIS ISN'T MY FAULT! IT'S TERRORISM! TERRORISM!
WHERE'S ILIE?

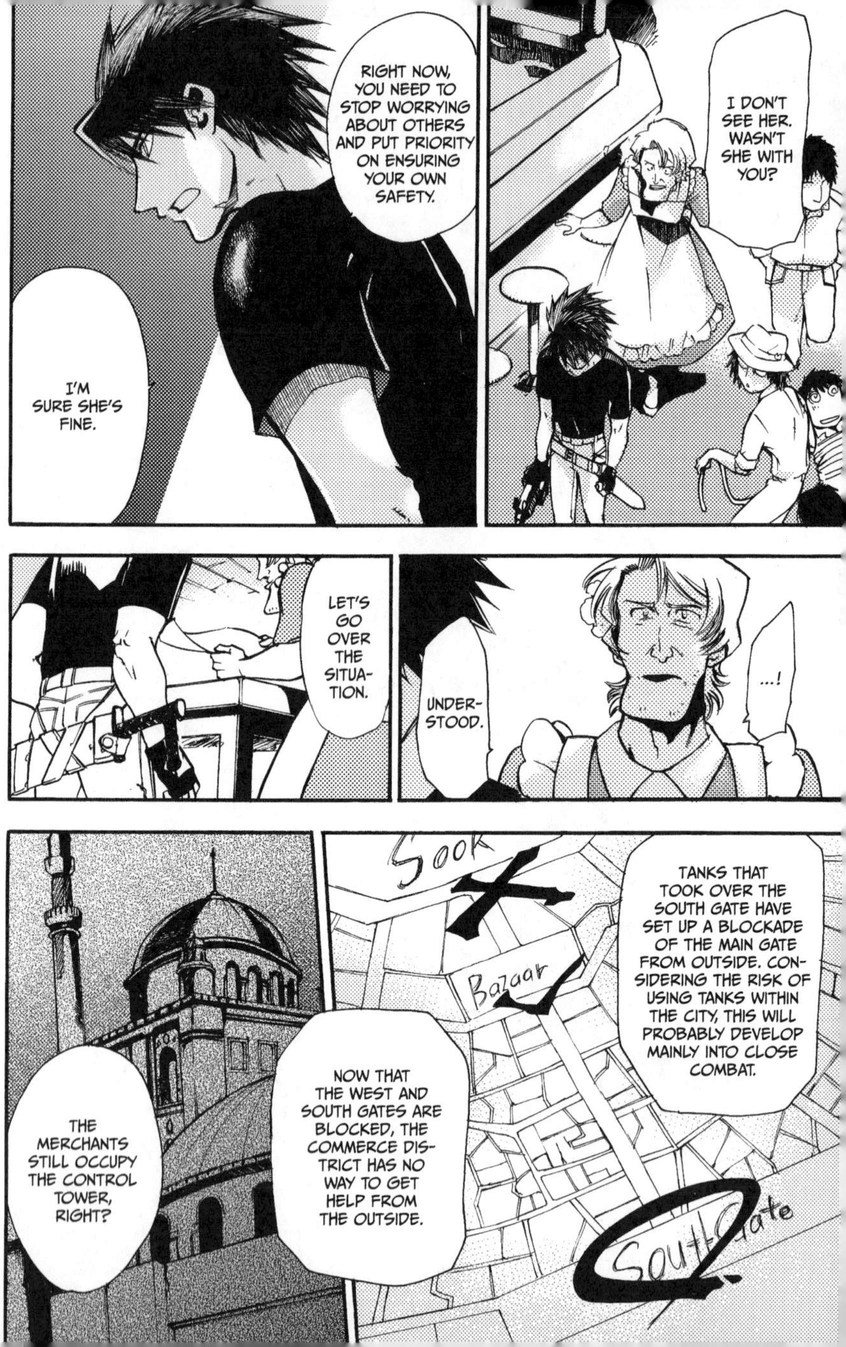
I DON'T SEE HER. WASN'T SHE WITH YOU?
RIGHT NOW, YOU NEED TO STOP WORRYING ABOUT OTHERS AND PUT PRIORITY ON ENSURING YOUR OWN SAFETY.
I'M SURE SHE'S FINE.
...!
UNDER-STOOD.
LET'S GO OVER THE SITUATION.
Sook
Bazaar
TANKS THAT TOOK OVER THE SOUTH GATE HAVE SET UP A BLOCKADE OF THE MAIN GATE FROM OUTSIDE. CON-SIDERING THE RISK OF USING TANKS WITHIN THE CITY, THIS WILL PROBABLY DEVELOP MAINLY INTO CLOSE COMBAT.
NOW THAT THE WEST AND SOUTH GATES ARE BLOCKED, THE COMMERCE DIS-TRICT HAS NO WAY TO GET HELP FROM THE OUTSIDE.
SouthGate
THE MERCHANTS STILL OCCUPY THE CONTROL TOWER, RIGHT?

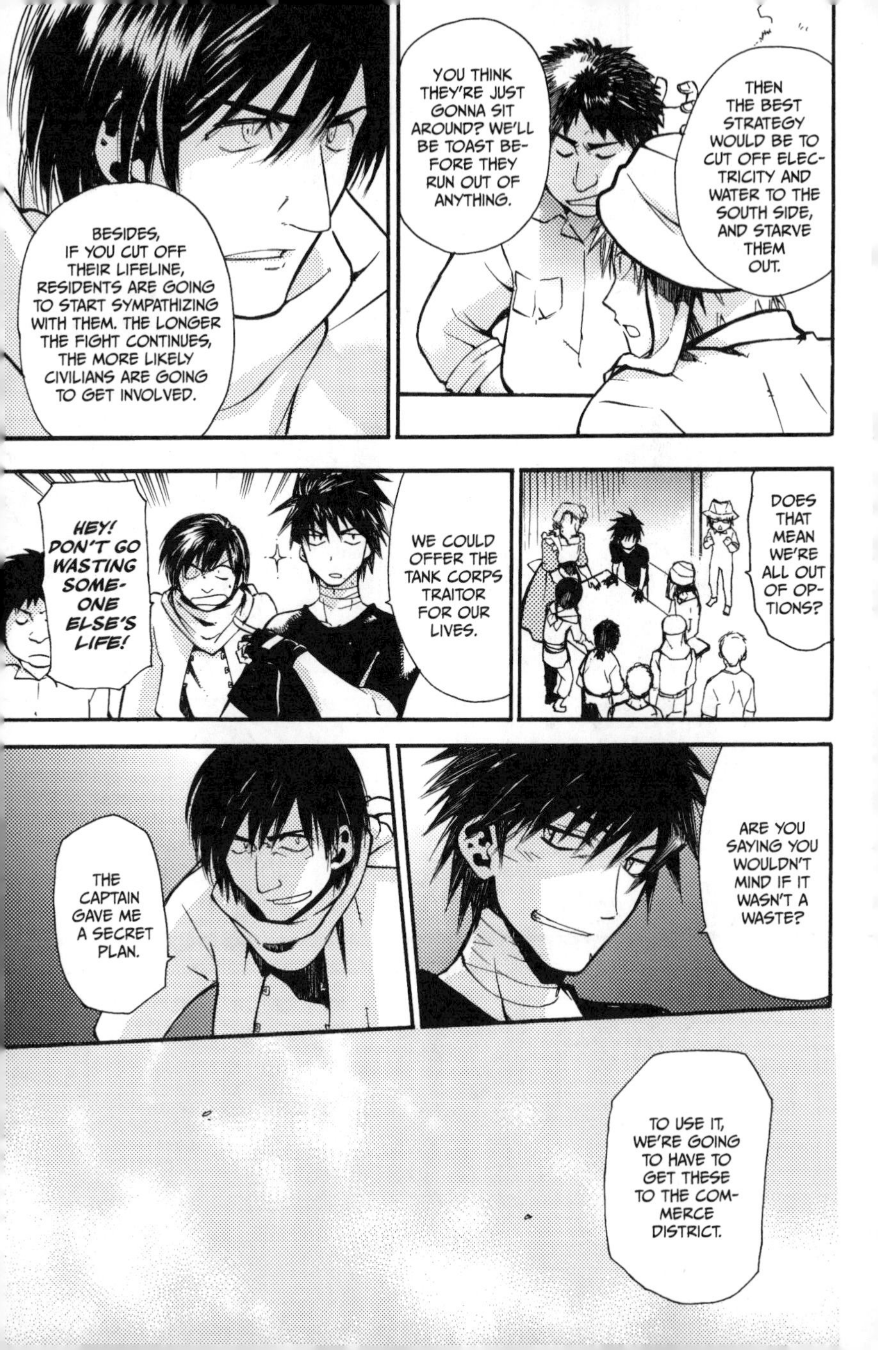
THEN THE BEST STRATEGY WOULD BE TO CUT OFF ELECTRICITY AND WATER TO THE SOUTH SIDE, AND STARVE THEM OUT.
YOU THINK THEY'RE JUST GONNA SIT AROUND? WE'LL BE TOAST BEFORE THEY RUN OUT OF ANYTHING.
BESIDES, IF YOU CUT OFF THEIR LIFELINE, RESIDENTS ARE GOING TO START SYMPATHIZING WITH THEM. THE LONGER THE FIGHT CONTINUES, THE MORE LIKELY CIVILIANS ARE GOING TO GET INVOLVED.
DOES THAT MEAN WE'RE ALL OUT OF OPTIONS?
WE COULD OFFER THE TANK CORPS TRAITOR FOR OUR LIVES.
HEY! DON'T GO WASTING SOMEONE ELSE'S LIFE!
ARE YOU SAYING YOU WOULDN'T MIND IF IT WASN'T A WASTE?
THE CAPTAIN GAVE ME A SECRET PLAN.
TO USE IT, WE'RE GOING TO HAVE TO GET THESE TO THE COMMERCE DISTRICT.

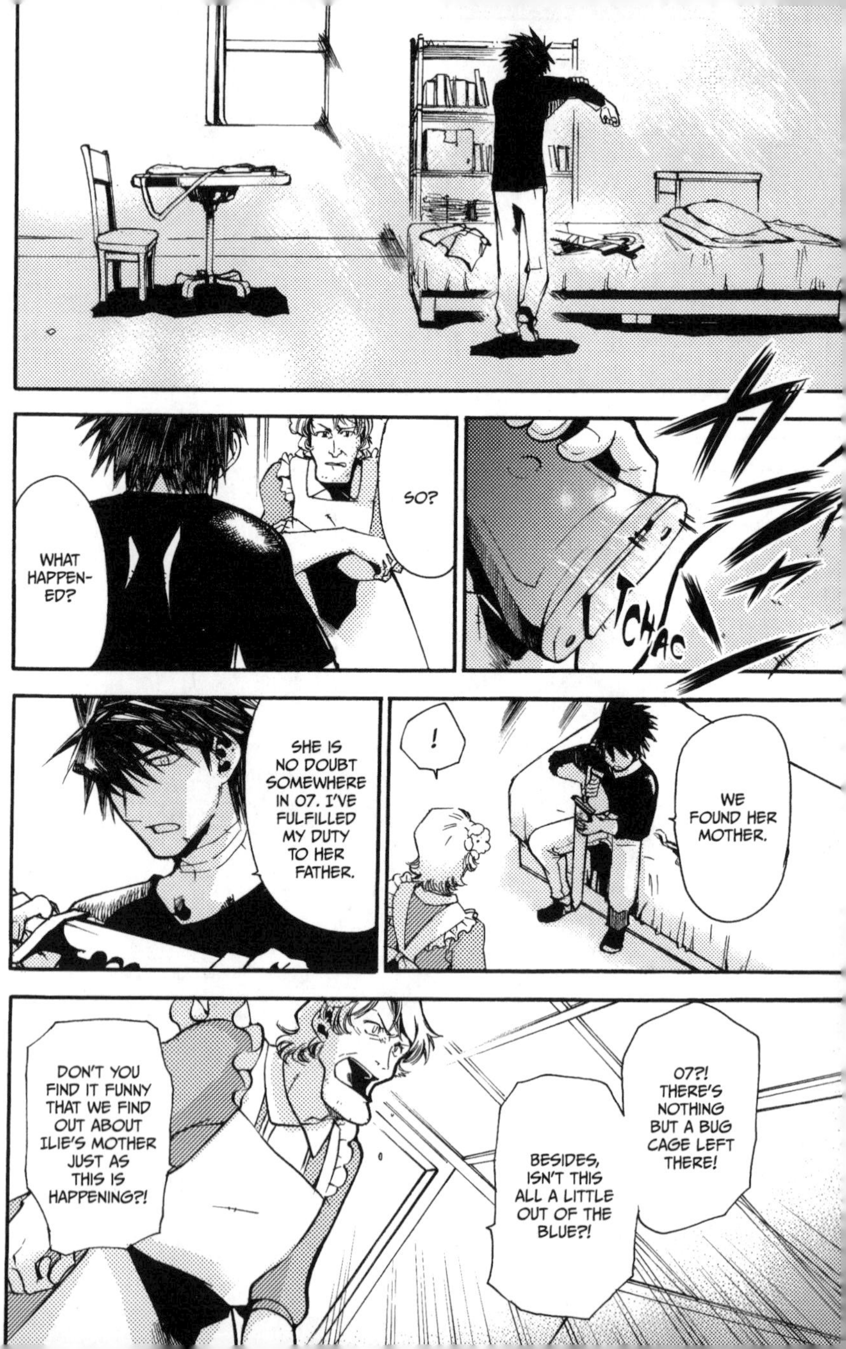
TCHAC
SO?
WHAT HAPPEN-ED?
WE FOUND HER MOTHER.
!
SHE IS NO DOUBT SOMEWHERE IN 07. I'VE FULFILLED MY DUTY TO HER FATHER.
07?! THERE'S NOTHING BUT A BUG CAGE LEFT THERE!
BESIDES, ISN'T THIS ALL A LITTLE OUT OF THE BLUE?!
DON'T YOU FIND IT FUNNY THAT WE FIND OUT ABOUT ILIE'S MOTHER JUST AS THIS IS HAPPENING?!

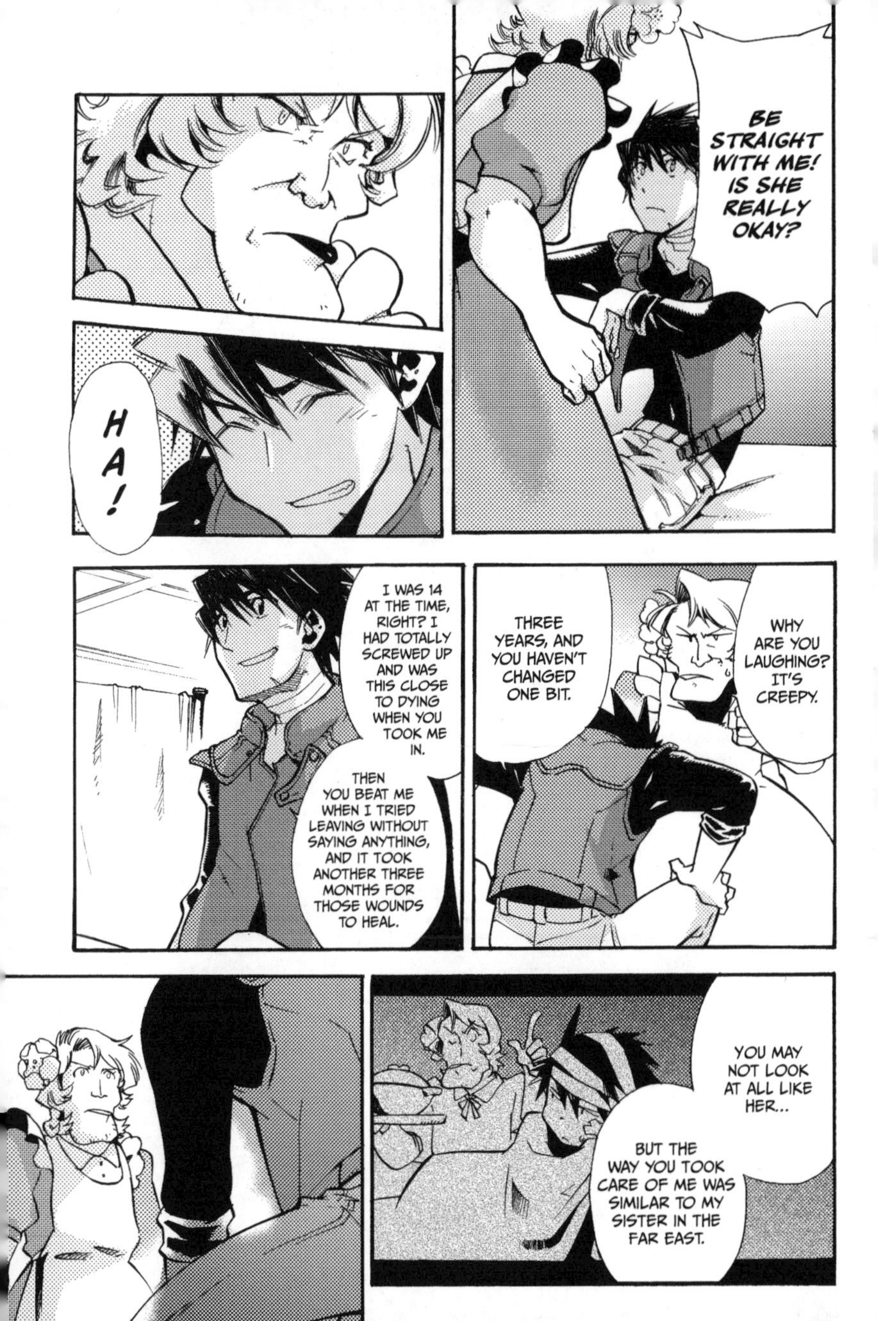
BE STRAIGHT WITH ME! IS SHE REALLY OKAY?
HA!
WHY ARE YOU LAUGHING? IT'S CREEPY.
THREE YEARS, AND YOU HAVEN'T CHANGED ONE BIT.
I WAS 14 AT THE TIME, RIGHT? I HAD TOTALLY SCREWED UP AND WAS THIS CLOSE TO DYING WHEN YOU TOOK ME IN.
THEN YOU BEAT ME WHEN I TRIED LEAVING WITHOUT SAYING ANYTHING, AND IT TOOK ANOTHER THREE MONTHS FOR THOSE WOUNDS TO HEAL.
YOU MAY NOT LOOK AT ALL LIKE HER...
BUT THE WAY YOU TOOK CARE OF ME WAS SIMILAR TO MY SISTER IN THE FAR EAST.

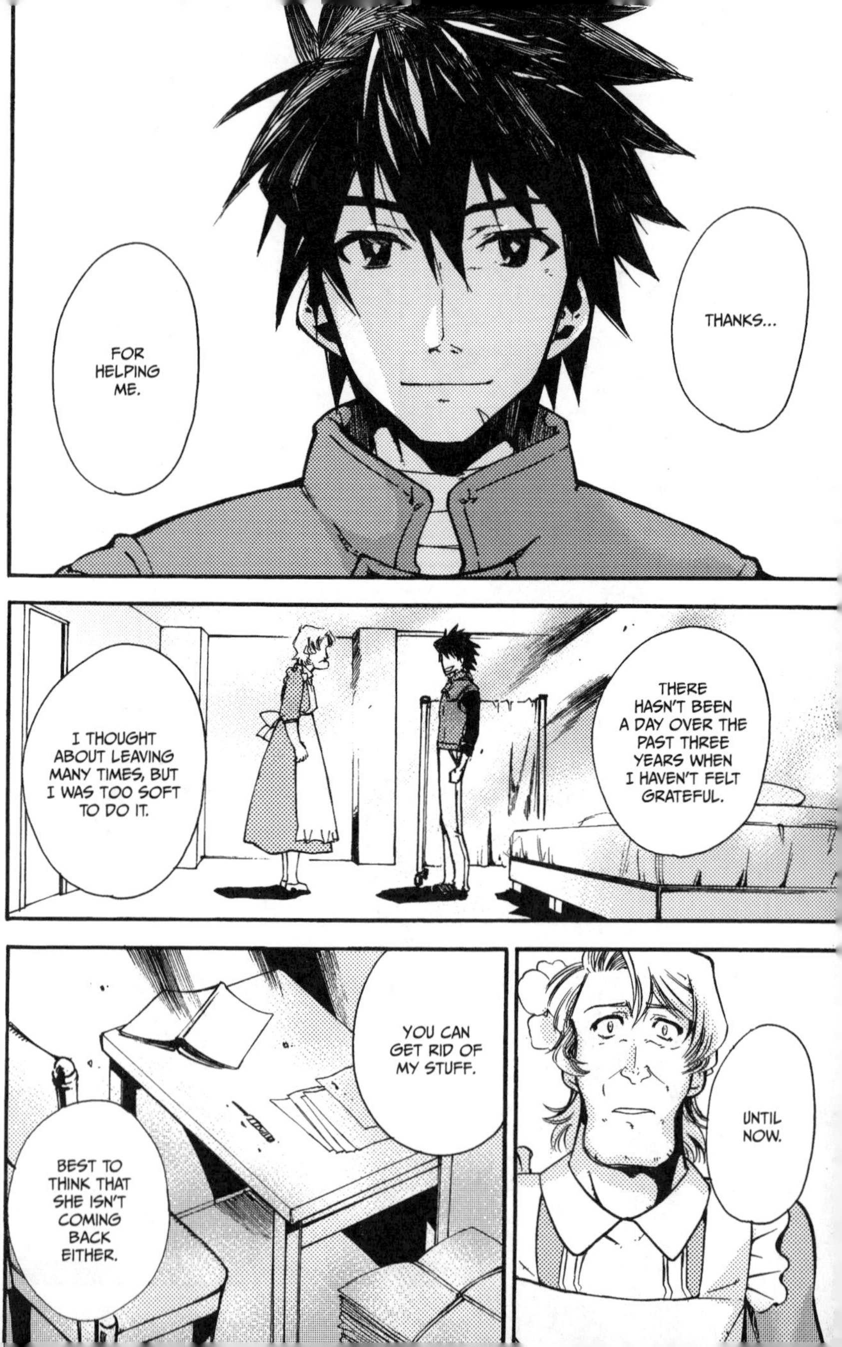
THANKS...
FOR HELPING ME.
THERE HASN'T BEEN A DAY OVER THE PAST THREE YEARS WHEN I HAVEN'T FELT GRATEFUL.
I THOUGHT ABOUT LEAVING MANY TIMES, BUT I WAS TOO SOFT TO DO IT.
UNTIL NOW.
YOU CAN GET RID OF MY STUFF.
BEST TO THINK THAT SHE ISN'T COMING BACK EITHER.

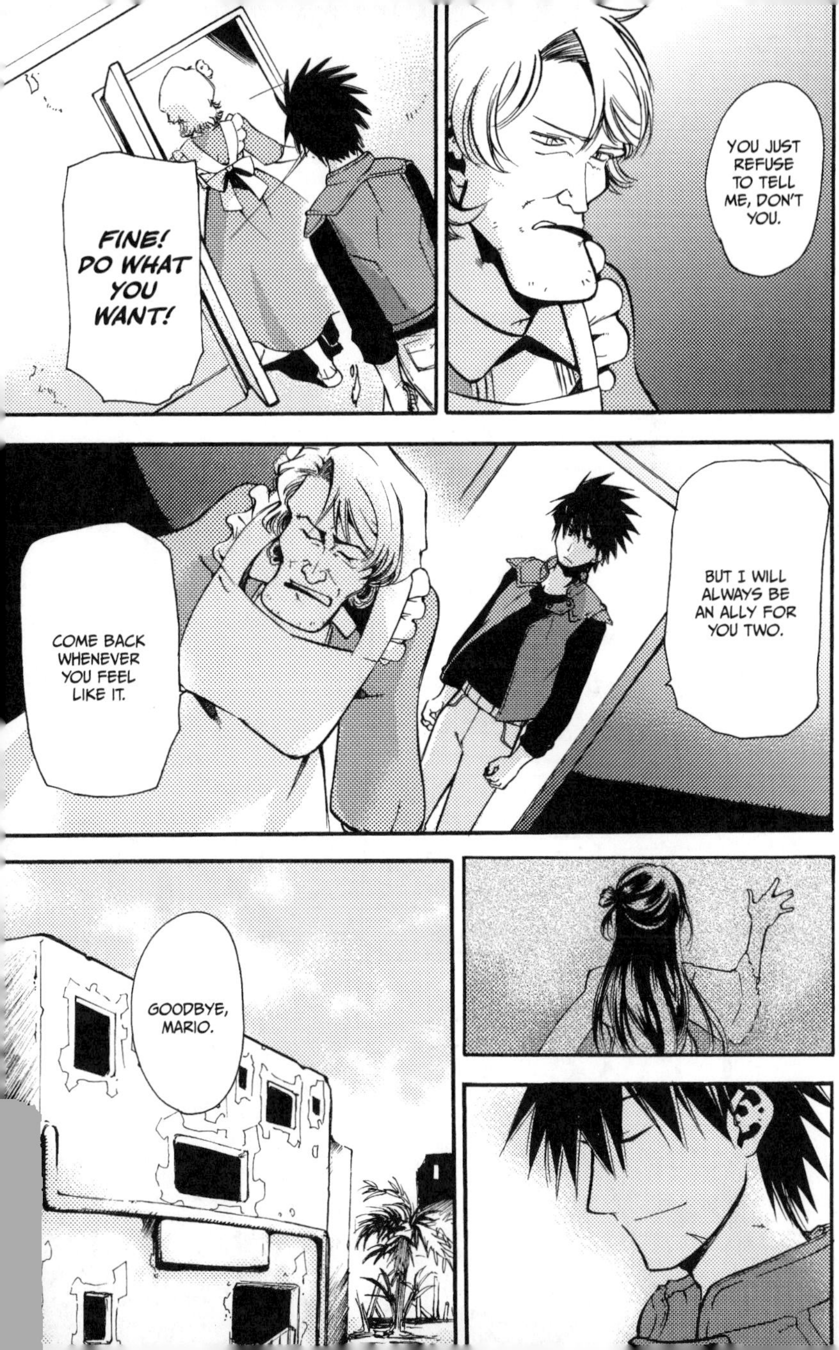
YOU JUST REFUSE TO TELL ME, DON'T YOU.
FINE! DO WHAT YOU WANT!
BUT I WILL ALWAYS BE AN ALLY FOR YOU TWO.
COME BACK WHENEVER YOU FEEL LIKE IT.
GOODBYE, MARIO.

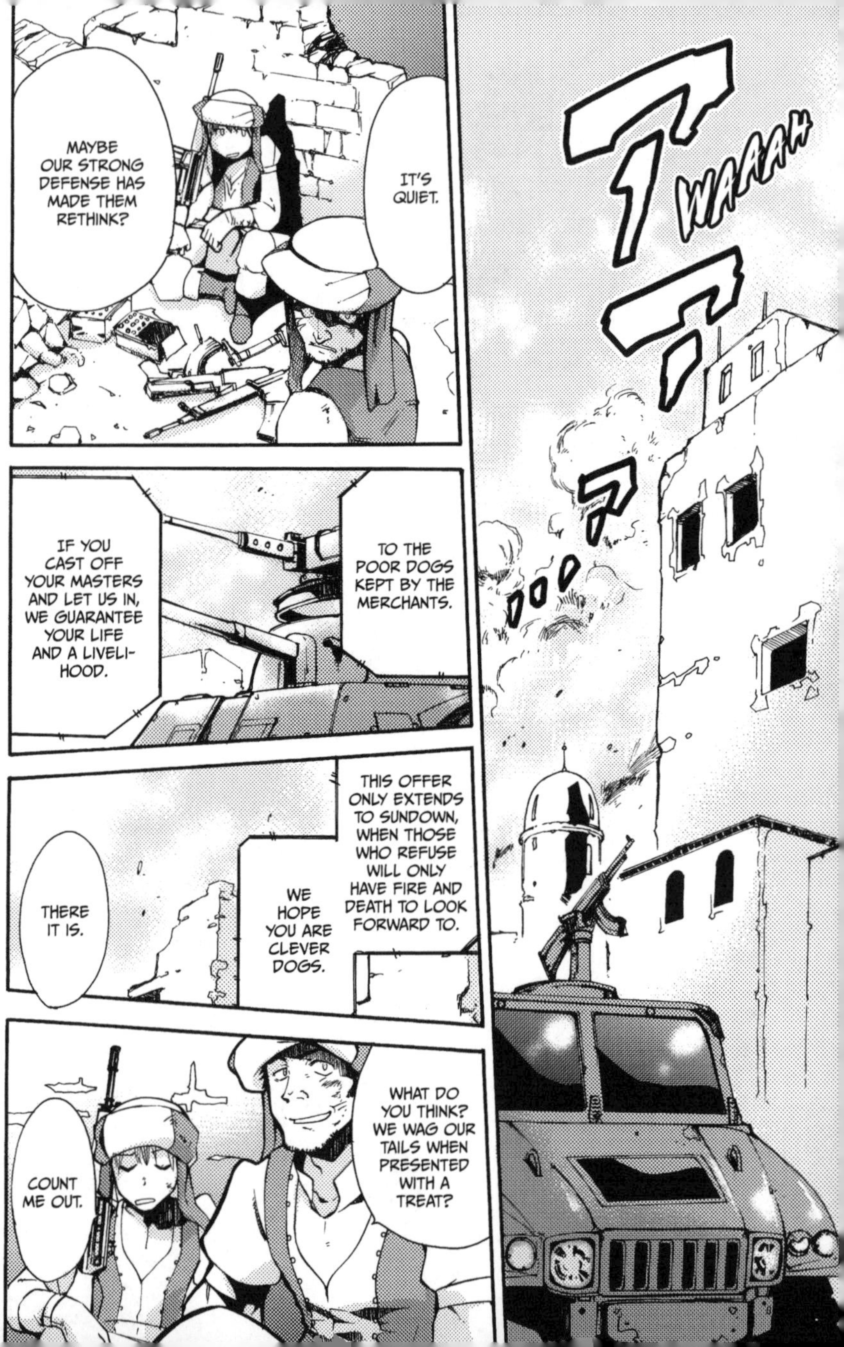

アァァ
WAAAH
IT'S QUIET.
MAYBE OUR STRONG DEFENSE HAS MADE THEM RETHINK?
TO THE POOR DOGS KEPT BY THE MERCHANTS.
IF YOU CAST OFF YOUR MASTERS AND LET US IN, WE GUARANTEE YOUR LIFE AND A LIVELI-HOOD.
THIS OFFER ONLY EXTENDS TO SUNDOWN, WHEN THOSE WHO REFUSE WILL ONLY HAVE FIRE AND DEATH TO LOOK FORWARD TO.
WE HOPE YOU ARE CLEVER DOGS.
THERE IT IS.
WHAT DO YOU THINK? WE WAG OUR TAILS WHEN PRESENTED WITH A TREAT?
COUNT ME OUT.

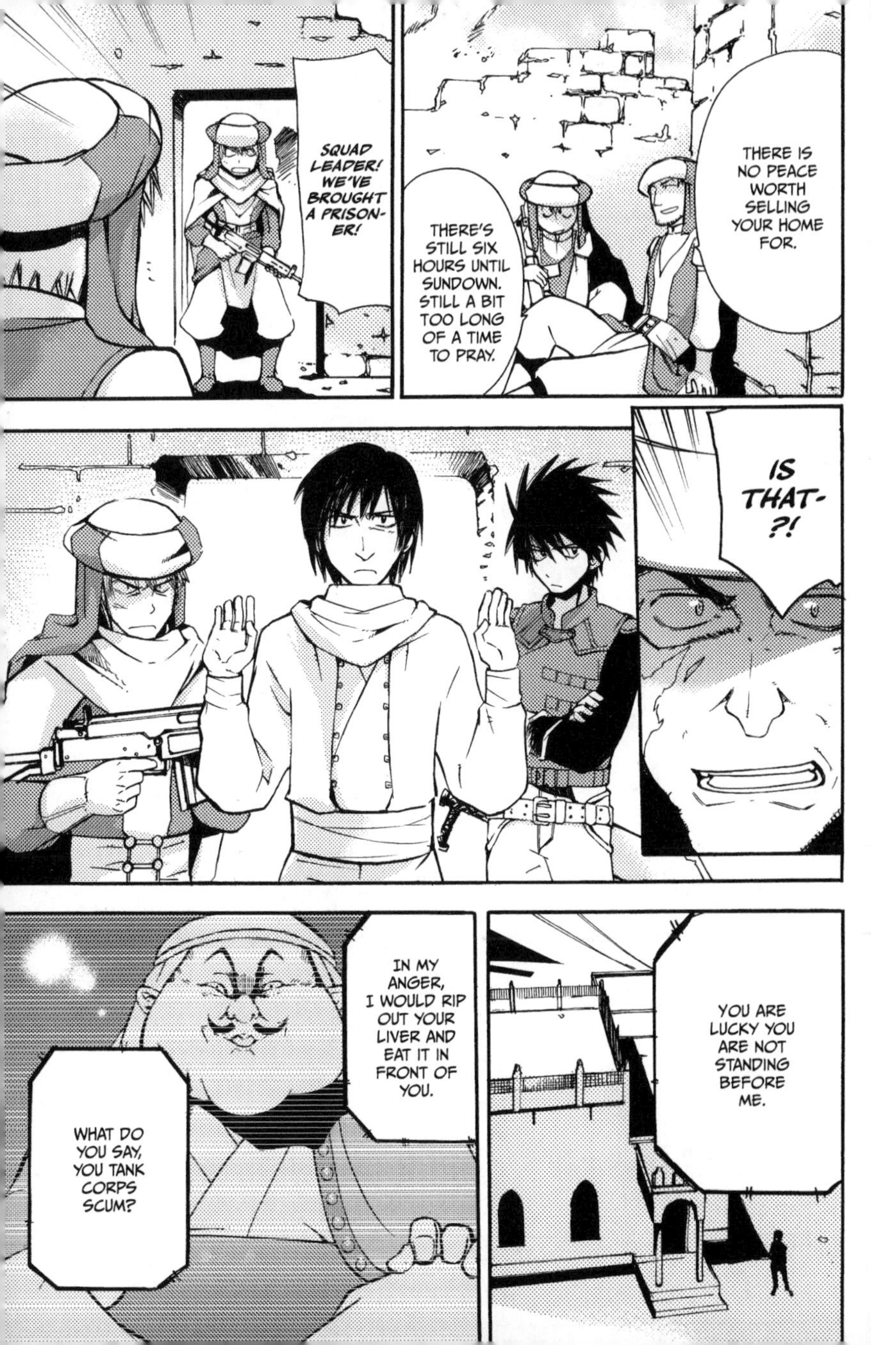
THERE IS NO PEACE WORTH SELLING YOUR HOME FOR.
THERE'S STILL SIX HOURS UNTIL SUNDOWN. STILL A BIT TOO LONG OF A TIME TO PRAY.
SQUAD LEADER! WE'VE BROUGHT A PRISONER!
IS THAT-?!
YOU ARE LUCKY YOU ARE NOT STANDING BEFORE ME.
IN MY ANGER, I WOULD RIP OUT YOUR LIVER AND EAT IT IN FRONT OF YOU.
WHAT DO YOU SAY, YOU TANK CORPS SCUM?

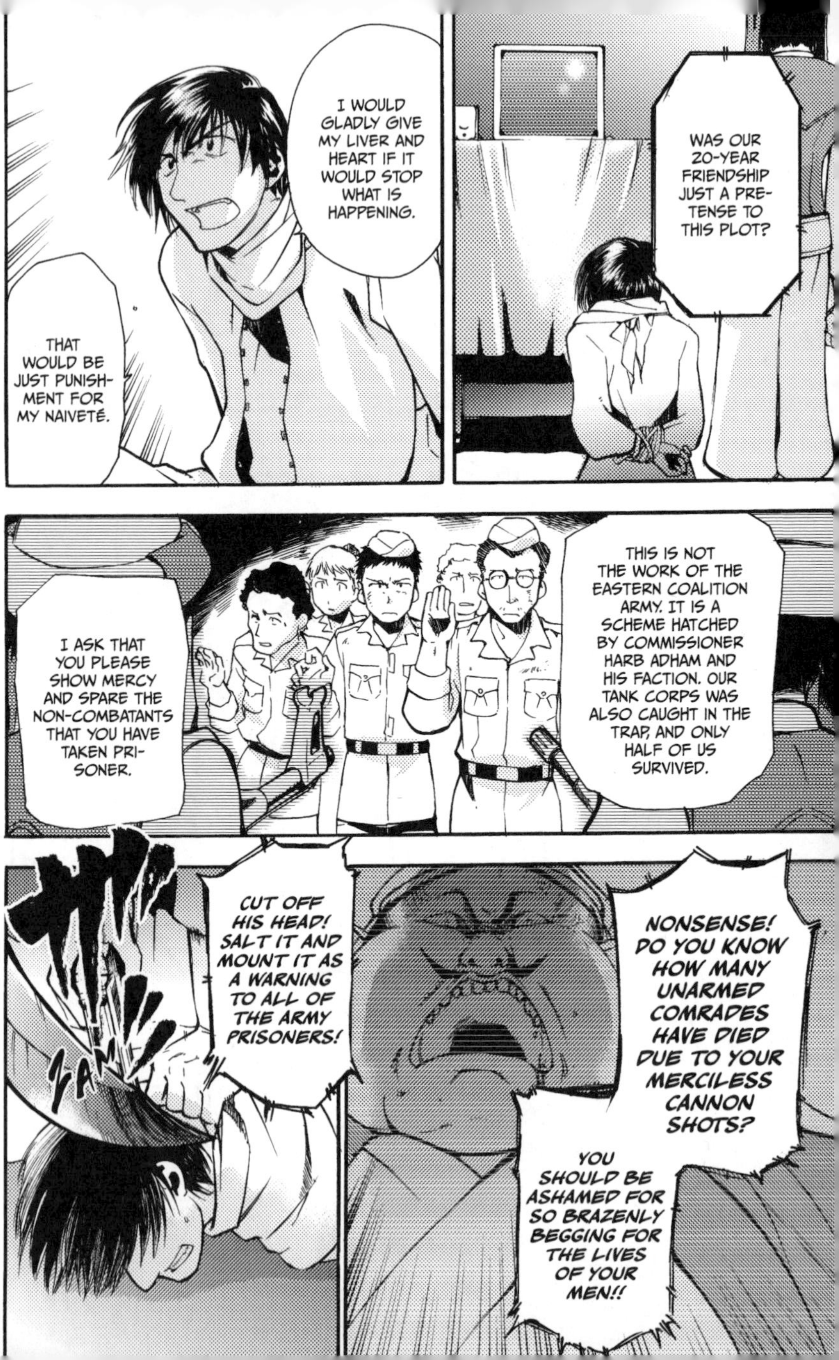
WAS OUR 20-YEAR FRIENDSHIP JUST A PRETENSE TO THIS PLOT?
I WOULD GLADLY GIVE MY LIVER AND HEART IF IT WOULD STOP WHAT IS HAPPENING.
THAT WOULD BE JUST PUNISHMENT FOR MY NAIVETÉ.
THIS IS NOT THE WORK OF THE EASTERN COALITION ARMY. IT IS A SCHEME HATCHED BY COMMISSIONER HARB ADHAM AND HIS FACTION. OUR TANK CORPS WAS ALSO CAUGHT IN THE TRAP, AND ONLY HALF OF US SURVIVED.
I ASK THAT YOU PLEASE SHOW MERCY AND SPARE THE NON-COMBATANTS THAT YOU HAVE TAKEN PRISONER.
NONSENSE! DO YOU KNOW HOW MANY UNARMED COMRADES HAVE DIED DUE TO YOUR MERCILESS CANNON SHOTS?
YOU SHOULD BE ASHAMED FOR SO BRAZENLY BEGGING FOR THE LIVES OF YOUR MEN!!
CUT OFF HIS HEAD! SALT IT AND MOUNT IT AS A WARNING TO ALL OF THE ARMY PRISONERS!

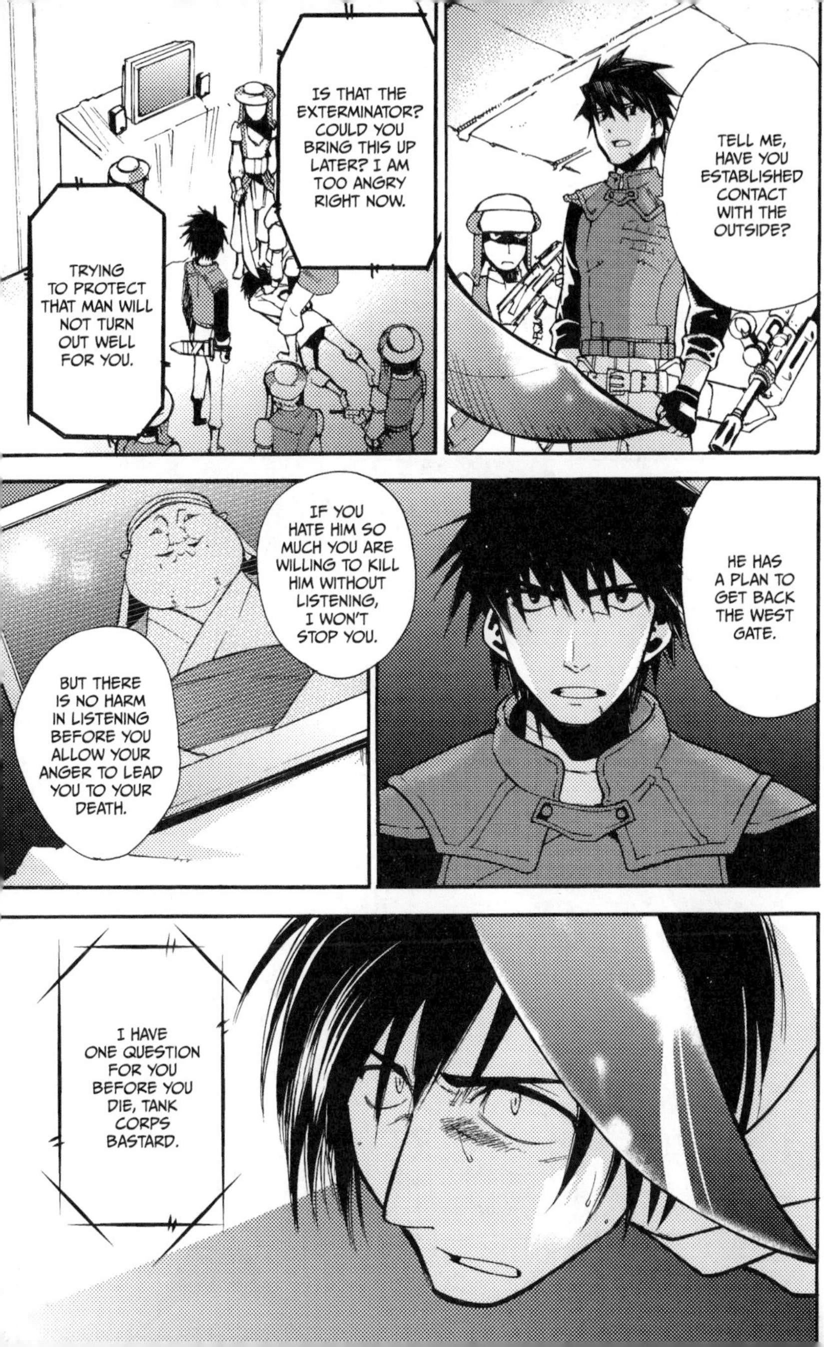
TELL ME, HAVE YOU ESTABLISHED CONTACT WITH THE OUTSIDE?
IS THAT THE EXTERMINATOR? COULD YOU BRING THIS UP LATER? I AM TOO ANGRY RIGHT NOW.
TRYING TO PROTECT THAT MAN WILL NOT TURN OUT WELL FOR YOU.
HE HAS A PLAN TO GET BACK THE WEST GATE.
IF YOU HATE HIM SO MUCH YOU ARE WILLING TO KILL HIM WITHOUT LISTENING, I WON'T STOP YOU.
BUT THERE IS NO HARM IN LISTENING BEFORE YOU ALLOW YOUR ANGER TO LEAD YOU TO YOUR DEATH.
I HAVE ONE QUESTION FOR YOU BEFORE YOU DIE, TANK CORPS BASTARD.

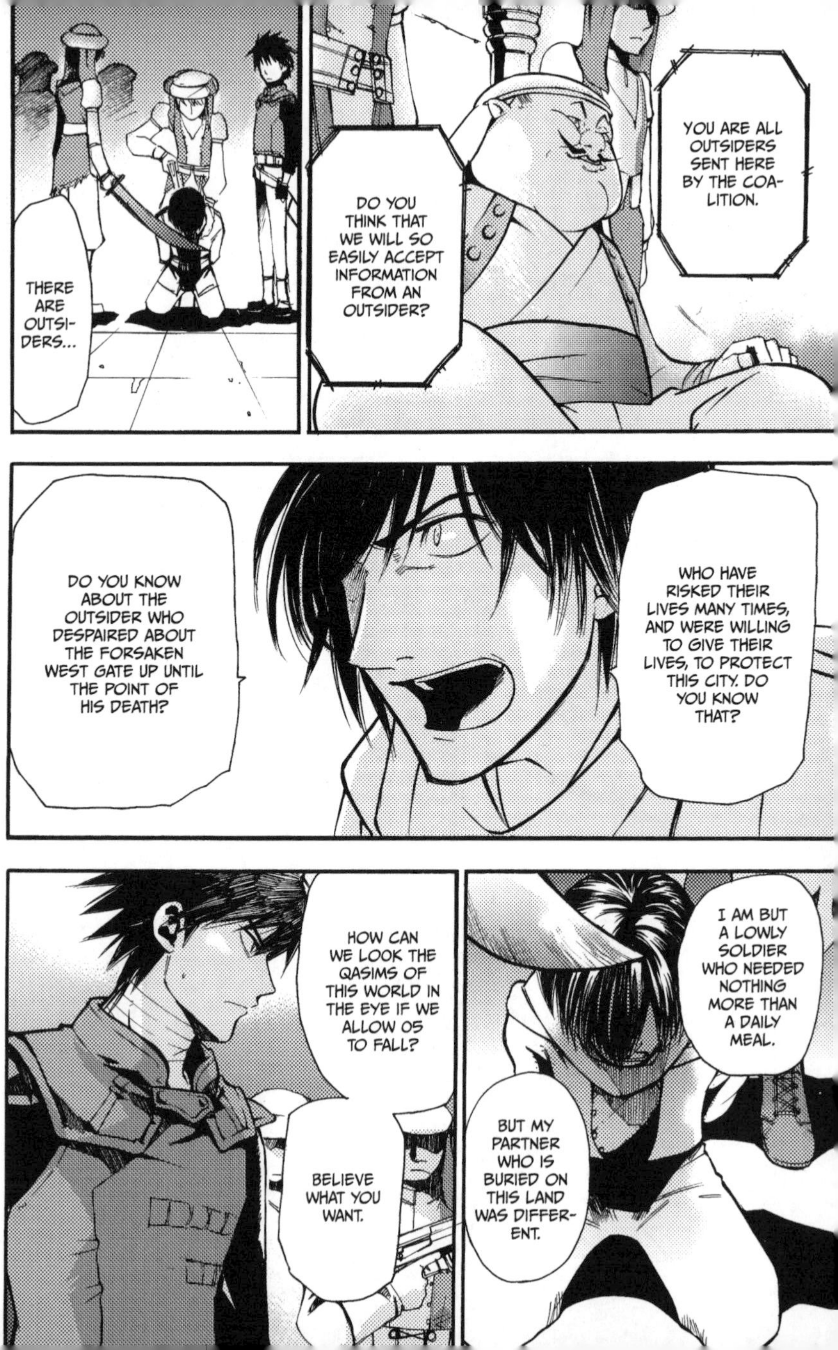
YOU ARE ALL OUTSIDERS SENT HERE BY THE COA-LITION.
DO YOU THINK THAT WE WILL SO EASILY ACCEPT INFORMATION FROM AN OUTSIDER?
THERE ARE OUTSI-DERS...
WHO HAVE RISKED THEIR LIVES MANY TIMES, AND WERE WILLING TO GIVE THEIR LIVES, TO PROTECT THIS CITY. DO YOU KNOW THAT?
DO YOU KNOW ABOUT THE OUTSIDER WHO DESPAIRED ABOUT THE FORSAKEN WEST GATE UP UNTIL THE POINT OF HIS DEATH?
I AM BUT A LOWLY SOLDIER WHO NEEDED NOTHING MORE THAN A DAILY MEAL.
BUT MY PARTNER WHO IS BURIED ON THIS LAND WAS DIFFER-ENT.
HOW CAN WE LOOK THE QASIMS OF THIS WORLD IN THE EYE IF WE ALLOW 05 TO FALL?
BELIEVE WHAT YOU WANT.

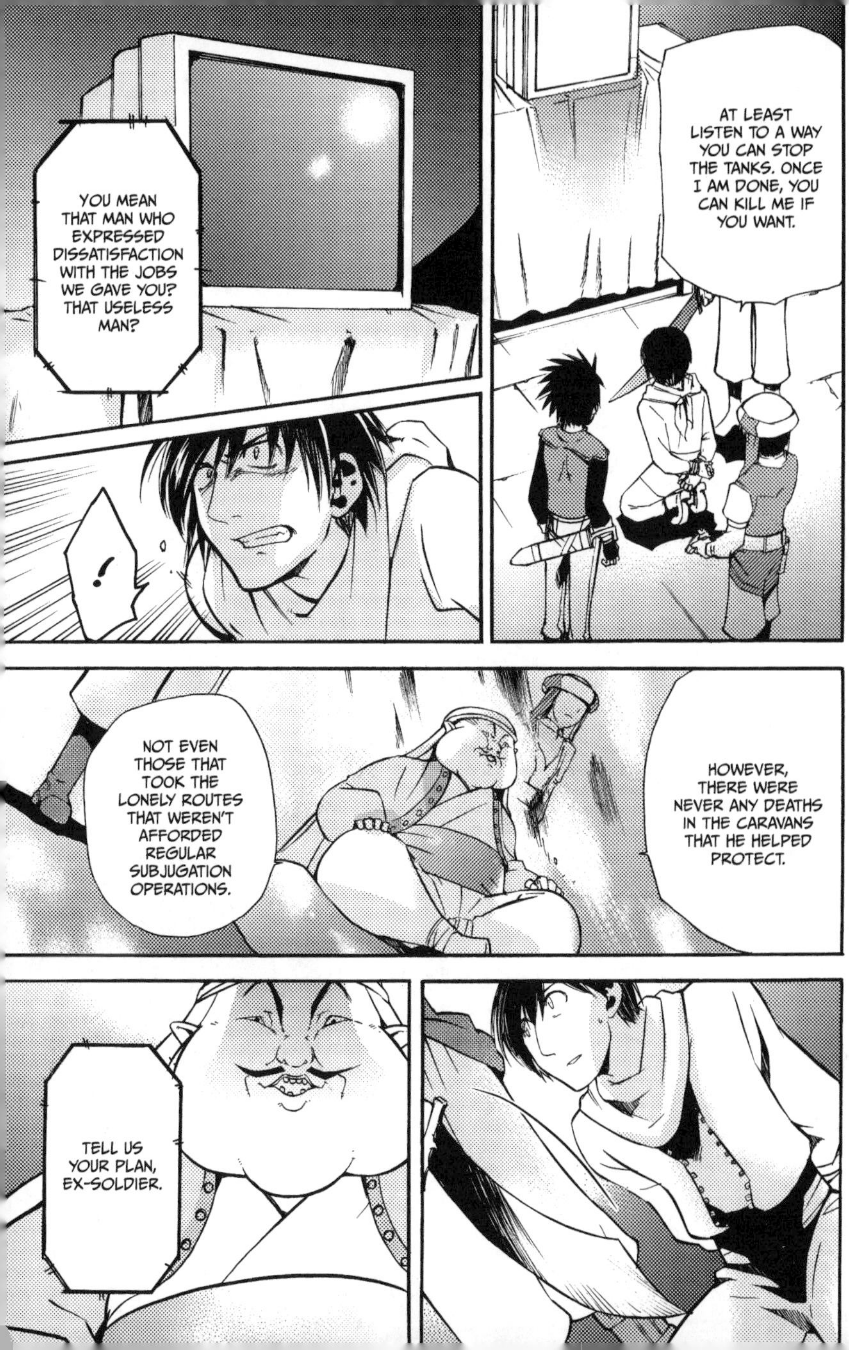
AT LEAST LISTEN TO A WAY YOU CAN STOP THE TANKS. ONCE I AM DONE, YOU CAN KILL ME IF YOU WANT.
YOU MEAN THAT MAN WHO EXPRESSED DISSATISFACTION WITH THE JOBS WE GAVE YOU? THAT USELESS MAN?
!
HOWEVER, THERE WERE NEVER ANY DEATHS IN THE CARAVANS THAT HE HELPED PROTECT.
NOT EVEN THOSE THAT TOOK THE LONELY ROUTES THAT WEREN'T AFFORDED REGULAR SUBJUGATION OPERATIONS.
TELL US YOUR PLAN, EX-SOLDIER.

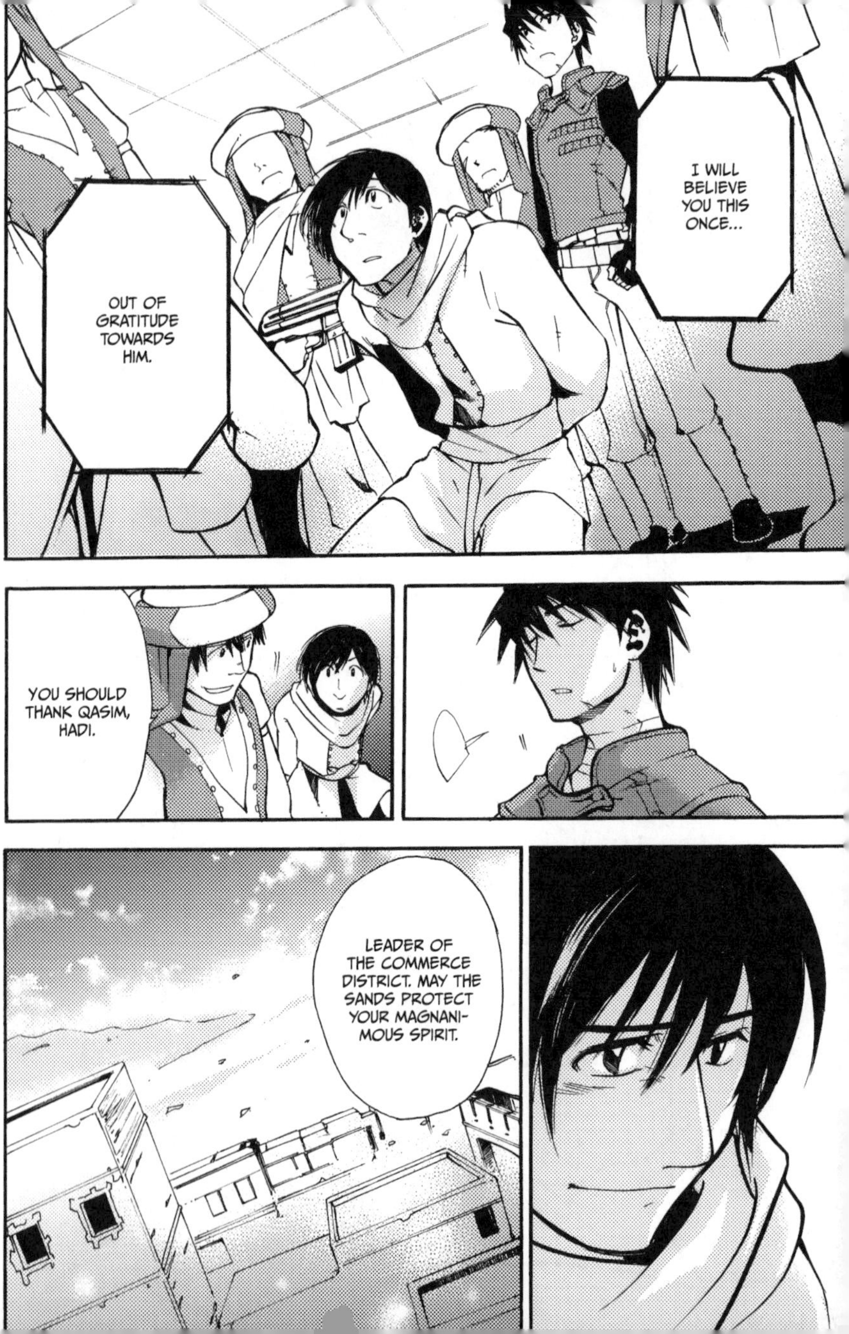
I WILL BELIEVE YOU THIS ONCE...
OUT OF GRATITUDE TOWARDS HIM.
YOU SHOULD THANK QASIM, HADI.
LEADER OF THE COMMERCE DISTRICT. MAY THE SANDS PROTECT YOUR MAGNANIMOUS SPIRIT.

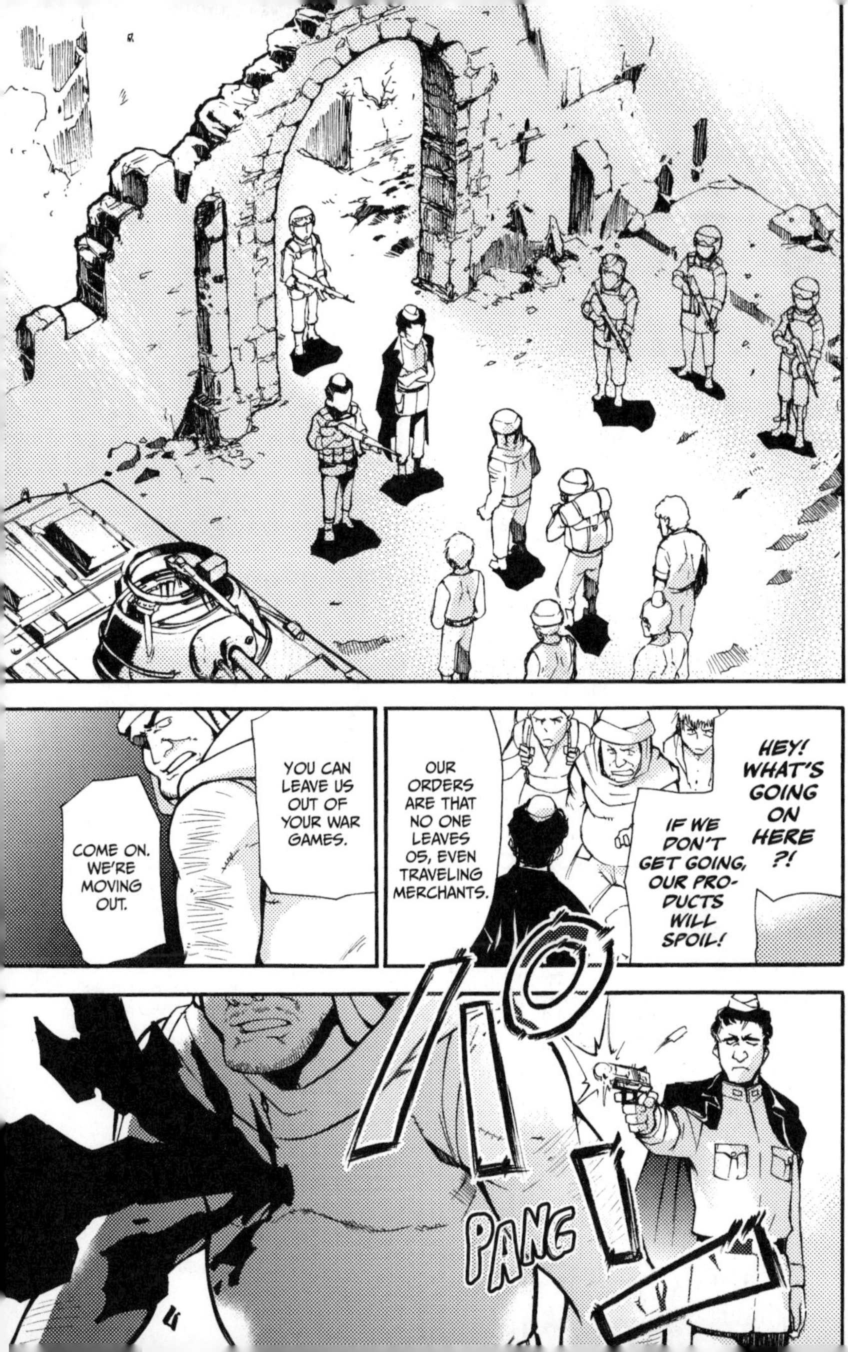
HEY! WHAT'S GOING ON HERE?!
IF WE DON'T GET GOING, OUR PRO-DUCTS WILL SPOIL!
OUR ORDERS ARE THAT NO ONE LEAVES 05, EVEN TRAVELING MERCHANTS.
YOU CAN LEAVE US OUT OF YOUR WAR GAMES.
COME ON. WE'RE MOVING OUT.
PANG

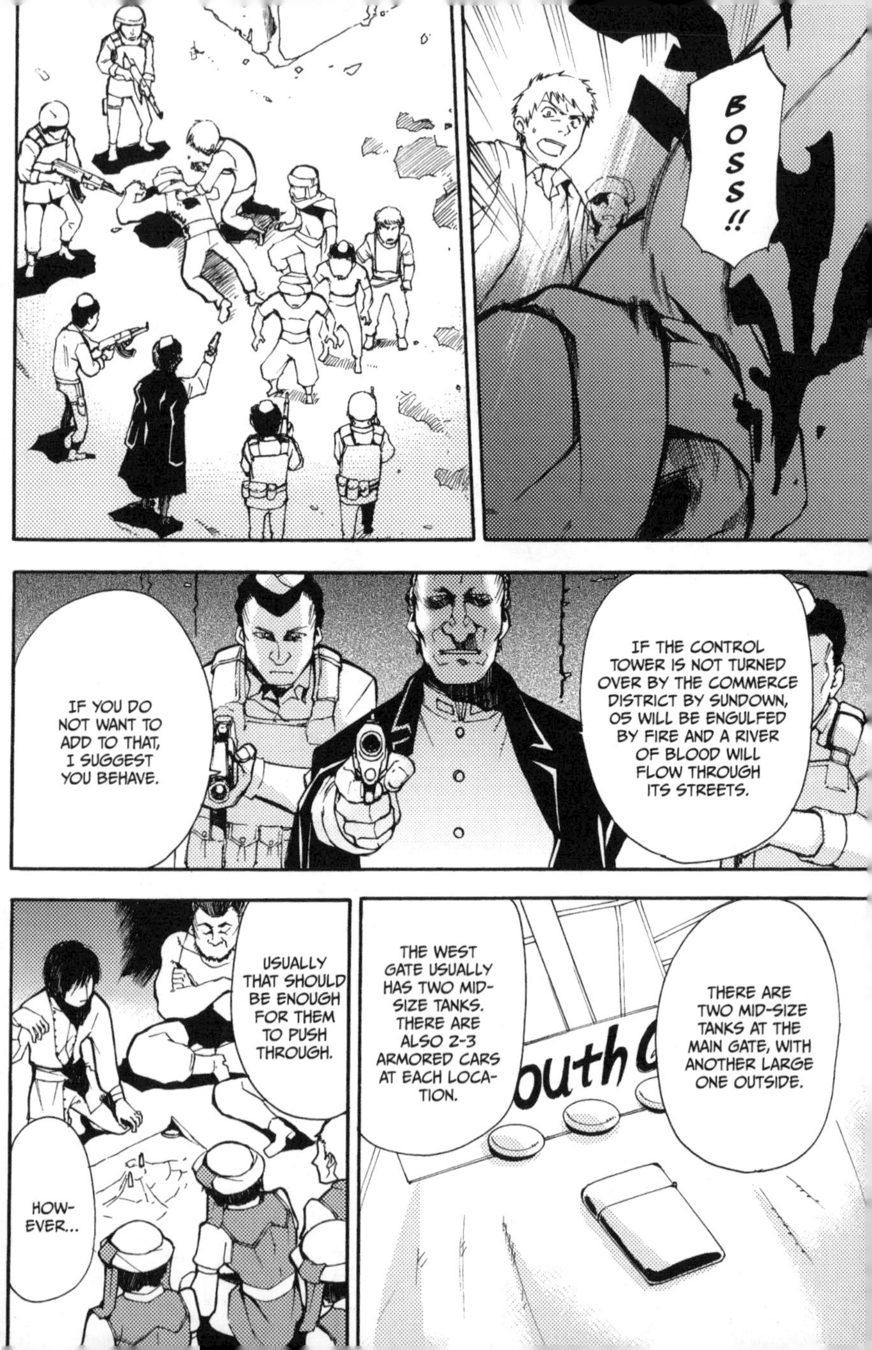
BOSS!!
IF THE CONTROL TOWER IS NOT TURNED OVER BY THE COMMERCE DISTRICT BY SUNDOWN, 05 WILL BE ENGULFED BY FIRE AND A RIVER OF BLOOD WILL FLOW THROUGH ITS STREETS.
IF YOU DO NOT WANT TO ADD TO THAT, I SUGGEST YOU BEHAVE.
THERE ARE TWO MID-SIZE TANKS AT THE MAIN GATE, WITH ANOTHER LARGE ONE OUTSIDE.
THE WEST GATE USUALLY HAS TWO MID-SIZE TANKS. THERE ARE ALSO 2-3 ARMORED CARS AT EACH LOCATION.
USUALLY THAT SHOULD BE ENOUGH FOR THEM TO PUSH THROUGH.
HOWEVER...

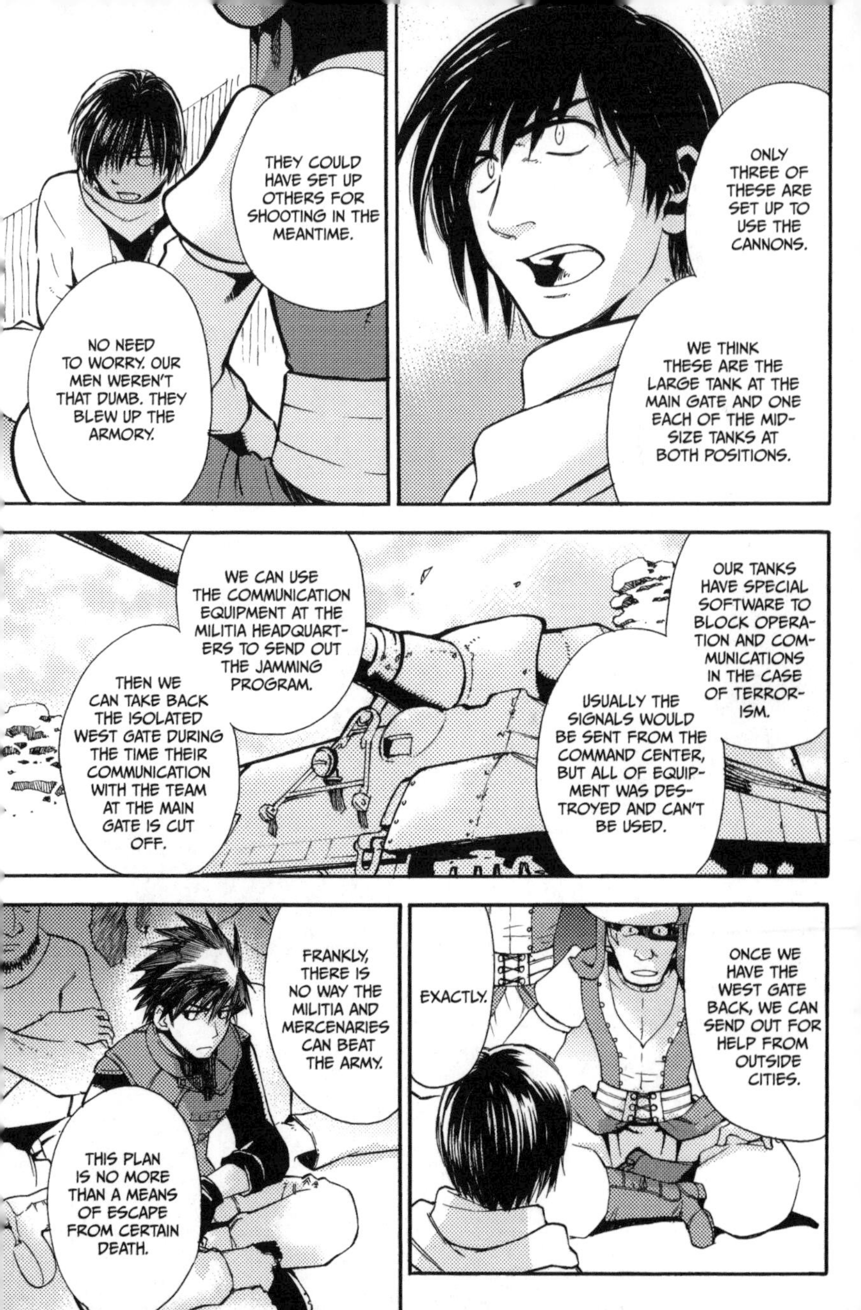
ONLY THREE OF THESE ARE SET UP TO USE THE CANNONS.
WE THINK THESE ARE THE LARGE TANK AT THE MAIN GATE AND ONE EACH OF THE MID-SIZE TANKS AT BOTH POSITIONS.
THEY COULD HAVE SET UP OTHERS FOR SHOOTING IN THE MEANTIME.
NO NEED TO WORRY. OUR MEN WEREN'T THAT DUMB. THEY BLEW UP THE ARMORY.
OUR TANKS HAVE SPECIAL SOFTWARE TO BLOCK OPERATION AND COMMUNICATIONS IN THE CASE OF TERRORISM.
USUALLY THE SIGNALS WOULD BE SENT FROM THE COMMAND CENTER, BUT ALL OF EQUIPMENT WAS DESTROYED AND CAN'T BE USED.
WE CAN USE THE COMMUNICATION EQUIPMENT AT THE MILITIA HEADQUARTERS TO SEND OUT THE JAMMING PROGRAM.
THEN WE CAN TAKE BACK THE ISOLATED WEST GATE DURING THE TIME THEIR COMMUNICATION WITH THE TEAM AT THE MAIN GATE IS CUT OFF.
ONCE WE HAVE THE WEST GATE BACK, WE CAN SEND OUT FOR HELP FROM OUTSIDE CITIES.
EXACTLY.
FRANKLY, THERE IS NO WAY THE MILITIA AND MERCENARIES CAN BEAT THE ARMY.
THIS PLAN IS NO MORE THAN A MEANS OF ESCAPE FROM CERTAIN DEATH.

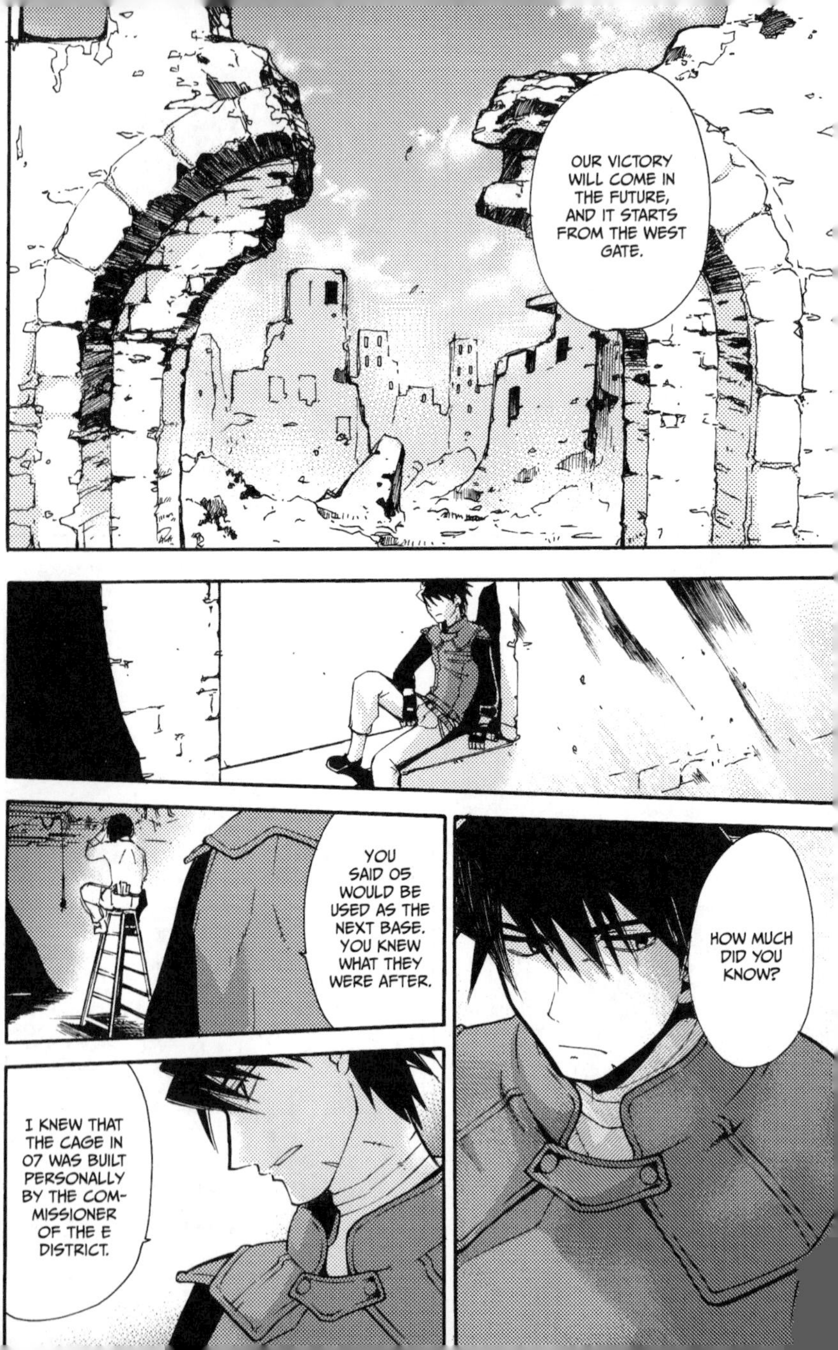
OUR VICTORY WILL COME IN THE FUTURE, AND IT STARTS FROM THE WEST GATE.
HOW MUCH DID YOU KNOW?
YOU SAID 05 WOULD BE USED AS THE NEXT BASE. YOU KNEW WHAT THEY WERE AFTER.
I KNEW THAT THE CAGE IN 07 WAS BUILT PERSONALLY BY THE COM- MISSIONER OF THE E DISTRICT.

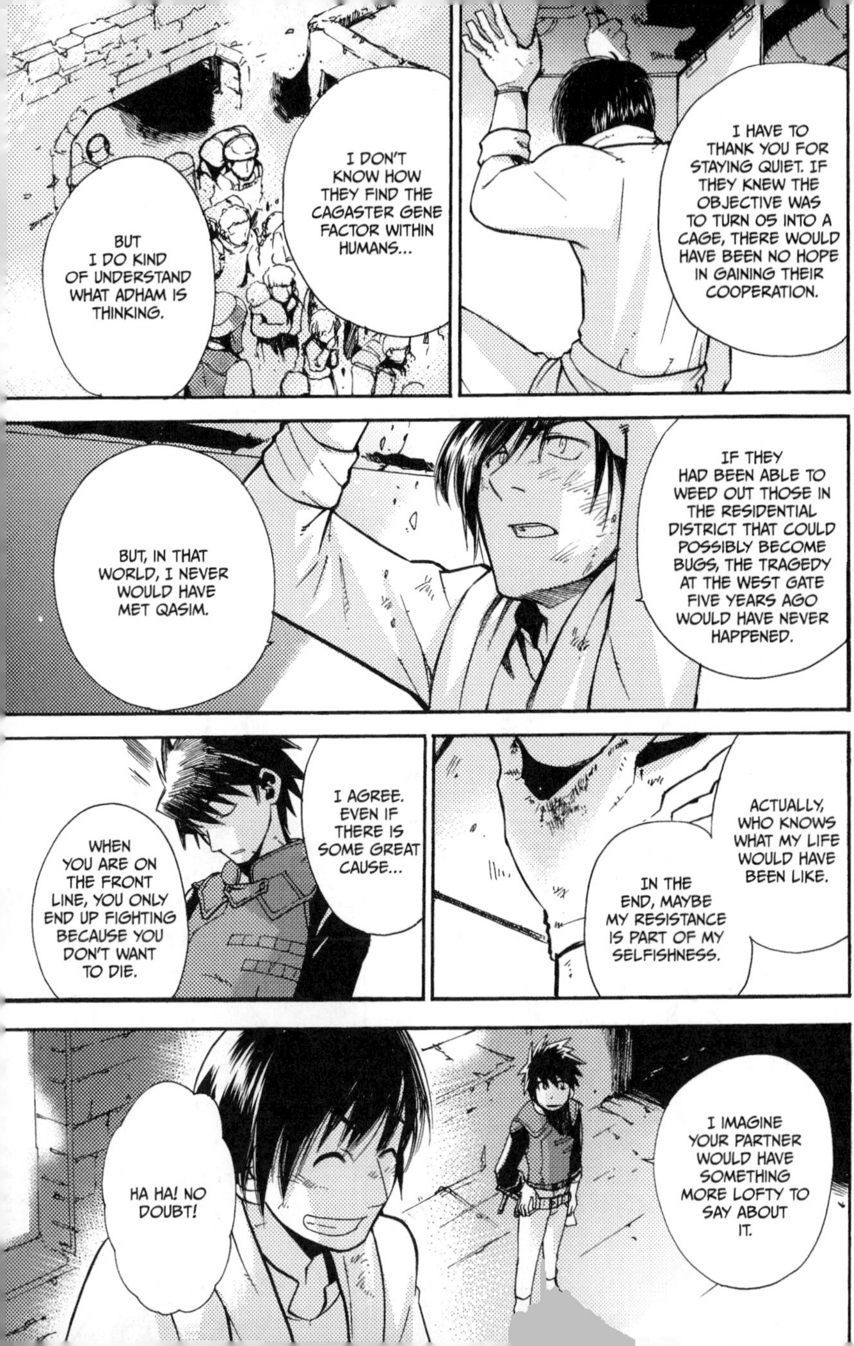
I HAVE TO THANK YOU FOR STAYING QUIET. IF THEY KNEW THE OBJECTIVE WAS TO TURN 05 INTO A CAGE, THERE WOULD HAVE BEEN NO HOPE IN GAINING THEIR COOPERATION.
I DON'T KNOW HOW THEY FIND THE CAGASTER GENE FACTOR WITHIN HUMANS...
BUT I DO KIND OF UNDERSTAND WHAT ADHAM IS THINKING.
IF THEY HAD BEEN ABLE TO WEED OUT THOSE IN THE RESIDENTIAL DISTRICT THAT COULD POSSIBLY BECOME BUGS, THE TRAGEDY AT THE WEST GATE FIVE YEARS AGO WOULD HAVE NEVER HAPPENED.
BUT, IN THAT WORLD, I NEVER WOULD HAVE MET QASIM.
ACTUALLY, WHO KNOWS WHAT MY LIFE WOULD HAVE BEEN LIKE.
IN THE END, MAYBE MY RESISTANCE IS PART OF MY SELFISHNESS.
I AGREE. EVEN IF THERE IS SOME GREAT CAUSE...
WHEN YOU ARE ON THE FRONT LINE, YOU ONLY END UP FIGHTING BECAUSE YOU DON'T WANT TO DIE.
I IMAGINE YOUR PARTNER WOULD HAVE SOMETHING MORE LOFTY TO SAY ABOUT IT.
HA HA! NO DOUBT!

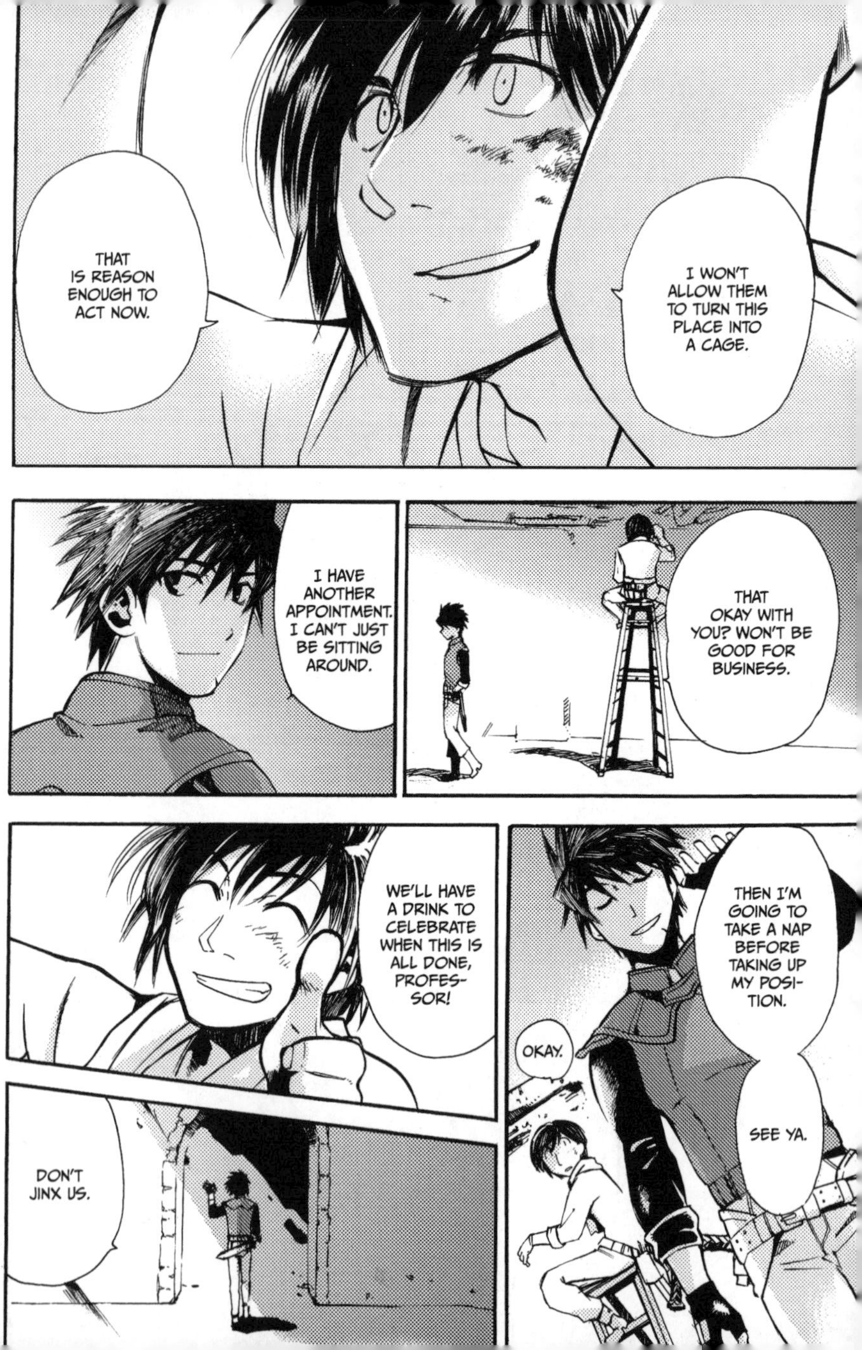
I WON'T ALLOW THEM TO TURN THIS PLACE INTO A CAGE.
THAT IS REASON ENOUGH TO ACT NOW.
THAT OKAY WITH YOU? WON'T BE GOOD FOR BUSINESS.
I HAVE ANOTHER APPOINTMENT. I CAN'T JUST BE SITTING AROUND.
THEN I'M GOING TO TAKE A NAP BEFORE TAKING UP MY POSI-TION.
OKAY.
SEE YA.
WE'LL HAVE A DRINK TO CELEBRATE WHEN THIS IS ALL DONE, PROFES-SOR!
DON'T JINX US.

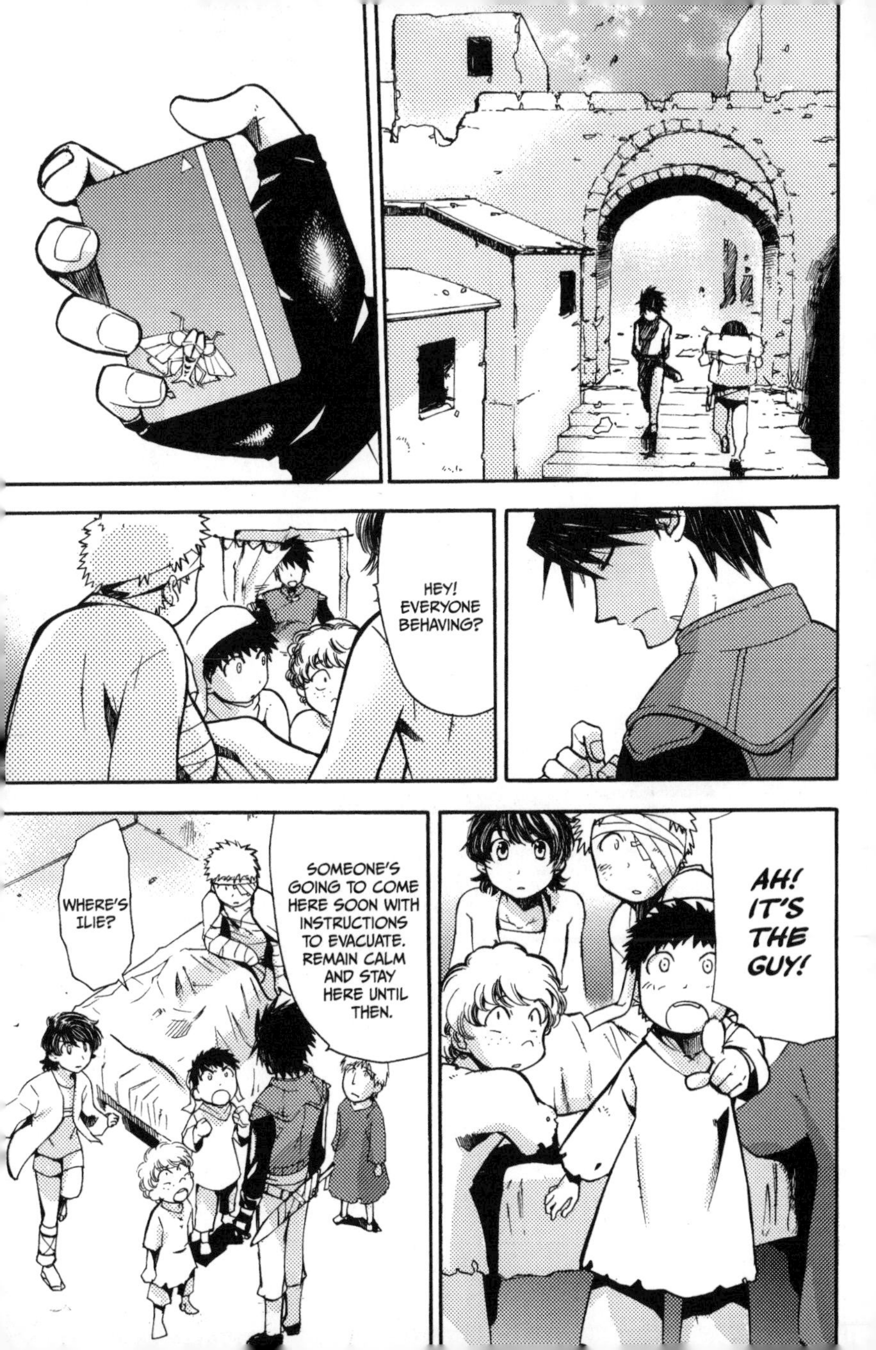
HEY! EVERYONE BEHAVING?
AH! IT'S THE GUY!
SOMEONE'S GOING TO COME HERE SOON WITH INSTRUCTIONS TO EVACUATE. REMAIN CALM AND STAY HERE UNTIL THEN.
WHERE'S ILIE?

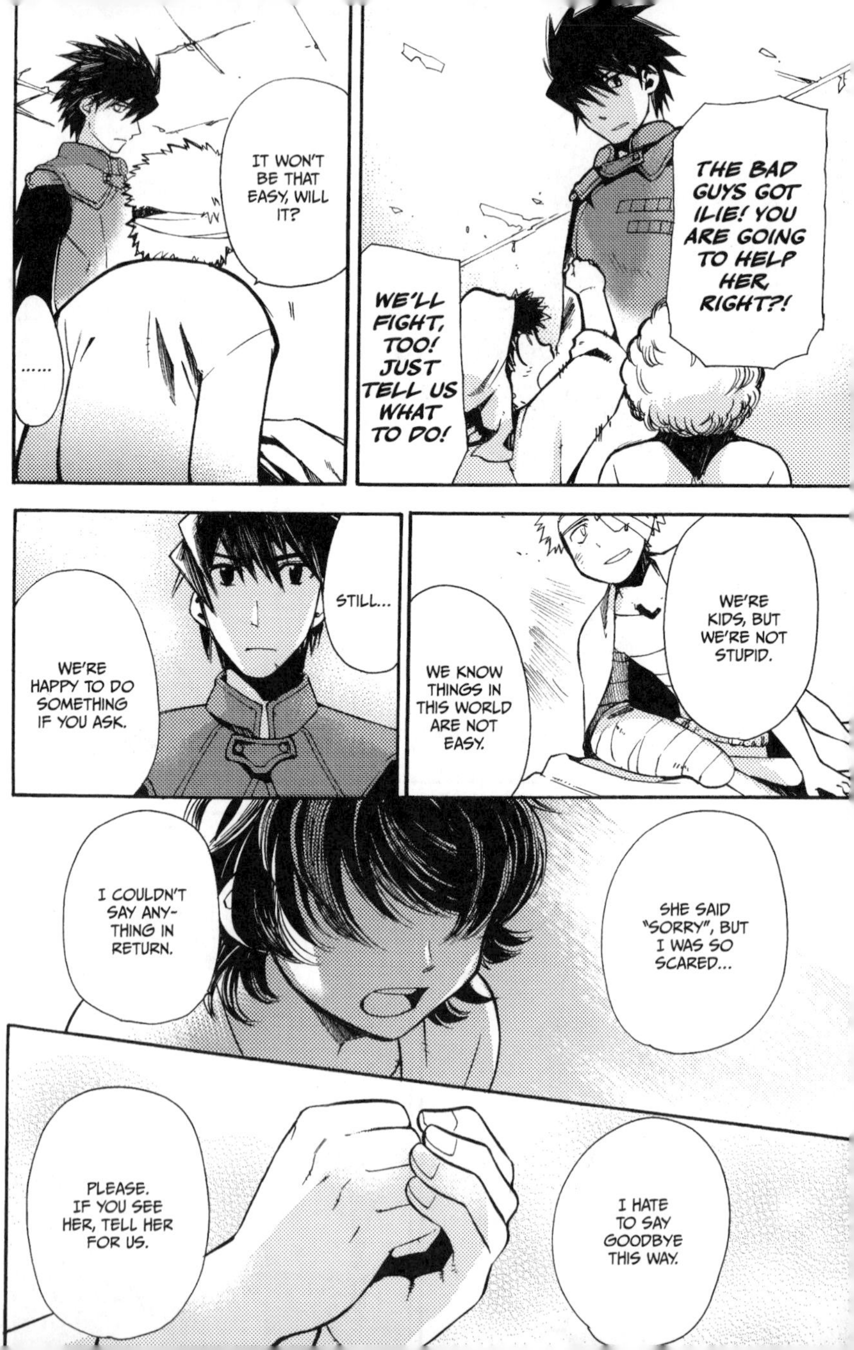
THE BAD GUYS GOT ILIE! YOU ARE GOING TO HELP HER, RIGHT?!
WE'LL FIGHT, TOO! JUST TELL US WHAT TO DO!
IT WON'T BE THAT EASY, WILL IT?
......
WE'RE KIDS, BUT WE'RE NOT STUPID.
WE KNOW THINGS IN THIS WORLD ARE NOT EASY.
STILL...
WE'RE HAPPY TO DO SOMETHING IF YOU ASK.
SHE SAID "SORRY", BUT I WAS SO SCARED...
I COULDN'T SAY ANY-THING IN RETURN.
I HATE TO SAY GOODBYE THIS WAY.
PLEASE. IF YOU SEE HER, TELL HER FOR US.

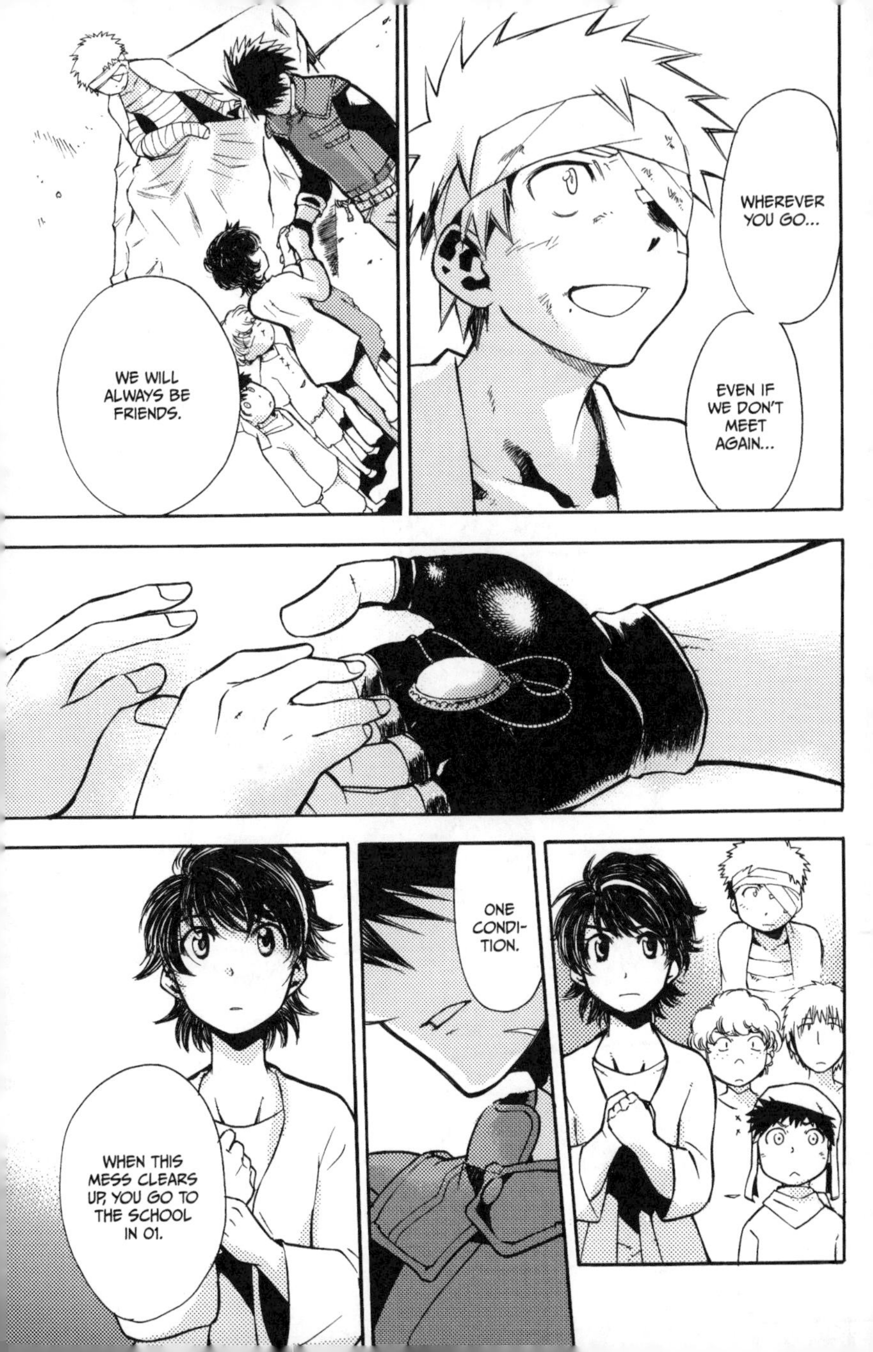
WHEREVER YOU GO...
EVEN IF WE DON'T MEET AGAIN...
WE WILL ALWAYS BE FRIENDS.
ONE CONDI-TION.
WHEN THIS MESS CLEARS UP, YOU GO TO THE SCHOOL IN 01.

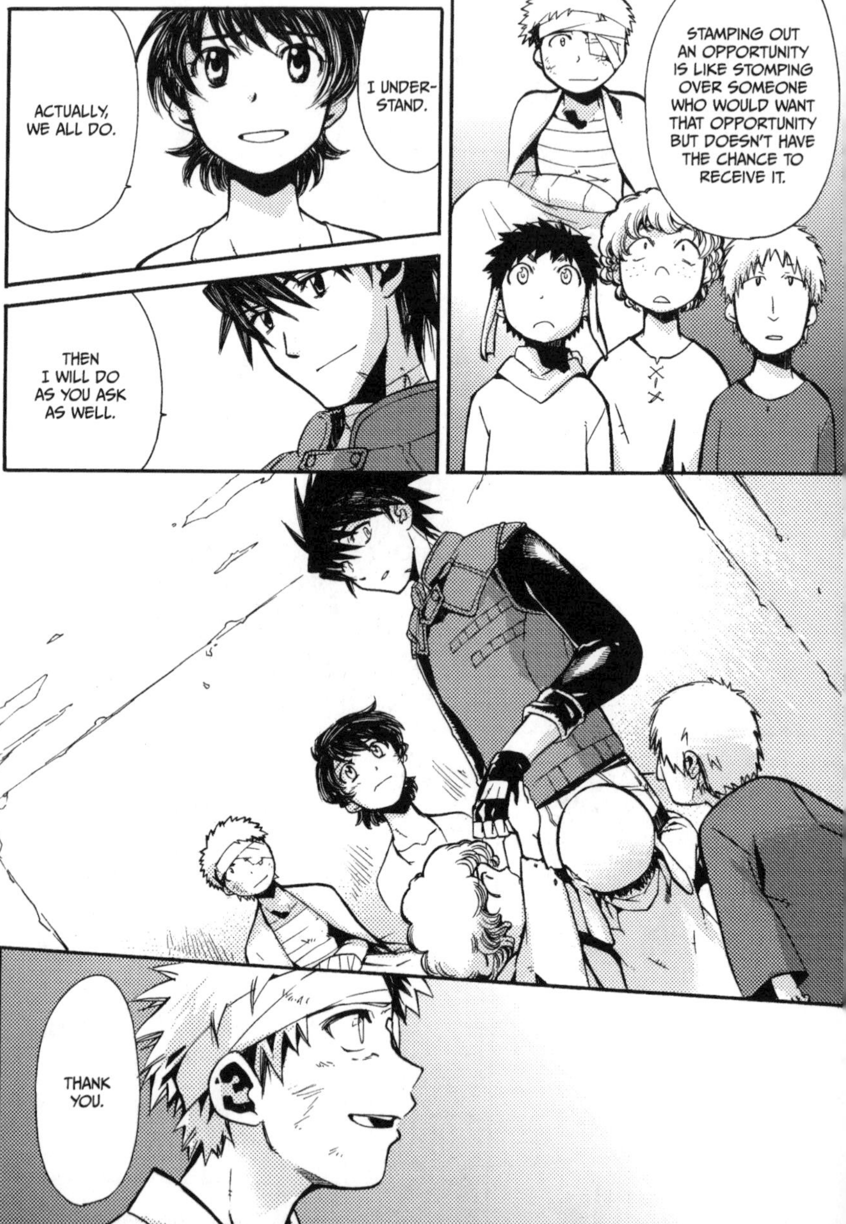
STAMPING OUT AN OPPORTUNITY IS LIKE STOMPING OVER SOMEONE WHO WOULD WANT THAT OPPORTUNITY BUT DOESN'T HAVE THE CHANCE TO RECEIVE IT.
I UNDER-STAND.
ACTUALLY, WE ALL DO.
THEN I WILL DO AS YOU ASK AS WELL.
THANK YOU.

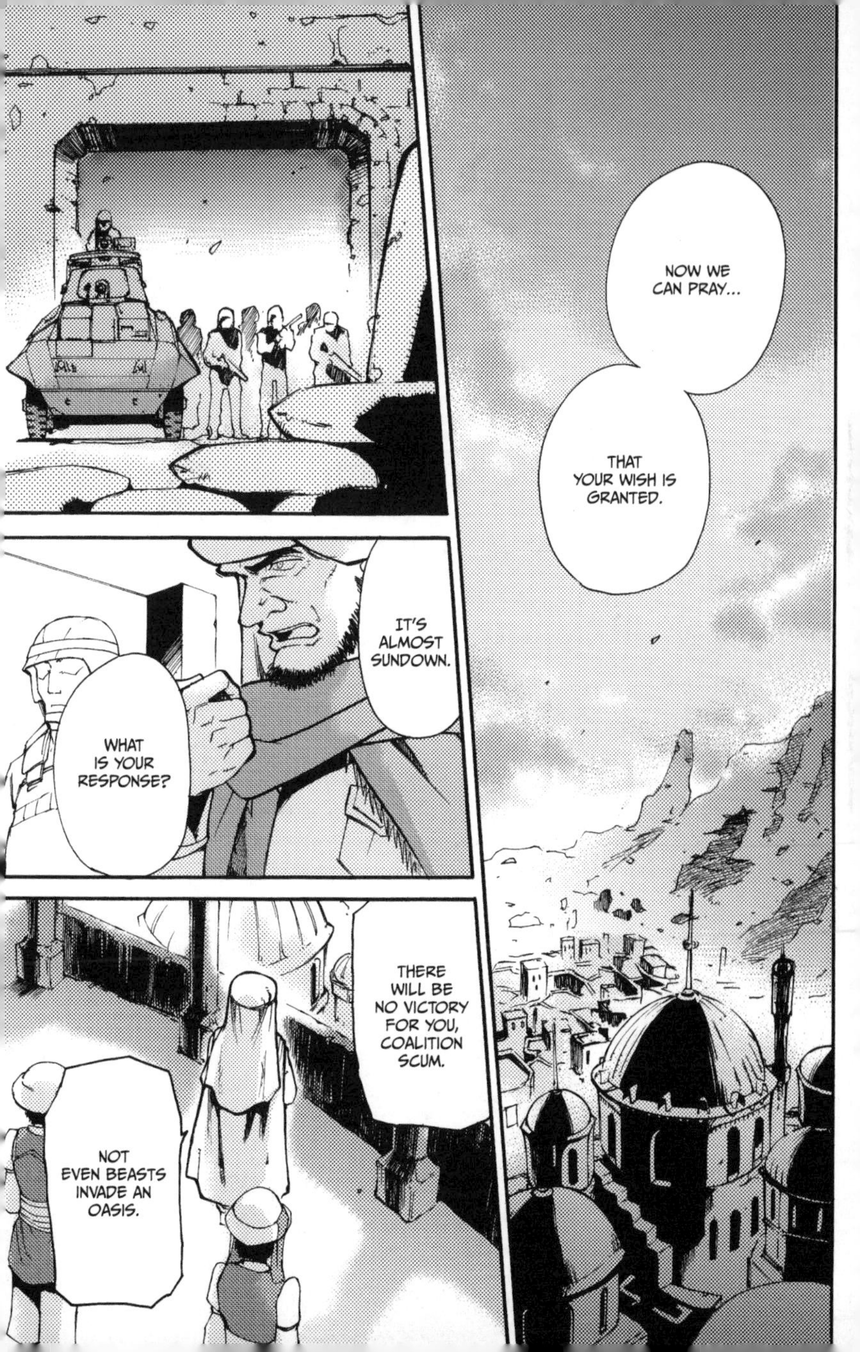
NOW WE CAN PRAY...
THAT YOUR WISH IS GRANTED.
IT'S ALMOST SUNDOWN.
WHAT IS YOUR RESPONSE?
THERE WILL BE NO VICTORY FOR YOU, COALITION SCUM.
NOT EVEN BEASTS INVADE AN OASIS.

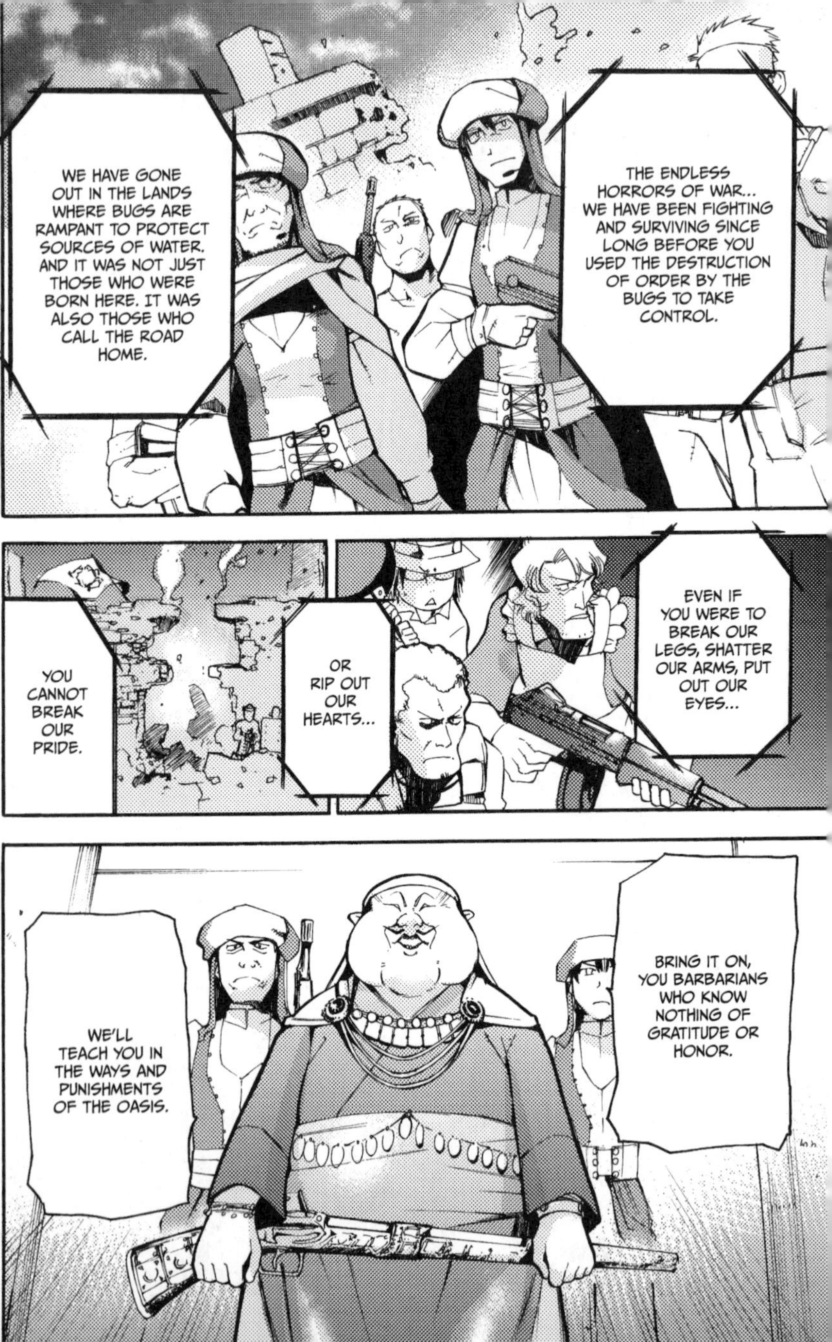
THE ENDLESS HORRORS OF WAR... WE HAVE BEEN FIGHTING AND SURVIVING SINCE LONG BEFORE YOU USED THE DESTRUCTION OF ORDER BY THE BUGS TO TAKE CONTROL.
WE HAVE GONE OUT IN THE LANDS WHERE BUGS ARE RAMPANT TO PROTECT SOURCES OF WATER. AND IT WAS NOT JUST THOSE WHO WERE BORN HERE. IT WAS ALSO THOSE WHO CALL THE ROAD HOME.
EVEN IF YOU WERE TO BREAK OUR LEGS, SHATTER OUR ARMS, PUT OUT OUR EYES...
OR RIP OUT OUR HEARTS...
YOU CANNOT BREAK OUR PRIDE.
BRING IT ON, YOU BARBARIANS WHO KNOW NOTHING OF GRATITUDE OR HONOR.
WE'LL TEACH YOU IN THE WAYS AND PUNISHMENTS OF THE OASIS.

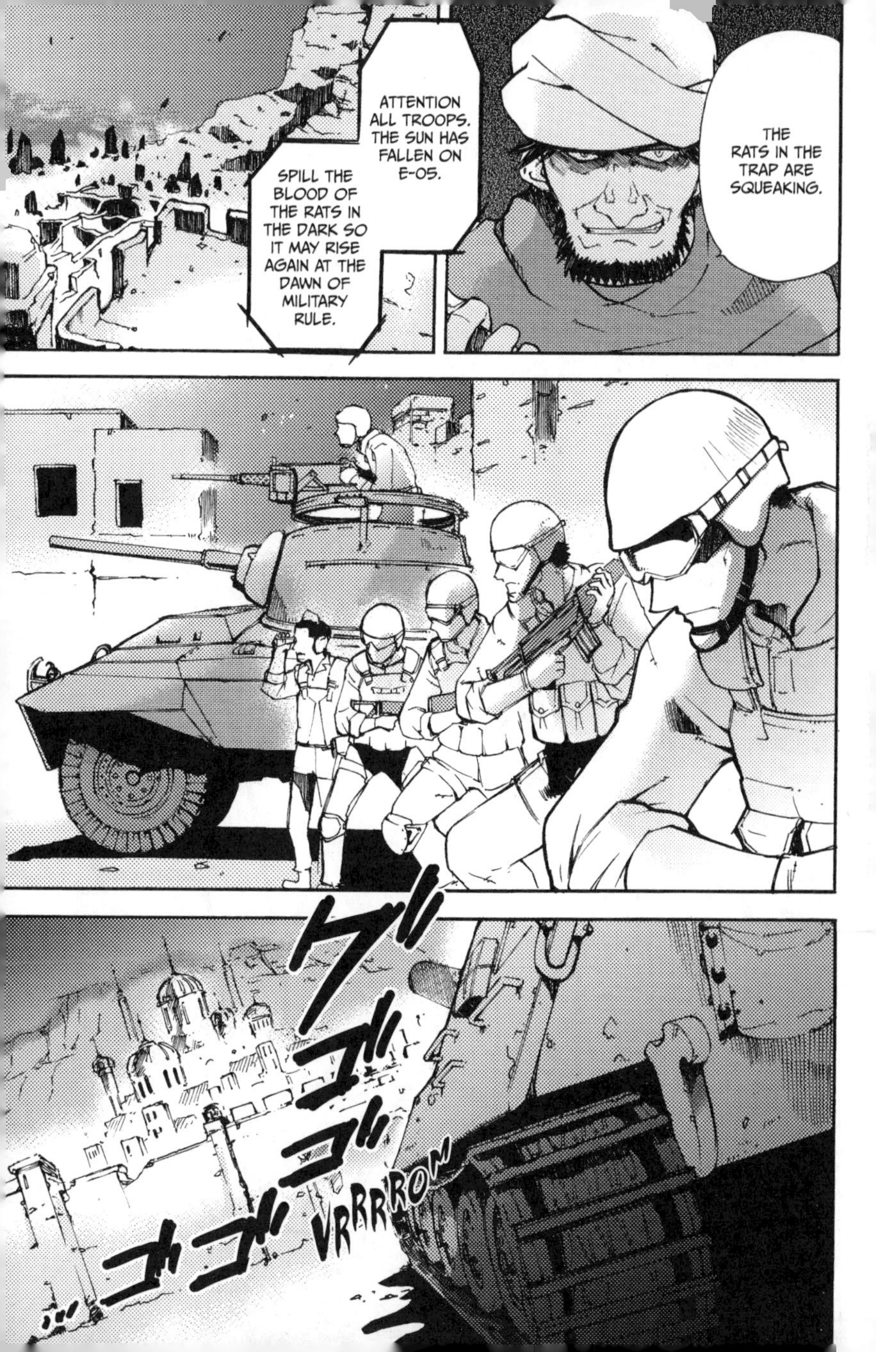
THE RATS IN THE TRAP ARE SQUEAKING.
ATTENTION ALL TROOPS. THE SUN HAS FALLEN ON E-05.
SPILL THE BLOOD OF THE RATS IN THE DARK SO IT MAY RISE AGAIN AT THE DAWN OF MILITARY RULE.
VRRRROM

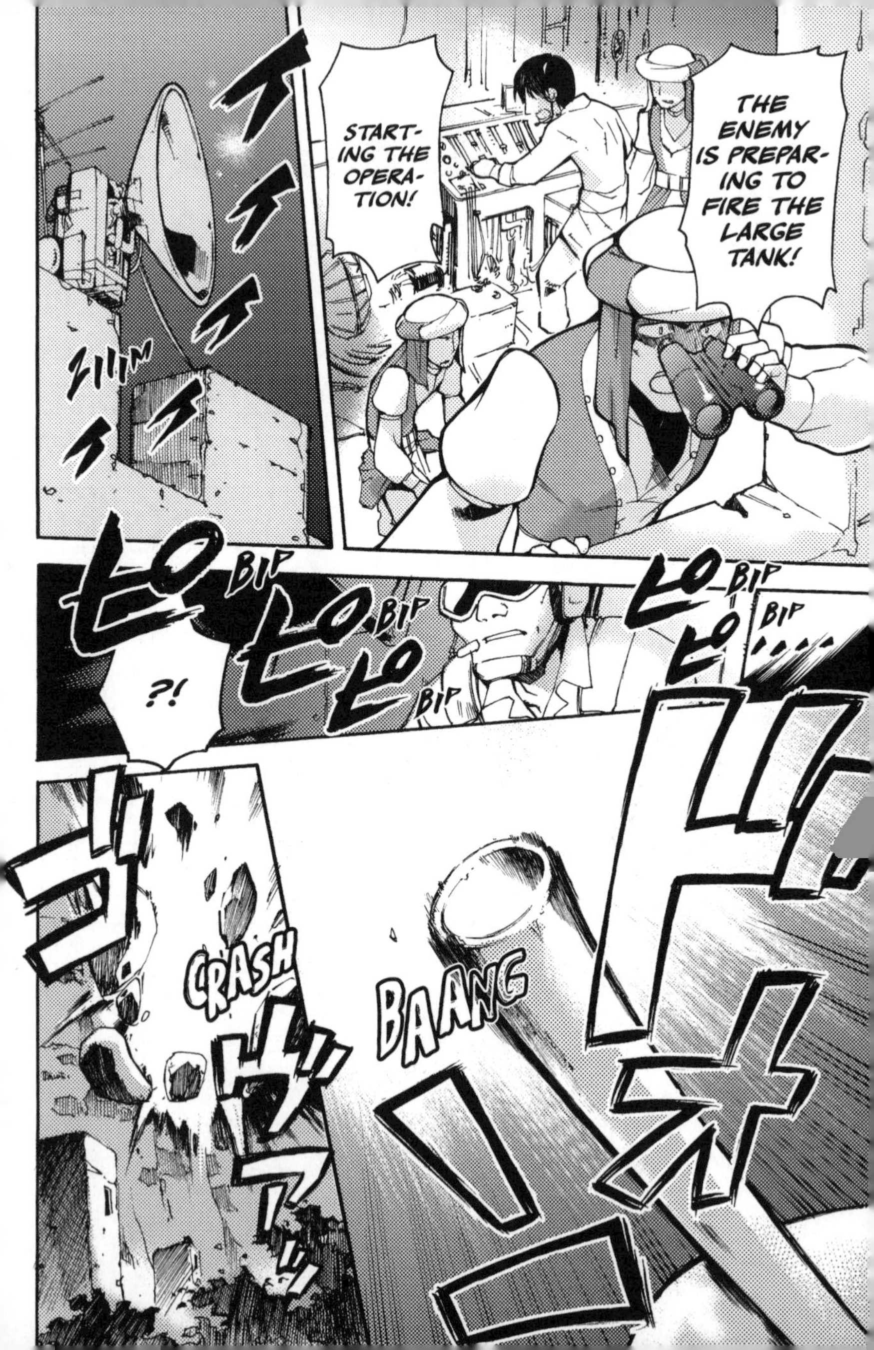
THE ENEMY IS PREPARING TO FIRE THE LARGE TANK!
STARTING THE OPERATION!
ZIIIM
BIP
BIP
BIP
BIP
BIP
?!
BAANG
CRASH

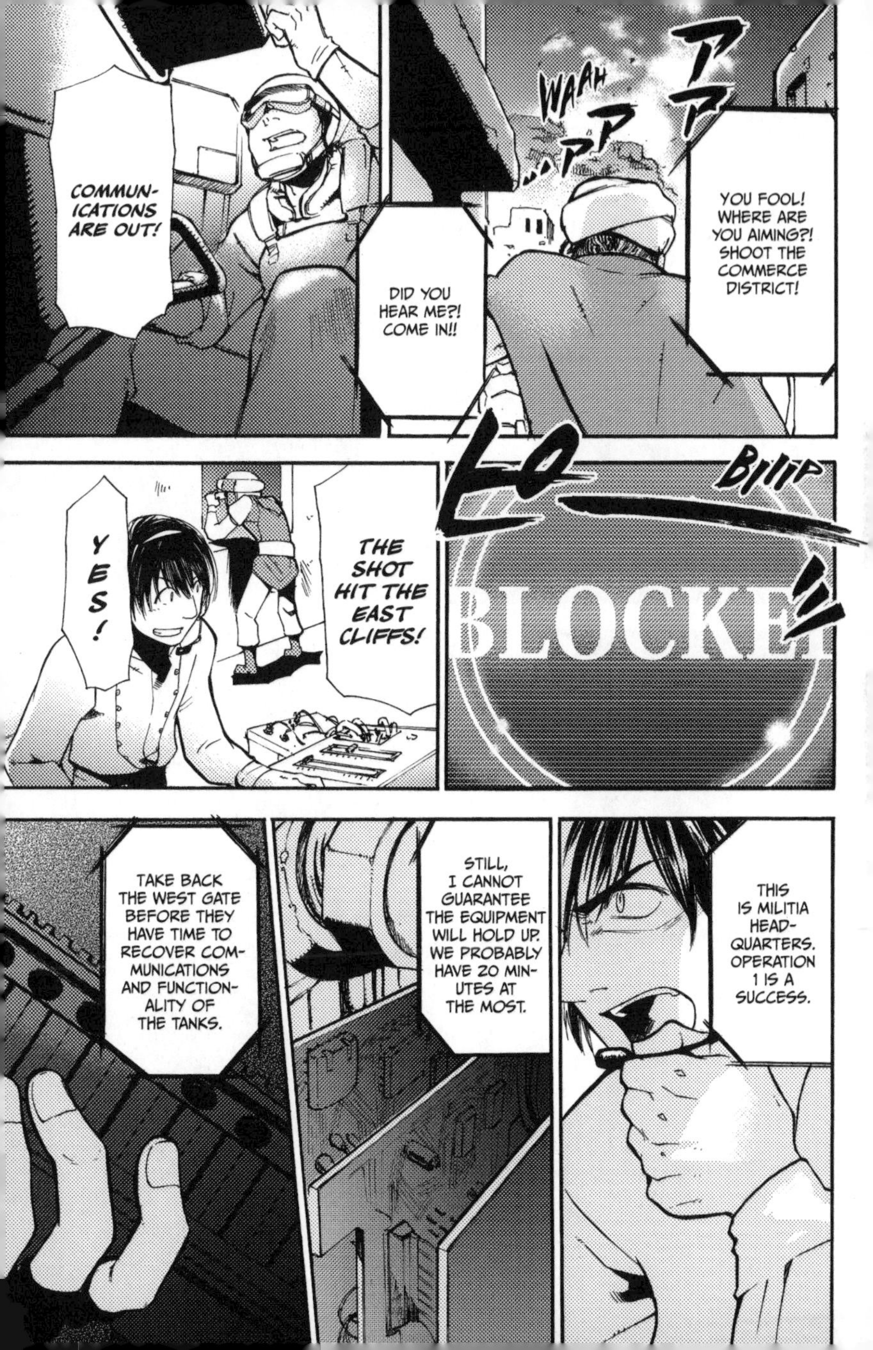
WAAH
YOU FOOL! WHERE ARE YOU AIMING?! SHOOT THE COMMERCE DISTRICT!
DID YOU HEAR ME?! COME IN!!
COMMUNICATIONS ARE OUT!
BLIIP
BLOCKE
THE SHOT HIT THE EAST CLIFFS!
YES!
THIS IS MILITIA HEADQUARTERS. OPERATION 1 IS A SUCCESS.
STILL, I CANNOT GUARANTEE THE EQUIPMENT WILL HOLD UP. WE PROBABLY HAVE 20 MINUTES AT THE MOST.
TAKE BACK THE WEST GATE BEFORE THEY HAVE TIME TO RECOVER COMMUNICATIONS AND FUNCTIONALITY OF THE TANKS.

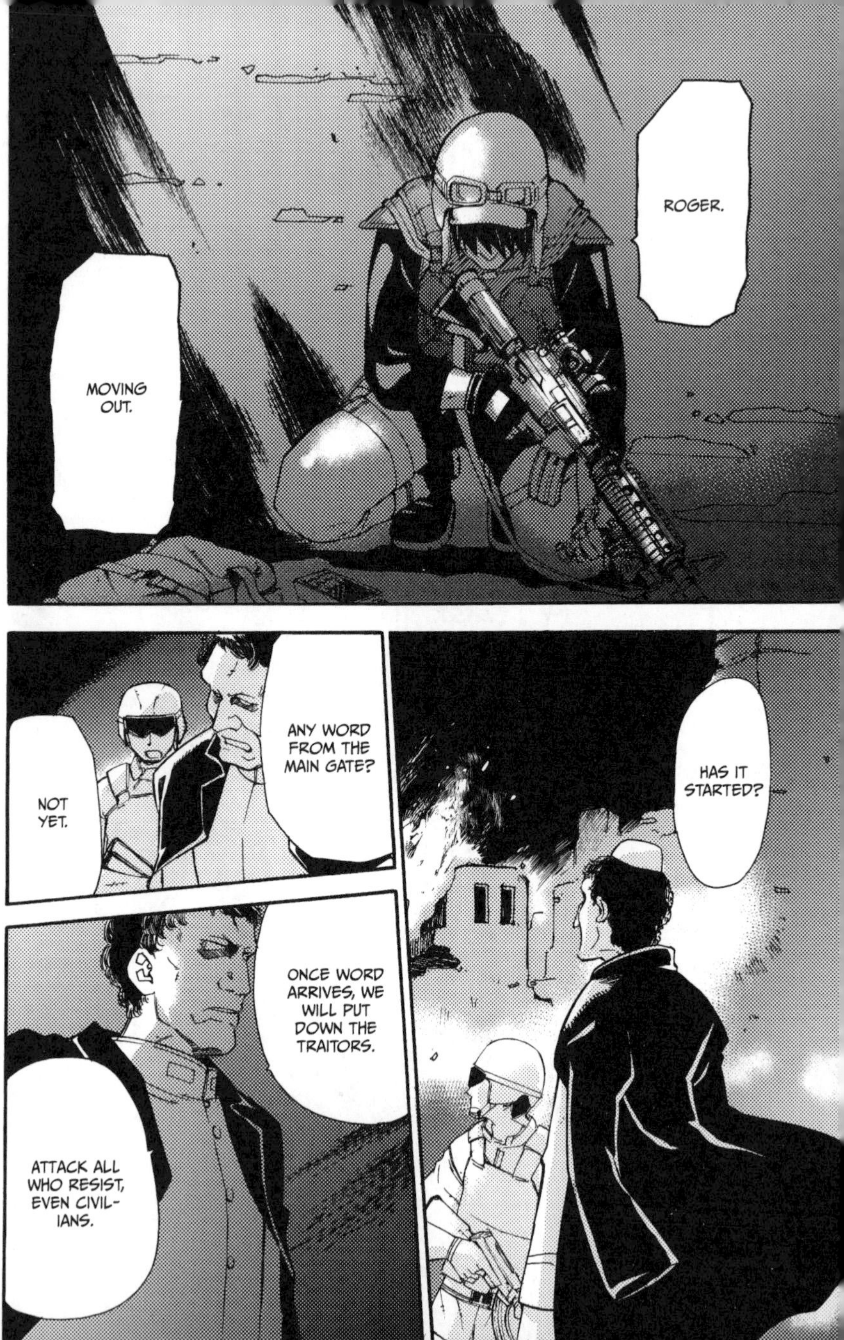
ROGER.
MOVING OUT.
HAS IT STARTED?
ANY WORD FROM THE MAIN GATE?
NOT YET.
ONCE WORD ARRIVES, WE WILL PUT DOWN THE TRAITORS.
ATTACK ALL WHO RESIST, EVEN CIVIL-IANS.

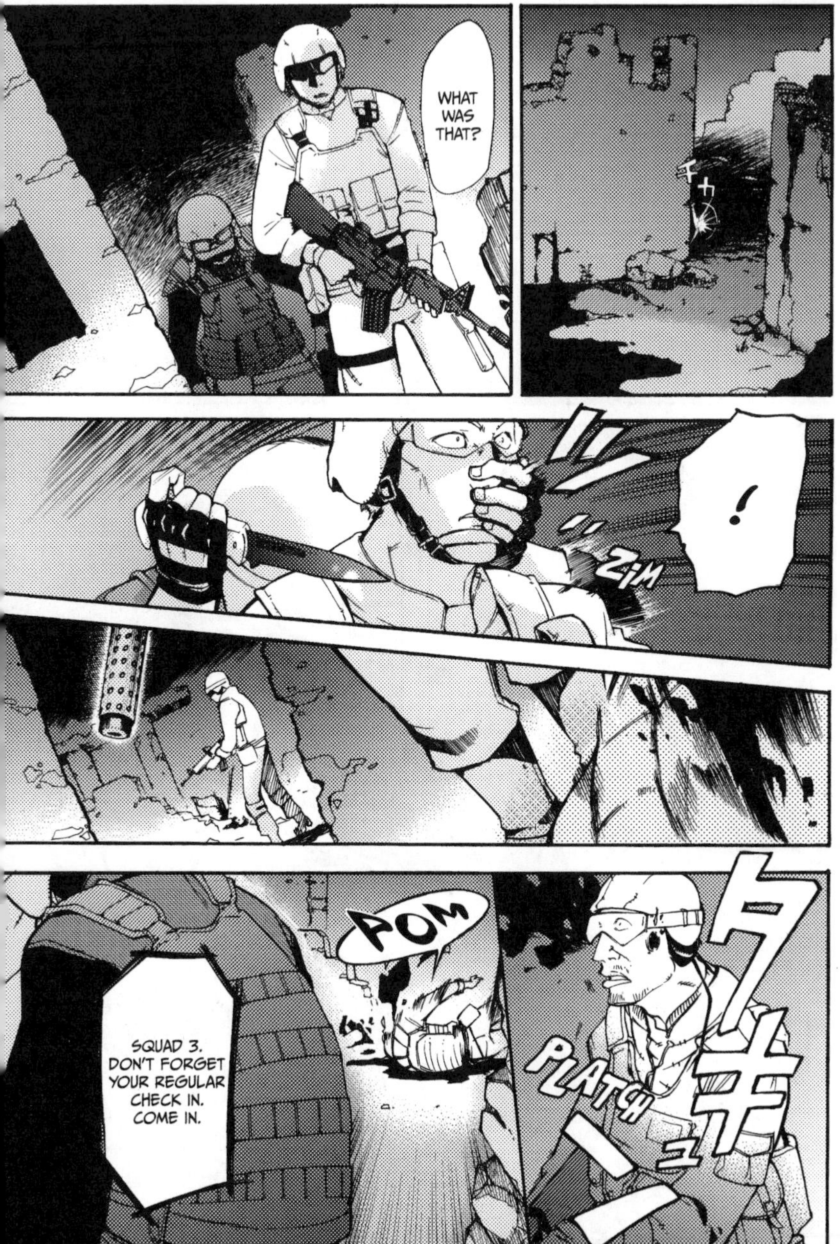

チカ
WHAT WAS THAT?
!
ZIM
タキュ
PLATCH
POM
SQUAD 3. DON'T FORGET YOUR REGULAR CHECK IN. COME IN.

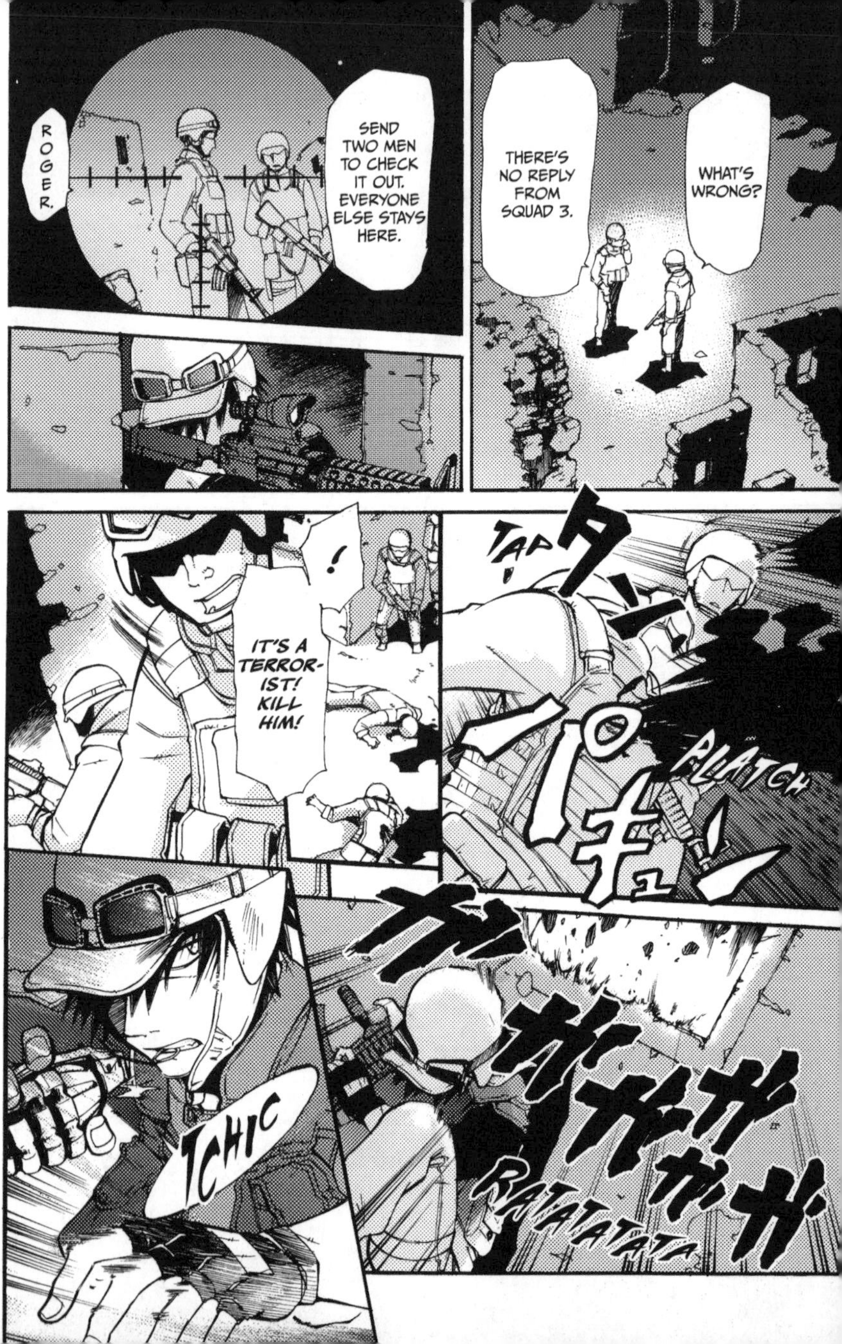
WHAT'S WRONG?
THERE'S NO REPLY FROM SQUAD 3.
SEND TWO MEN TO CHECK IT OUT. EVERYONE ELSE STAYS HERE.
ROGER.
TAP
PLATCH
!
IT'S A TERRORIST! KILL HIM!
RATATATATA
TCHIC

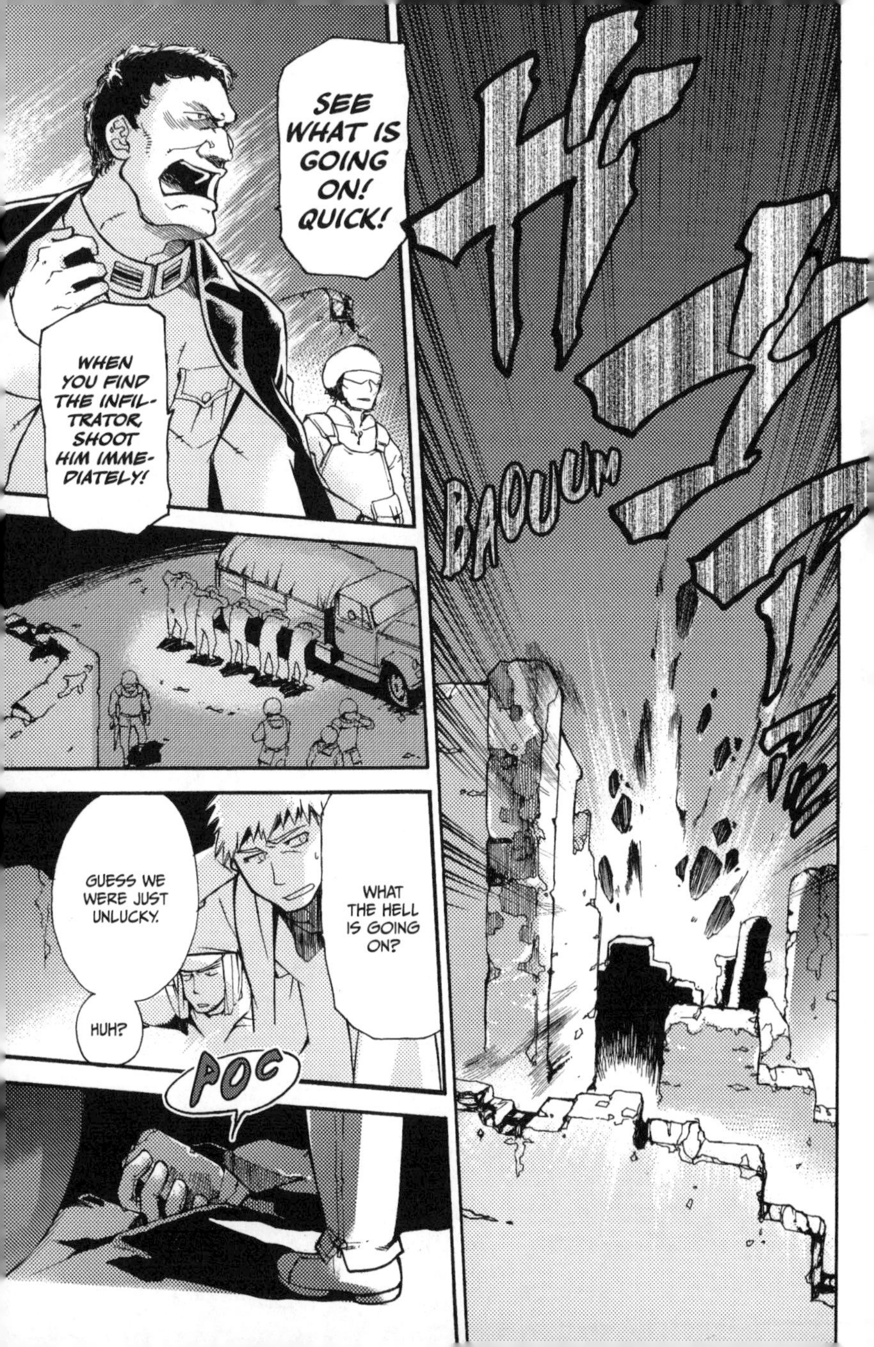
BAOUUM
SEE WHAT IS GOING ON! QUICK!
WHEN YOU FIND THE INFIL-TRATOR, SHOOT HIM IMME-DIATELY!
WHAT THE HELL IS GOING ON?
GUESS WE WERE JUST UNLUCKY.
HUH?
POC

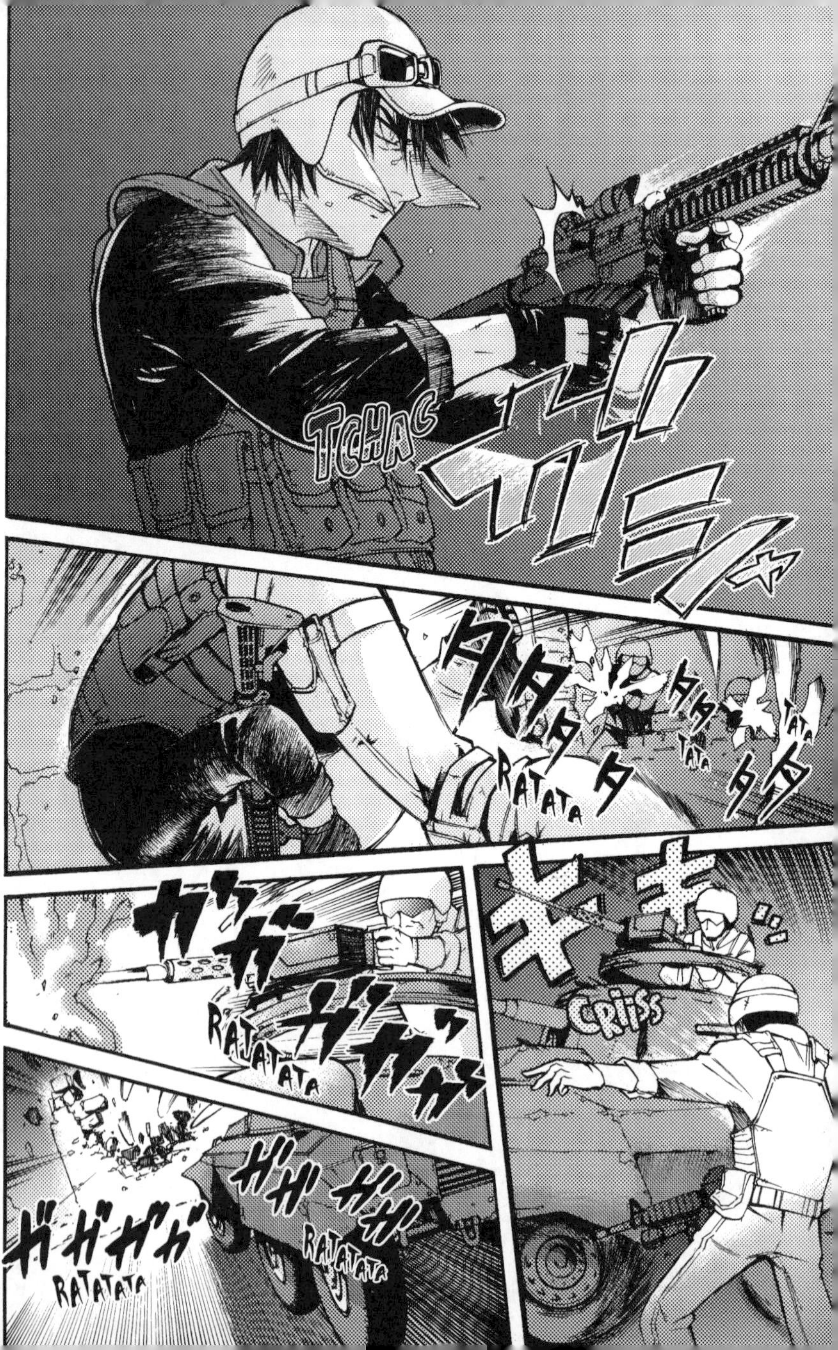
TCHAC
TATA
TATA
RATATATA
CRISS
RATATATATA
RATATATA
RATATATA

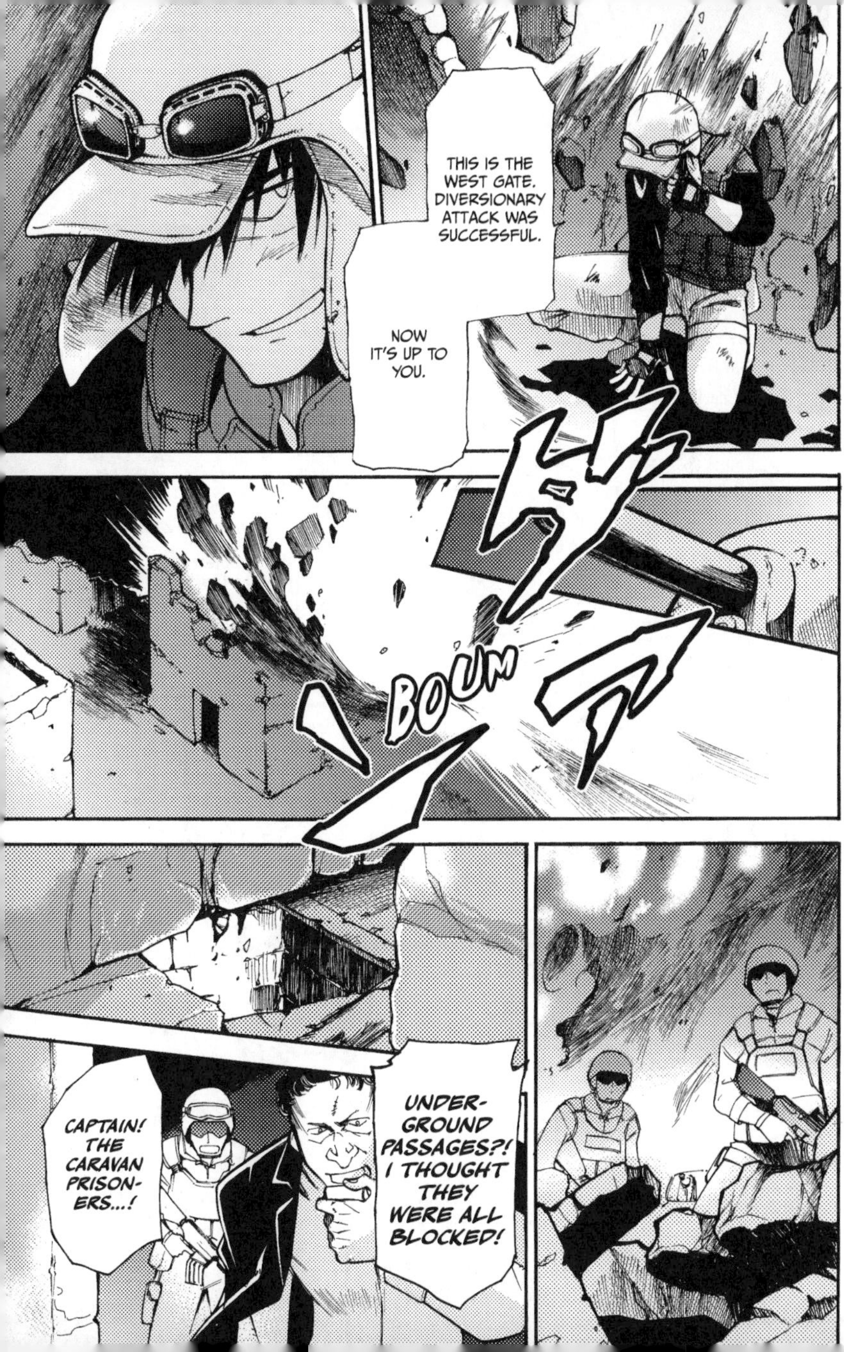
THIS IS THE WEST GATE. DIVERSIONARY ATTACK WAS SUCCESSFUL.
NOW IT'S UP TO YOU.
BOUM
CAPTAIN! THE CARAVAN PRISON-ERS...!
UNDER-GROUND PASSAGES?! I THOUGHT THEY WERE ALL BLOCKED!

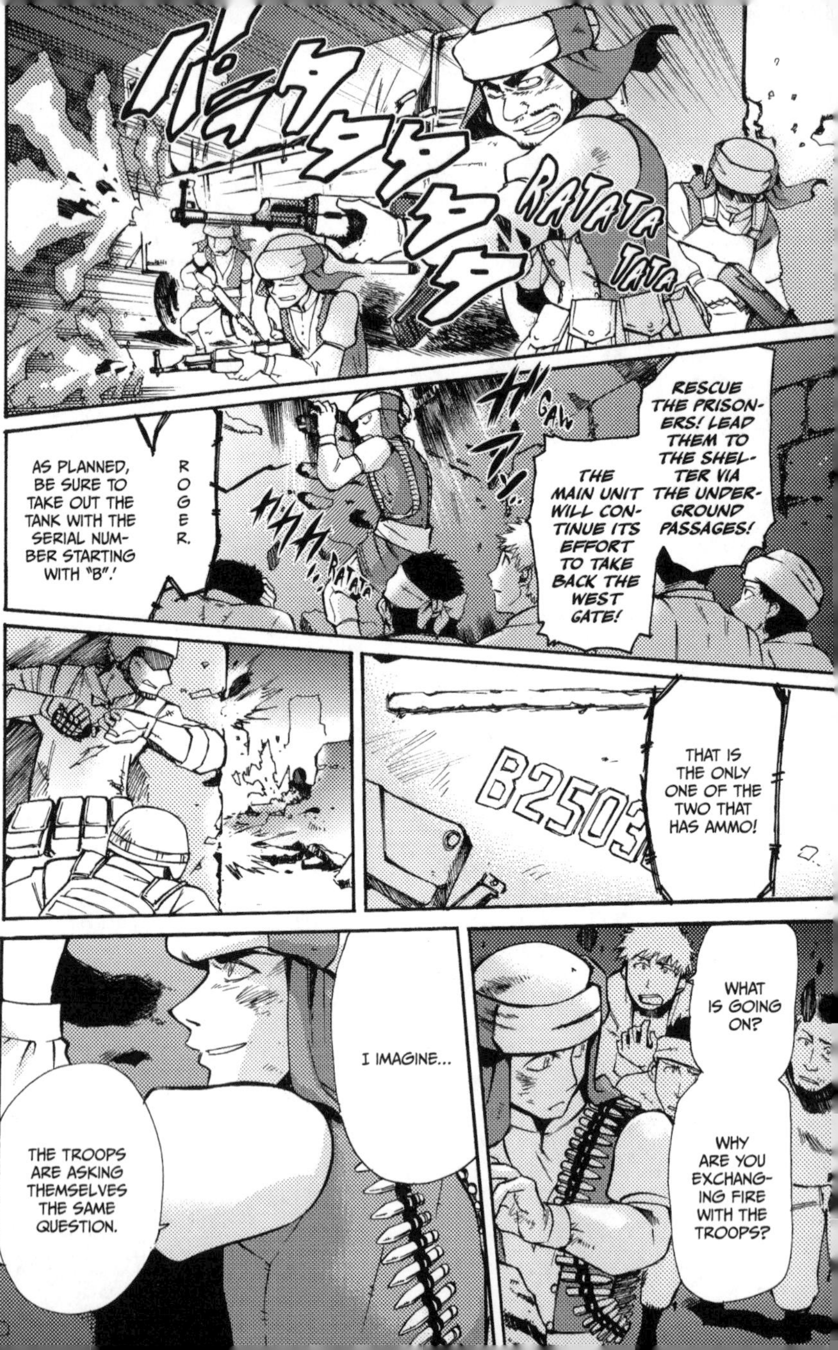
RATATA TATA
RESCUE THE PRISONERS! LEAD THEM TO THE SHELTER VIA THE UNDERGROUND PASSAGES!
GAW
THE MAIN UNIT WILL CONTINUE ITS EFFORT TO TAKE BACK THE WEST GATE!
RATATA
ROGER.
AS PLANNED, BE SURE TO TAKE OUT THE TANK WITH THE SERIAL NUMBER STARTING WITH "B".'
THAT IS THE ONLY ONE OF THE TWO THAT HAS AMMO!
B2503
WHAT IS GOING ON?
WHY ARE YOU EXCHANGING FIRE WITH THE TROOPS?
I IMAGINE...
THE TROOPS ARE ASKING THEMSELVES THE SAME QUESTION.

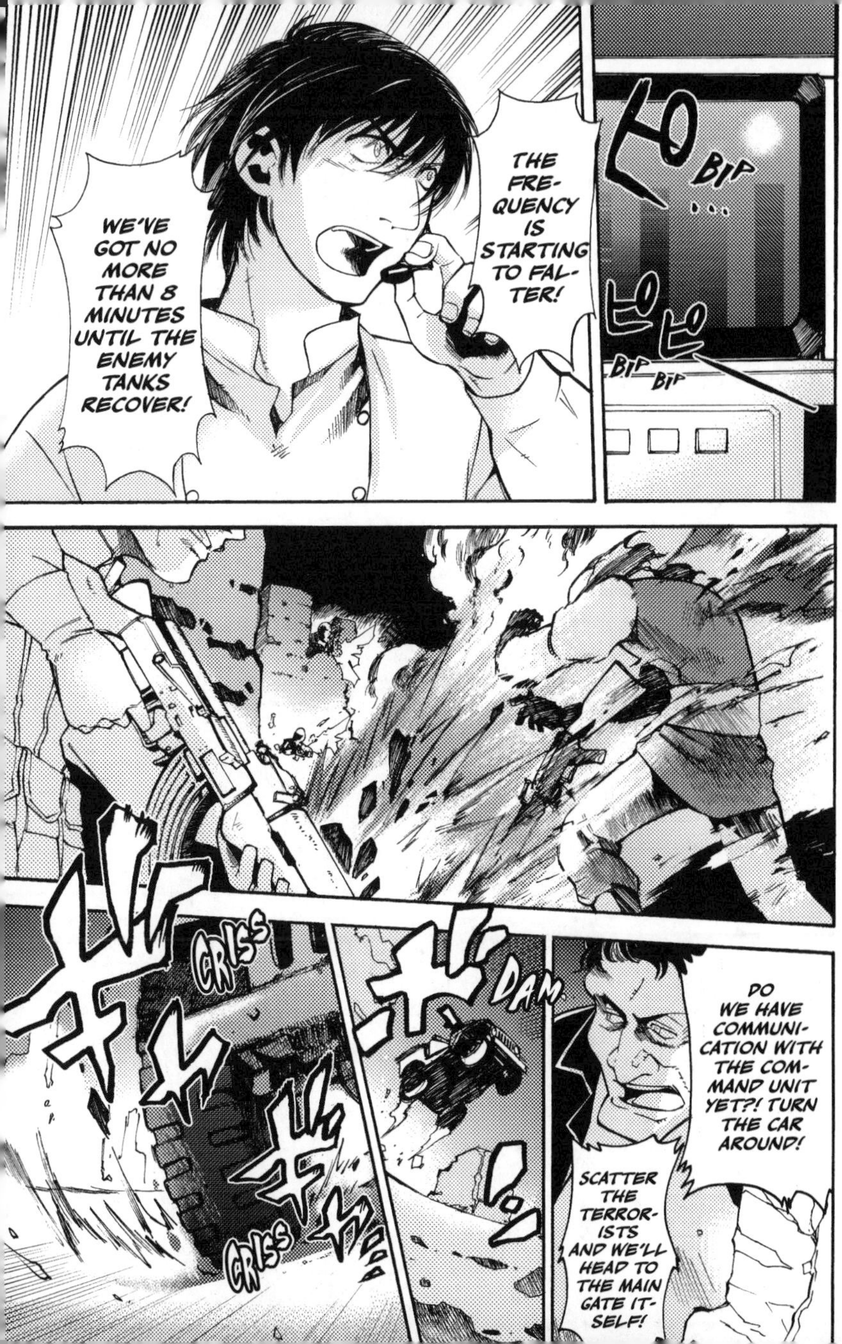
BIP ...
BIP BIP
THE FREQUENCY IS STARTING TO FALTER!
WE'VE GOT NO MORE THAN 8 MINUTES UNTIL THE ENEMY TANKS RECOVER!
DO WE HAVE COMMUNICATION WITH THE COMMAND UNIT YET?! TURN THE CAR AROUND!
SCATTER THE TERRORISTS AND WE'LL HEAD TO THE MAIN GATE ITSELF!
DAM.
CRISS
CRISS

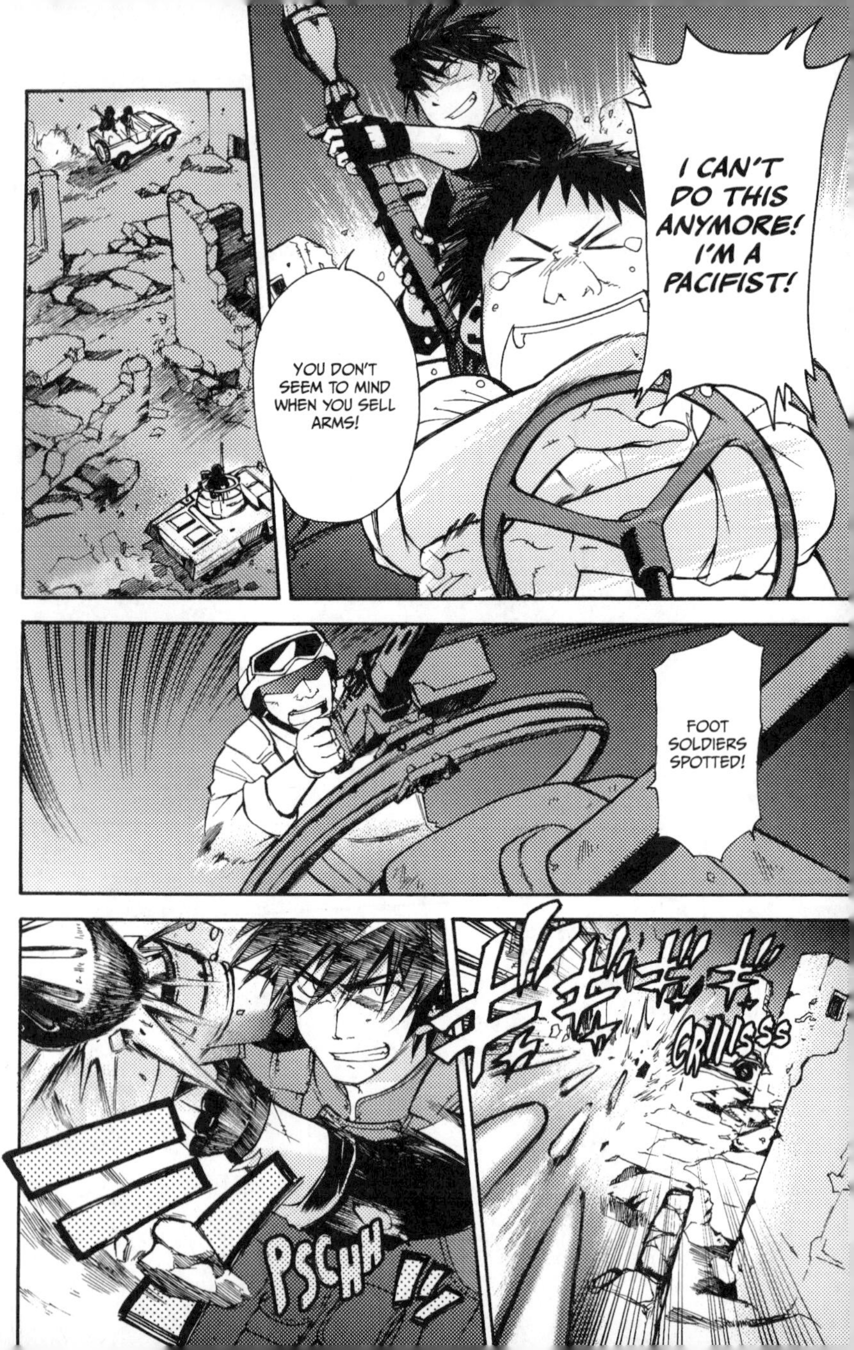
I CAN'T DO THIS ANYMORE! I'M A PACIFIST!
YOU DON'T SEEM TO MIND WHEN YOU SELL ARMS!
FOOT SOLDIERS SPOTTED!
CRIISSS
PSCHH !!

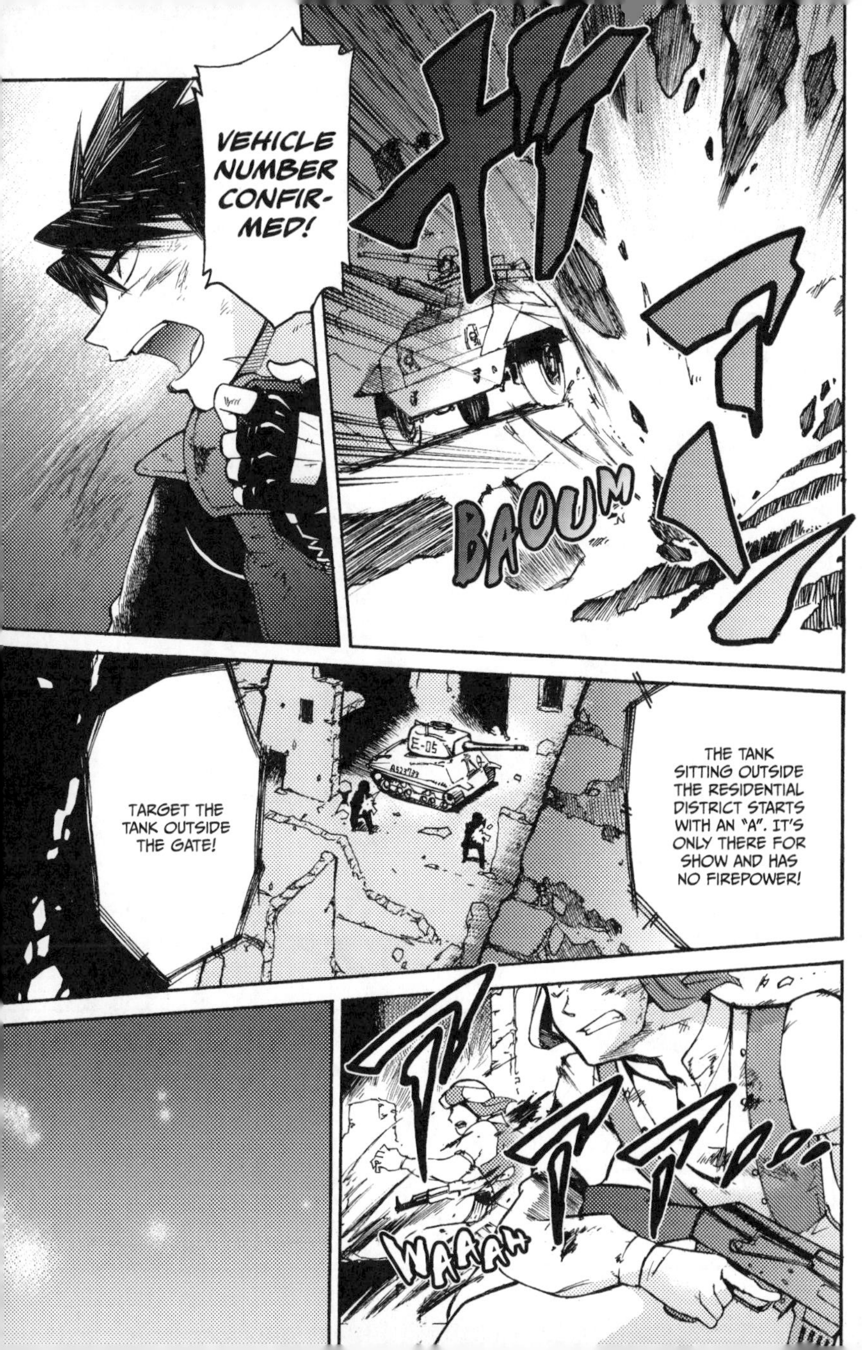
BAOUM
VEHICLE NUMBER CONFIRMED!
THE TANK SITTING OUTSIDE THE RESIDENTIAL DISTRICT STARTS WITH AN "A". IT'S ONLY THERE FOR SHOW AND HAS NO FIREPOWER!
E-05
TARGET THE TANK OUTSIDE THE GATE!
WAAAH

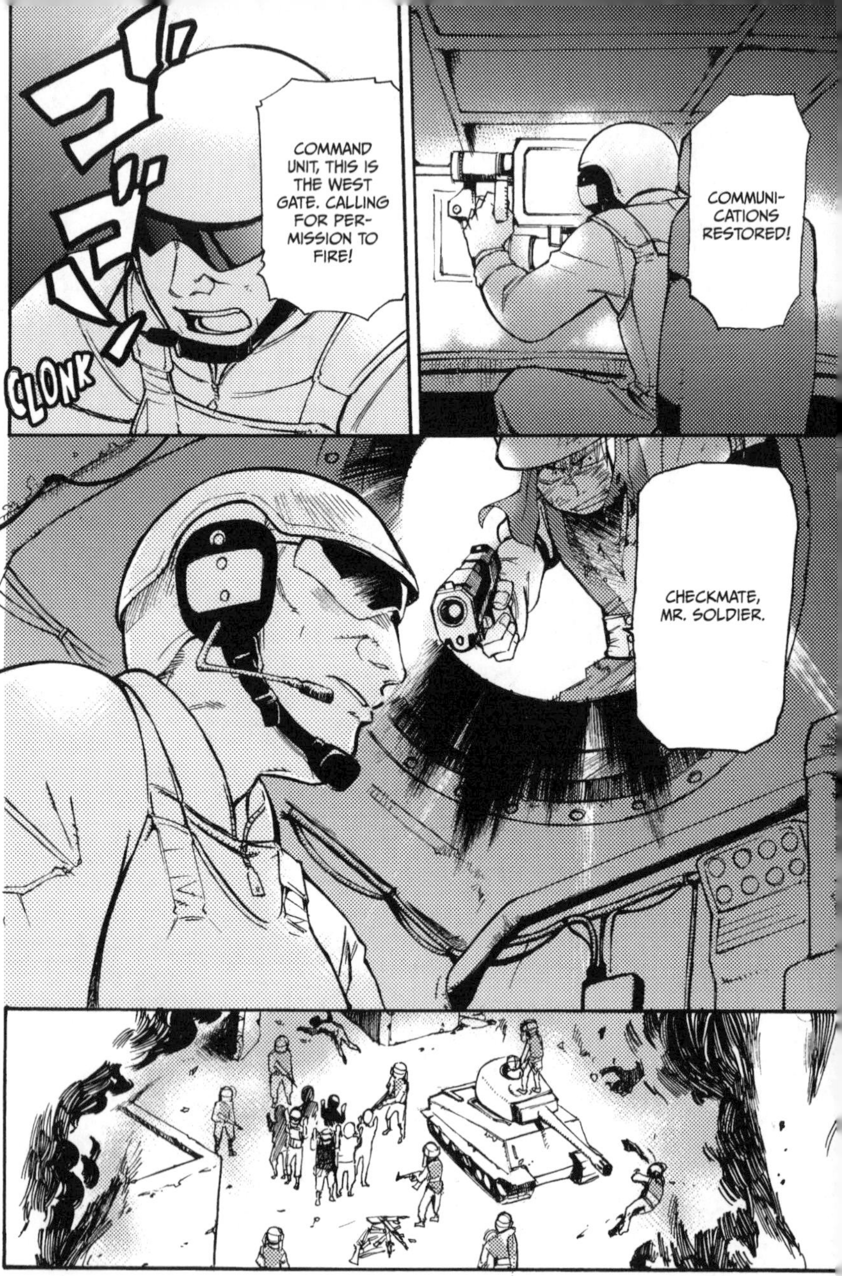
COMMUNI-CATIONS RESTORED!
COMMAND UNIT, THIS IS THE WEST GATE. CALLING FOR PER-MISSION TO FIRE!
CLONK
CHECKMATE, MR. SOLDIER.

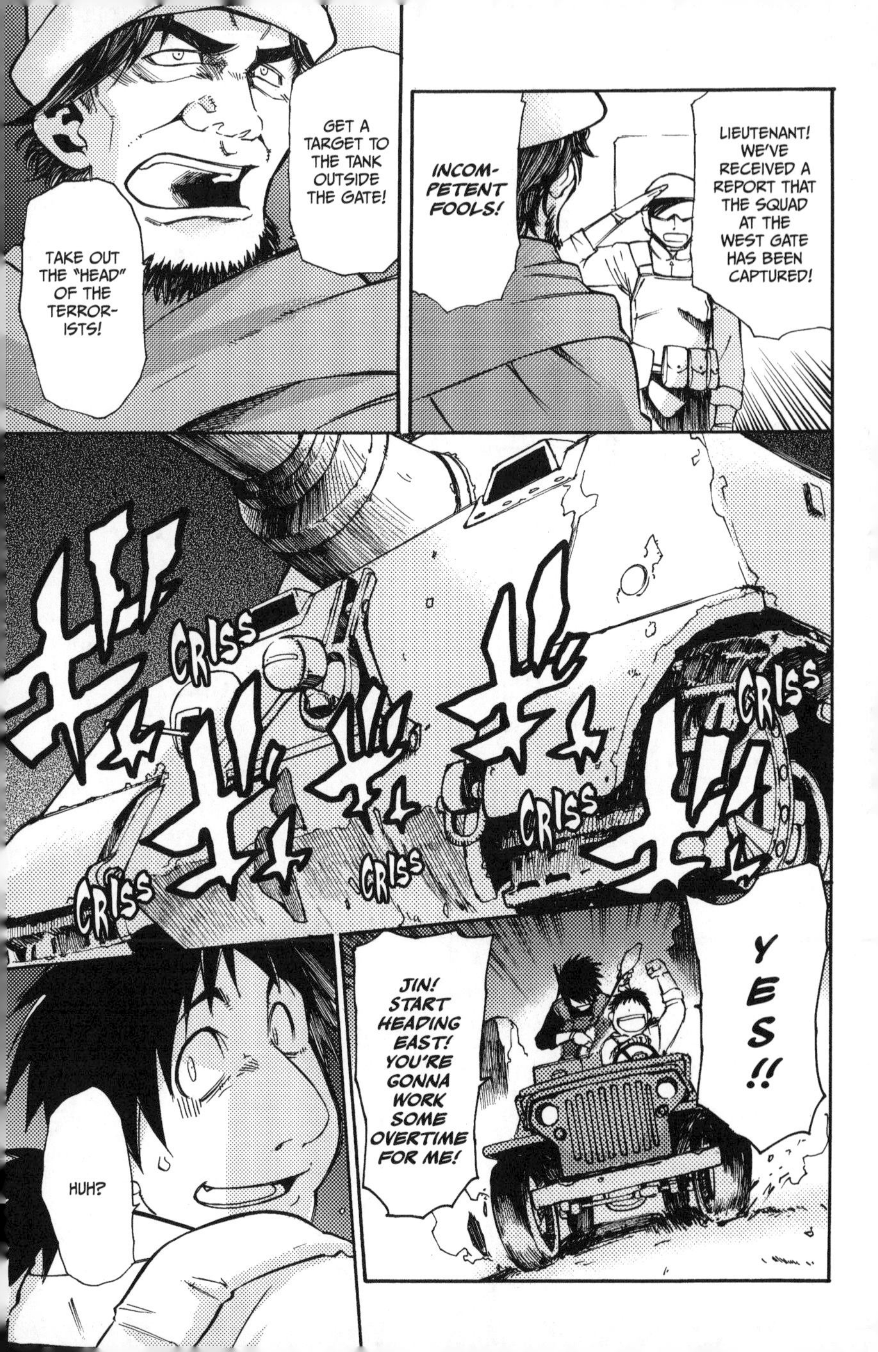
LIEUTENANT! WE'VE RECEIVED A REPORT THAT THE SQUAD AT THE WEST GATE HAS BEEN CAPTURED!
INCOM-PETENT FOOLS!
GET A TARGET TO THE TANK OUTSIDE THE GATE!
TAKE OUT THE "HEAD" OF THE TERROR-ISTS!
CRISS
CRISS
CRISS
CRISS
CRISS
YES!!
JIN! START HEADING EAST! YOU'RE GONNA WORK SOME OVERTIME FOR ME!
HUH?

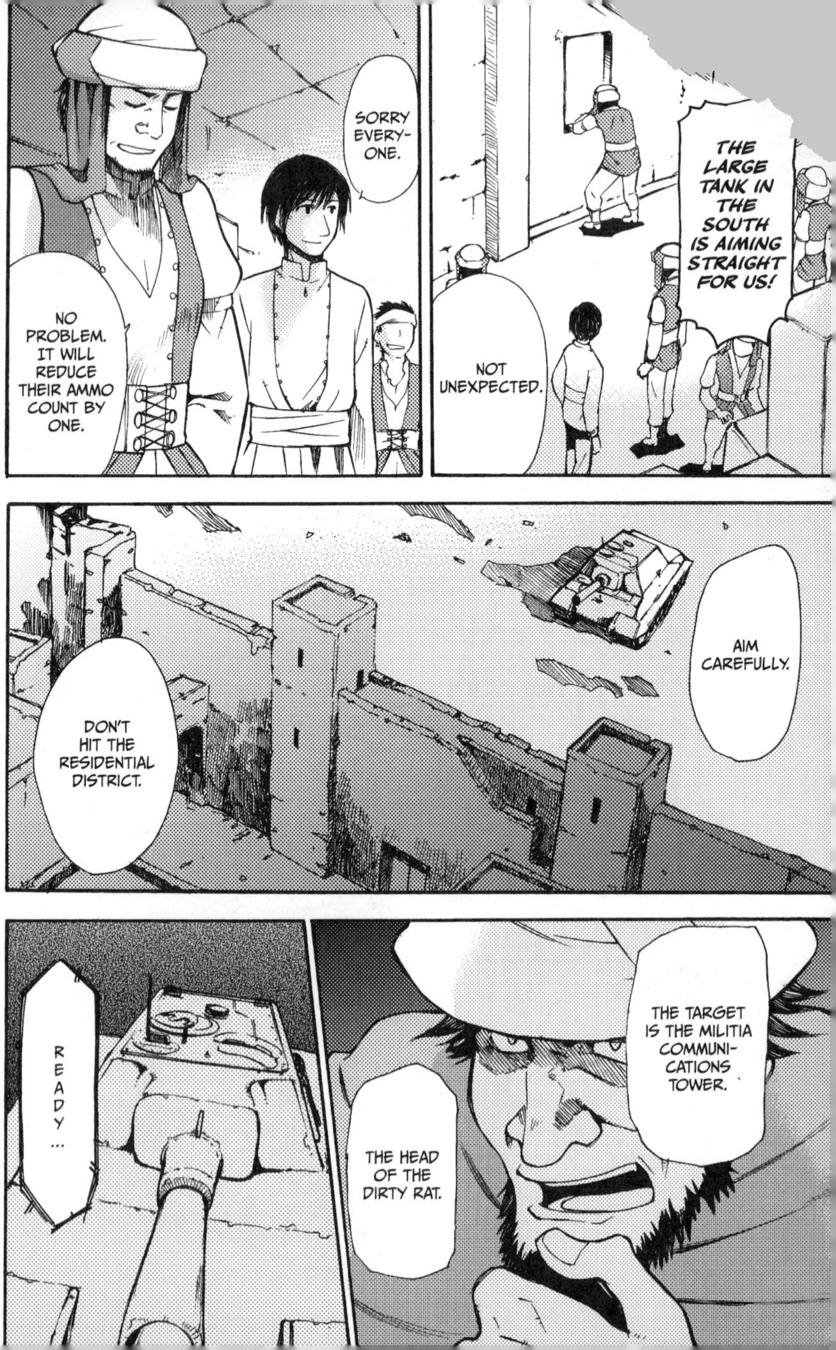
THE LARGE TANK IN THE SOUTH IS AIMING STRAIGHT FOR US!
NOT UNEXPECTED.
SORRY EVERY-ONE.
NO PROBLEM. IT WILL REDUCE THEIR AMMO COUNT BY ONE.
AIM CAREFULLY.
DON'T HIT THE RESIDENTIAL DISTRICT.
THE TARGET IS THE MILITIA COMMUNI-CATIONS TOWER.
THE HEAD OF THE DIRTY RAT.
READY...

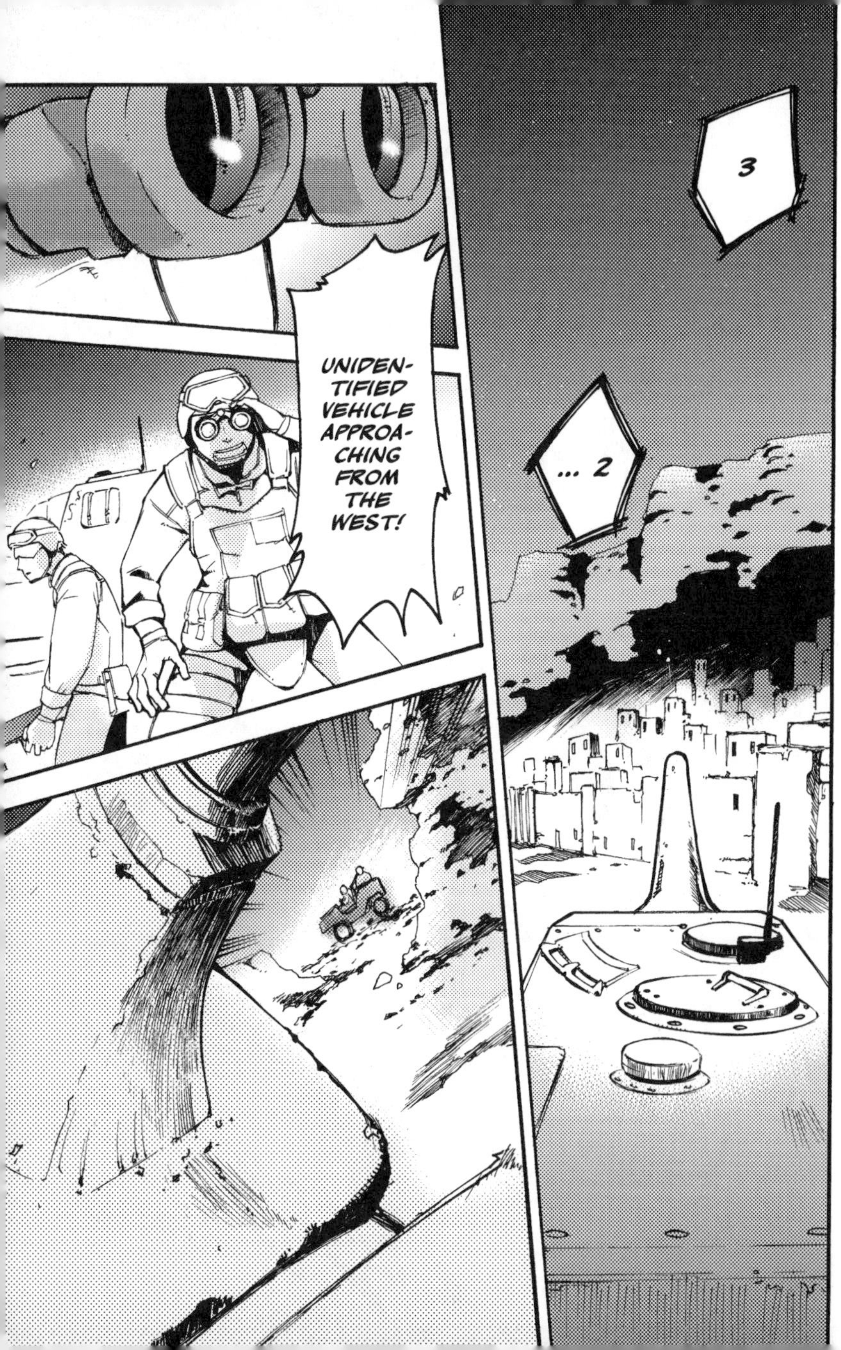
3
... 2
UNIDENTIFIED VEHICLE APPROACHING FROM THE WEST!

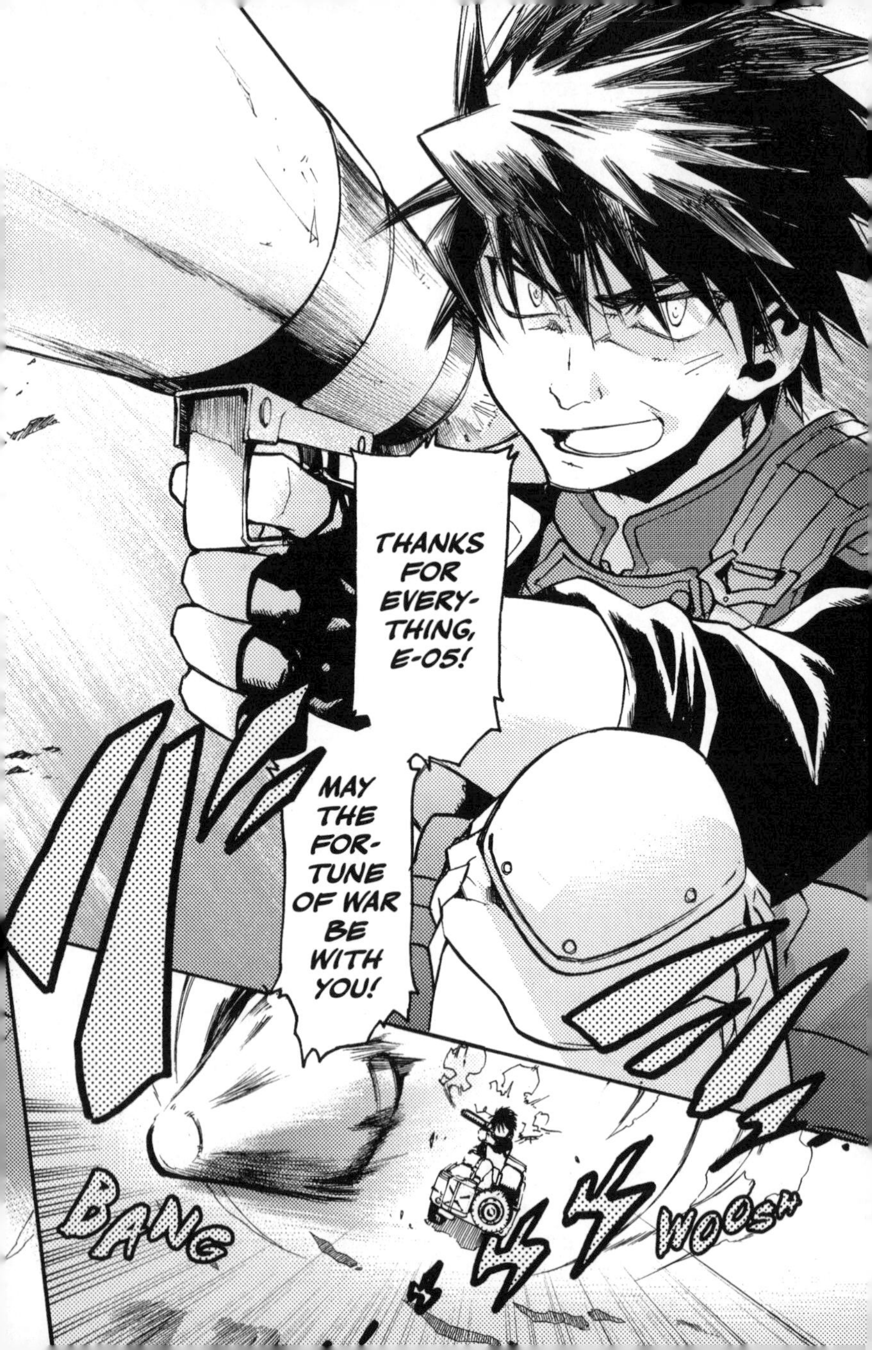
THANKS FOR EVERYTHING, E-05!
MAY THE FORTUNE OF WAR BE WITH YOU!
BANG
WOOSH

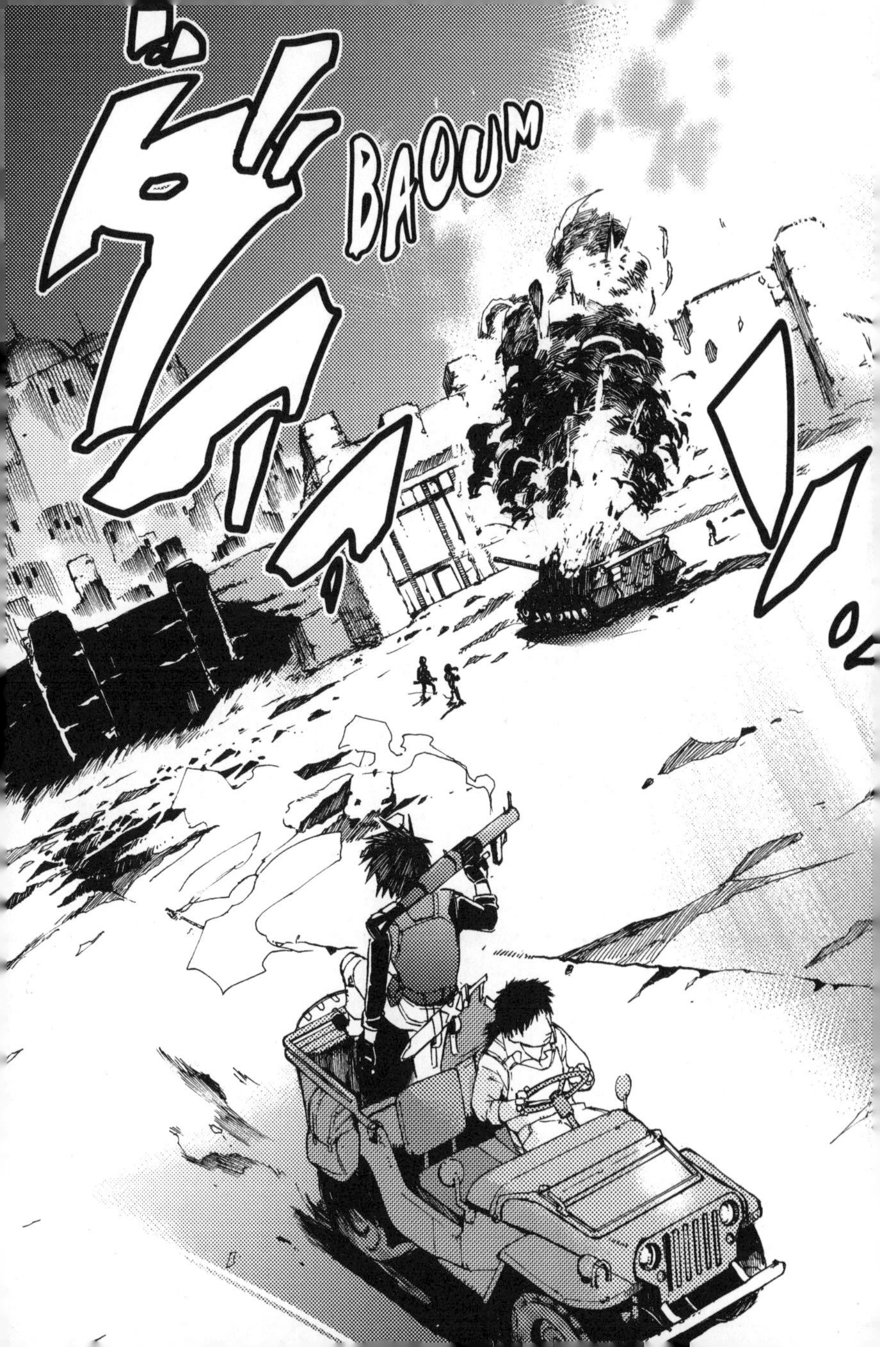
ドーン!!
BAOUM

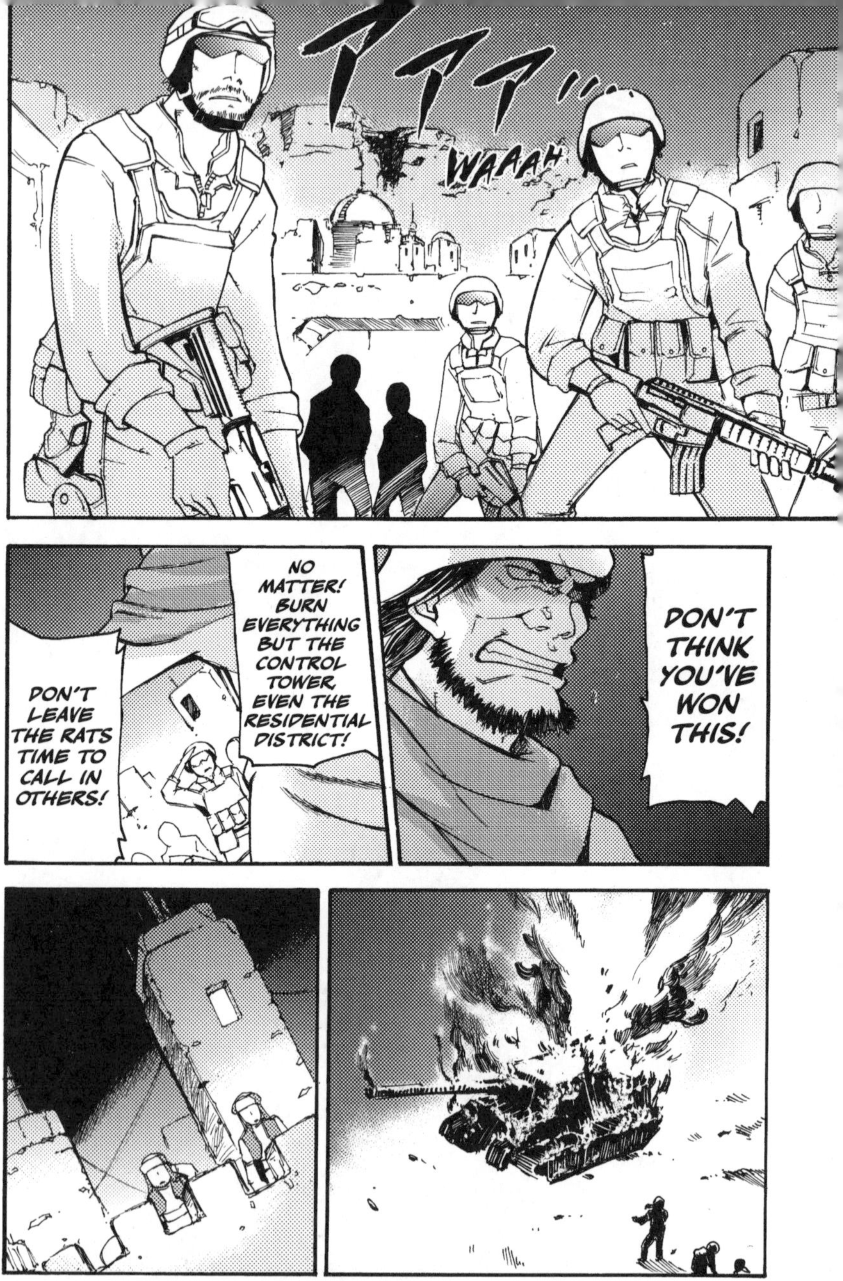
アアア…
WAAAH
DON'T THINK YOU'VE WON THIS!
NO MATTER! BURN EVERYTHING BUT THE CONTROL TOWER, EVEN THE RESIDENTIAL DISTRICT!
DON'T LEAVE THE RATS TIME TO CALL IN OTHERS!

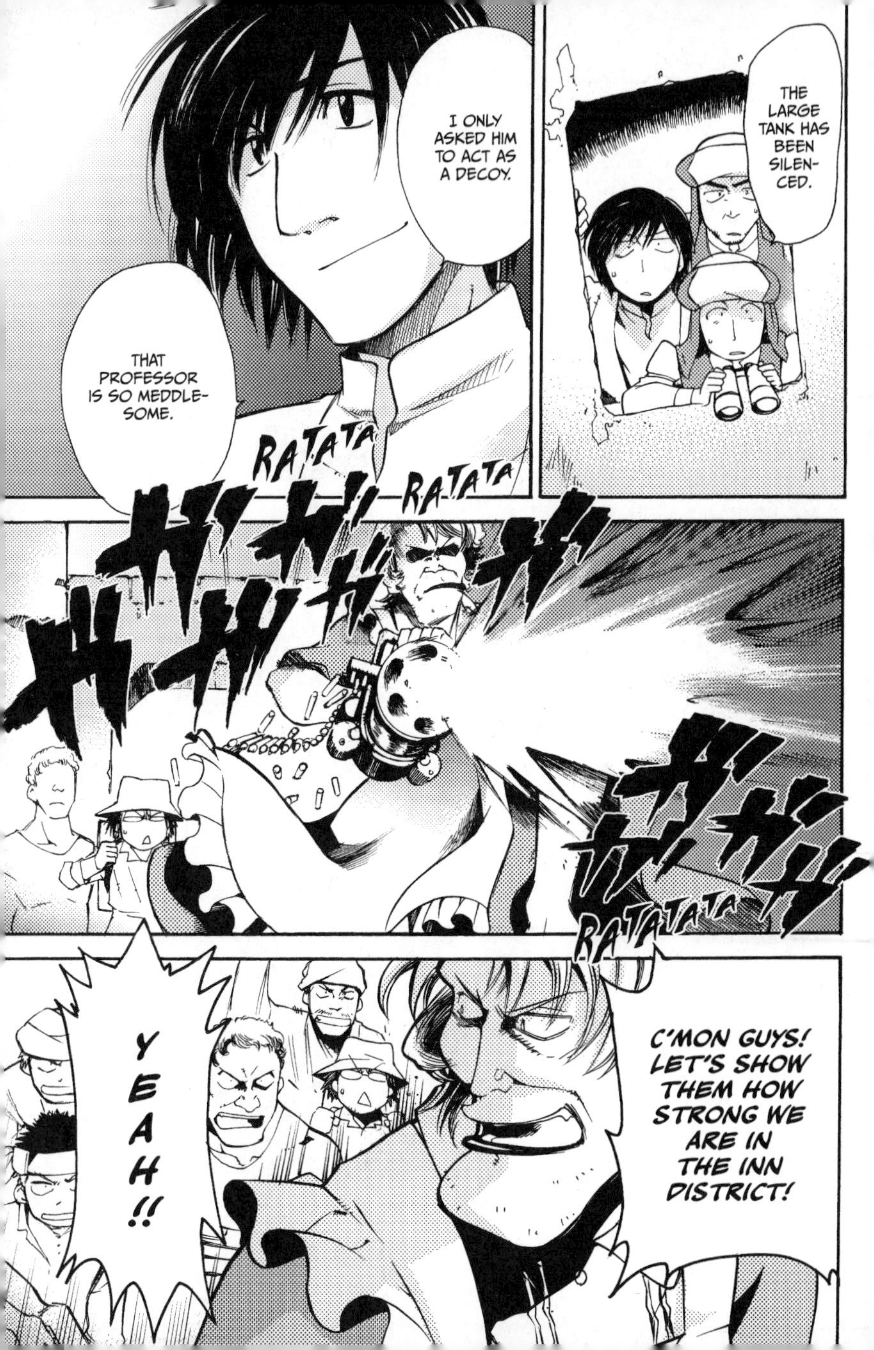
THE LARGE TANK HAS BEEN SILEN-CED.
I ONLY ASKED HIM TO ACT AS A DECOY.
THAT PROFESSOR IS SO MEDDLE-SOME.
RATATA
RATATA
RATATATA
C'MON GUYS! LET'S SHOW THEM HOW STRONG WE ARE IN THE INN DISTRICT!
YEAH!!

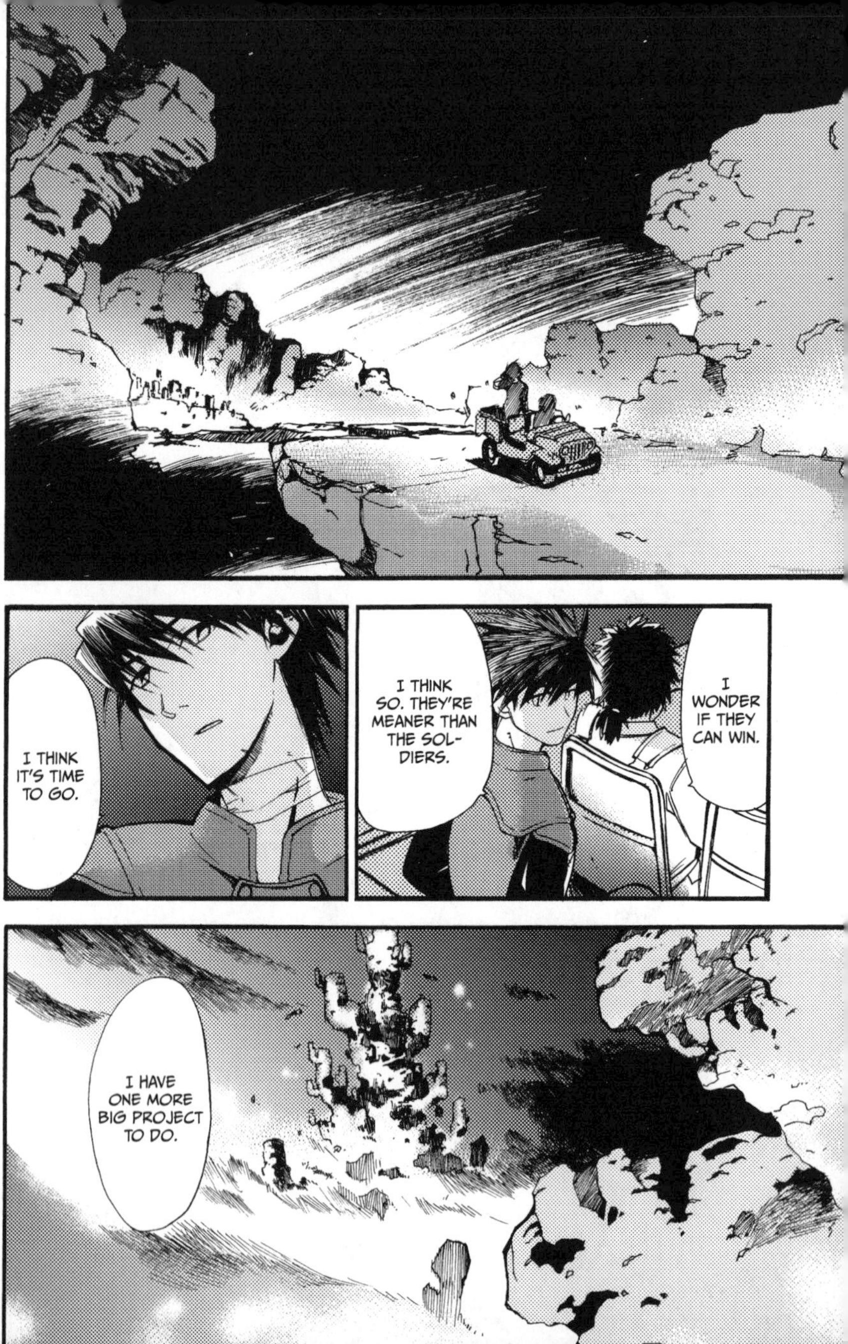
I WONDER IF THEY CAN WIN.
I THINK SO. THEY'RE MEANER THAN THE SOL-DIERS.
I THINK IT'S TIME TO GO.
I HAVE ONE MORE BIG PROJECT TO DO.

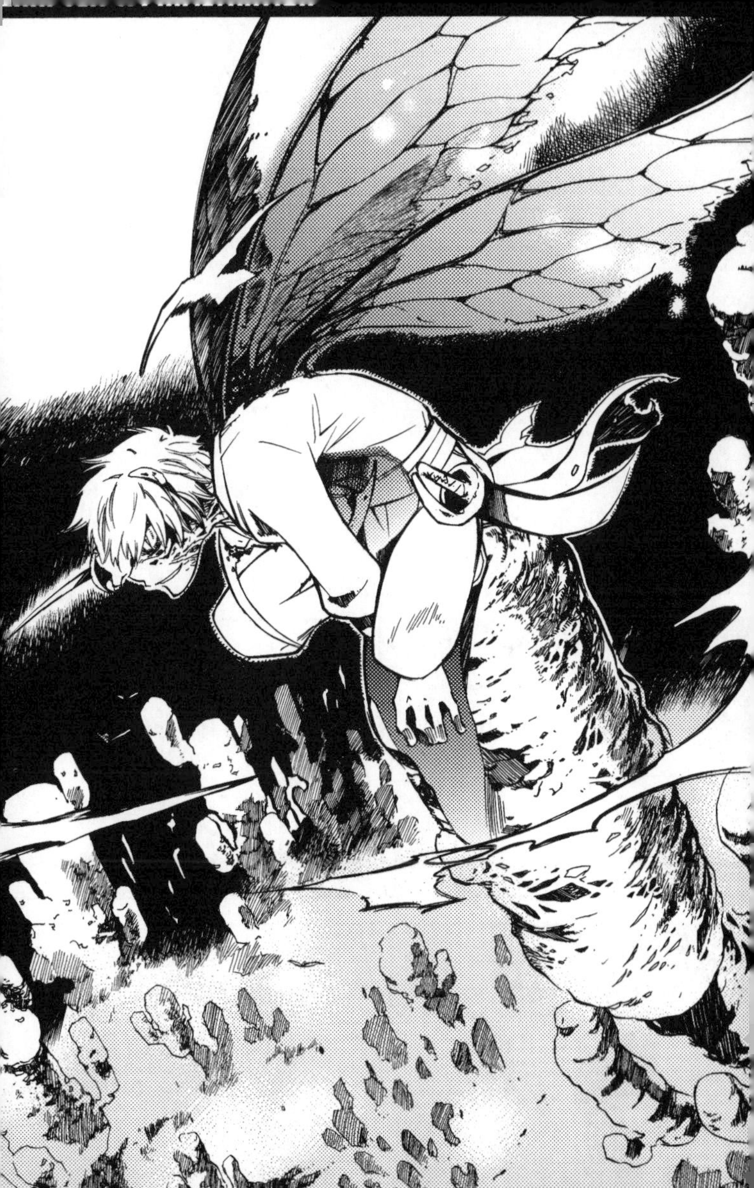

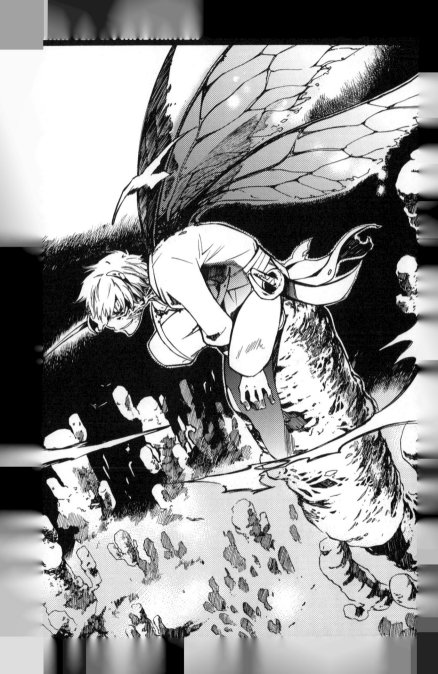

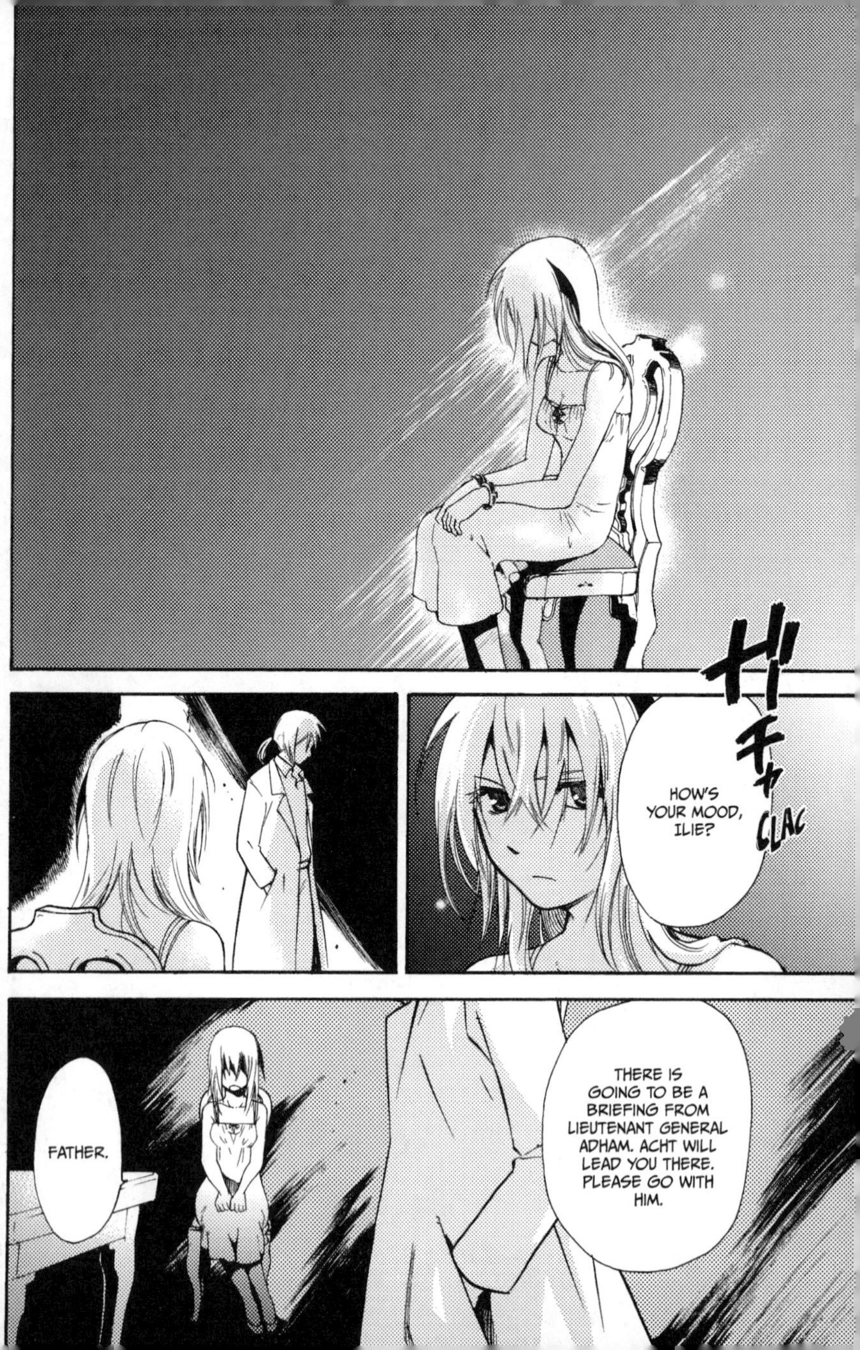
ガチャ
CLAC
HOW'S YOUR MOOD, ILIE?
THERE IS GOING TO BE A BRIEFING FROM LIEUTENANT GENERAL ADHAM. ACHT WILL LEAD YOU THERE. PLEASE GO WITH HIM.
FATHER.

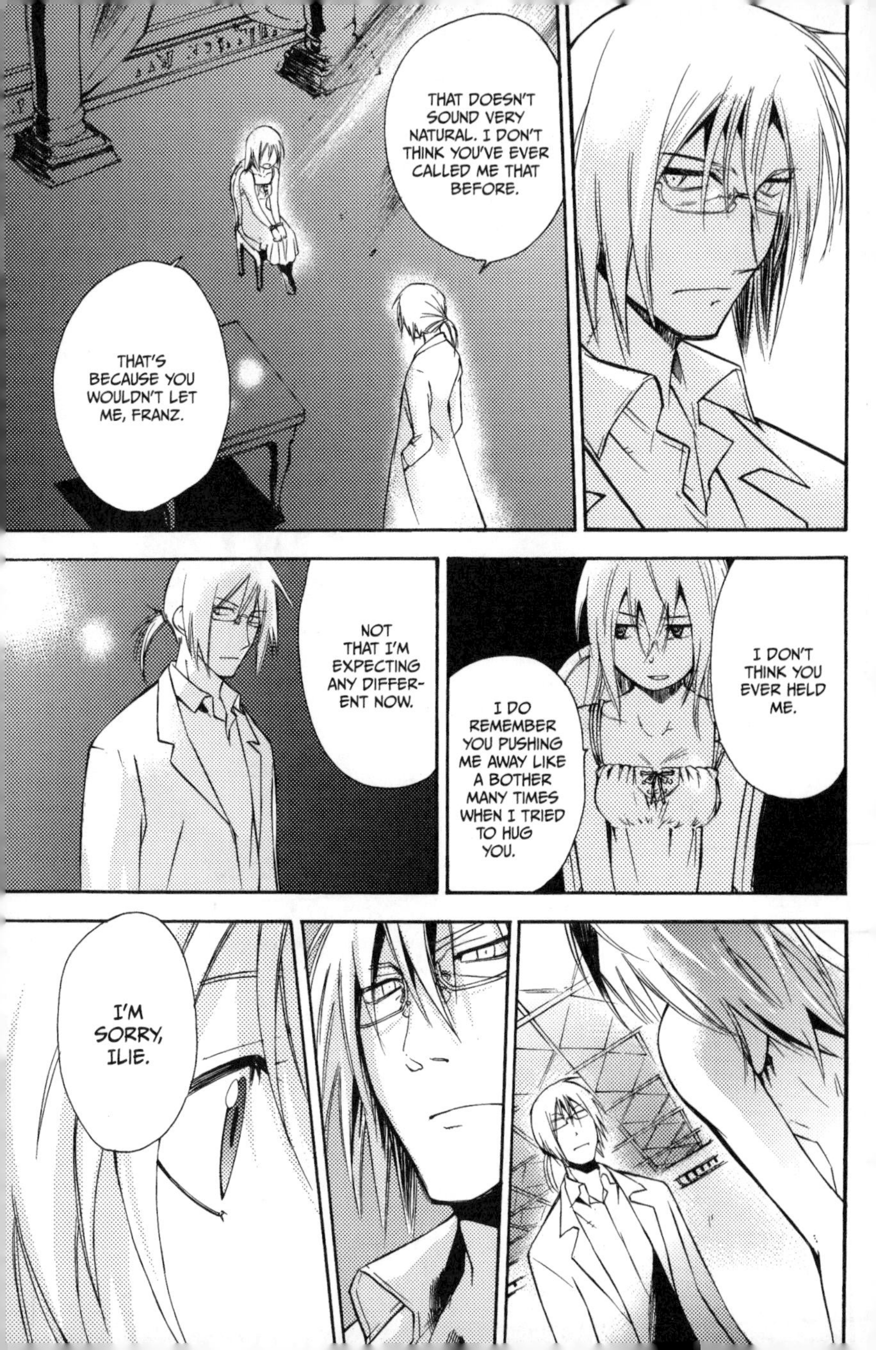
THAT DOESN'T SOUND VERY NATURAL. I DON'T THINK YOU'VE EVER CALLED ME THAT BEFORE.
THAT'S BECAUSE YOU WOULDN'T LET ME, FRANZ.
I DON'T THINK YOU EVER HELD ME.
I DO REMEMBER YOU PUSHING ME AWAY LIKE A BOTHER MANY TIMES WHEN I TRIED TO HUG YOU.
NOT THAT I'M EXPECTING ANY DIFFER-ENT NOW.
I'M SORRY, ILIE.

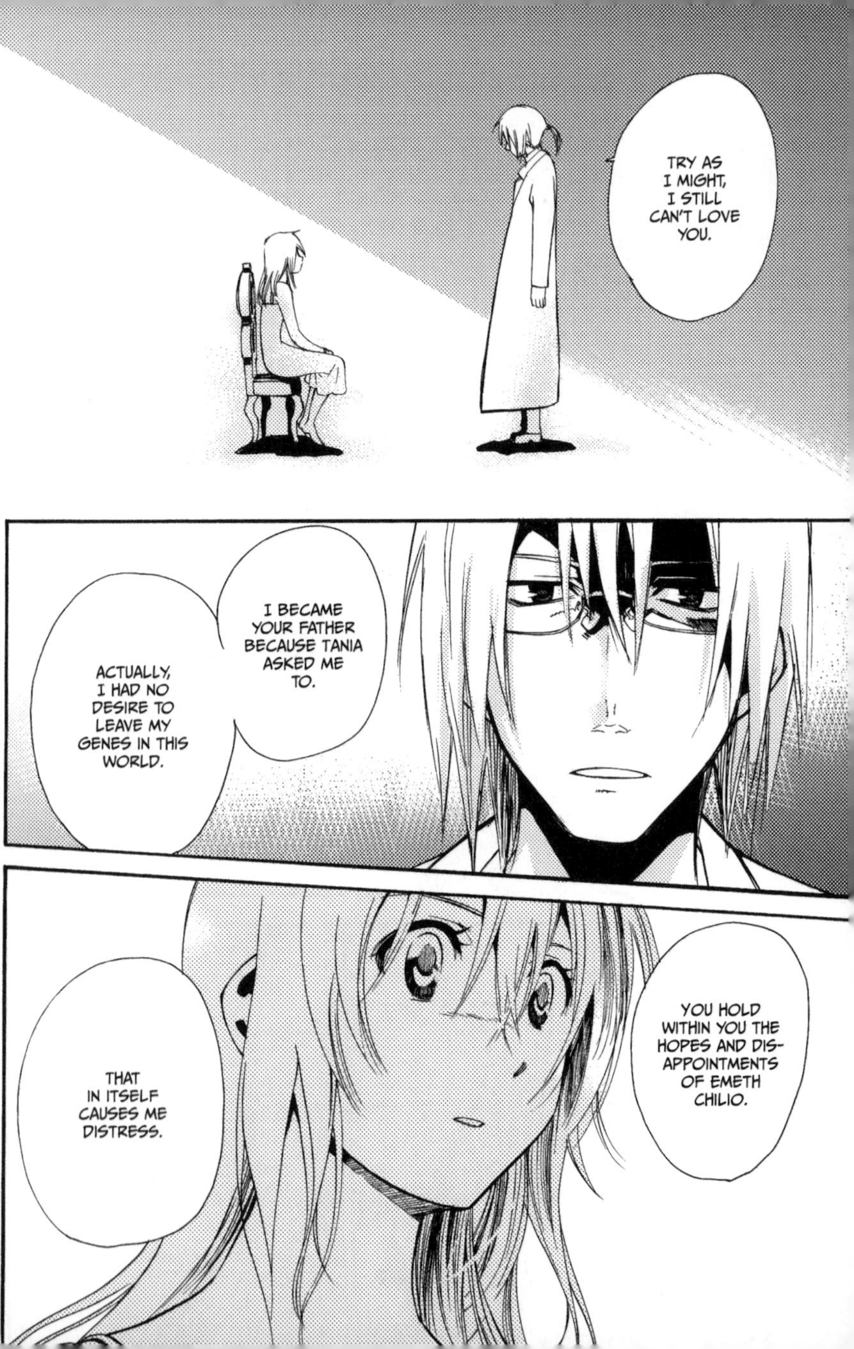
TRY AS I MIGHT, I STILL CAN'T LOVE YOU.
I BECAME YOUR FATHER BECAUSE TANIA ASKED ME TO.
ACTUALLY, I HAD NO DESIRE TO LEAVE MY GENES IN THIS WORLD.
YOU HOLD WITHIN YOU THE HOPES AND DIS-APPOINTMENTS OF EMETH CHILIO.
THAT IN ITSELF CAUSES ME DISTRESS.

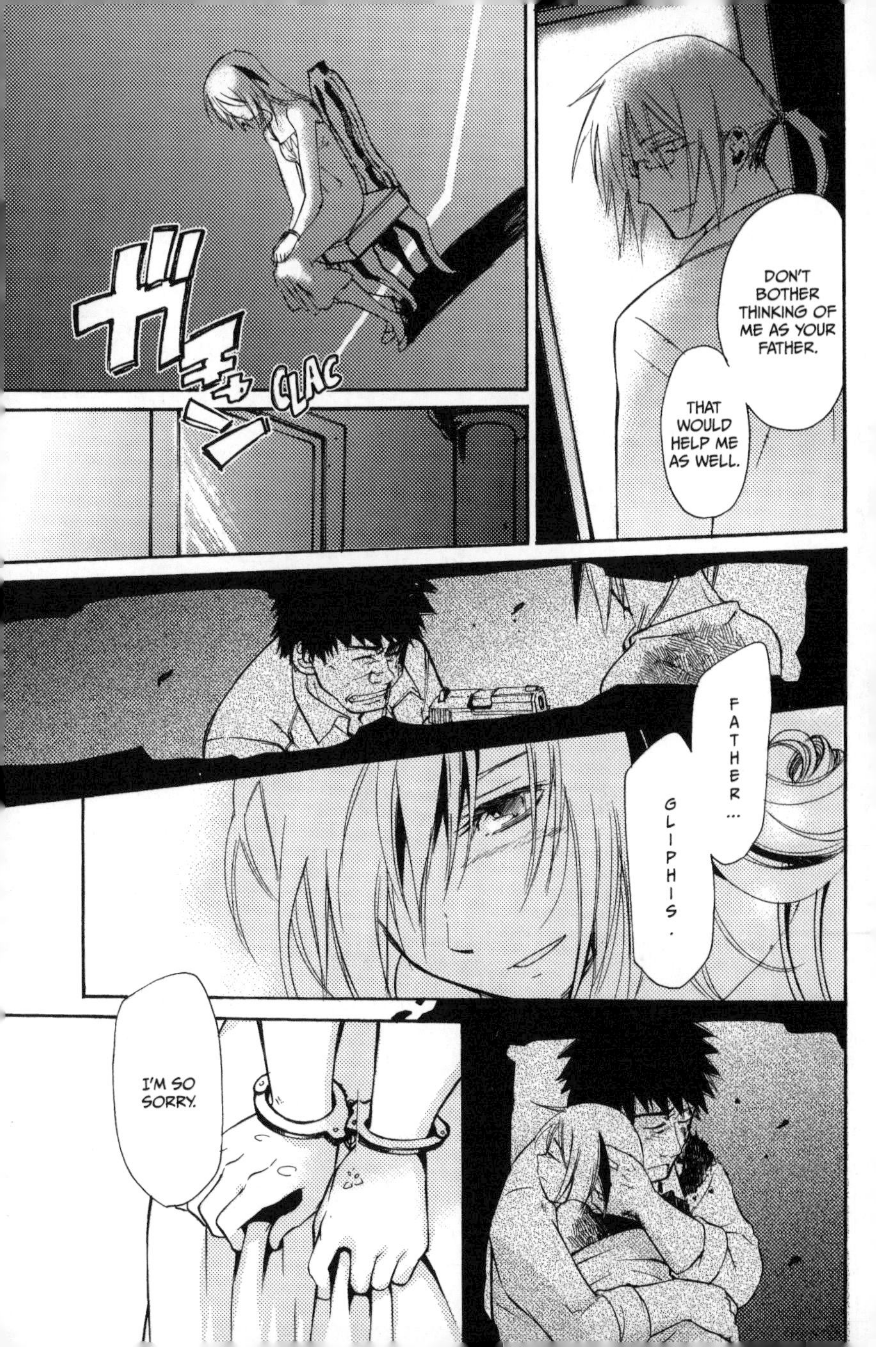
DON'T BOTHER THINKING OF ME AS YOUR FATHER.
THAT WOULD HELP ME AS WELL.
ガチャン
CLAC
FATHER...
GLIPHIS.
I'M SO SORRY.

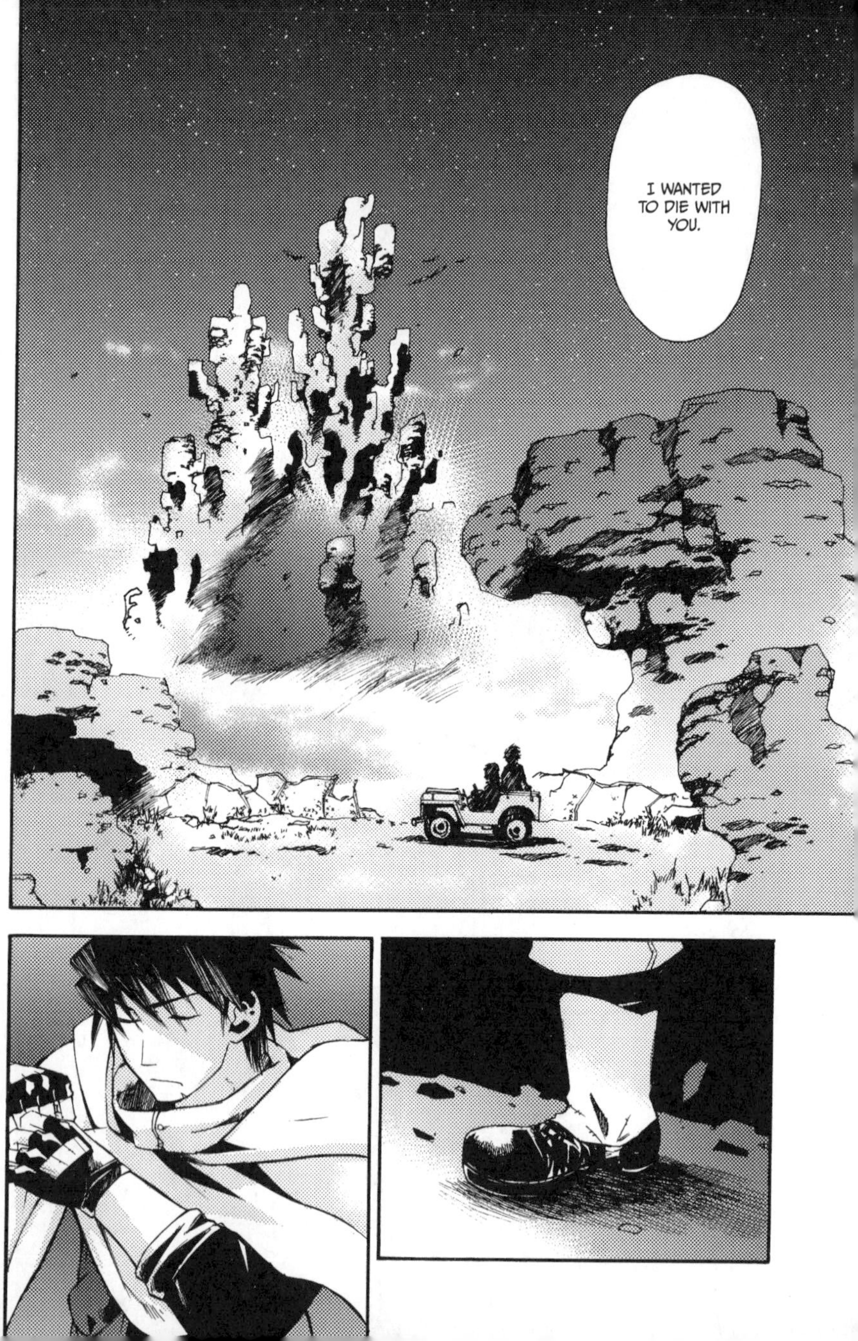
I WANTED TO DIE WITH YOU.

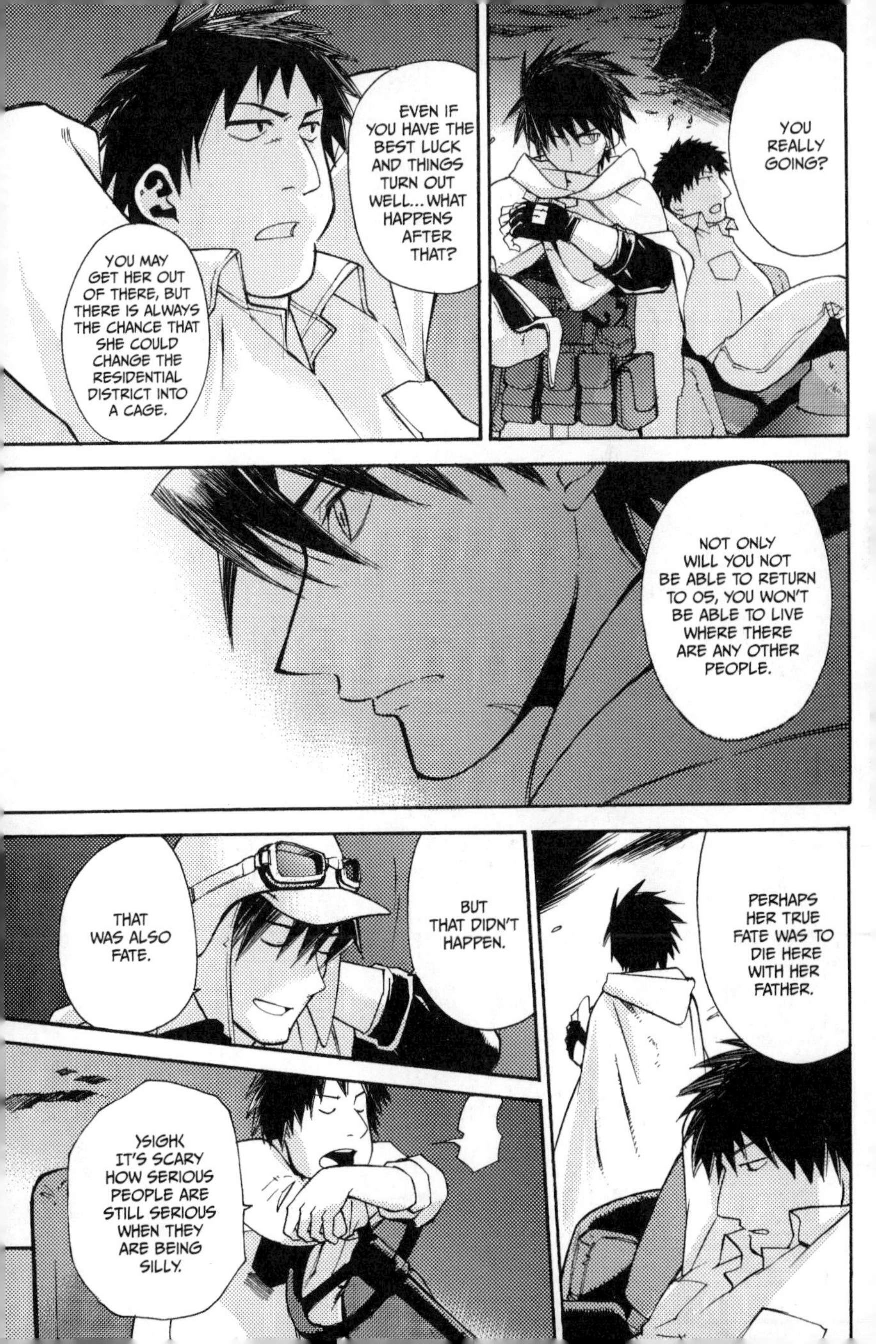

YOU REALLY GOING?
EVEN IF YOU HAVE THE BEST LUCK AND THINGS TURN OUT WELL...WHAT HAPPENS AFTER THAT?
YOU MAY GET HER OUT OF THERE, BUT THERE IS ALWAYS THE CHANCE THAT SHE COULD CHANGE THE RESIDENTIAL DISTRICT INTO A CAGE.
NOT ONLY WILL YOU NOT BE ABLE TO RETURN TO 05, YOU WON'T BE ABLE TO LIVE WHERE THERE ARE ANY OTHER PEOPLE.
PERHAPS HER TRUE FATE WAS TO DIE HERE WITH HER FATHER.
BUT THAT DIDN'T HAPPEN.
THAT WAS ALSO FATE.
›SIGH‹ IT'S SCARY HOW SERIOUS PEOPLE ARE STILL SERIOUS WHEN THEY ARE BEING SILLY.

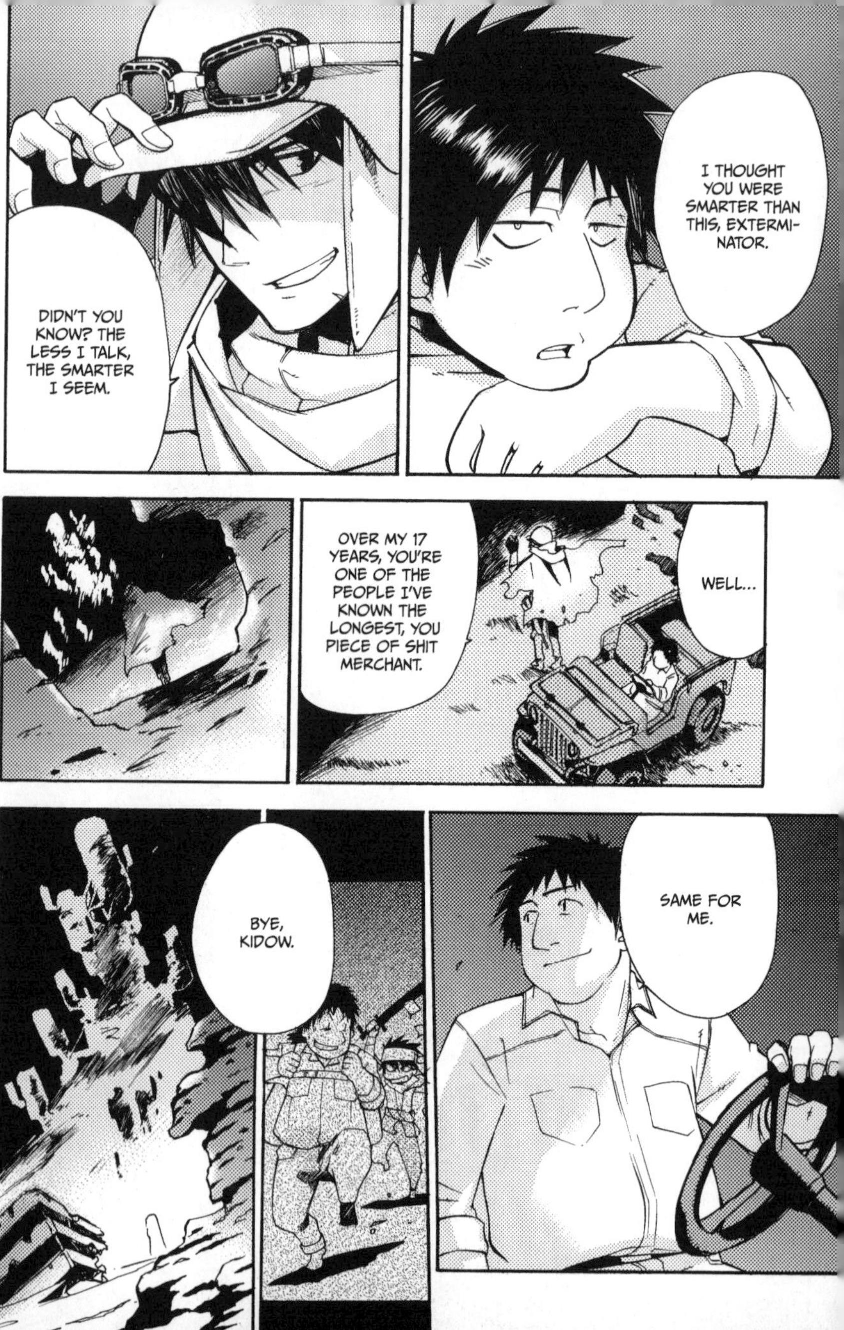
I THOUGHT YOU WERE SMARTER THAN THIS, EXTERMI-NATOR.
DIDN'T YOU KNOW? THE LESS I TALK, THE SMARTER I SEEM.
WELL...
OVER MY 17 YEARS, YOU'RE ONE OF THE PEOPLE I'VE KNOWN THE LONGEST, YOU PIECE OF SHIT MERCHANT.
SAME FOR ME.
BYE, KIDOW.

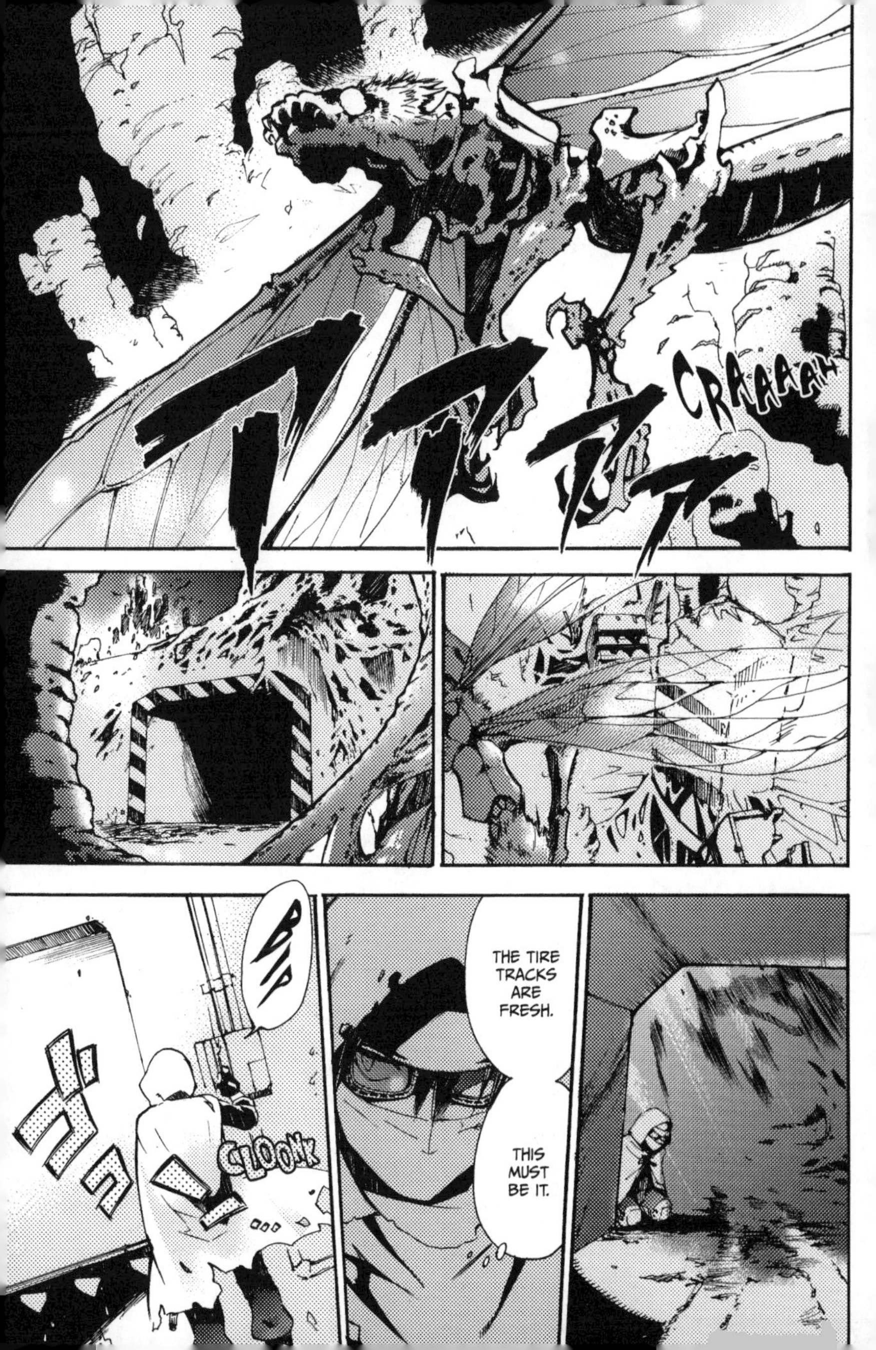
CRAAAAH
THE TIRE TRACKS ARE FRESH.
THIS MUST BE IT.
BLIP
CLOONK

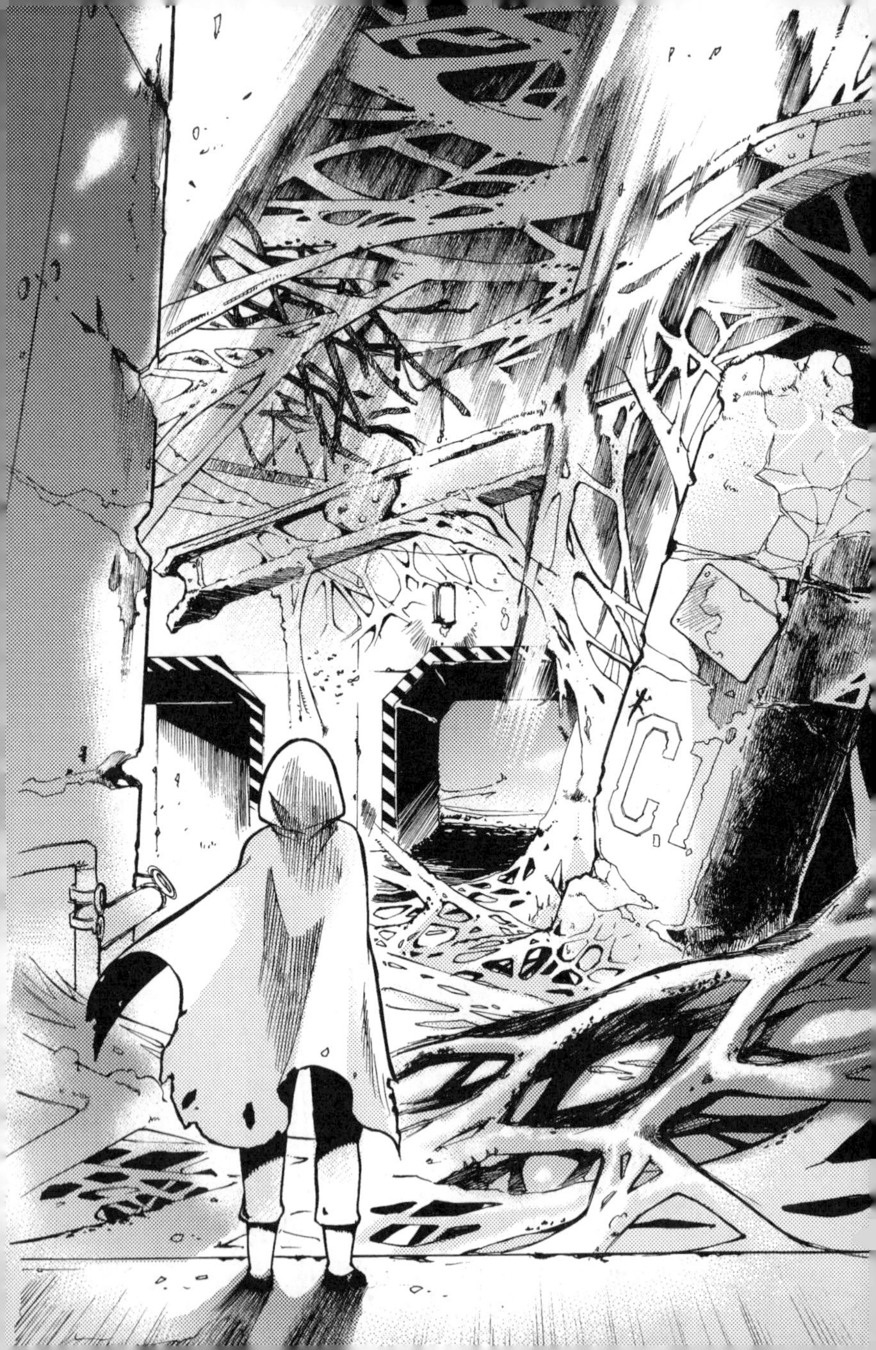
C1

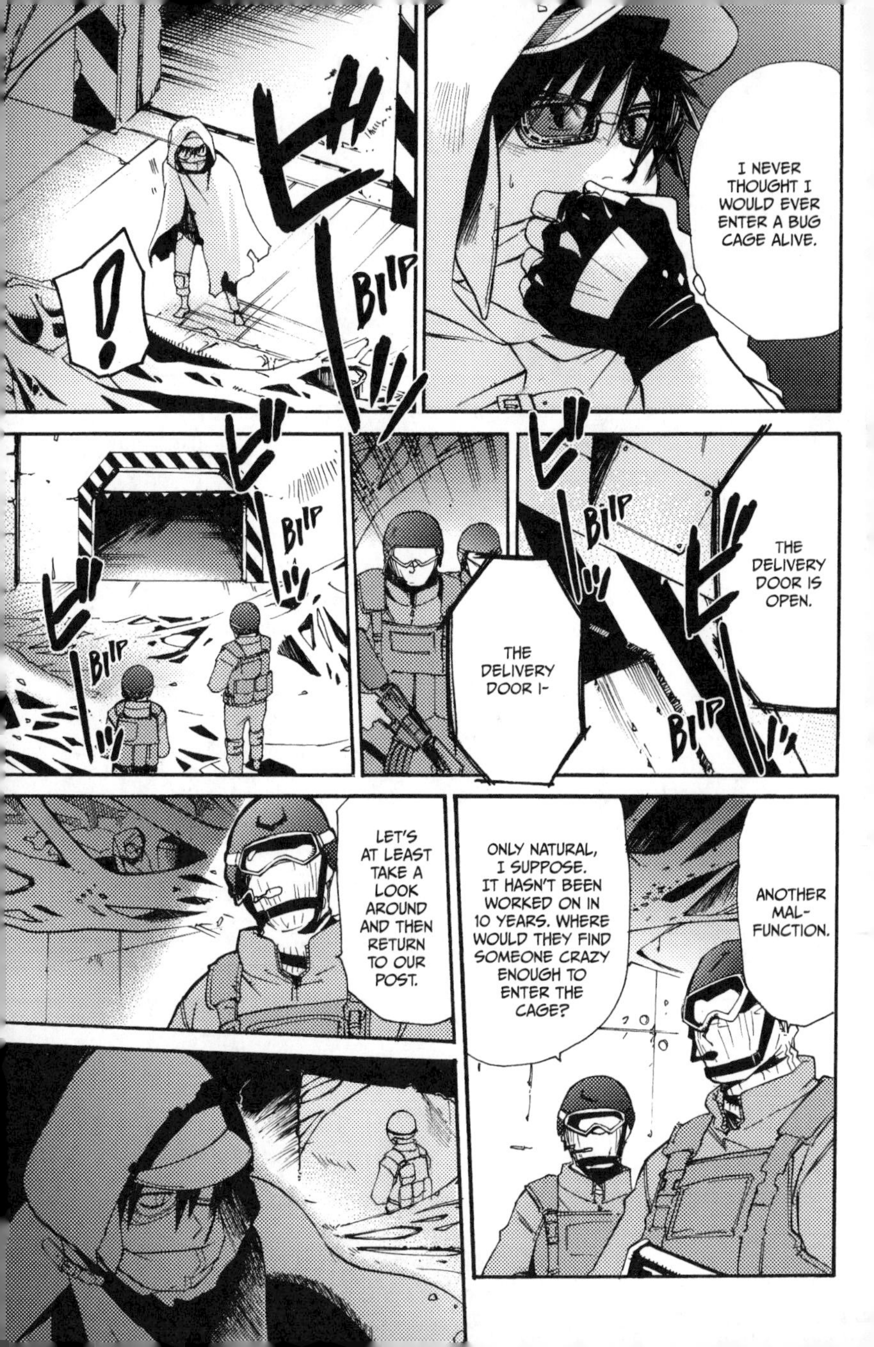

I NEVER THOUGHT I WOULD EVER ENTER A BUG CAGE ALIVE.
BIIP
!?
BIIP
THE DELIVERY DOOR IS OPEN.
BIIP
THE DELIVERY DOOR I-
BIIP
BIIP
ANOTHER MAL-FUNCTION.
ONLY NATURAL, I SUPPOSE. IT HASN'T BEEN WORKED ON IN 10 YEARS. WHERE WOULD THEY FIND SOMEONE CRAZY ENOUGH TO ENTER THE CAGE?
LET'S AT LEAST TAKE A LOOK AROUND AND THEN RETURN TO OUR POST.

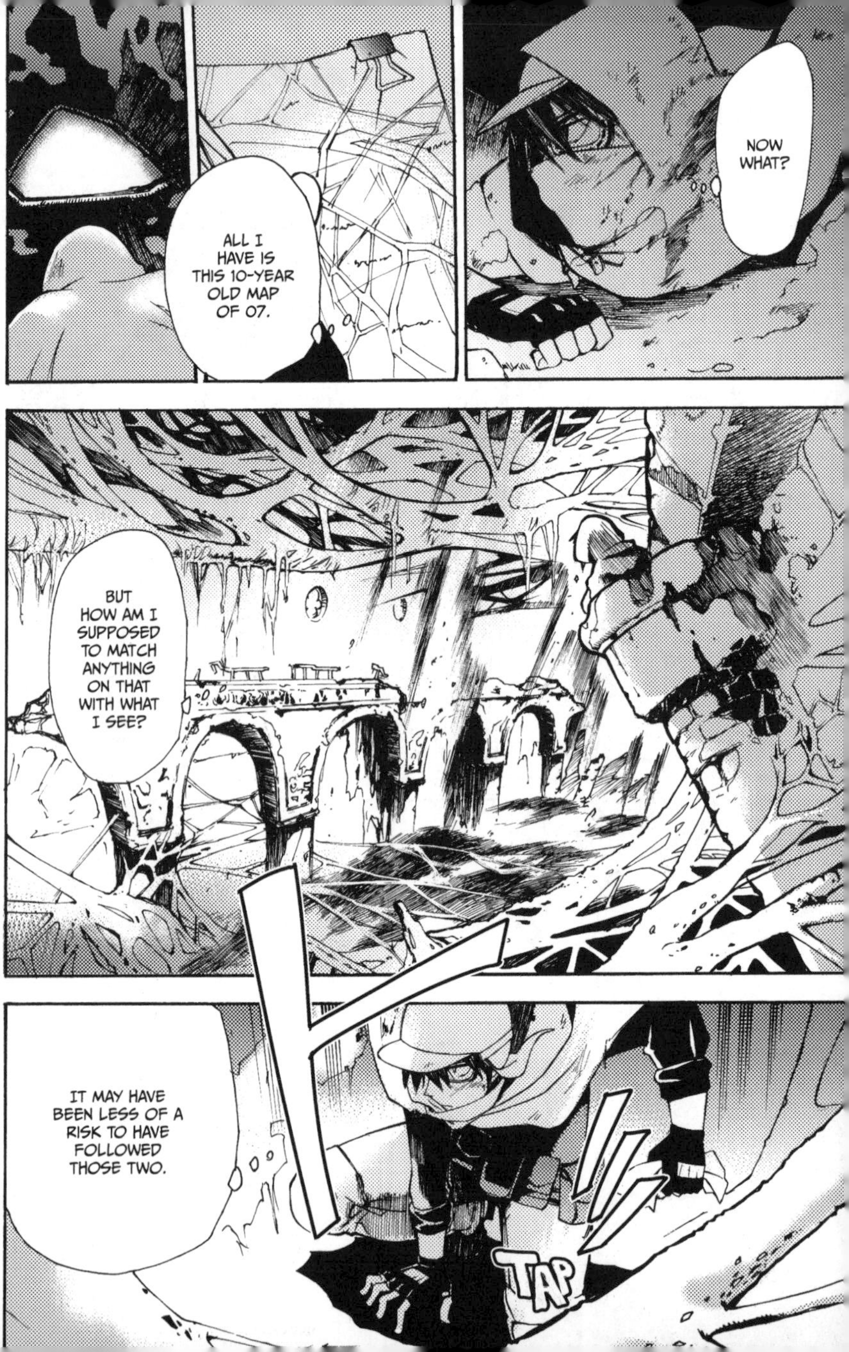
NOW WHAT?
ALL I HAVE IS THIS 10-YEAR OLD MAP OF 07.
BUT HOW AM I SUPPOSED TO MATCH ANYTHING ON THAT WITH WHAT I SEE?
IT MAY HAVE BEEN LESS OF A RISK TO HAVE FOLLOWED THOSE TWO.
TAP

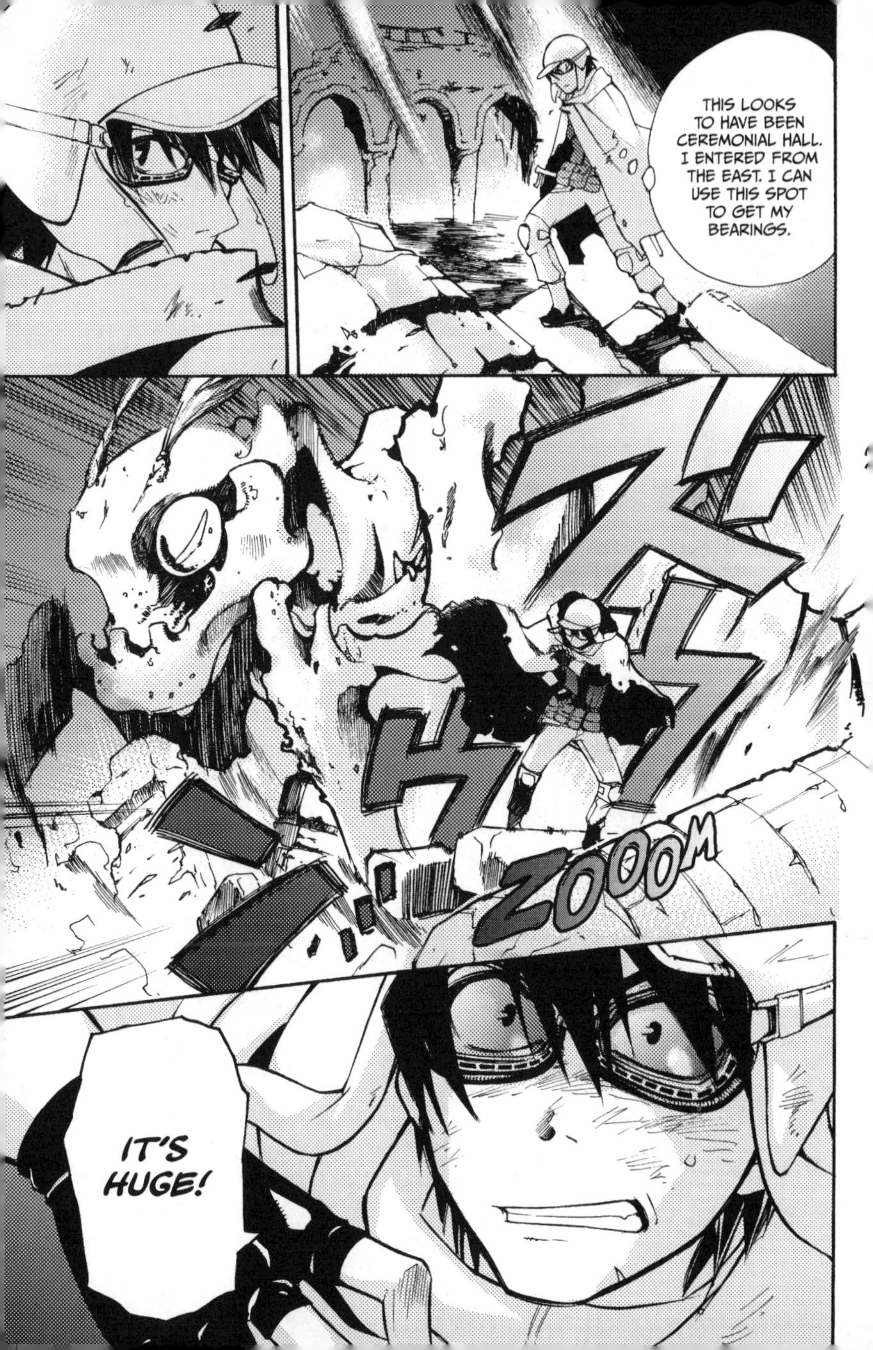
THIS LOOKS TO HAVE BEEN CEREMONIAL HALL. I ENTERED FROM THE EAST. I CAN USE THIS SPOT TO GET MY BEARINGS.
ZOOOM
IT'S HUGE!

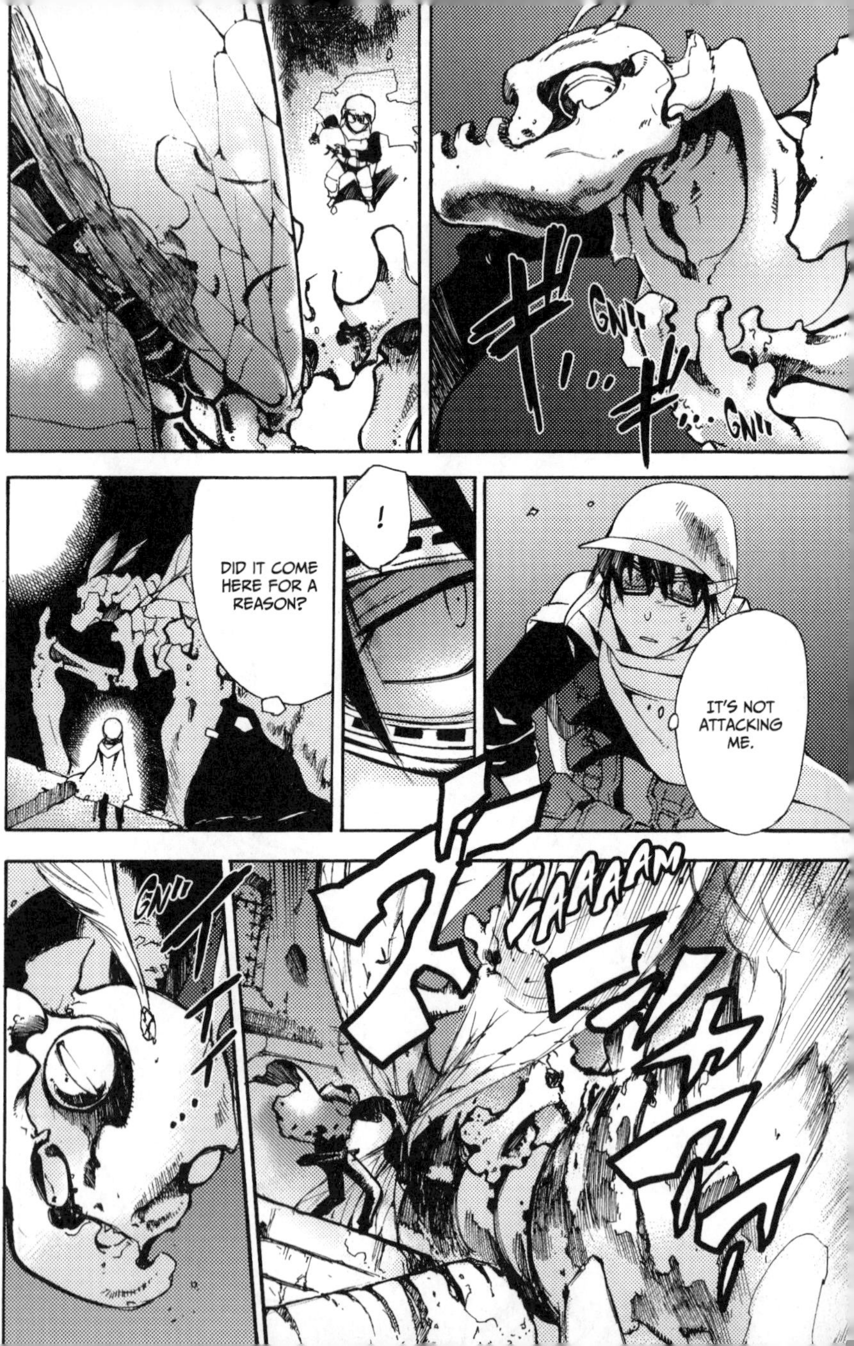
GN!!
GN!!
IT'S NOT ATTACKING ME.
!
DID IT COME HERE FOR A REASON?
ZAAAAAM
GN!!

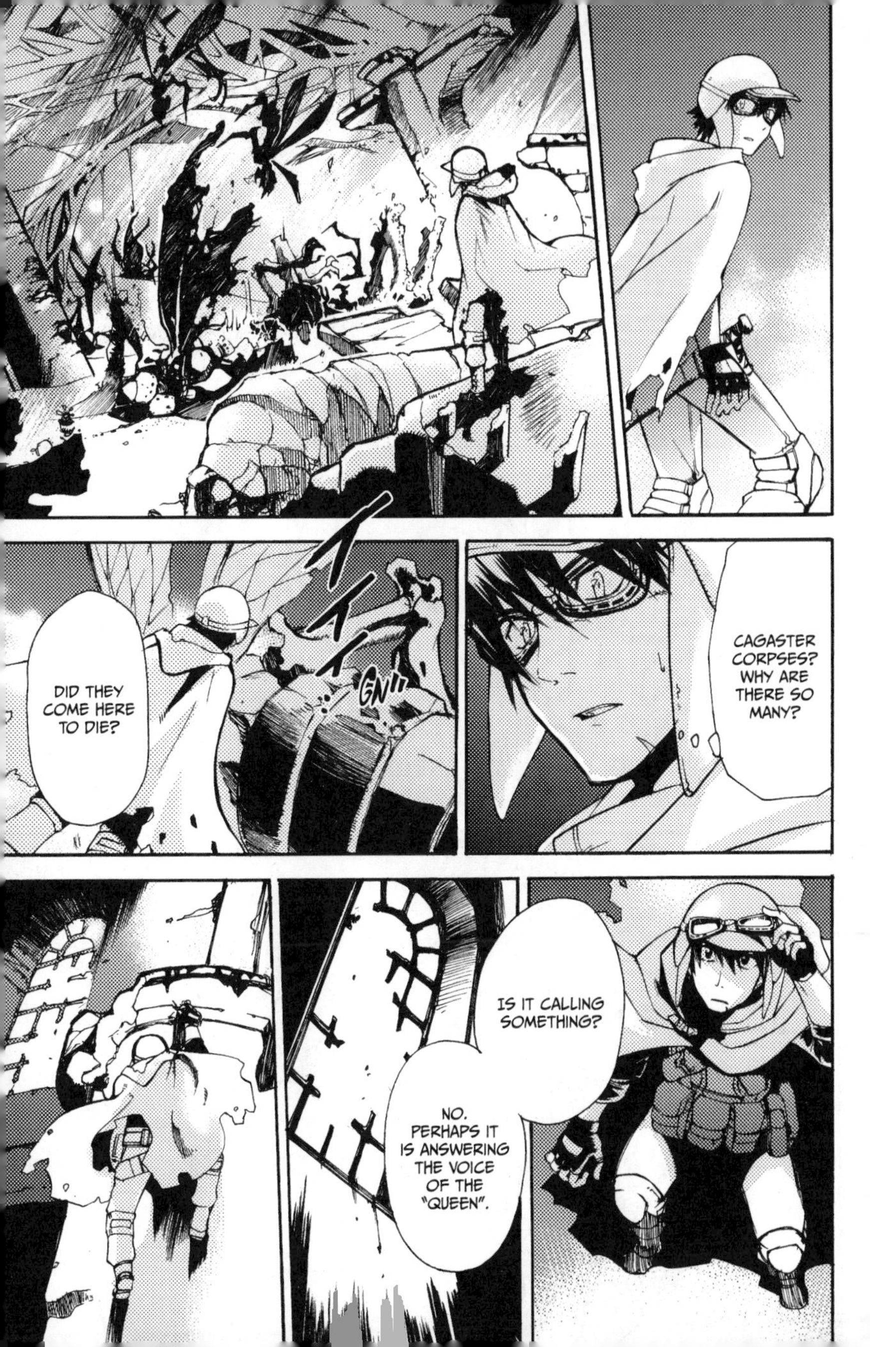
CAGASTER CORPSES? WHY ARE THERE SO MANY?
GN''
DID THEY COME HERE TO DIE?
IS IT CALLING SOMETHING?
NO. PERHAPS IT IS ANSWERING THE VOICE OF THE "QUEEN".

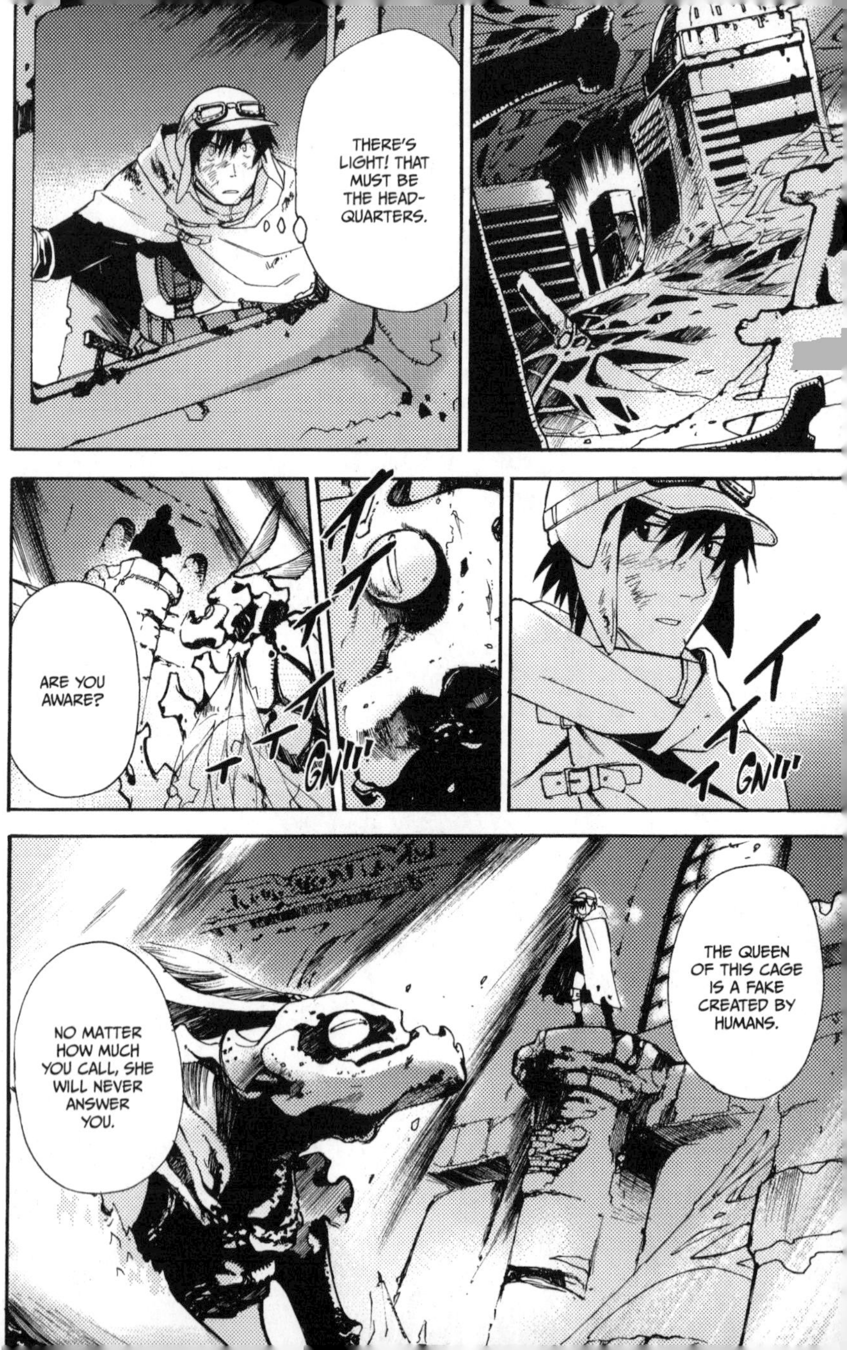
THERE'S LIGHT! THAT MUST BE THE HEAD-QUARTERS.
GN''
GN''
ARE YOU AWARE?
THE QUEEN OF THIS CAGE IS A FAKE CREATED BY HUMANS.
NO MATTER HOW MUCH YOU CALL, SHE WILL NEVER ANSWER YOU.

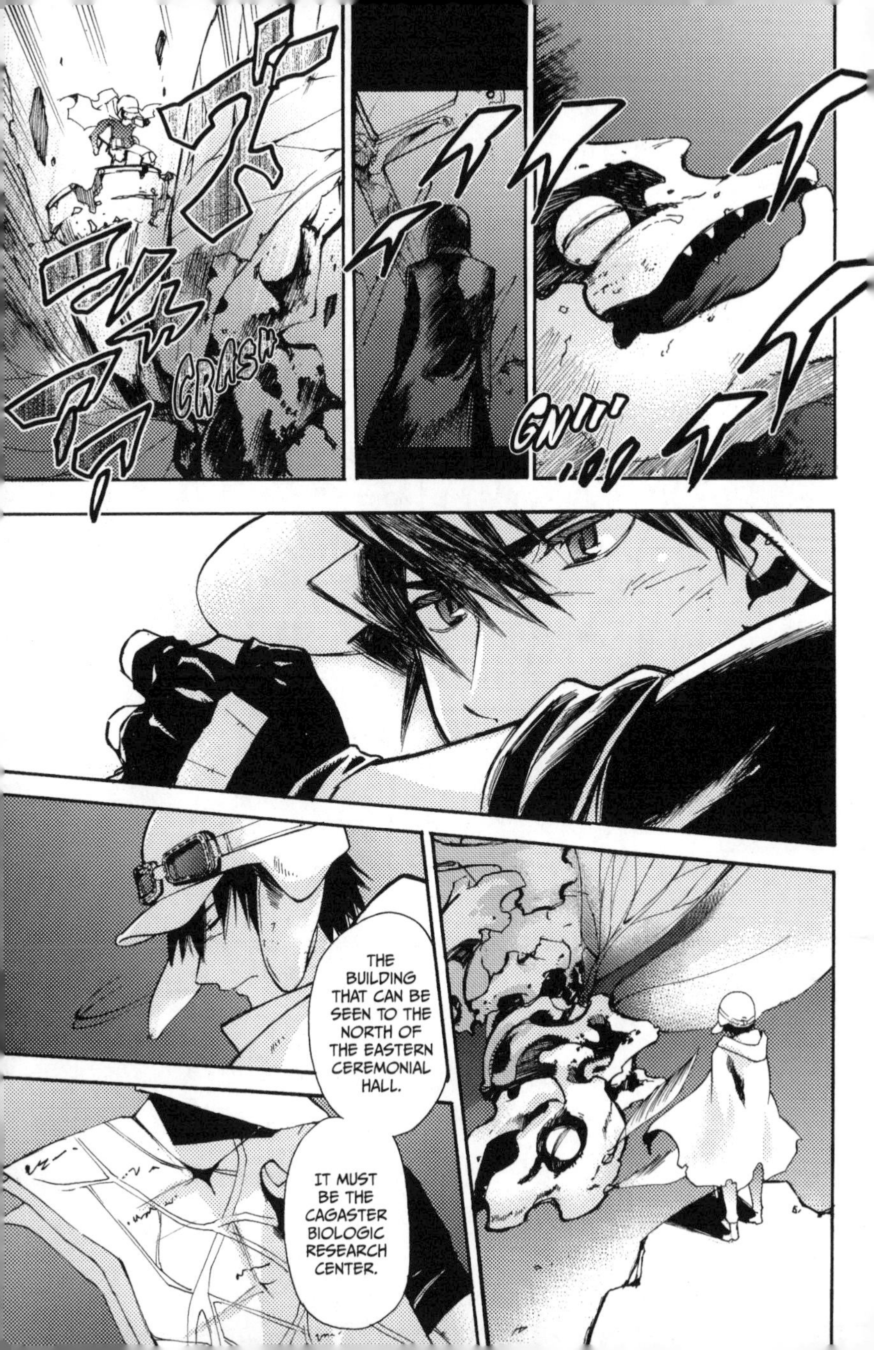
GN!!
CRASH
THE BUILDING THAT CAN BE SEEN TO THE NORTH OF THE EASTERN CEREMONIAL HALL.
IT MUST BE THE CAGASTER BIOLOGIC RESEARCH CENTER.

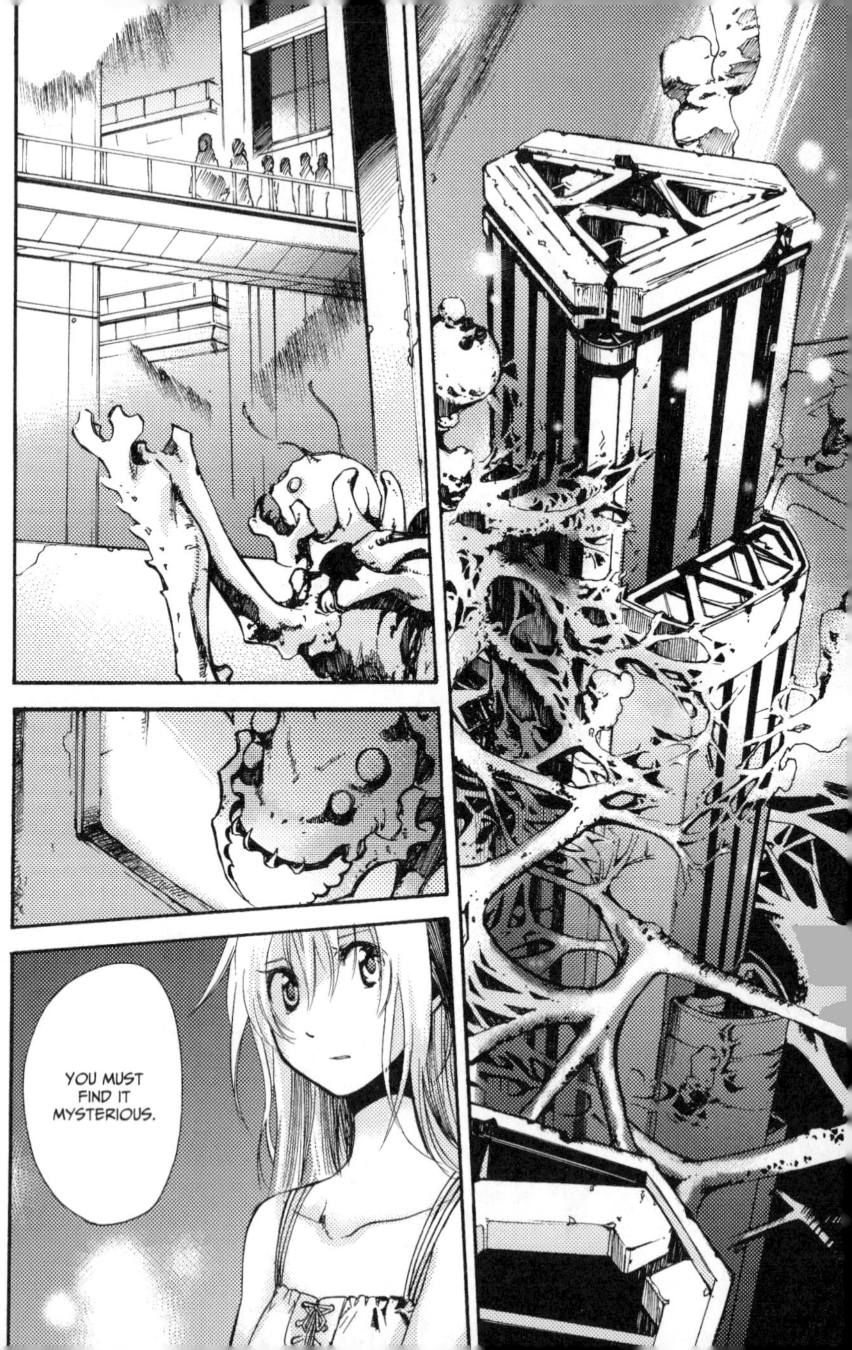
YOU MUST FIND IT MYSTERIOUS.

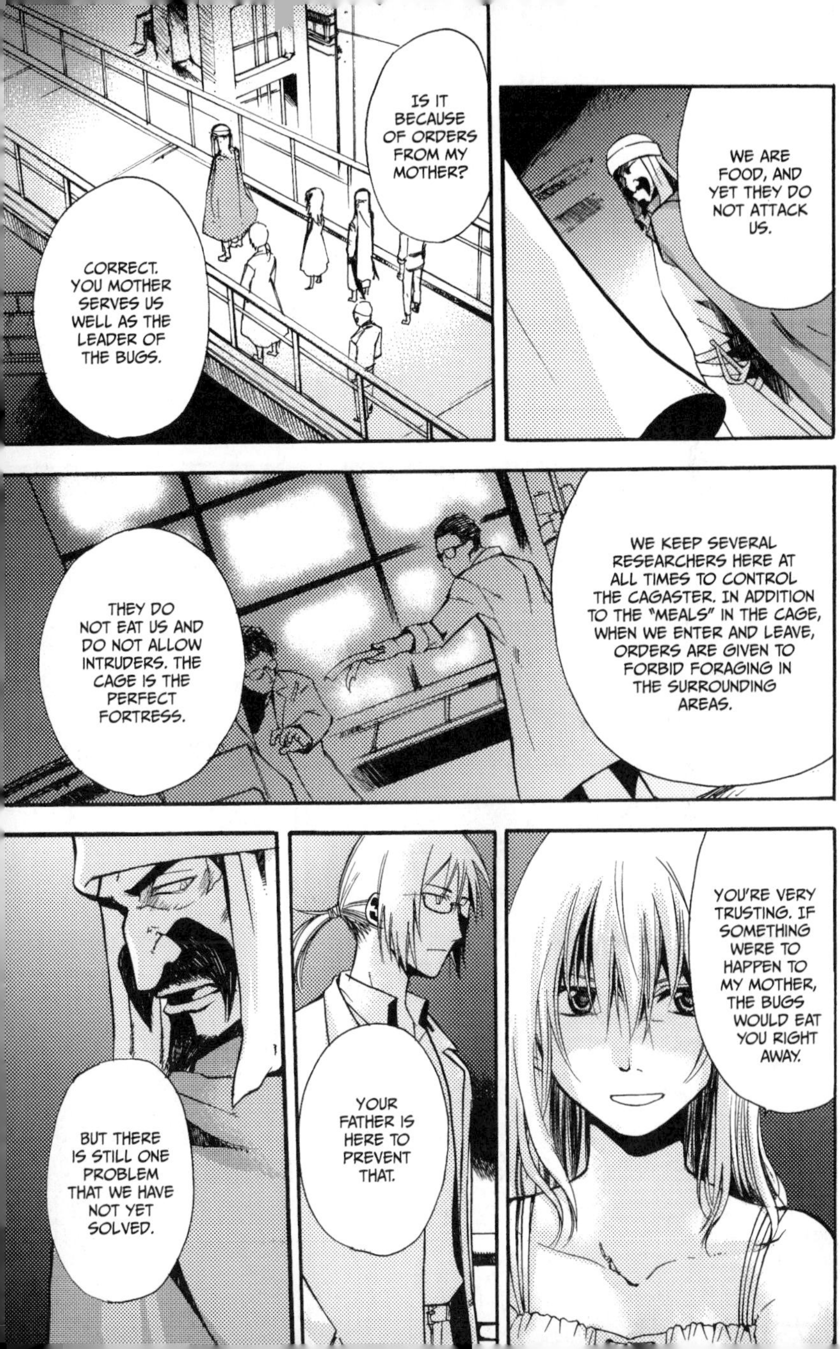
WE ARE FOOD, AND YET THEY DO NOT ATTACK US.
IS IT BECAUSE OF ORDERS FROM MY MOTHER?
CORRECT. YOU MOTHER SERVES US WELL AS THE LEADER OF THE BUGS.
WE KEEP SEVERAL RESEARCHERS HERE AT ALL TIMES TO CONTROL THE CAGASTER. IN ADDITION TO THE "MEALS" IN THE CAGE, WHEN WE ENTER AND LEAVE, ORDERS ARE GIVEN TO FORBID FORAGING IN THE SURROUNDING AREAS.
THEY DO NOT EAT US AND DO NOT ALLOW INTRUDERS. THE CAGE IS THE PERFECT FORTRESS.
YOU'RE VERY TRUSTING. IF SOMETHING WERE TO HAPPEN TO MY MOTHER, THE BUGS WOULD EAT YOU RIGHT AWAY.
YOUR FATHER IS HERE TO PREVENT THAT.
BUT THERE IS STILL ONE PROBLEM THAT WE HAVE NOT YET SOLVED.

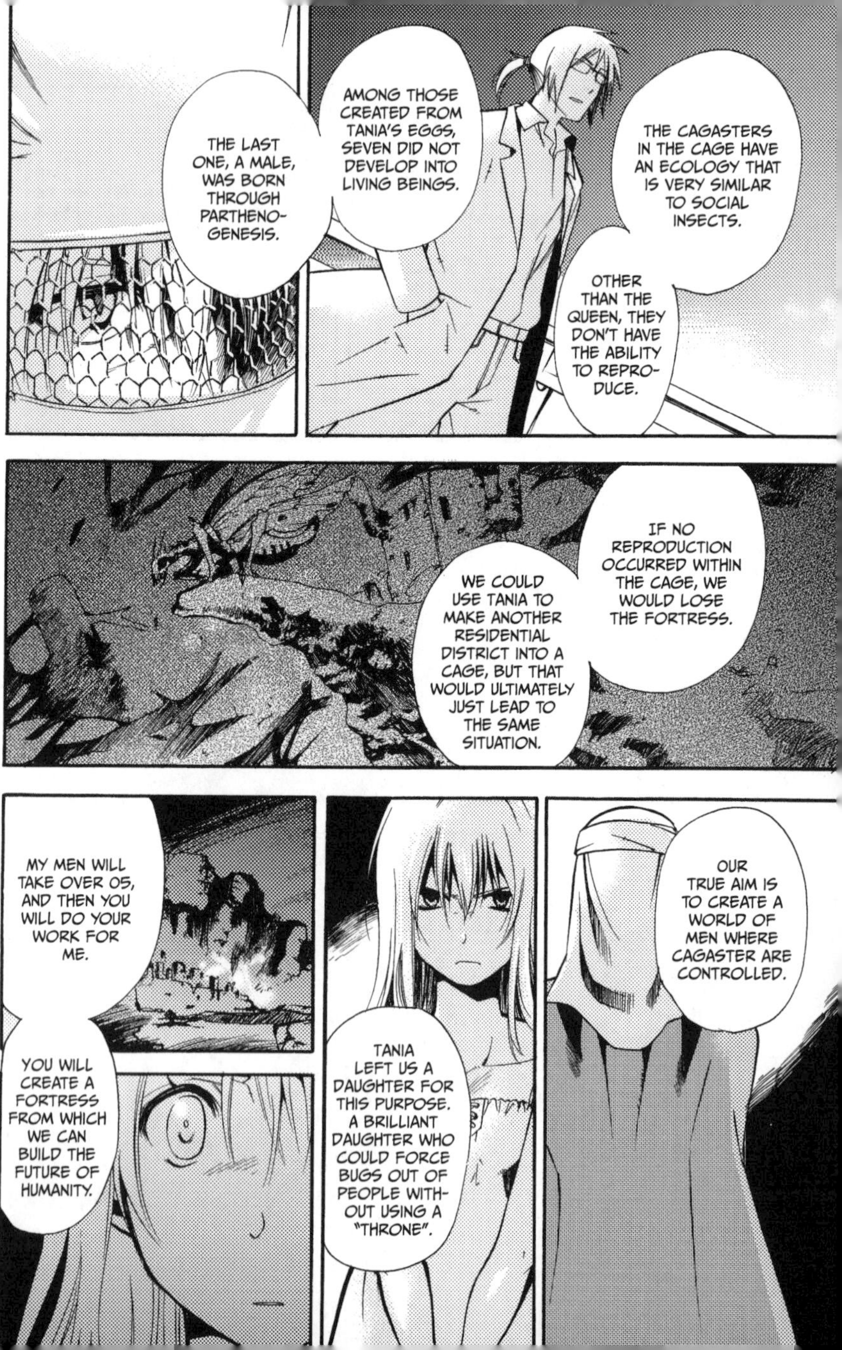
THE CAGASTERS IN THE CAGE HAVE AN ECOLOGY THAT IS VERY SIMILAR TO SOCIAL INSECTS.
OTHER THAN THE QUEEN, THEY DON'T HAVE THE ABILITY TO REPRO-DUCE.
AMONG THOSE CREATED FROM TANIA'S EGGS, SEVEN DID NOT DEVELOP INTO LIVING BEINGS.
THE LAST ONE, A MALE, WAS BORN THROUGH PARTHENO-GENESIS.
IF NO REPRODUCTION OCCURRED WITHIN THE CAGE, WE WOULD LOSE THE FORTRESS.
WE COULD USE TANIA TO MAKE ANOTHER RESIDENTIAL DISTRICT INTO A CAGE, BUT THAT WOULD ULTIMATELY JUST LEAD TO THE SAME SITUATION.
OUR TRUE AIM IS TO CREATE A WORLD OF MEN WHERE CAGASTER ARE CONTROLLED.
TANIA LEFT US A DAUGHTER FOR THIS PURPOSE. A BRILLIANT DAUGHTER WHO COULD FORCE BUGS OUT OF PEOPLE WITH-OUT USING A "THRONE".
MY MEN WILL TAKE OVER 05, AND THEN YOU WILL DO YOUR WORK FOR ME.
YOU WILL CREATE A FORTRESS FROM WHICH WE CAN BUILD THE FUTURE OF HUMANITY.

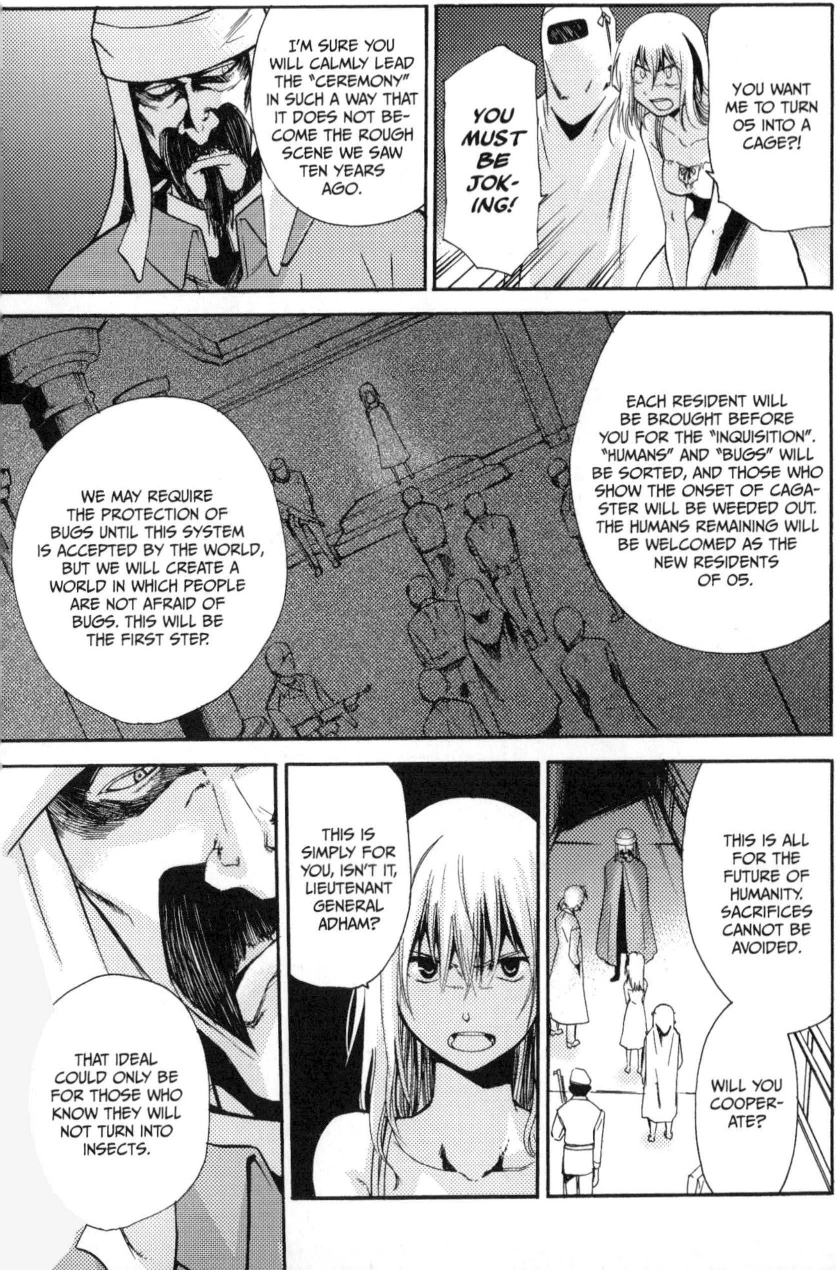
YOU WANT ME TO TURN 05 INTO A CAGE?!
YOU MUST BE JOK-ING!
I'M SURE YOU WILL CALMLY LEAD THE "CEREMONY" IN SUCH A WAY THAT IT DOES NOT BE-COME THE ROUGH SCENE WE SAW TEN YEARS AGO.
EACH RESIDENT WILL BE BROUGHT BEFORE YOU FOR THE "INQUISITION". "HUMANS" AND "BUGS" WILL BE SORTED, AND THOSE WHO SHOW THE ONSET OF CAGA-STER WILL BE WEEDED OUT. THE HUMANS REMAINING WILL BE WELCOMED AS THE NEW RESIDENTS OF 05.
WE MAY REQUIRE THE PROTECTION OF BUGS UNTIL THIS SYSTEM IS ACCEPTED BY THE WORLD, BUT WE WILL CREATE A WORLD IN WHICH PEOPLE ARE NOT AFRAID OF BUGS. THIS WILL BE THE FIRST STEP.
THIS IS ALL FOR THE FUTURE OF HUMANITY. SACRIFICES CANNOT BE AVOIDED.
WILL YOU COOPER-ATE?
THIS IS SIMPLY FOR YOU, ISN'T IT, LIEUTENANT GENERAL ADHAM?
THAT IDEAL COULD ONLY BE FOR THOSE WHO KNOW THEY WILL NOT TURN INTO INSECTS.

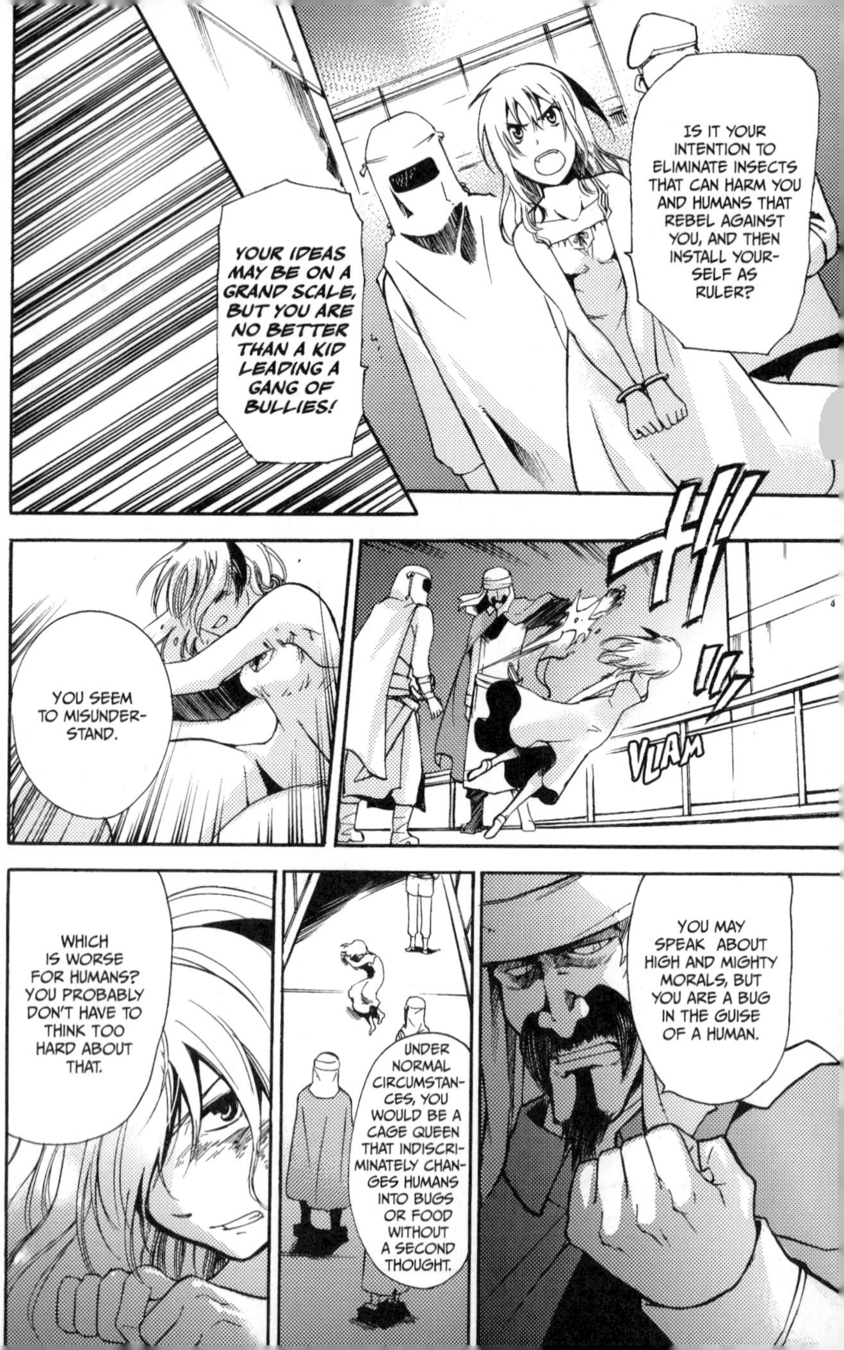
IS IT YOUR INTENTION TO ELIMINATE INSECTS THAT CAN HARM YOU AND HUMANS THAT REBEL AGAINST YOU, AND THEN INSTALL YOUR-SELF AS RULER?
YOUR IDEAS MAY BE ON A GRAND SCALE, BUT YOU ARE NO BETTER THAN A KID LEADING A GANG OF BULLIES!
VLAM
YOU SEEM TO MISUNDER-STAND.
YOU MAY SPEAK ABOUT HIGH AND MIGHTY MORALS, BUT YOU ARE A BUG IN THE GUISE OF A HUMAN.
UNDER NORMAL CIRCUMSTANCES, YOU WOULD BE A CAGE QUEEN THAT INDISCRIMINATELY CHANGES HUMANS INTO BUGS OR FOOD WITHOUT A SECOND THOUGHT.
WHICH IS WORSE FOR HUMANS? YOU PROBABLY DON'T HAVE TO THINK TOO HARD ABOUT THAT.

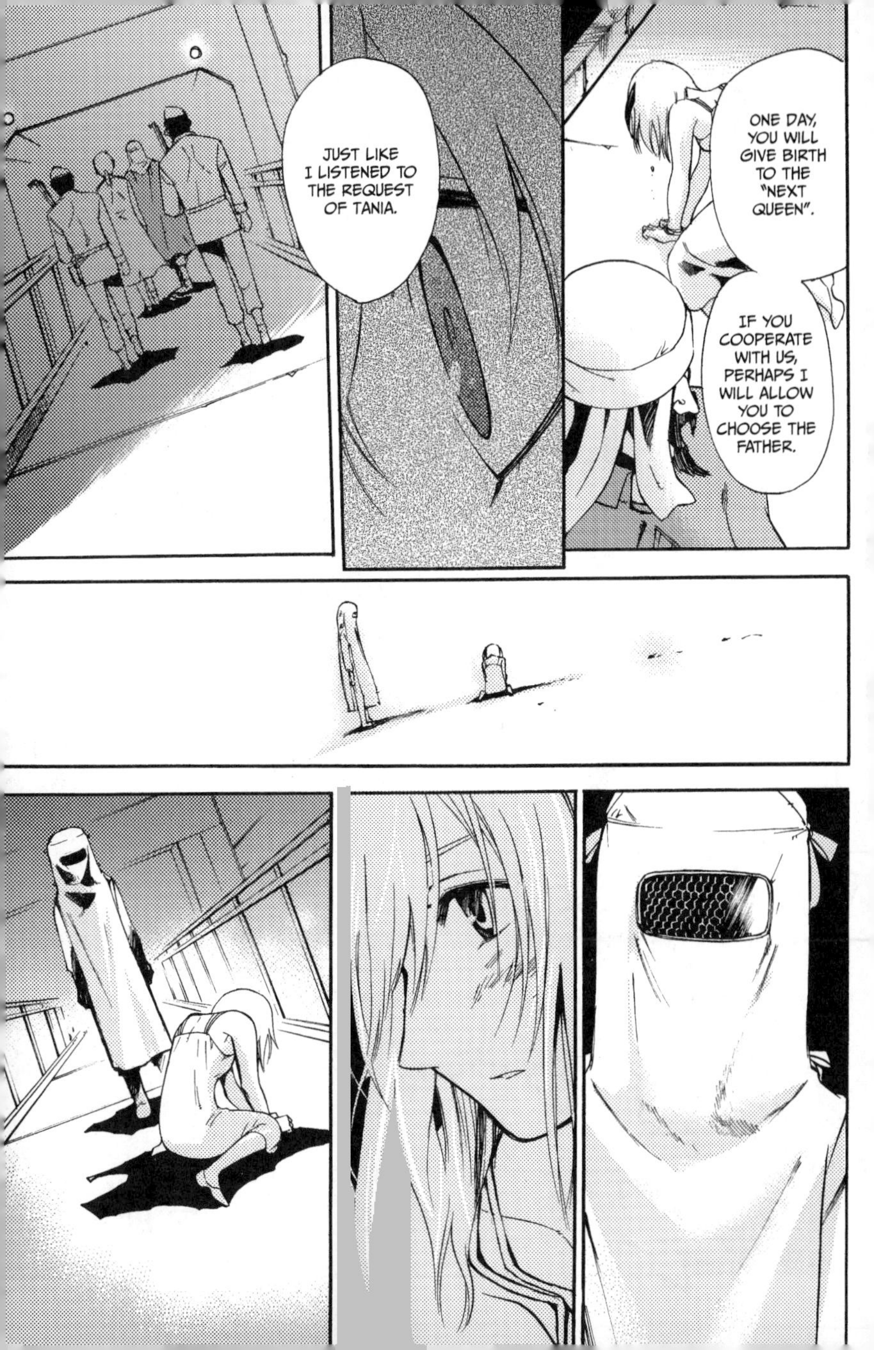
ONE DAY, YOU WILL GIVE BIRTH TO THE "NEXT QUEEN".
IF YOU COOPERATE WITH US, PERHAPS I WILL ALLOW YOU TO CHOOSE THE FATHER.
JUST LIKE I LISTENED TO THE REQUEST OF TANIA.

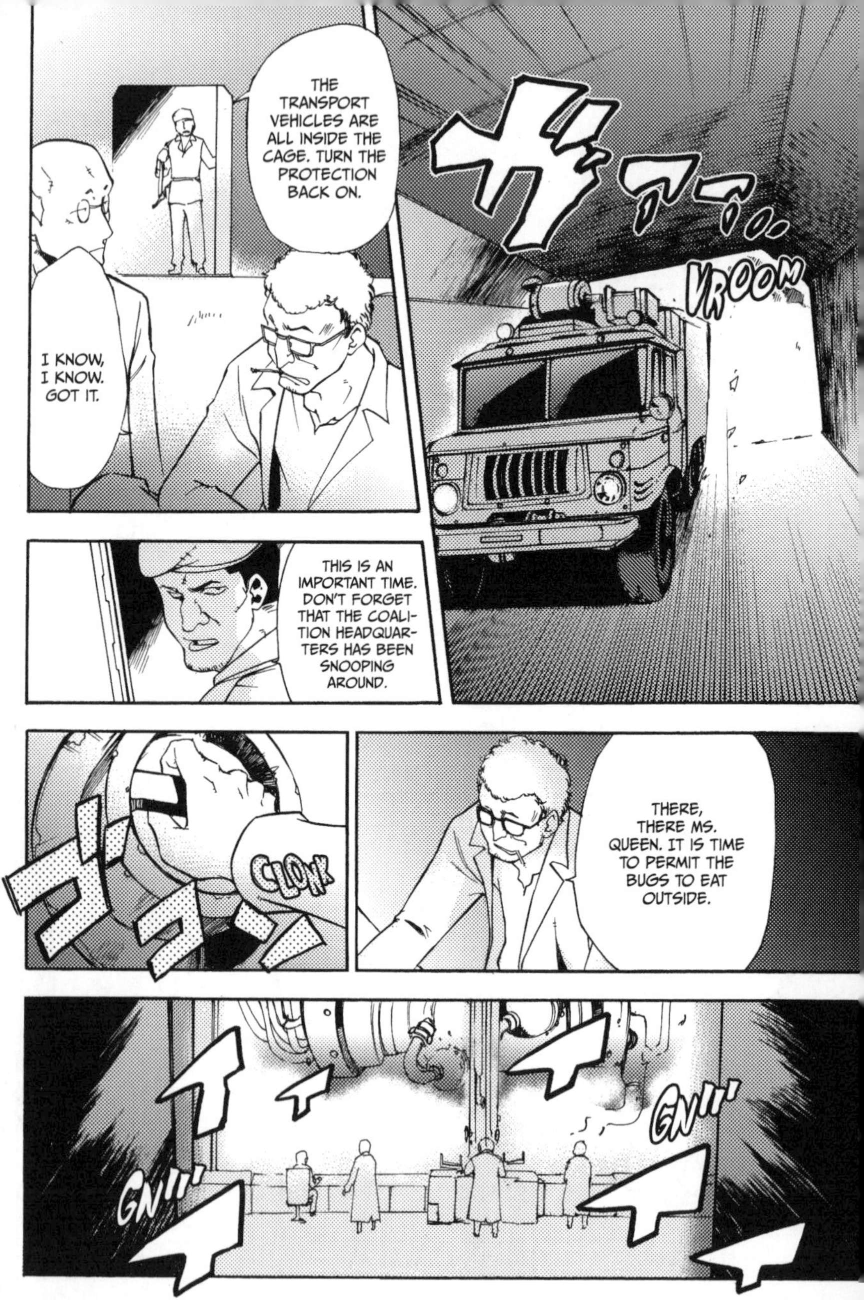
VROOM
THE TRANSPORT VEHICLES ARE ALL INSIDE THE CAGE. TURN THE PROTECTION BACK ON.
I KNOW, I KNOW. GOT IT.
THIS IS AN IMPORTANT TIME. DON'T FORGET THAT THE COALITION HEADQUARTERS HAS BEEN SNOOPING AROUND.
THERE, THERE MS. QUEEN. IT IS TIME TO PERMIT THE BUGS TO EAT OUTSIDE.
CLONK
GN''
GN''

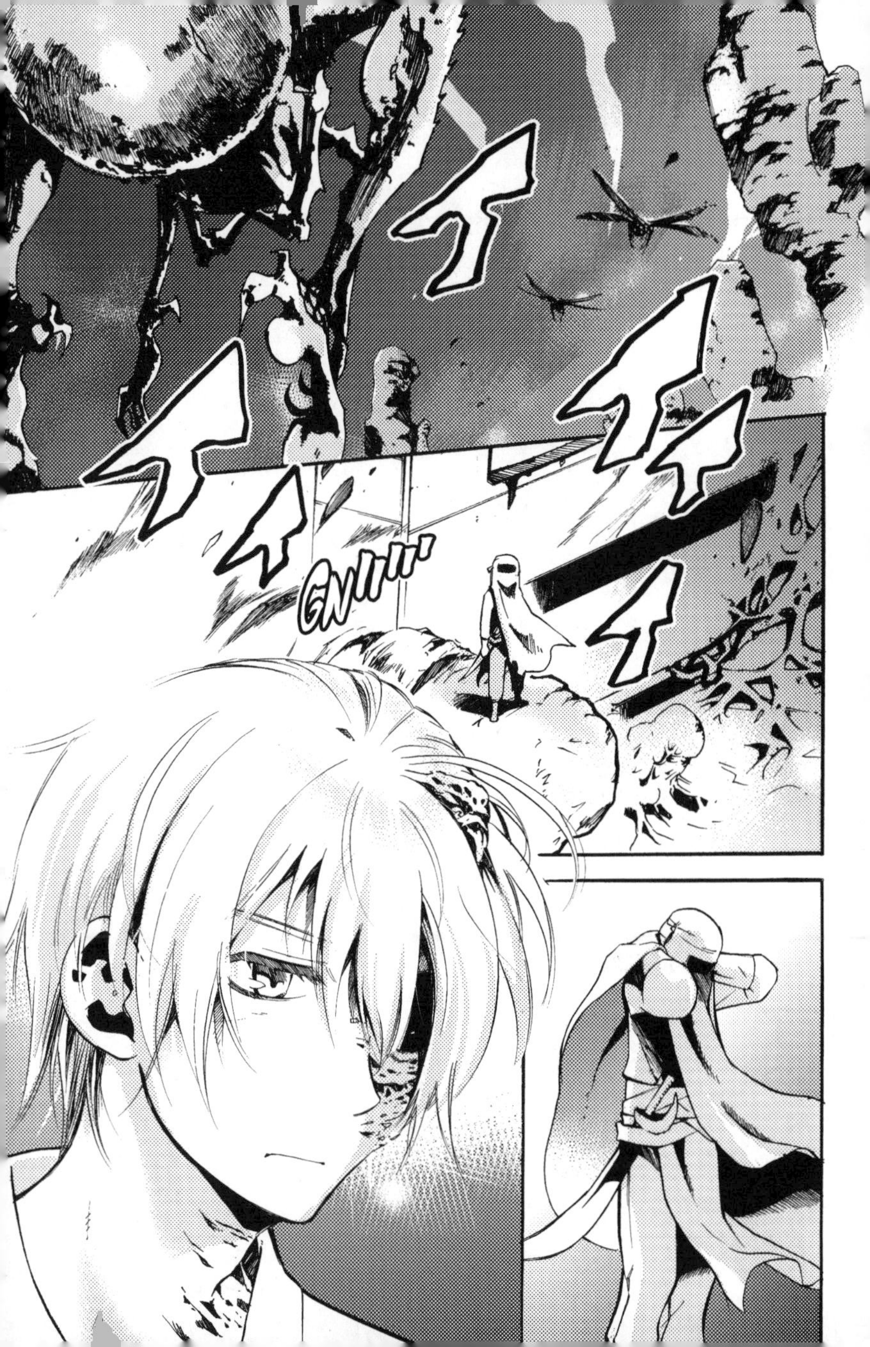
GNIIII

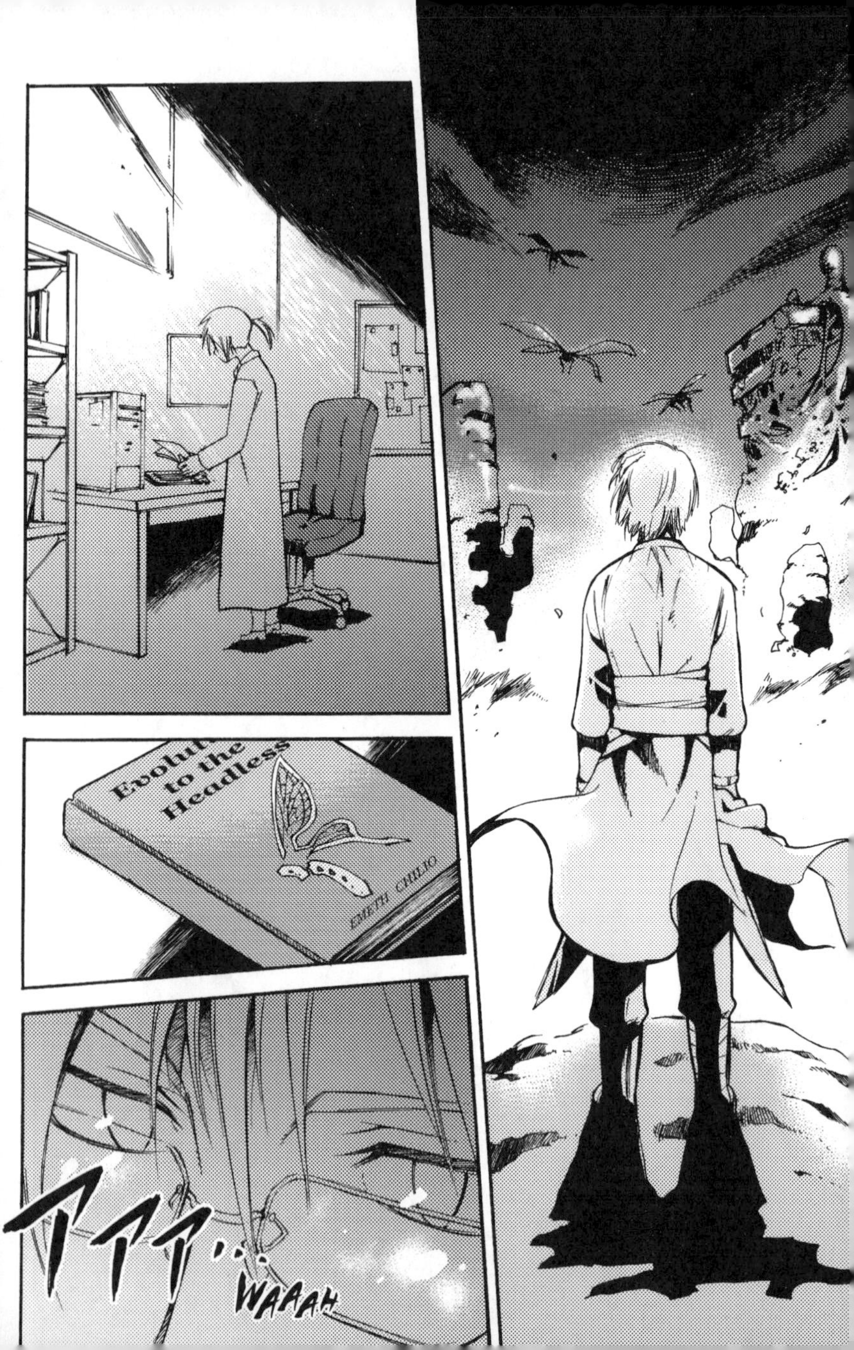
Evolu
to the
Headless
EMETH CHILIO
アアア…
WAAAH

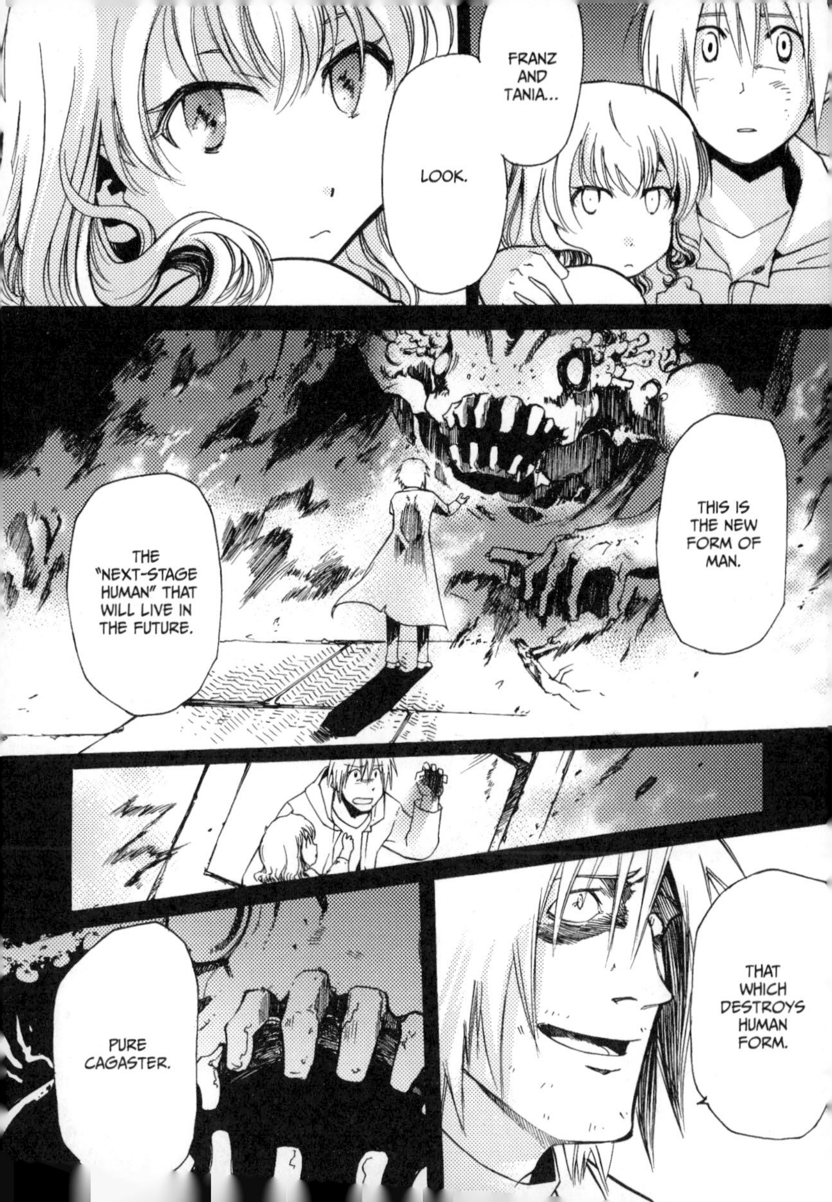
FRANZ AND TANIA...
LOOK.
THIS IS THE NEW FORM OF MAN.
THE "NEXT-STAGE HUMAN" THAT WILL LIVE IN THE FUTURE.
THAT WHICH DESTROYS HUMAN FORM.
PURE CAGASTER.

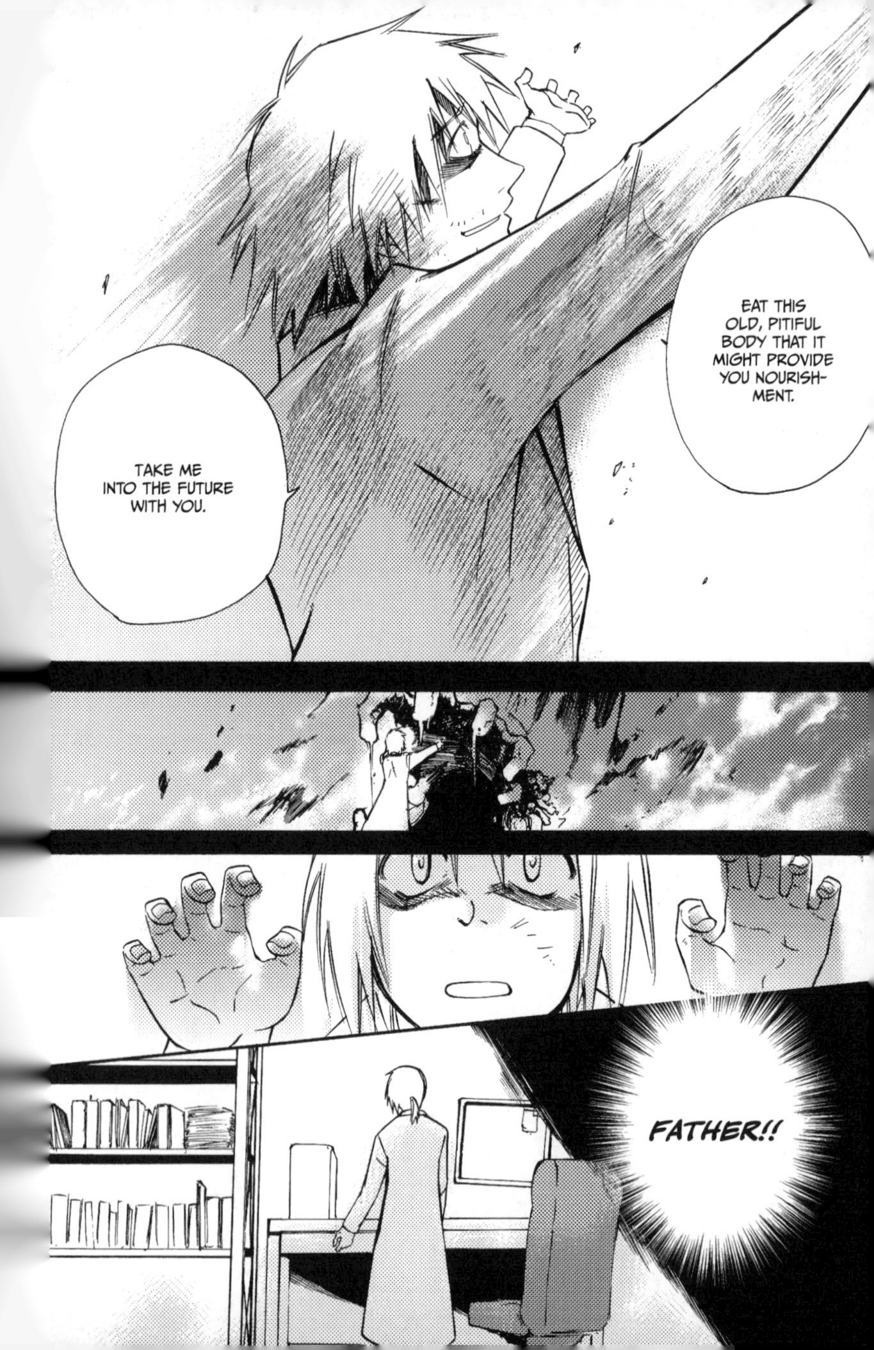
EAT THIS OLD, PITIFUL BODY THAT IT MIGHT PROVIDE YOU NOURISH-MENT.
TAKE ME INTO THE FUTURE WITH YOU.
FATHER!!

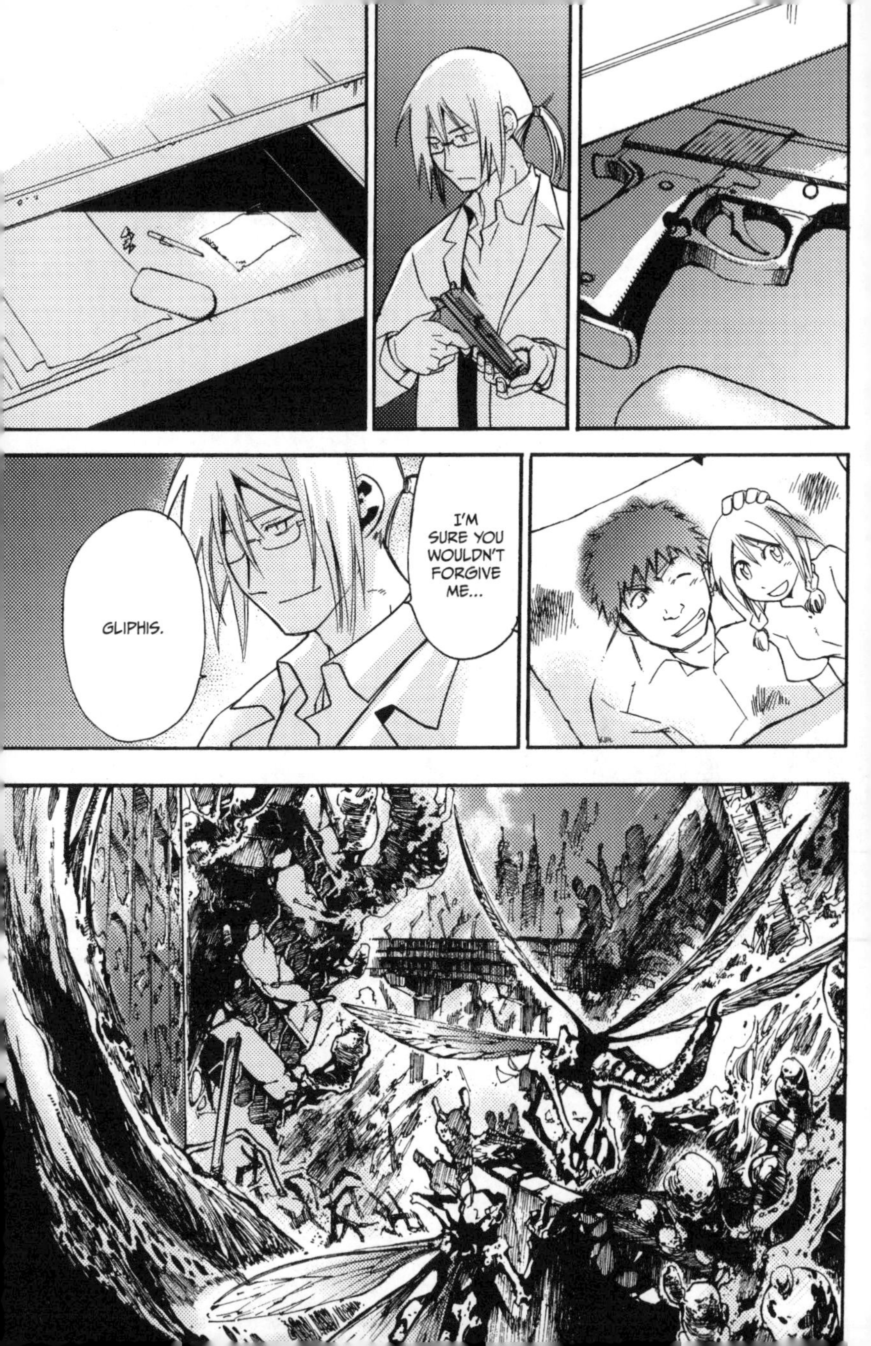
I'M SURE YOU WOULDN'T FORGIVE ME...
GLIPHIS.

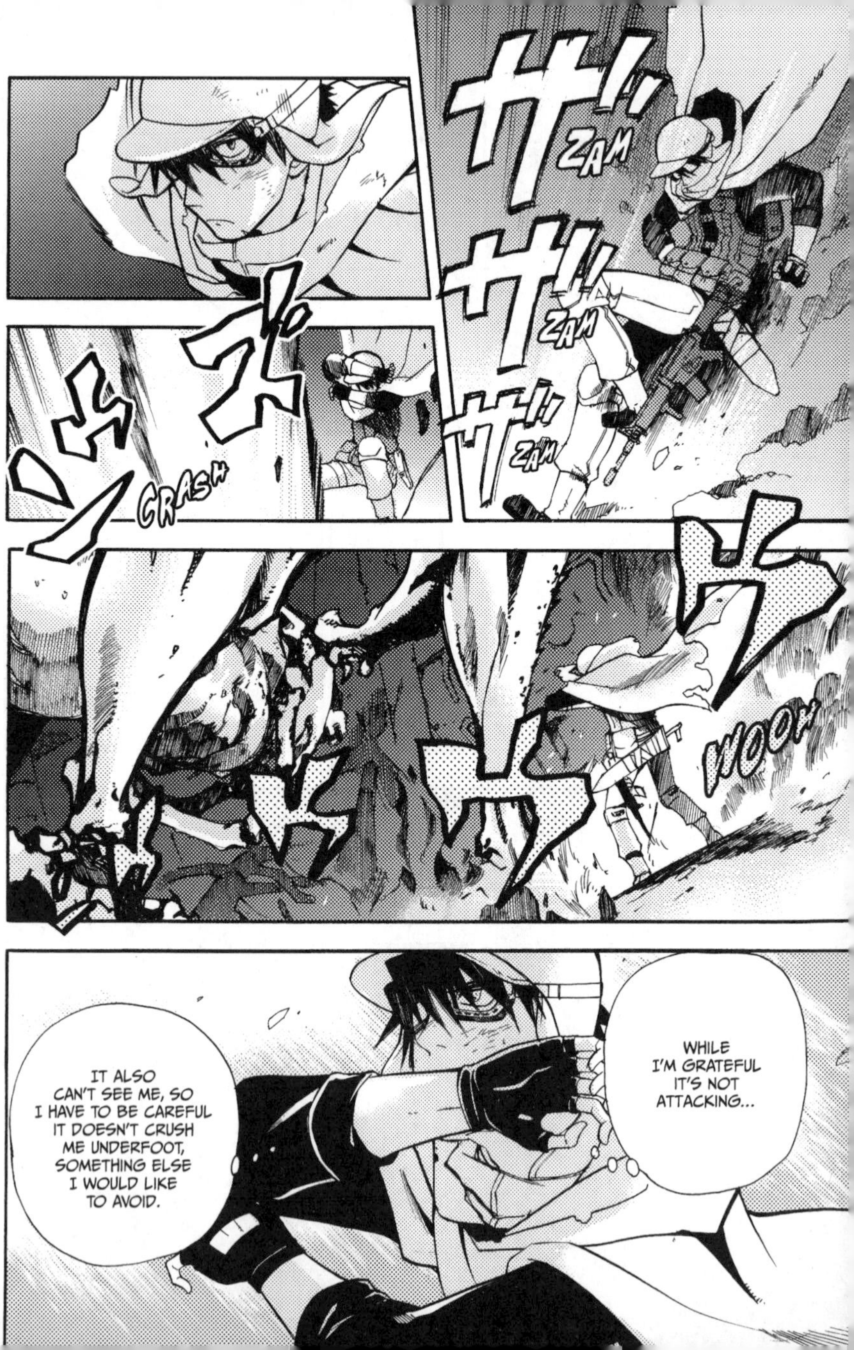
ZAM
ZAM
ZAM
CRASH
WOOOH
WHILE I'M GRATEFUL IT'S NOT ATTACKING...
IT ALSO CAN'T SEE ME, SO I HAVE TO BE CAREFUL IT DOESN'T CRUSH ME UNDERFOOT, SOMETHING ELSE I WOULD LIKE TO AVOID.

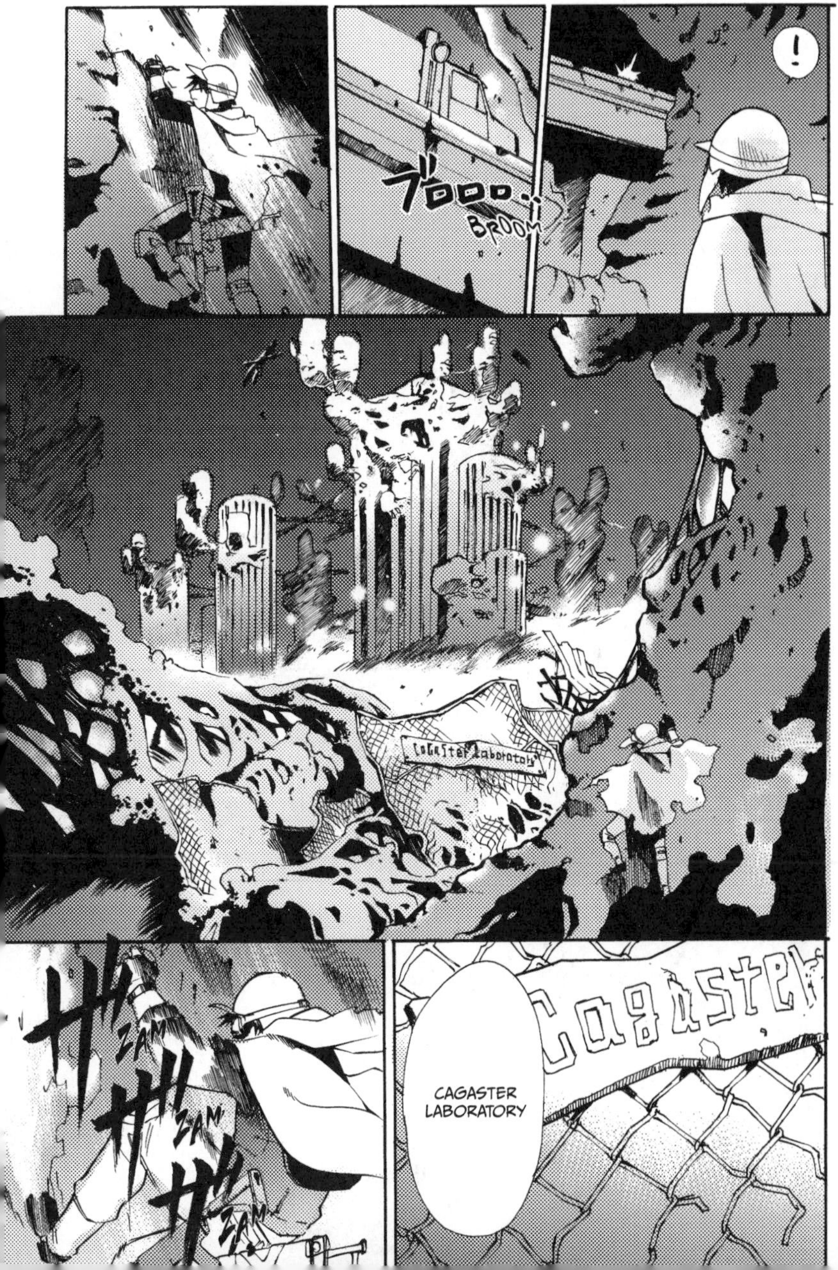
!
ブロロロ…
BROOM
Cagaster Laboratory
CAGASTER LABORATORY
Cagaster
ZAM
ZAM
ZAM

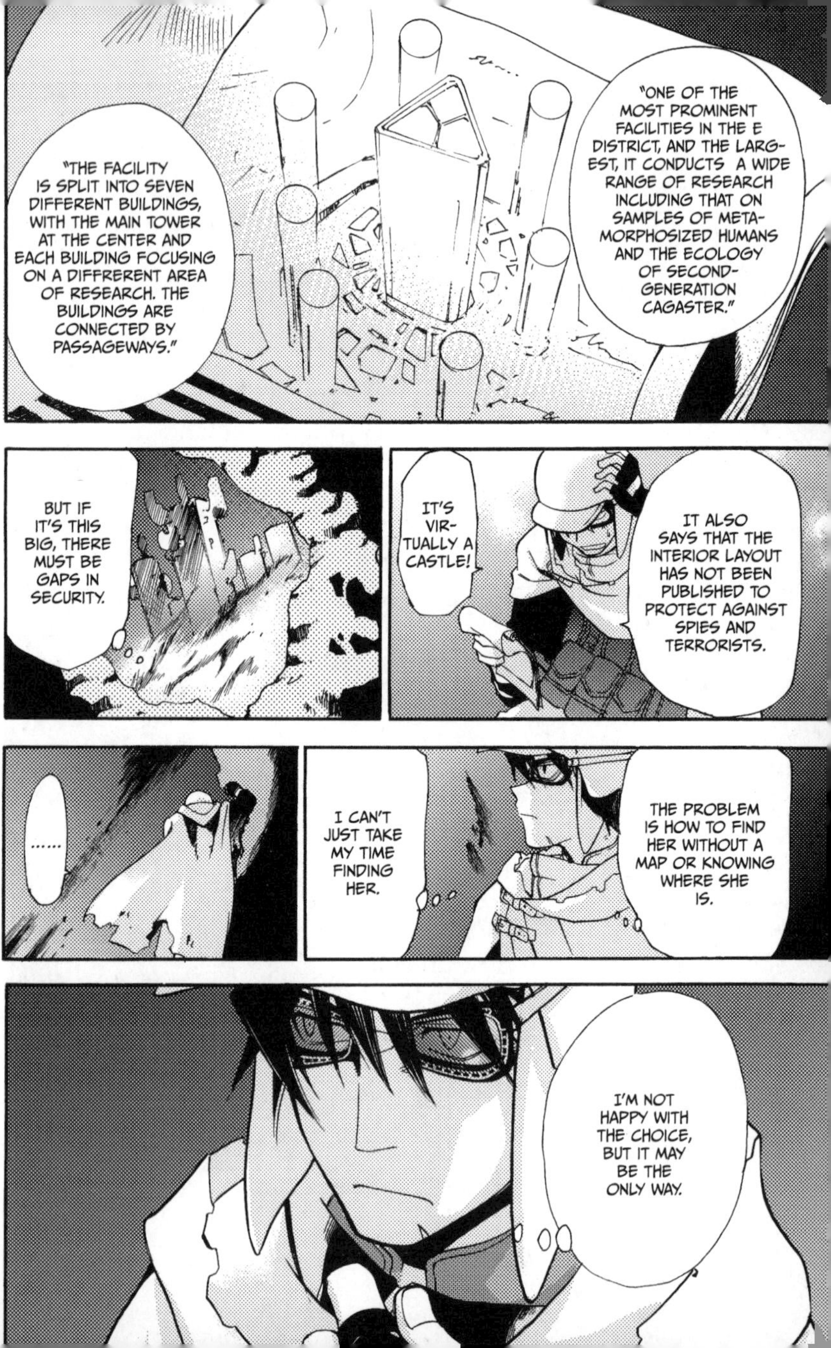
"ONE OF THE MOST PROMINENT FACILITIES IN THE E DISTRICT, AND THE LARGEST, IT CONDUCTS A WIDE RANGE OF RESEARCH INCLUDING THAT ON SAMPLES OF METAMORPHOSIZED HUMANS AND THE ECOLOGY OF SECOND-GENERATION CAGASTER."
"THE FACILITY IS SPLIT INTO SEVEN DIFFERENT BUILDINGS, WITH THE MAIN TOWER AT THE CENTER AND EACH BUILDING FOCUSING ON A DIFFRERENT AREA OF RESEARCH. THE BUILDINGS ARE CONNECTED BY PASSAGEWAYS."
IT ALSO SAYS THAT THE INTERIOR LAYOUT HAS NOT BEEN PUBLISHED TO PROTECT AGAINST SPIES AND TERRORISTS.
IT'S VIRTUALLY A CASTLE!
BUT IF IT'S THIS BIG, THERE MUST BE GAPS IN SECURITY.
THE PROBLEM IS HOW TO FIND HER WITHOUT A MAP OR KNOWING WHERE SHE IS.
I CAN'T JUST TAKE MY TIME FINDING HER.
......
I'M NOT HAPPY WITH THE CHOICE, BUT IT MAY BE THE ONLY WAY.

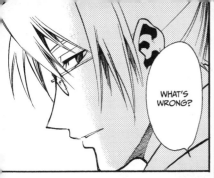

WHAT'S WRONG?
HAVE YOU FALLEN INTO SENTIMENTALITY RIGHT BEFORE ACHIEVING YOUR GREATEST DESIRE?
DESIRE?
THE "SEIZURE OF THE HUMAN WORLD" THAT ADHAM TALKS ABOUT.
EVEN THOUGH YOU CAN'T RID THE WORLD OF CAGASTERS, YOU CAN NOW CONTROL THEM.
IN THE FUTURE, YOU WILL BE WOR-SHIPPED AS THE SAVIOR OF HUMANITY.

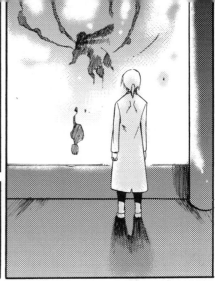

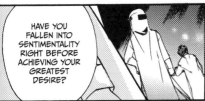

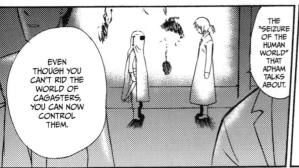

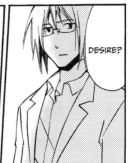

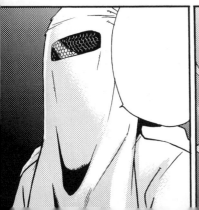

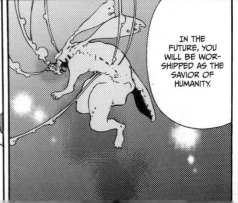

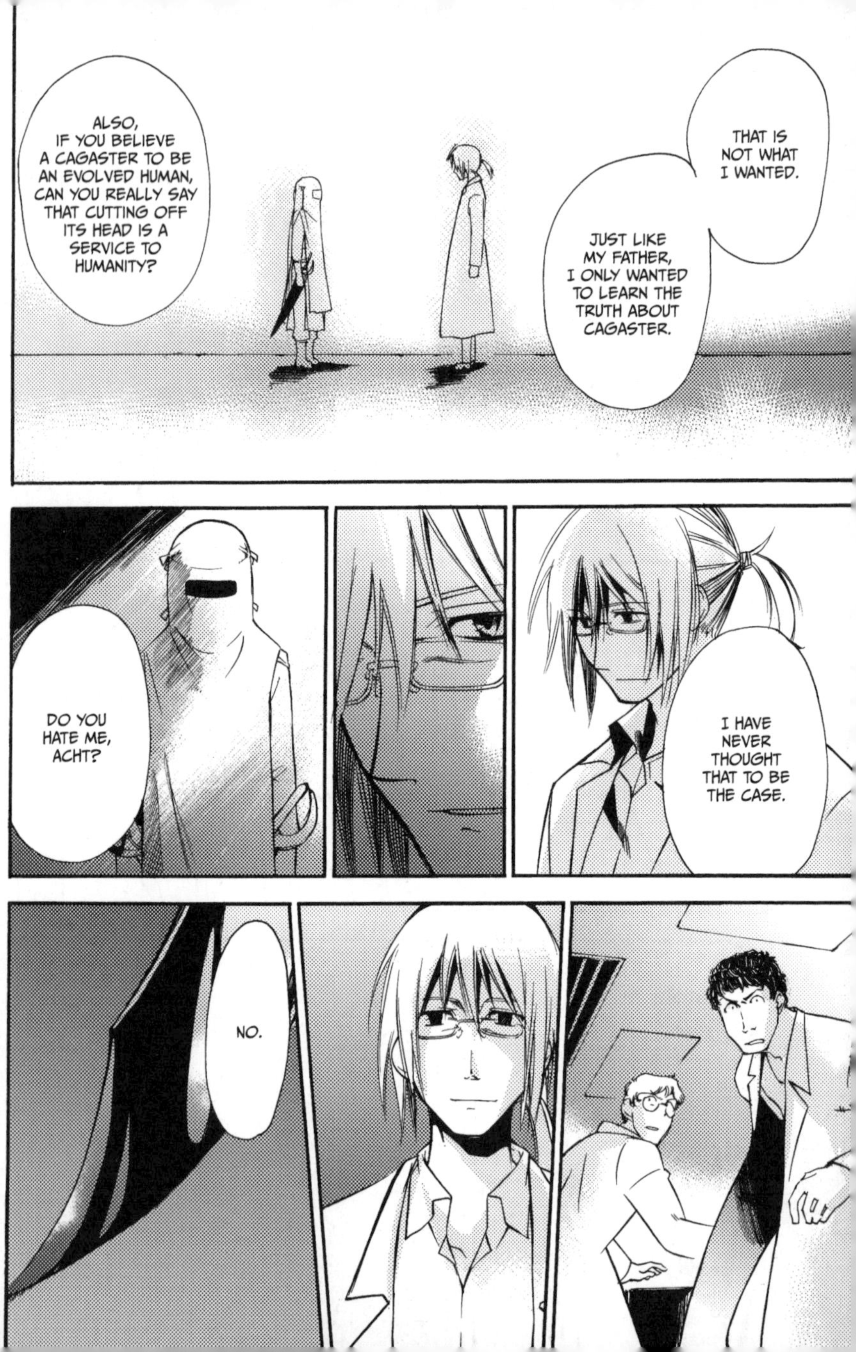
THAT IS NOT WHAT I WANTED.
JUST LIKE MY FATHER, I ONLY WANTED TO LEARN THE TRUTH ABOUT CAGASTER.
ALSO, IF YOU BELIEVE A CAGASTER TO BE AN EVOLVED HUMAN, CAN YOU REALLY SAY THAT CUTTING OFF ITS HEAD IS A SERVICE TO HUMANITY?
I HAVE NEVER THOUGHT THAT TO BE THE CASE.
DO YOU HATE ME, ACHT?
NO.

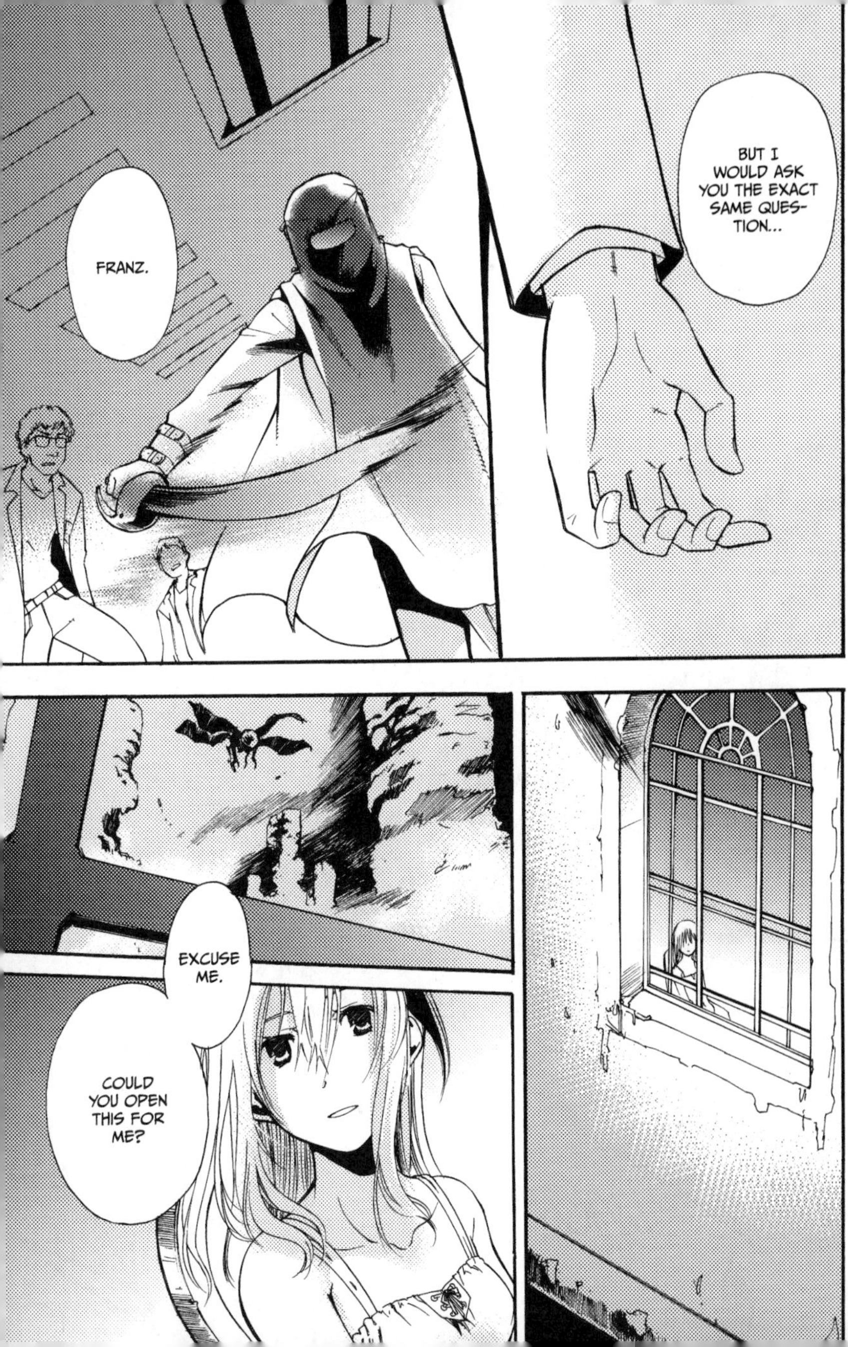
BUT I WOULD ASK YOU THE EXACT SAME QUES-TION...
FRANZ.
EXCUSE ME.
COULD YOU OPEN THIS FOR ME?

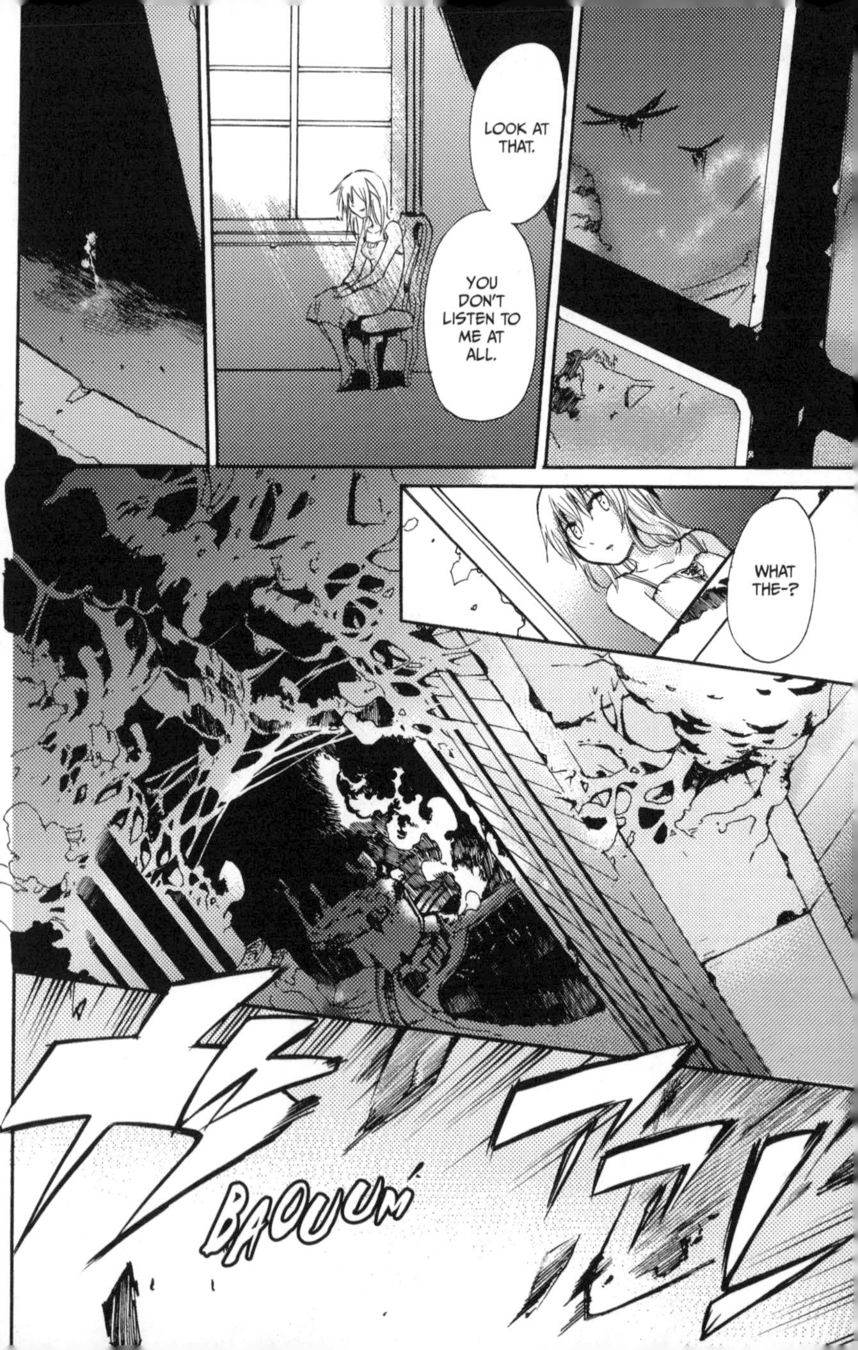
LOOK AT THAT.
YOU DON'T LISTEN TO ME AT ALL.
WHAT THE-?
BAOUUM

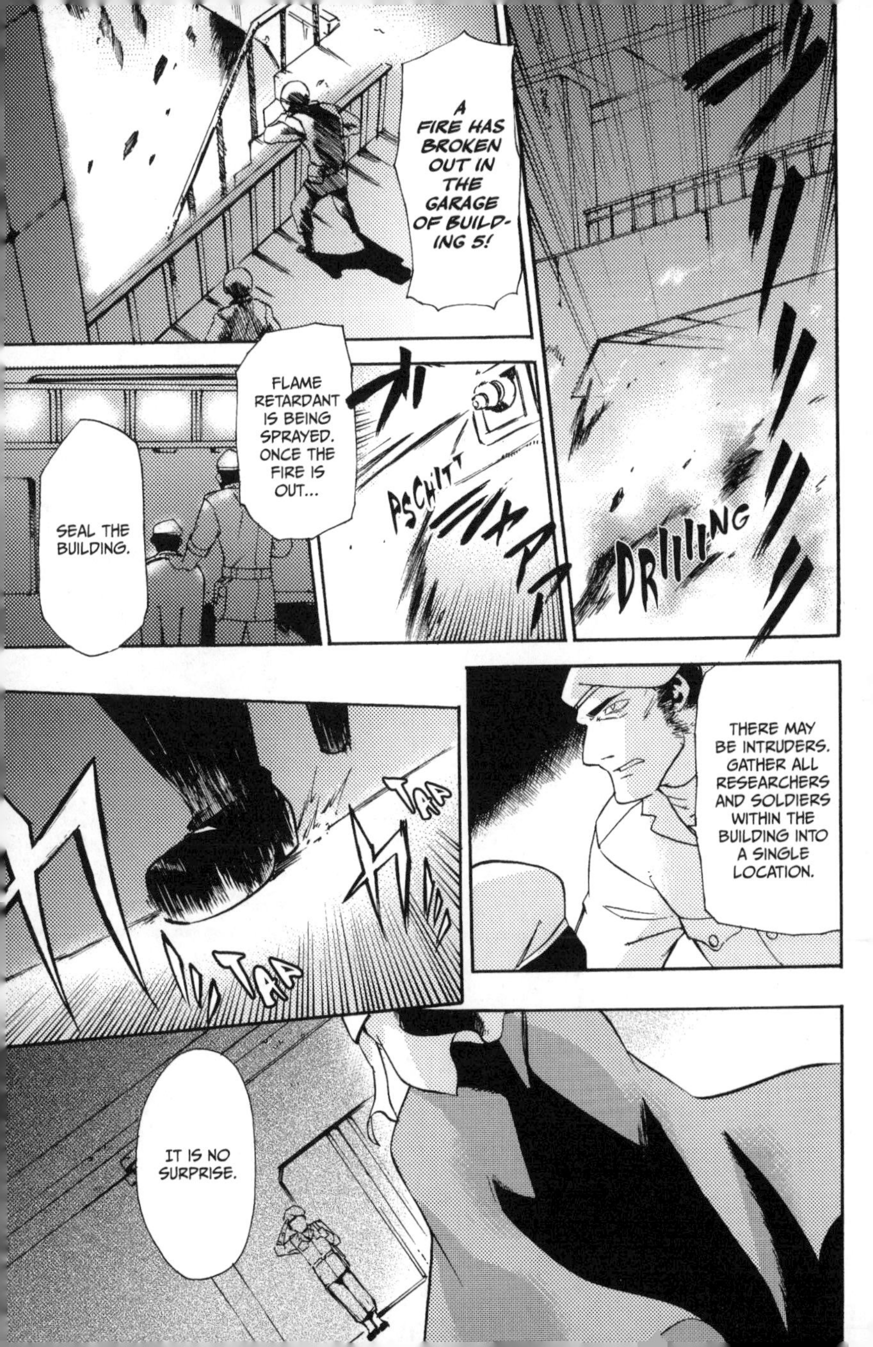
DRIIIING
A FIRE HAS BROKEN OUT IN THE GARAGE OF BUILD-ING 5!
FLAME RETARDANT IS BEING SPRAYED. ONCE THE FIRE IS OUT...
PSCHITT
SEAL THE BUILDING.
THERE MAY BE INTRUDERS. GATHER ALL RESEARCHERS AND SOLDIERS WITHIN THE BUILDING INTO A SINGLE LOCATION.
TAP
TAP
IT IS NO SURPRISE.

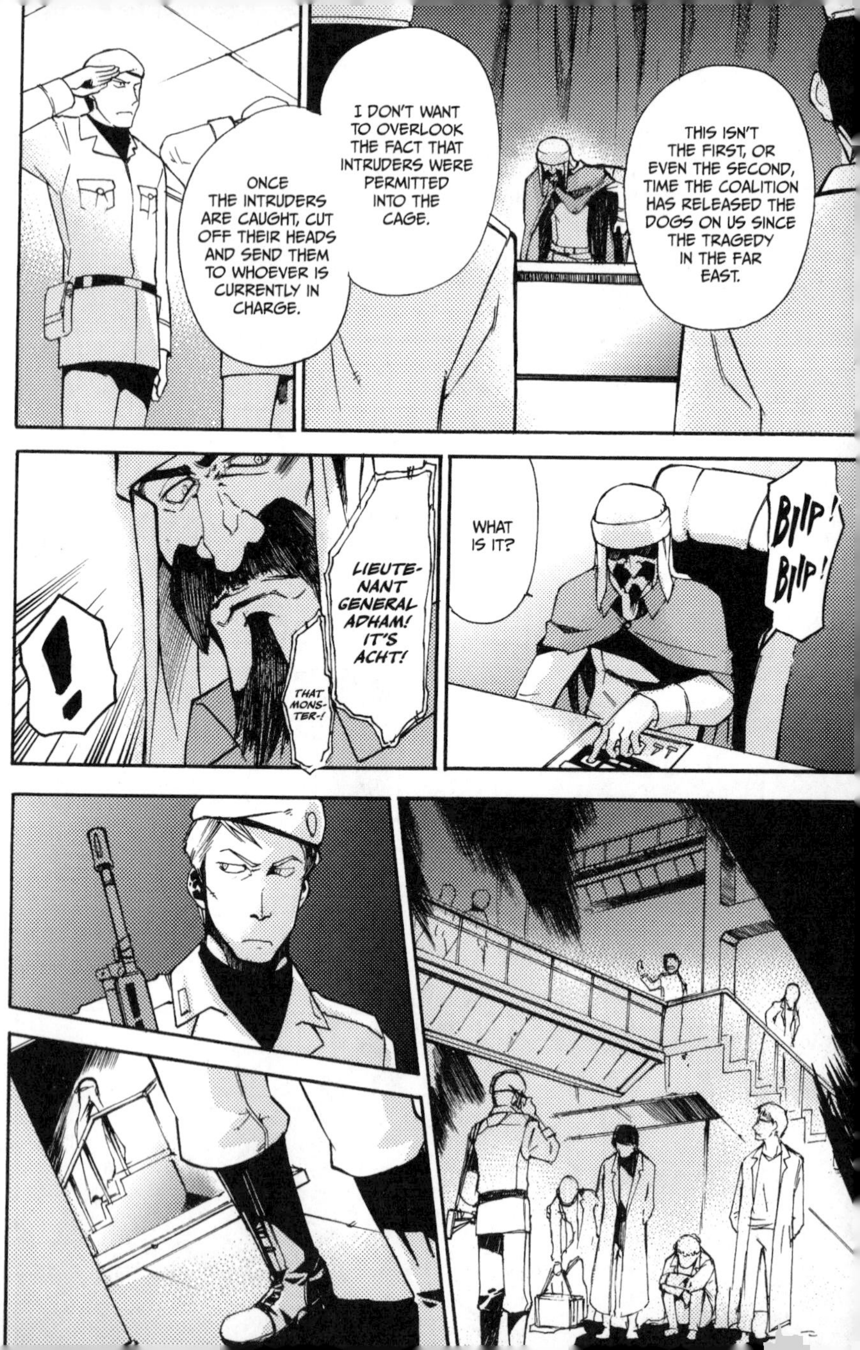
THIS ISN'T THE FIRST, OR EVEN THE SECOND, TIME THE COALITION HAS RELEASED THE DOGS ON US SINCE THE TRAGEDY IN THE FAR EAST.
I DON'T WANT TO OVERLOOK THE FACT THAT INTRUDERS WERE PERMITTED INTO THE CAGE.
ONCE THE INTRUDERS ARE CAUGHT, CUT OFF THEIR HEADS AND SEND THEM TO WHOEVER IS CURRENTLY IN CHARGE.
BIIP! BIIP!
WHAT IS IT?
LIEUTE-NANT GENERAL ADHAM! IT'S ACHT!
THAT MONS-TER-!
!

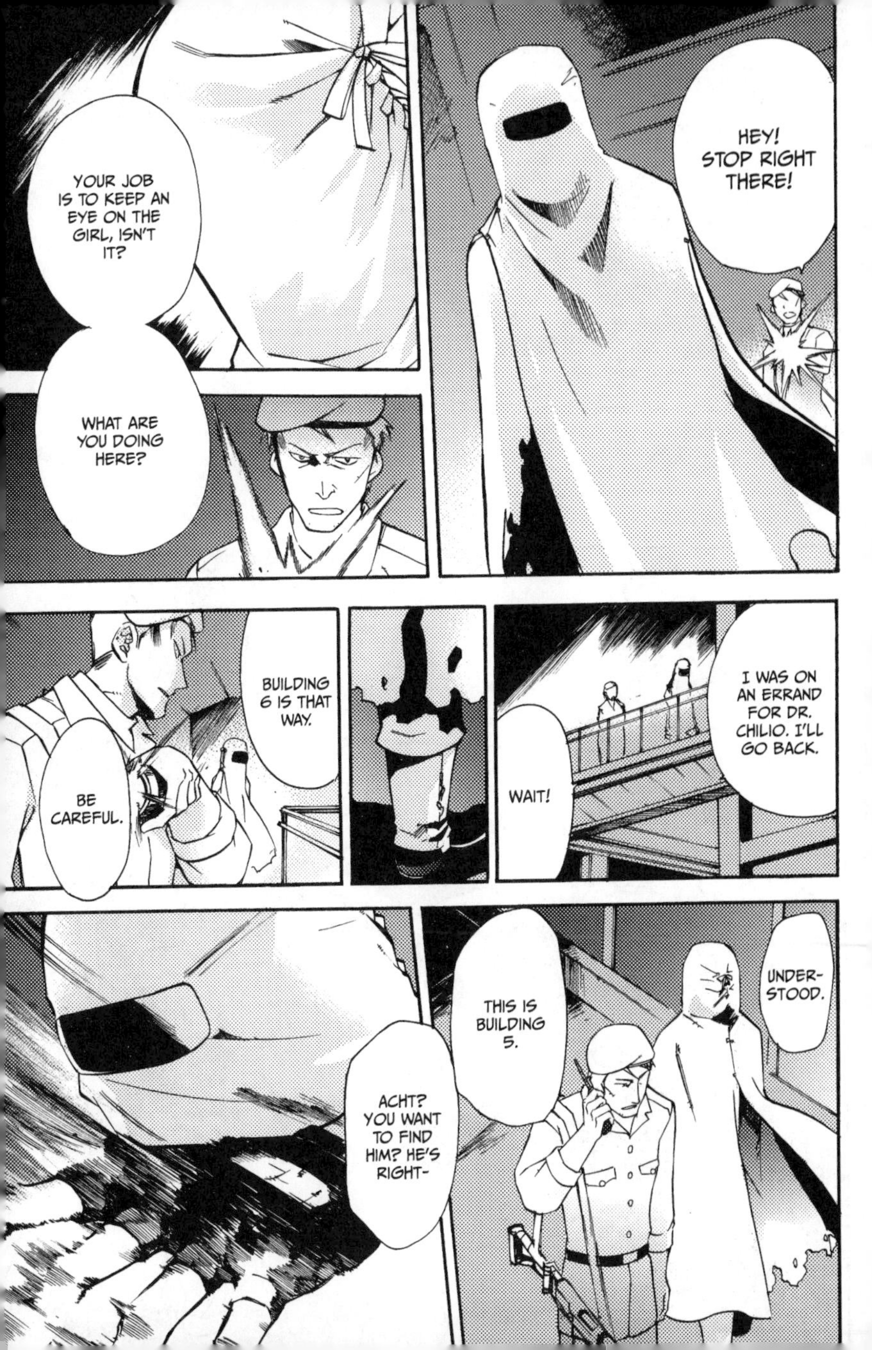
HEY! STOP RIGHT THERE!
YOUR JOB IS TO KEEP AN EYE ON THE GIRL, ISN'T IT?
WHAT ARE YOU DOING HERE?
I WAS ON AN ERRAND FOR DR. CHILIO. I'LL GO BACK.
WAIT!
BUILDING 6 IS THAT WAY.
BE CAREFUL.
UNDER-STOOD.
THIS IS BUILDING 5.
ACHT? YOU WANT TO FIND HIM? HE'S RIGHT-

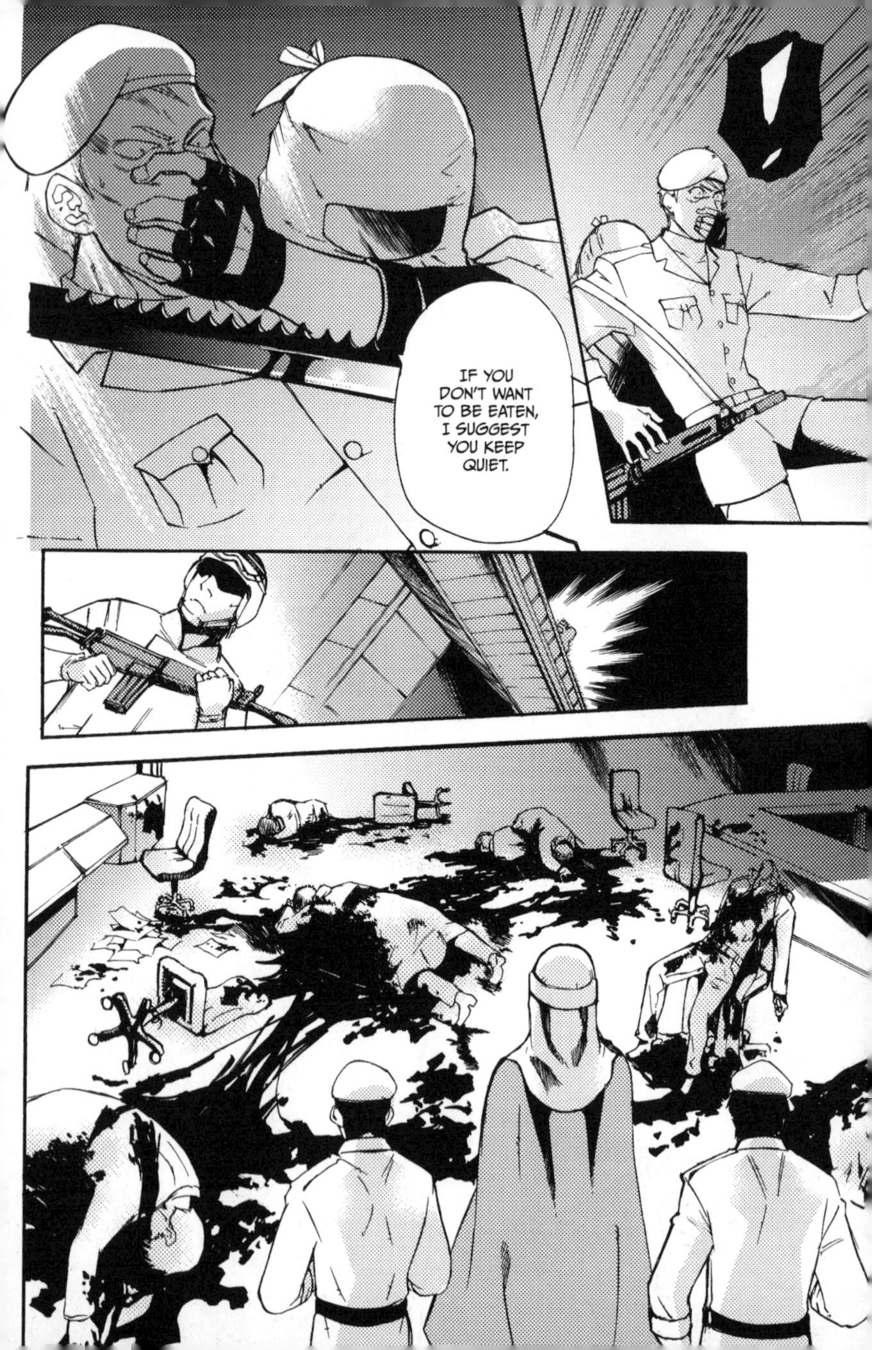
IF YOU DON'T WANT TO BE EATEN, I SUGGEST YOU KEEP QUIET.

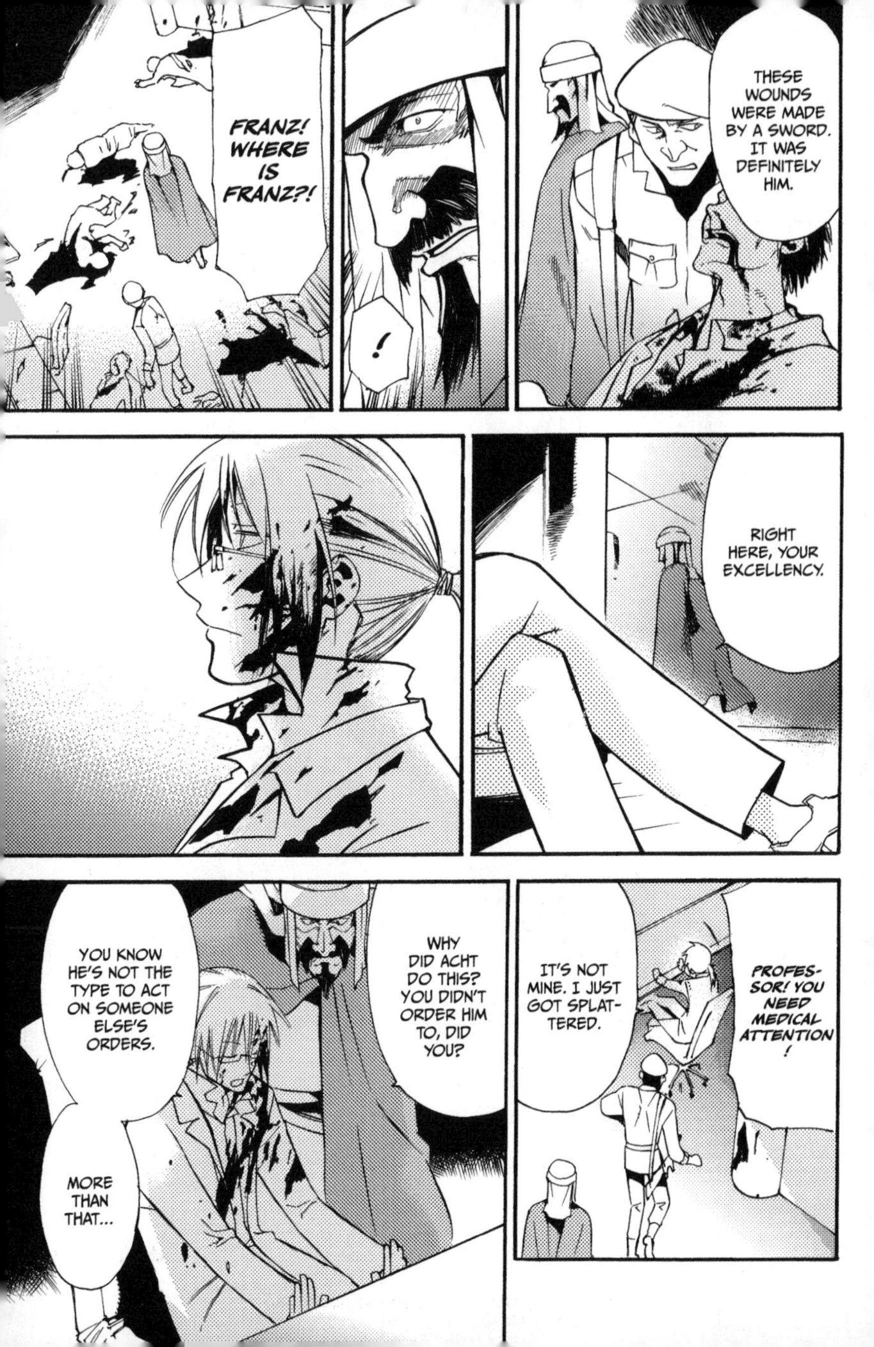
THESE WOUNDS WERE MADE BY A SWORD. IT WAS DEFINITELY HIM.
!
FRANZ! WHERE IS FRANZ?!
RIGHT HERE, YOUR EXCELLENCY.
PROFES-SOR! YOU NEED MEDICAL ATTENTION!
IT'S NOT MINE. I JUST GOT SPLAT-TERED.
WHY DID ACHT DO THIS? YOU DIDN'T ORDER HIM TO, DID YOU?
YOU KNOW HE'S NOT THE TYPE TO ACT ON SOMEONE ELSE'S ORDERS.
MORE THAN THAT...

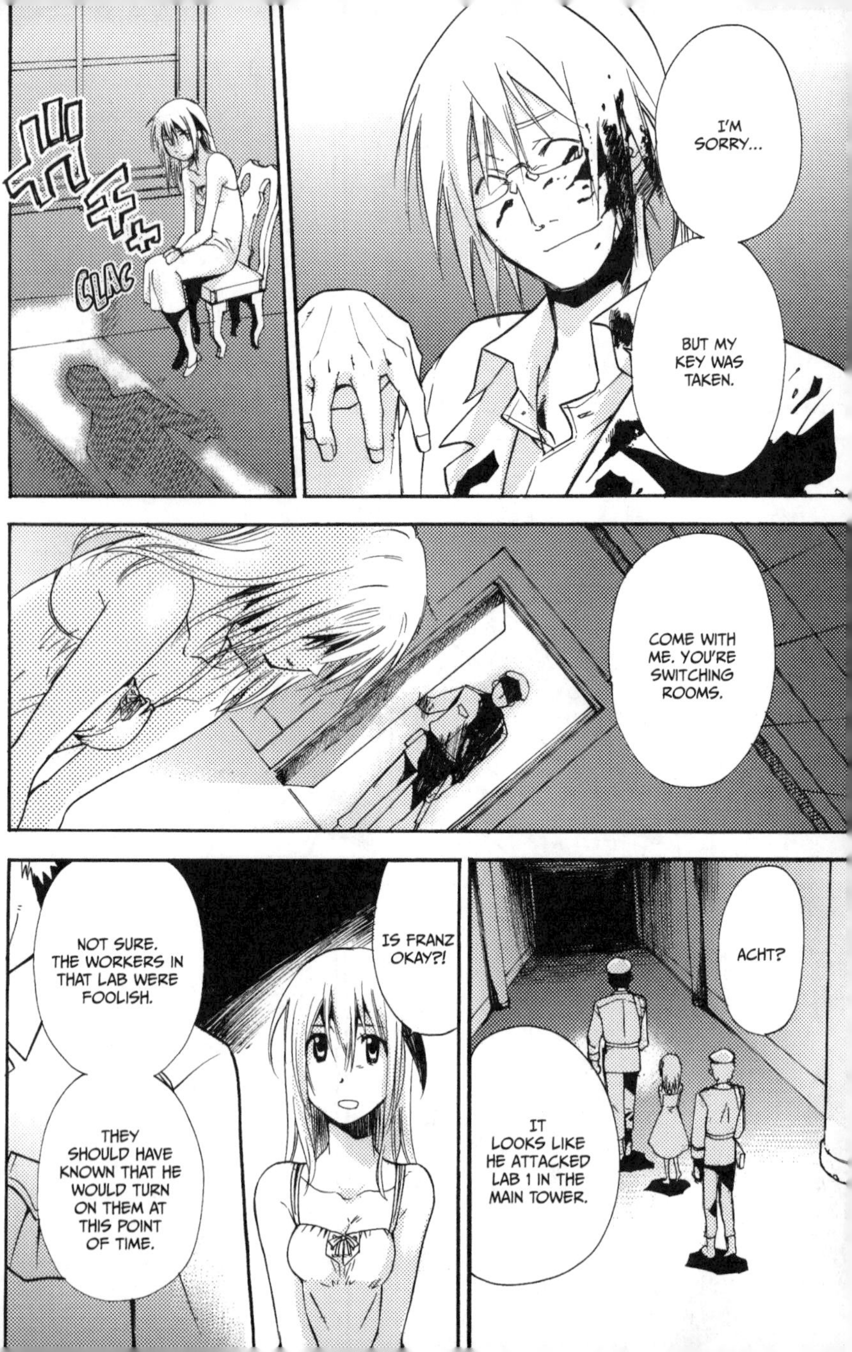
I'M SORRY...
BUT MY KEY WAS TAKEN.
ガチャ
CLAC
COME WITH ME. YOU'RE SWITCHING ROOMS.
ACHT?
IT LOOKS LIKE HE ATTACKED LAB 1 IN THE MAIN TOWER.
IS FRANZ OKAY?!
NOT SURE. THE WORKERS IN THAT LAB WERE FOOLISH.
THEY SHOULD HAVE KNOWN THAT HE WOULD TURN ON THEM AT THIS POINT OF TIME.

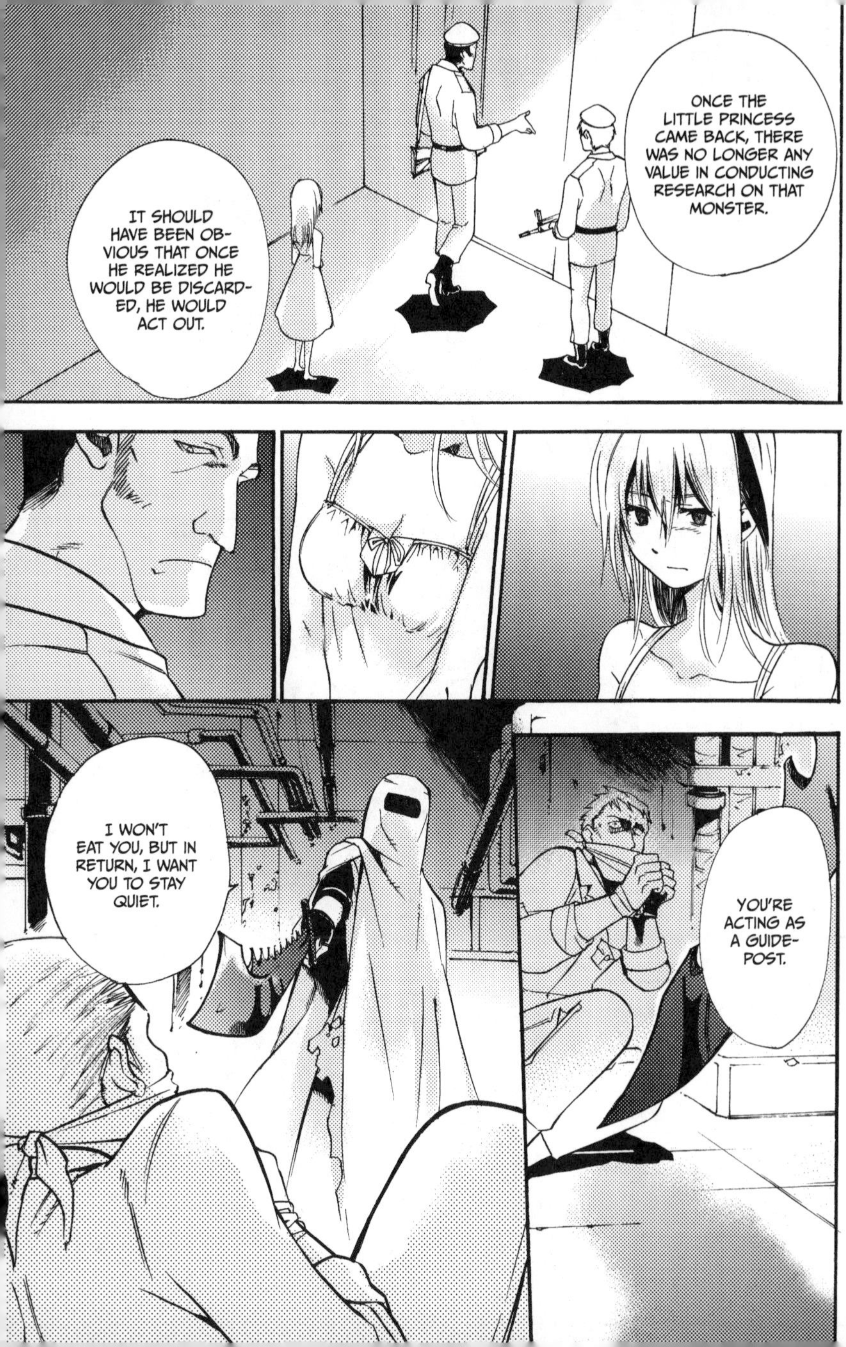
ONCE THE LITTLE PRINCESS CAME BACK, THERE WAS NO LONGER ANY VALUE IN CONDUCTING RESEARCH ON THAT MONSTER.
IT SHOULD HAVE BEEN OB- VIOUS THAT ONCE HE REALIZED HE WOULD BE DISCARD- ED, HE WOULD ACT OUT.
YOU'RE ACTING AS A GUIDE- POST.
I WON'T EAT YOU, BUT IN RETURN, I WANT YOU TO STAY QUIET.

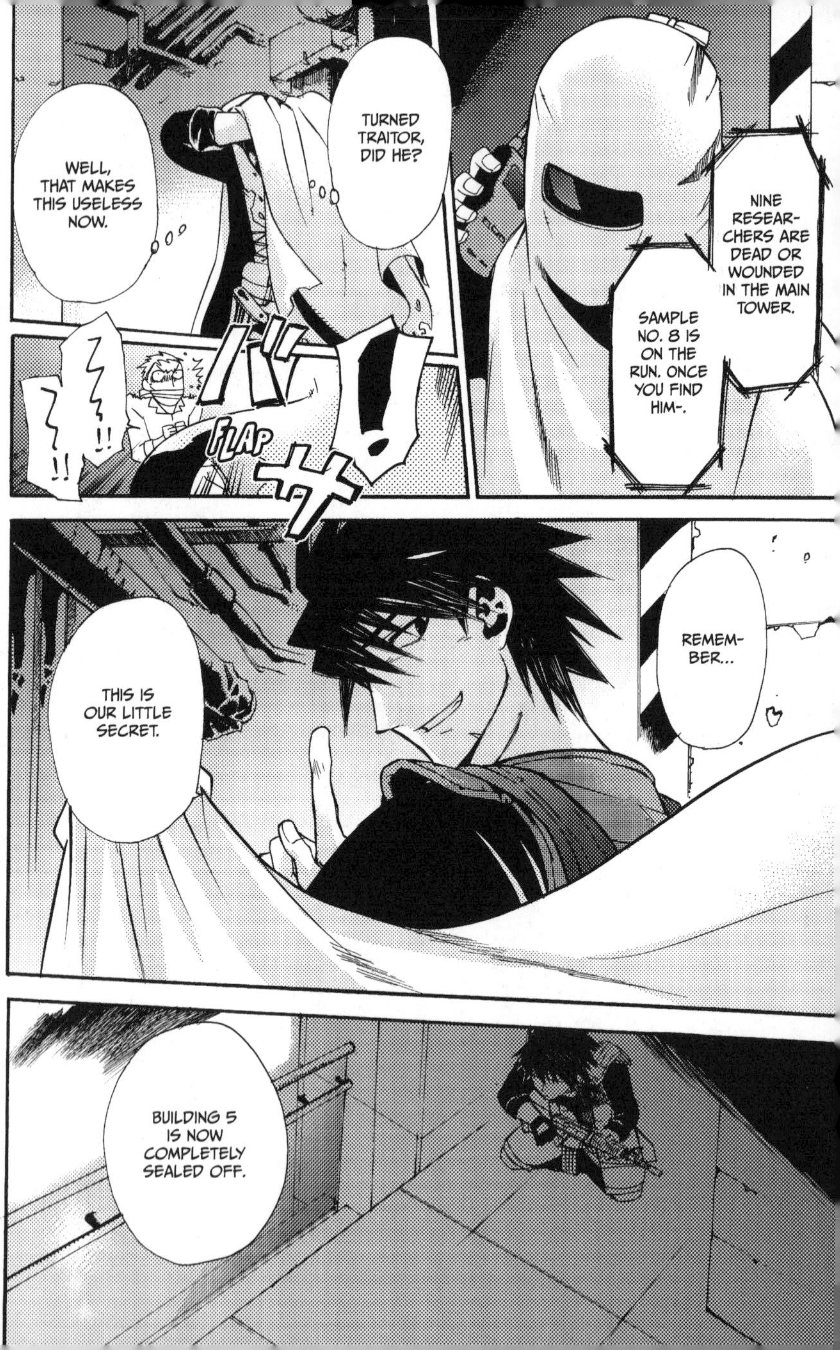

NINE RESEARCHERS ARE DEAD OR WOUNDED IN THE MAIN TOWER.
SAMPLE NO. 8 IS ON THE RUN. ONCE YOU FIND HIM-.
TURNED TRAITOR, DID HE?
WELL, THAT MAKES THIS USELESS NOW.
FLAP
REMEMBER...
THIS IS OUR LITTLE SECRET.
BUILDING 5 IS NOW COMPLETELY SEALED OFF.

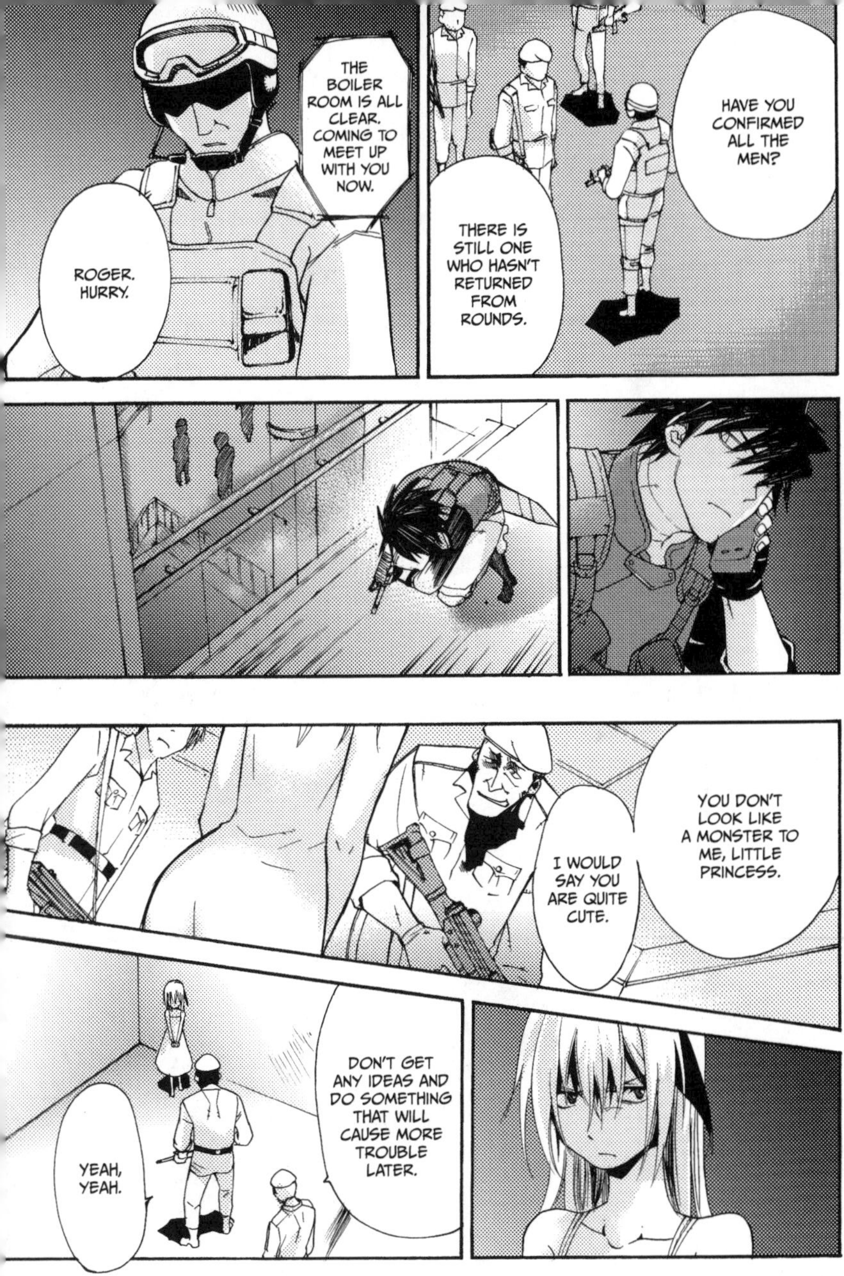
HAVE YOU CONFIRMED ALL THE MEN?
THERE IS STILL ONE WHO HASN'T RETURNED FROM ROUNDS.
THE BOILER ROOM IS ALL CLEAR. COMING TO MEET UP WITH YOU NOW.
ROGER. HURRY.
YOU DON'T LOOK LIKE A MONSTER TO ME, LITTLE PRINCESS.
I WOULD SAY YOU ARE QUITE CUTE.
DON'T GET ANY IDEAS AND DO SOMETHING THAT WILL CAUSE MORE TROUBLE LATER.
YEAH, YEAH.

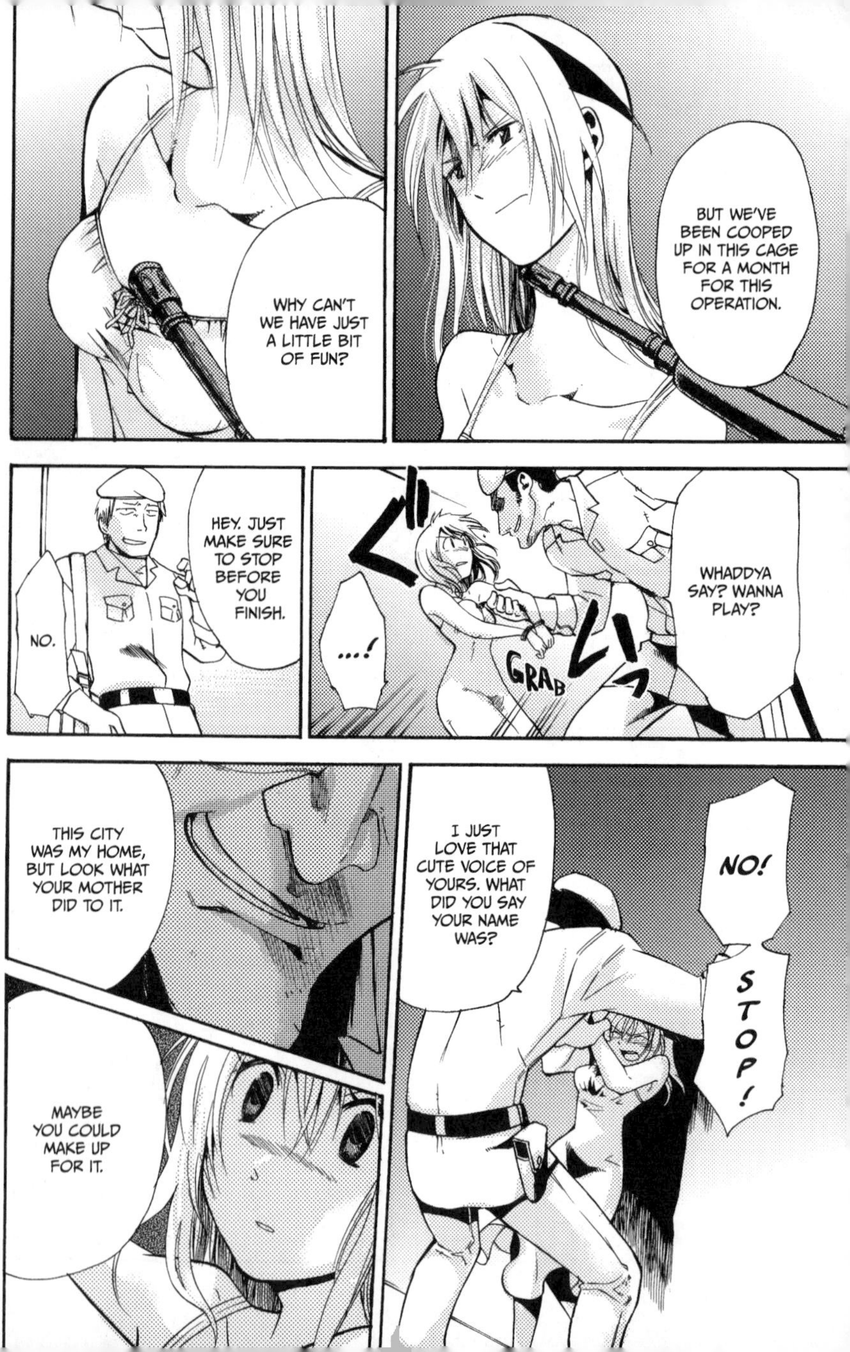
BUT WE'VE BEEN COOPED UP IN THIS CAGE FOR A MONTH FOR THIS OPERATION.
WHY CAN'T WE HAVE JUST A LITTLE BIT OF FUN?
WHADDYA SAY? WANNA PLAY?
GRAB
...!
HEY. JUST MAKE SURE TO STOP BEFORE YOU FINISH.
NO.
NO!
I JUST LOVE THAT CUTE VOICE OF YOURS. WHAT DID YOU SAY YOUR NAME WAS?
STOP!
THIS CITY WAS MY HOME, BUT LOOK WHAT YOUR MOTHER DID TO IT.
MAYBE YOU COULD MAKE UP FOR IT.

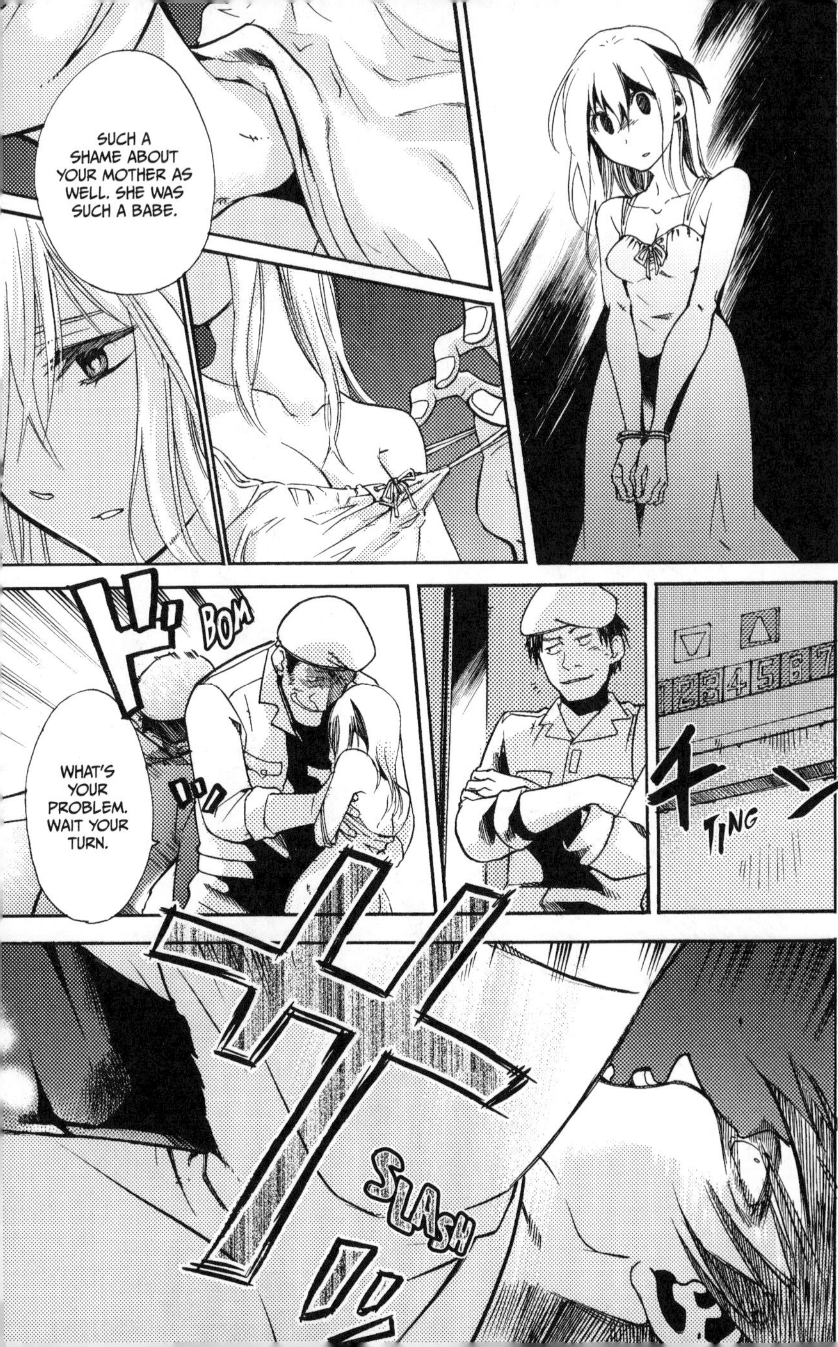
SUCH A SHAME ABOUT YOUR MOTHER AS WELL. SHE WAS SUCH A BABE.
TING
BOM
WHAT'S YOUR PROBLEM. WAIT YOUR TURN.
SLASH

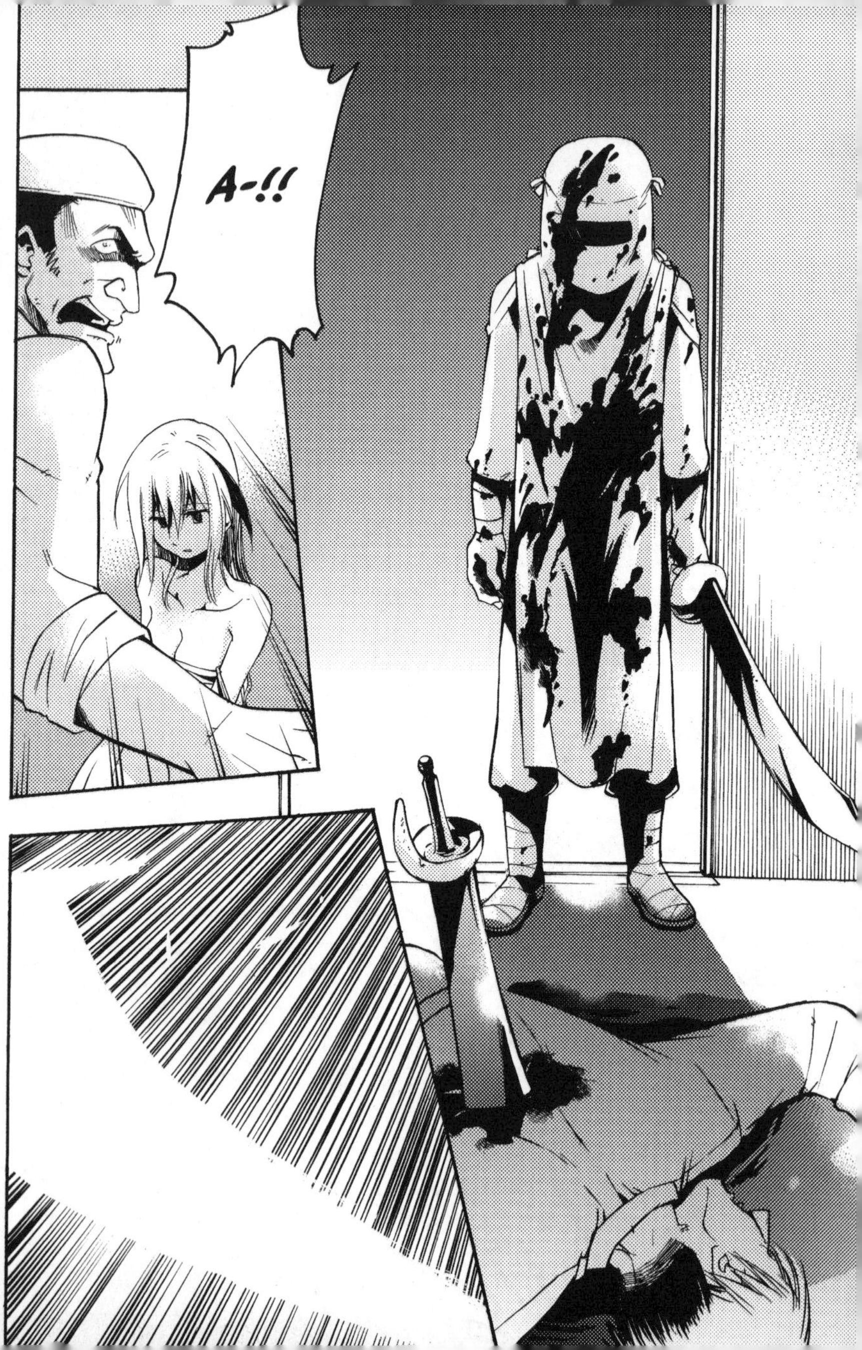
A-!!

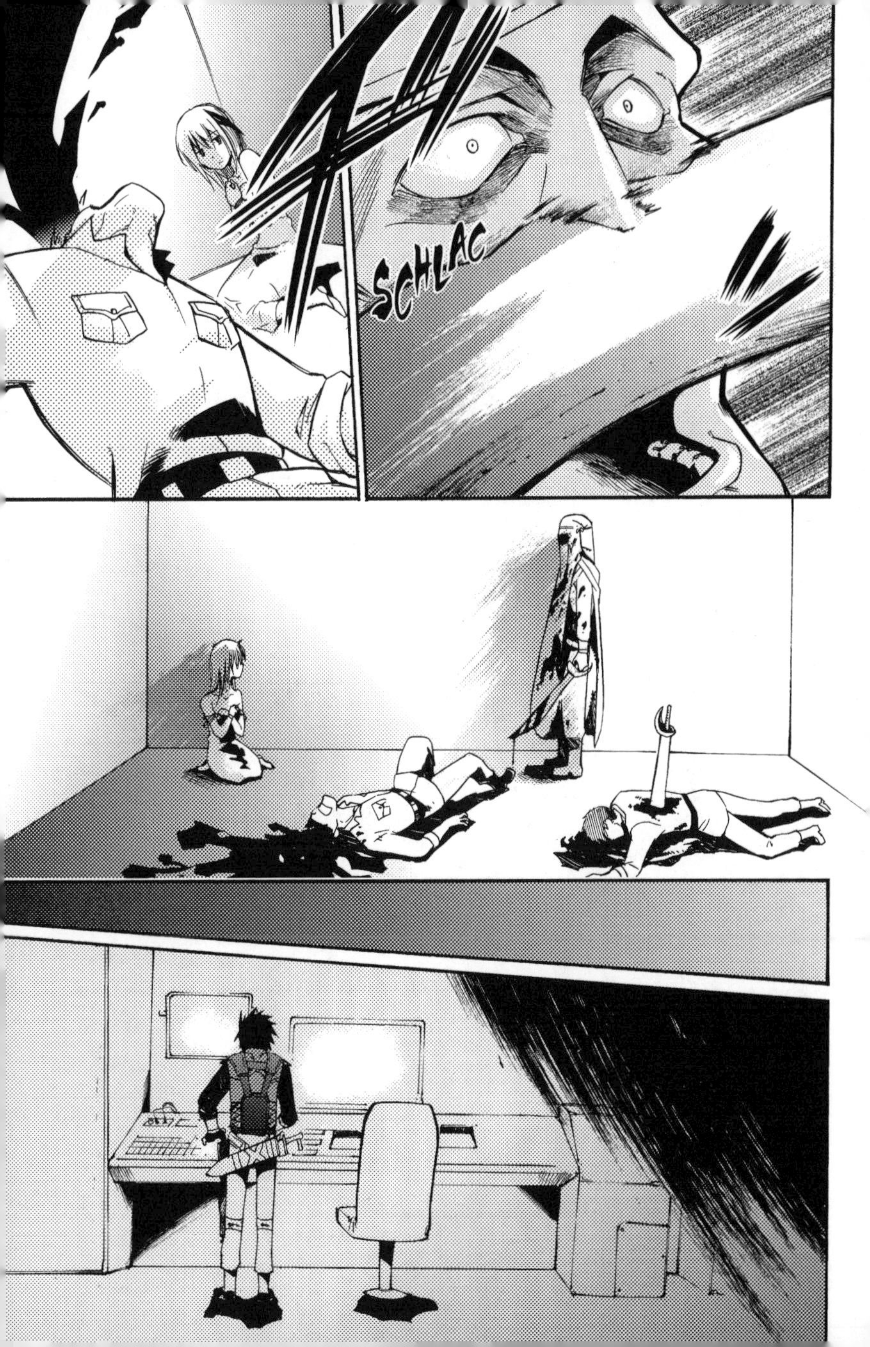
SCHLAC

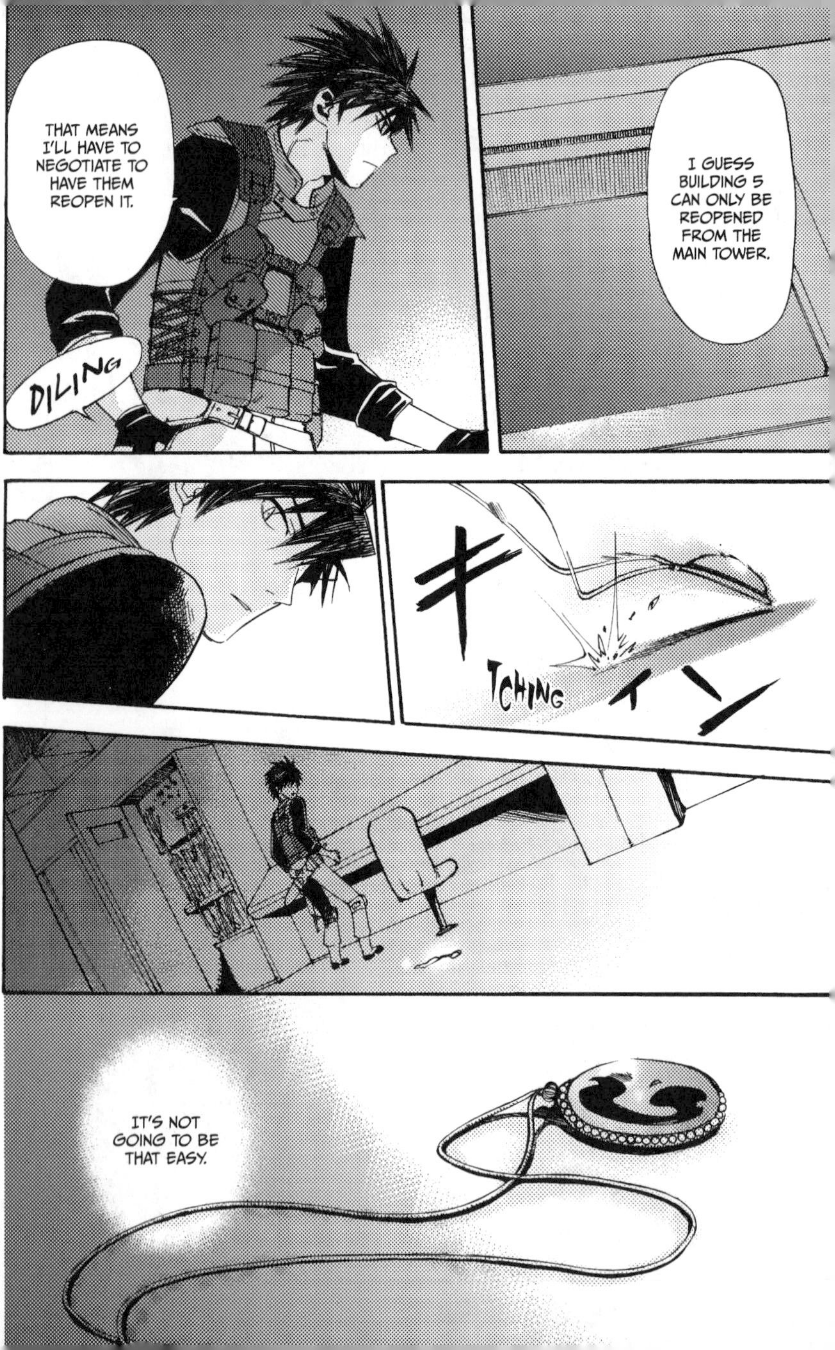
I GUESS BUILDING 5 CAN ONLY BE REOPENED FROM THE MAIN TOWER.
THAT MEANS I'LL HAVE TO NEGOTIATE TO HAVE THEM REOPEN IT.
DILING
TCHING
IT'S NOT GOING TO BE THAT EASY.

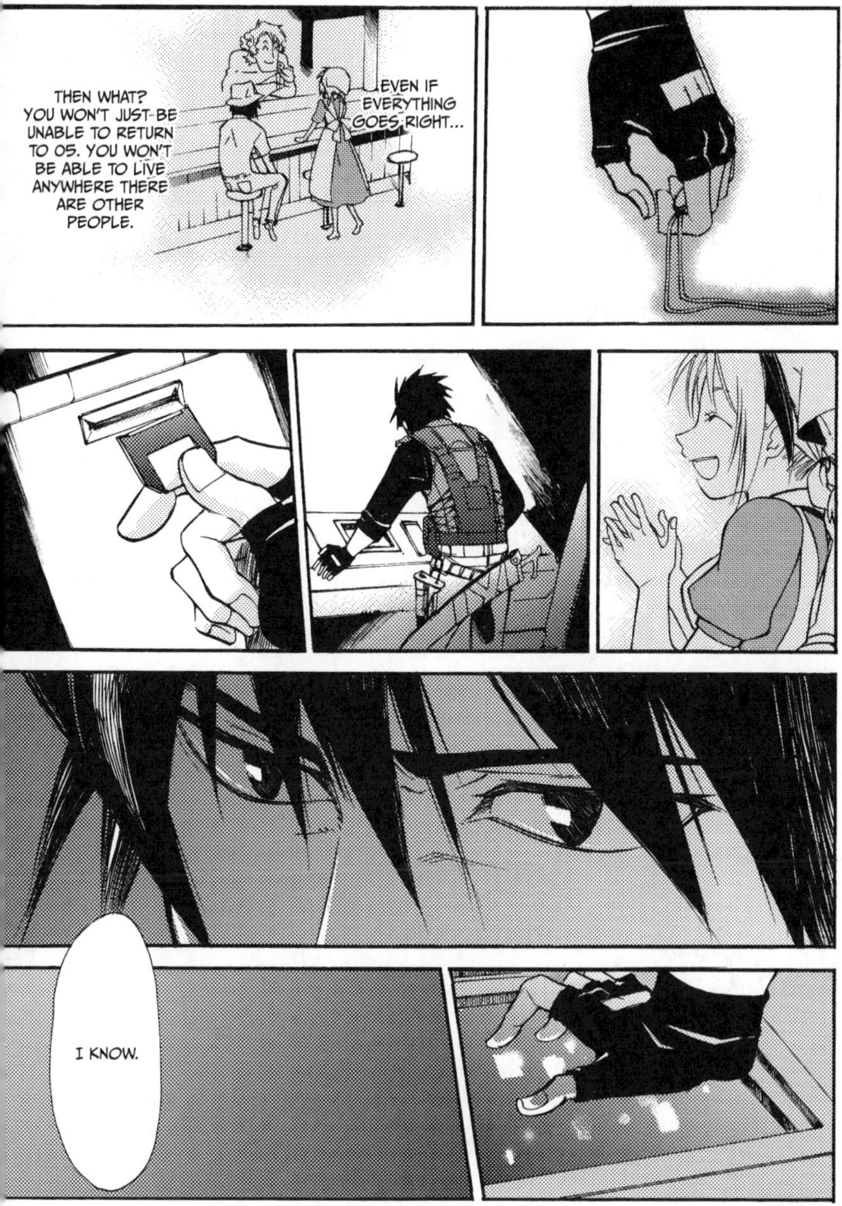
EVEN IF EVERYTHING GOES RIGHT...
THEN WHAT? YOU WON'T JUST BE UNABLE TO RETURN TO 05. YOU WON'T BE ABLE TO LIVE ANYWHERE THERE ARE OTHER PEOPLE.
I KNOW.

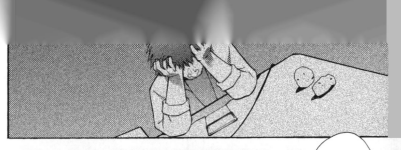

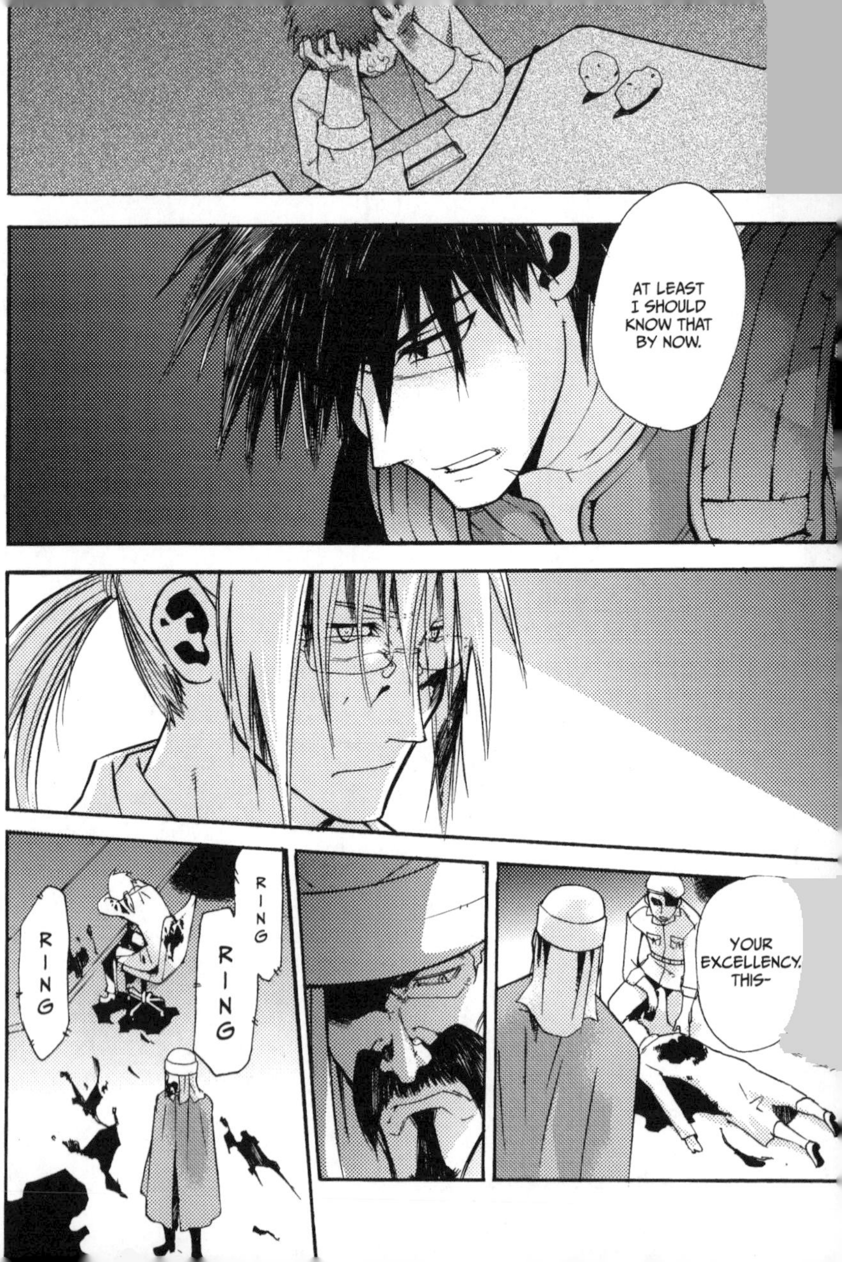
AT LEAST I SHOULD KNOW THAT BY NOW.
YOUR EXCELLENCY. THIS-
RING RING
RING RING

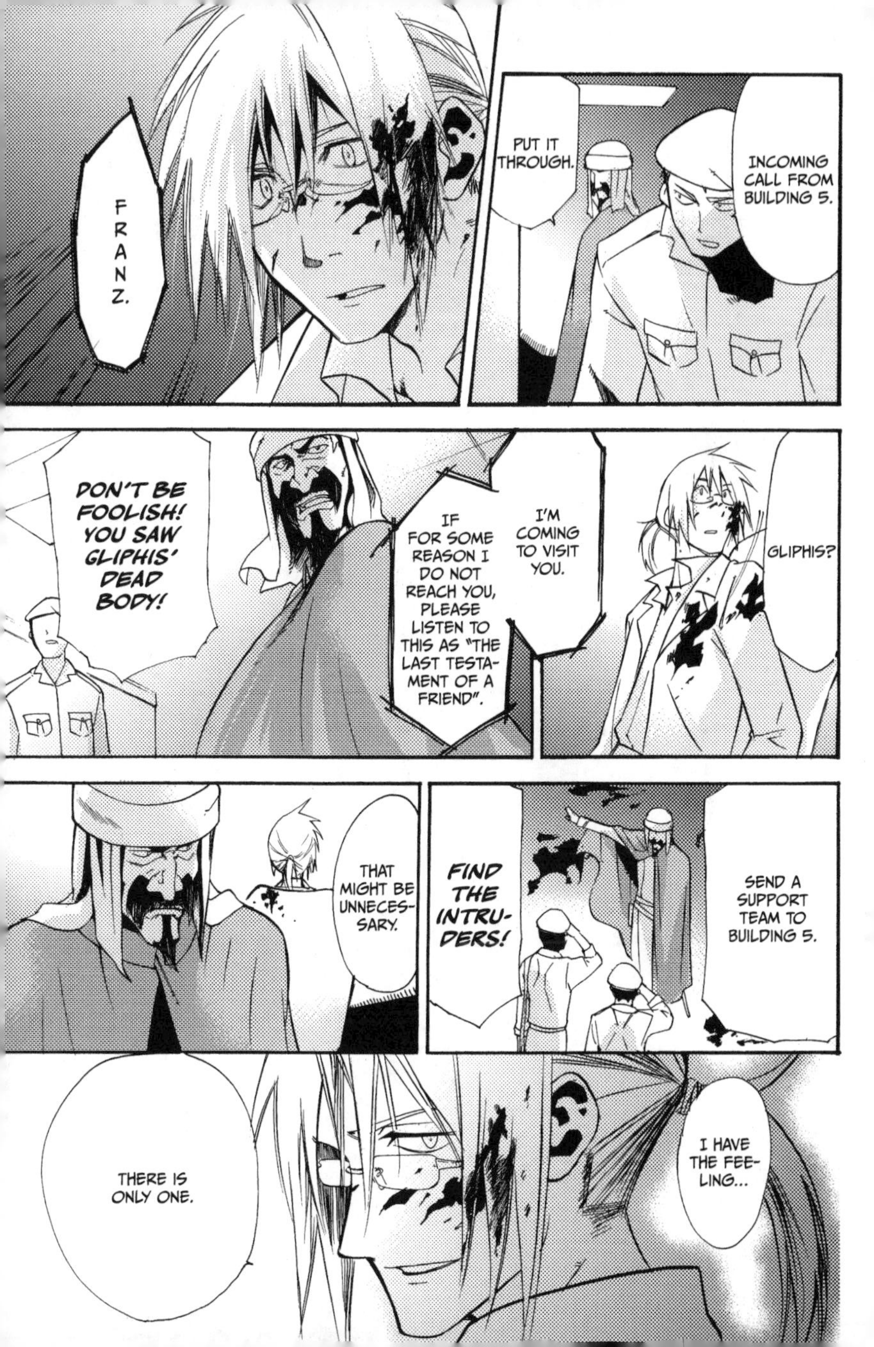
INCOMING CALL FROM BUILDING 5.
PUT IT THROUGH.
FRANZ.
GLIPHIS?
I'M COMING TO VISIT YOU.
IF FOR SOME REASON I DO NOT REACH YOU, PLEASE LISTEN TO THIS AS "THE LAST TESTAMENT OF A FRIEND".
DON'T BE FOOLISH! YOU SAW GLIPHIS' DEAD BODY!
SEND A SUPPORT TEAM TO BUILDING 5.
FIND THE INTRUDERS!
THAT MIGHT BE UNNECESSARY.
I HAVE THE FEELING...
THERE IS ONLY ONE.

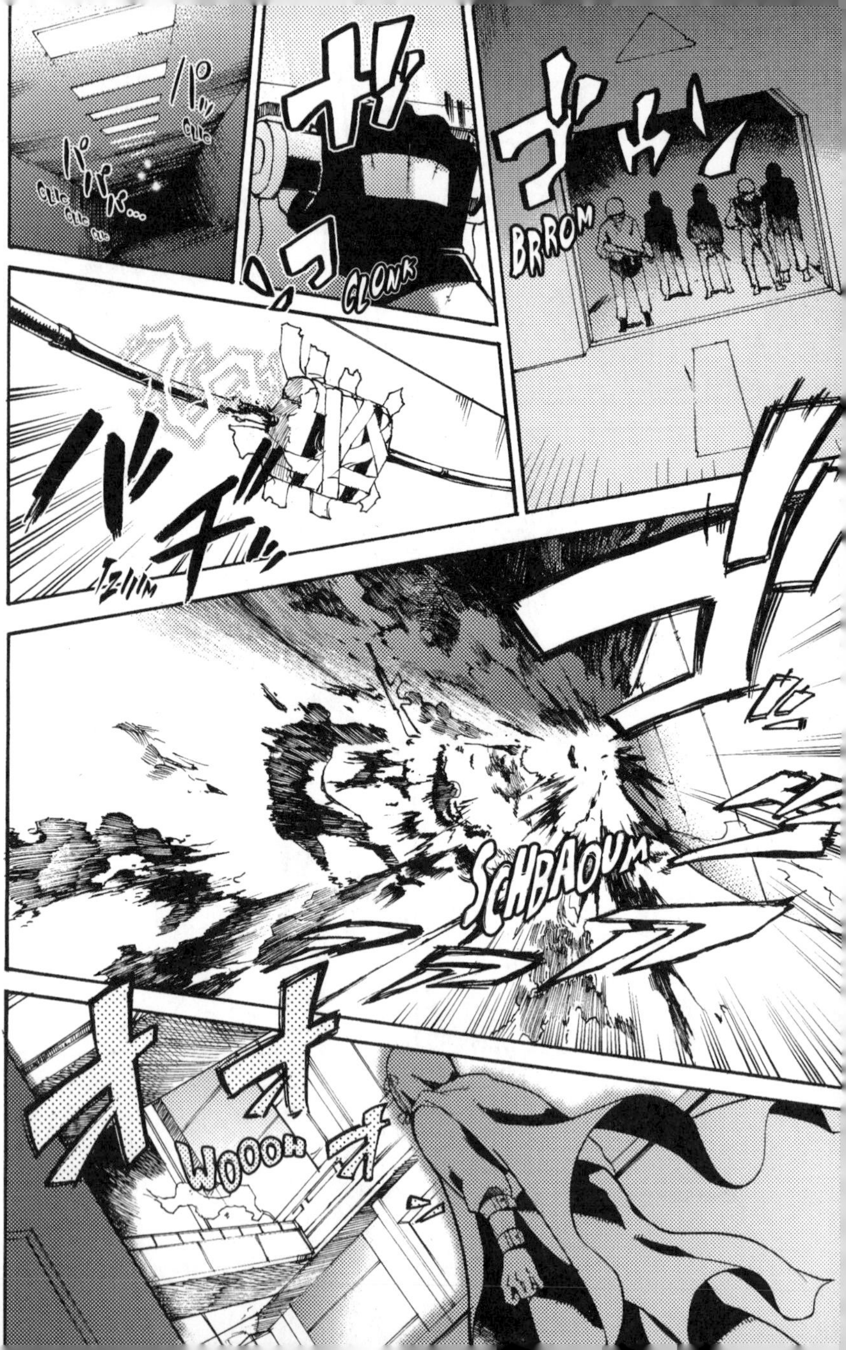
ゴゥン
BRROM
ガコッ
CLONK
パッ
CLIC
パパパ...
CLIC CLIC CLIC
バチッ
T-Z-IIIM
SCHBAOUM
オオオ
WOOOH

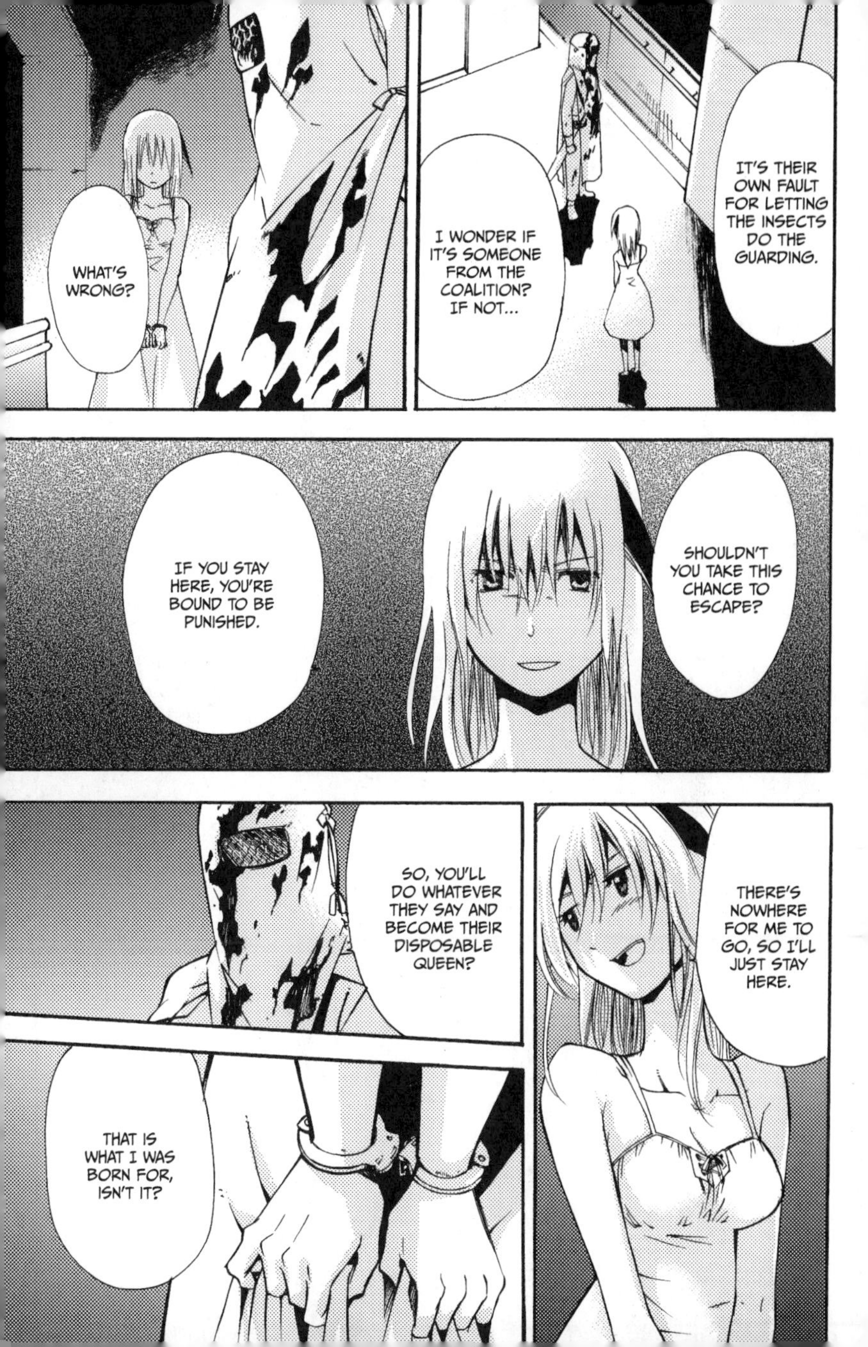
IT'S THEIR OWN FAULT FOR LETTING THE INSECTS DO THE GUARDING.
I WONDER IF IT'S SOMEONE FROM THE COALITION? IF NOT...
WHAT'S WRONG?
SHOULDN'T YOU TAKE THIS CHANCE TO ESCAPE?
IF YOU STAY HERE, YOU'RE BOUND TO BE PUNISHED.
THERE'S NOWHERE FOR ME TO GO, SO I'LL JUST STAY HERE.
SO, YOU'LL DO WHATEVER THEY SAY AND BECOME THEIR DISPOSABLE QUEEN?
THAT IS WHAT I WAS BORN FOR, ISN'T IT?

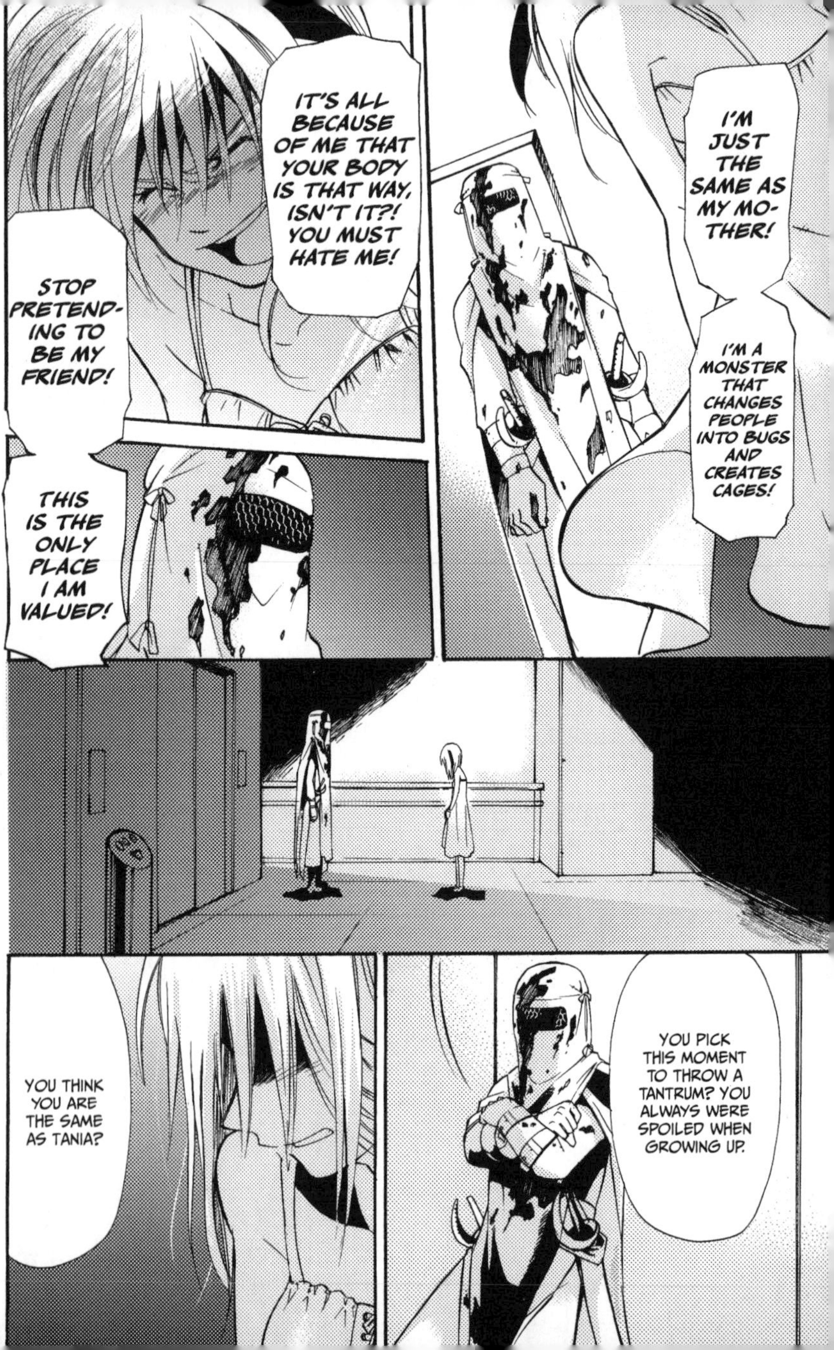
I'M JUST THE SAME AS MY MOTHER!
I'M A MONSTER THAT CHANGES PEOPLE INTO BUGS AND CREATES CAGES!
IT'S ALL BECAUSE OF ME THAT YOUR BODY IS THAT WAY, ISN'T IT?! YOU MUST HATE ME!
STOP PRETENDING TO BE MY FRIEND!
THIS IS THE ONLY PLACE I AM VALUED!
YOU PICK THIS MOMENT TO THROW A TANTRUM? YOU ALWAYS WERE SPOILED WHEN GROWING UP.
YOU THINK YOU ARE THE SAME AS TANIA?

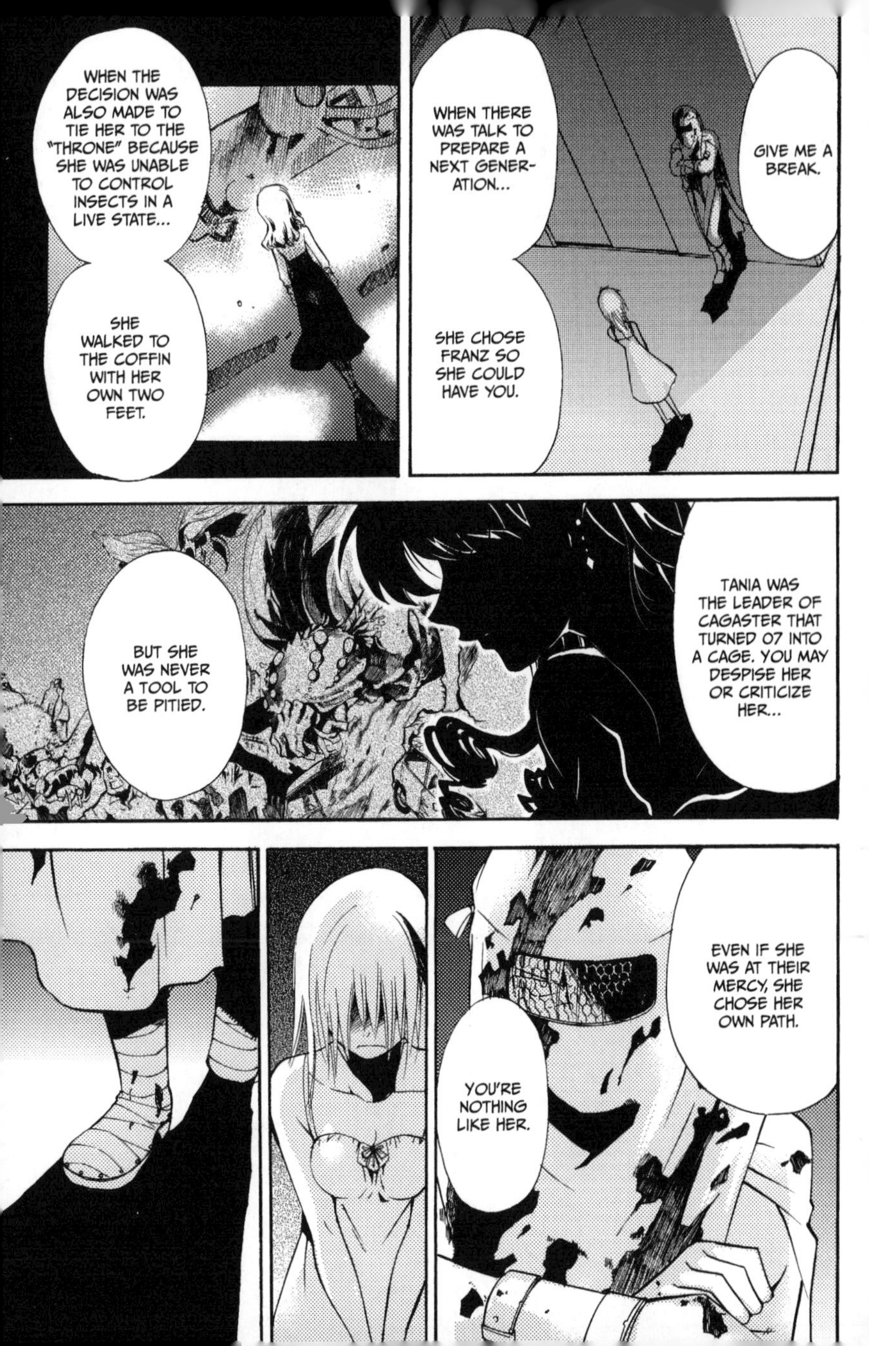
GIVE ME A BREAK.
WHEN THERE WAS TALK TO PREPARE A NEXT GENERATION...
SHE CHOSE FRANZ SO SHE COULD HAVE YOU.
WHEN THE DECISION WAS ALSO MADE TO TIE HER TO THE "THRONE" BECAUSE SHE WAS UNABLE TO CONTROL INSECTS IN A LIVE STATE...
SHE WALKED TO THE COFFIN WITH HER OWN TWO FEET.
TANIA WAS THE LEADER OF CAGASTER THAT TURNED 07 INTO A CAGE. YOU MAY DESPISE HER OR CRITICIZE HER...
BUT SHE WAS NEVER A TOOL TO BE PITIED.
EVEN IF SHE WAS AT THEIR MERCY, SHE CHOSE HER OWN PATH.
YOU'RE NOTHING LIKE HER.

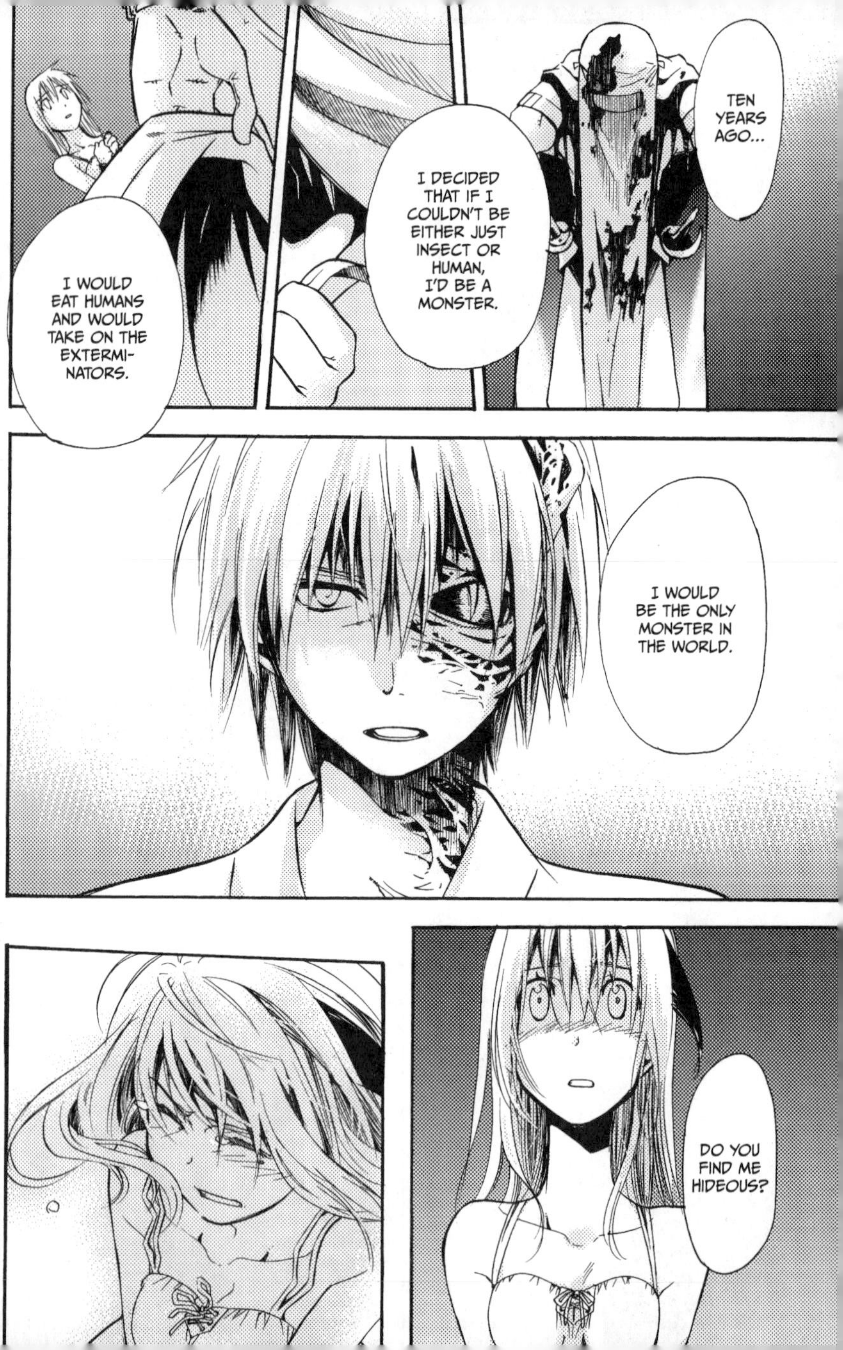
TEN YEARS AGO...
I DECIDED THAT IF I COULDN'T BE EITHER JUST INSECT OR HUMAN, I'D BE A MONSTER.
I WOULD EAT HUMANS AND WOULD TAKE ON THE EXTERMI-NATORS.
I WOULD BE THE ONLY MONSTER IN THE WORLD.
DO YOU FIND ME HIDEOUS?

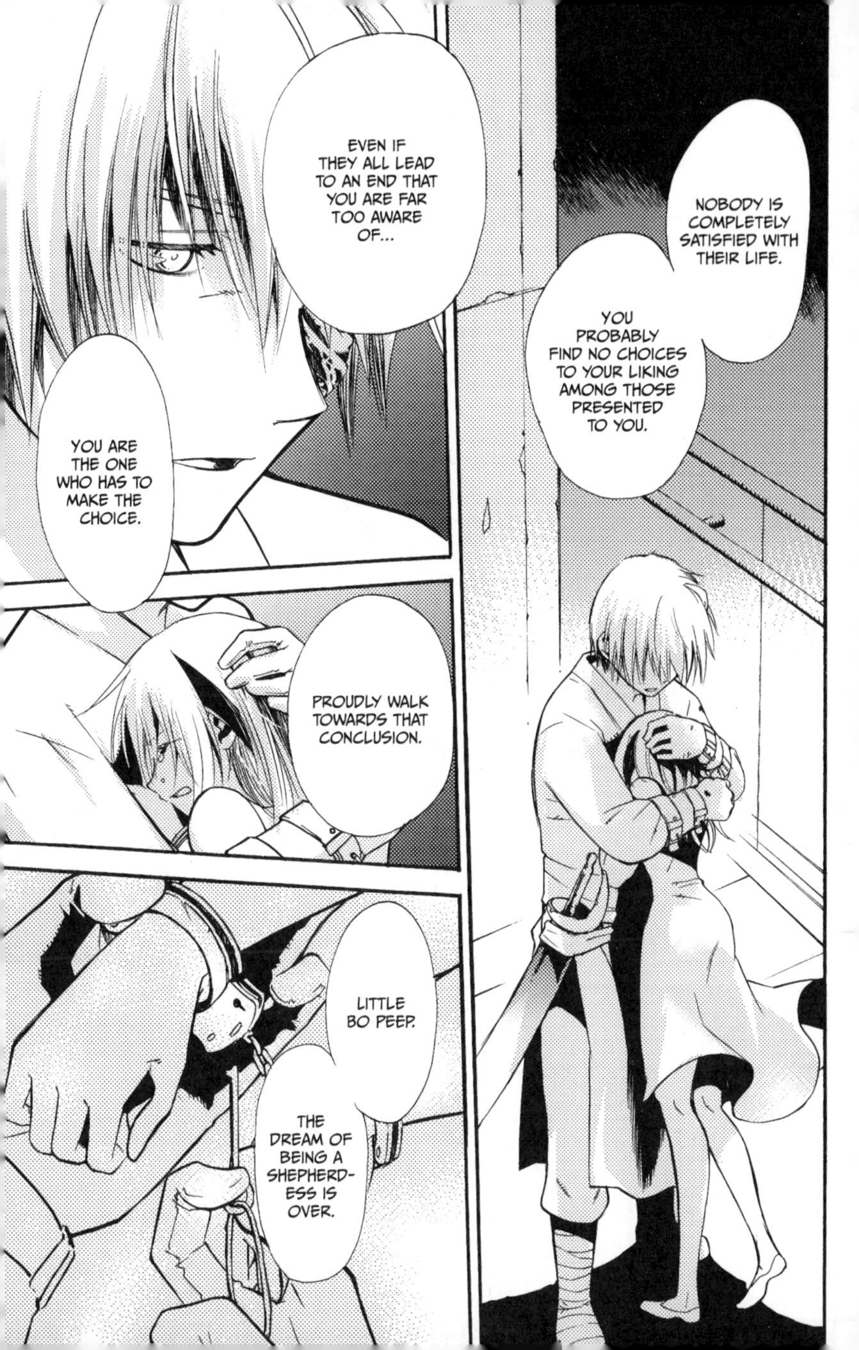
NOBODY IS COMPLETELY SATISFIED WITH THEIR LIFE.
YOU PROBABLY FIND NO CHOICES TO YOUR LIKING AMONG THOSE PRESENTED TO YOU.
EVEN IF THEY ALL LEAD TO AN END THAT YOU ARE FAR TOO AWARE OF...
YOU ARE THE ONE WHO HAS TO MAKE THE CHOICE.
PROUDLY WALK TOWARDS THAT CONCLUSION.
LITTLE BO PEEP.
THE DREAM OF BEING A SHEPHERDESS IS OVER.

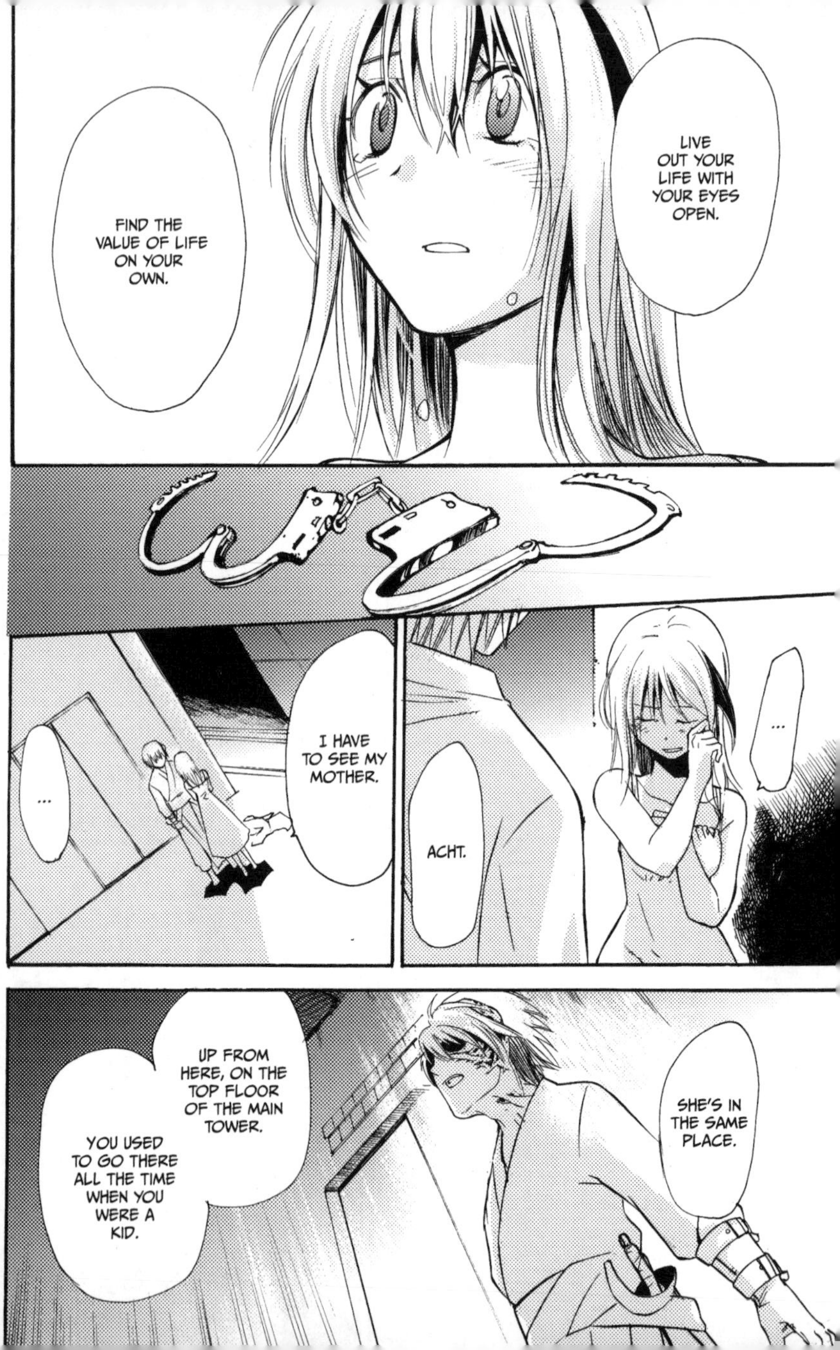
LIVE OUT YOUR LIFE WITH YOUR EYES OPEN.
FIND THE VALUE OF LIFE ON YOUR OWN.
...
ACHT.
I HAVE TO SEE MY MOTHER.
...
SHE'S IN THE SAME PLACE.
UP FROM HERE, ON THE TOP FLOOR OF THE MAIN TOWER.
YOU USED TO GO THERE ALL THE TIME WHEN YOU WERE A KID.

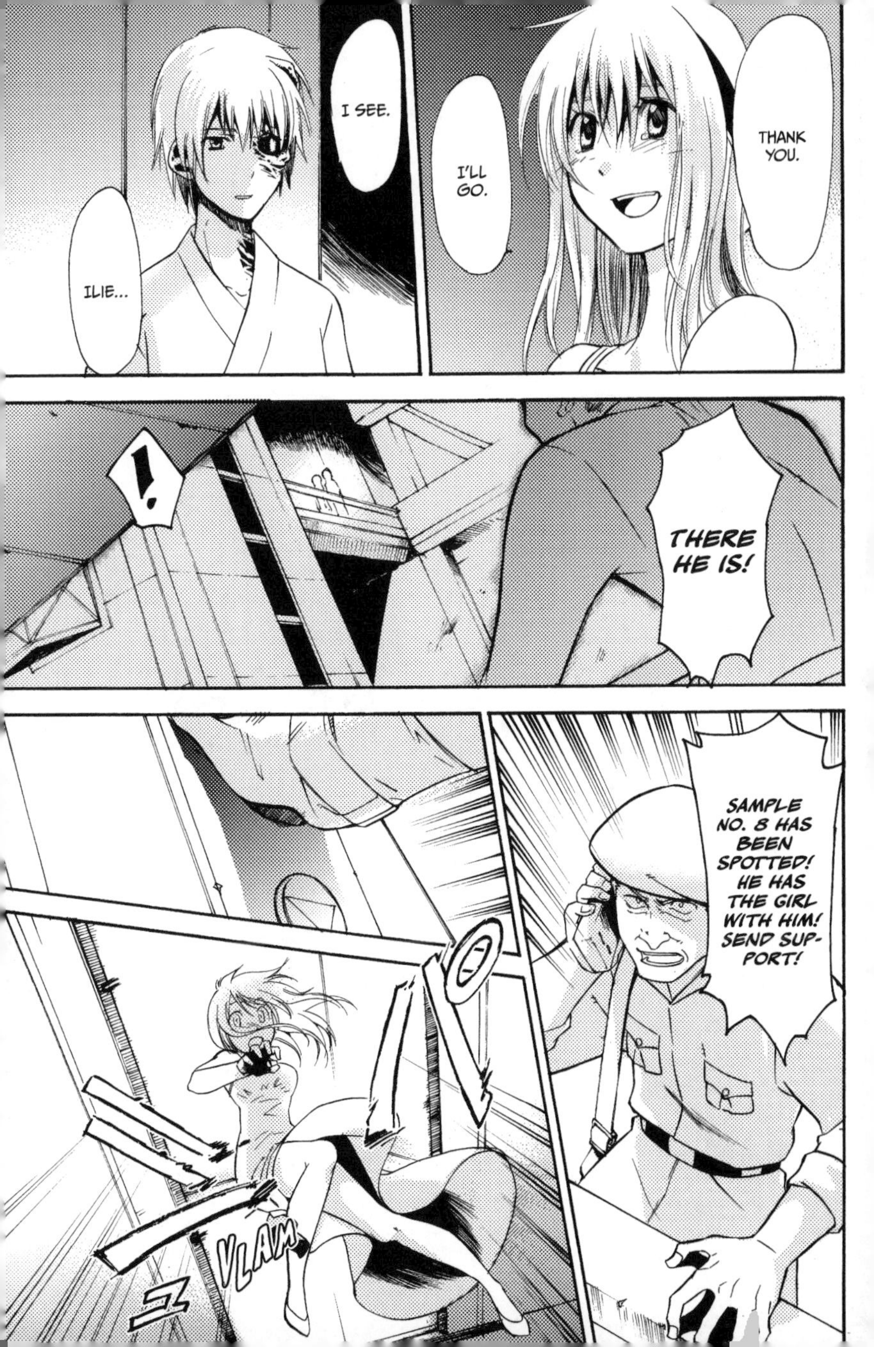
THANK YOU.
I'LL GO.
I SEE.
ILIE...
THERE HE IS!
!
SAMPLE NO. 8 HAS BEEN SPOTTED! HE HAS THE GIRL WITH HIM! SEND SUP-PORT!
VLAM

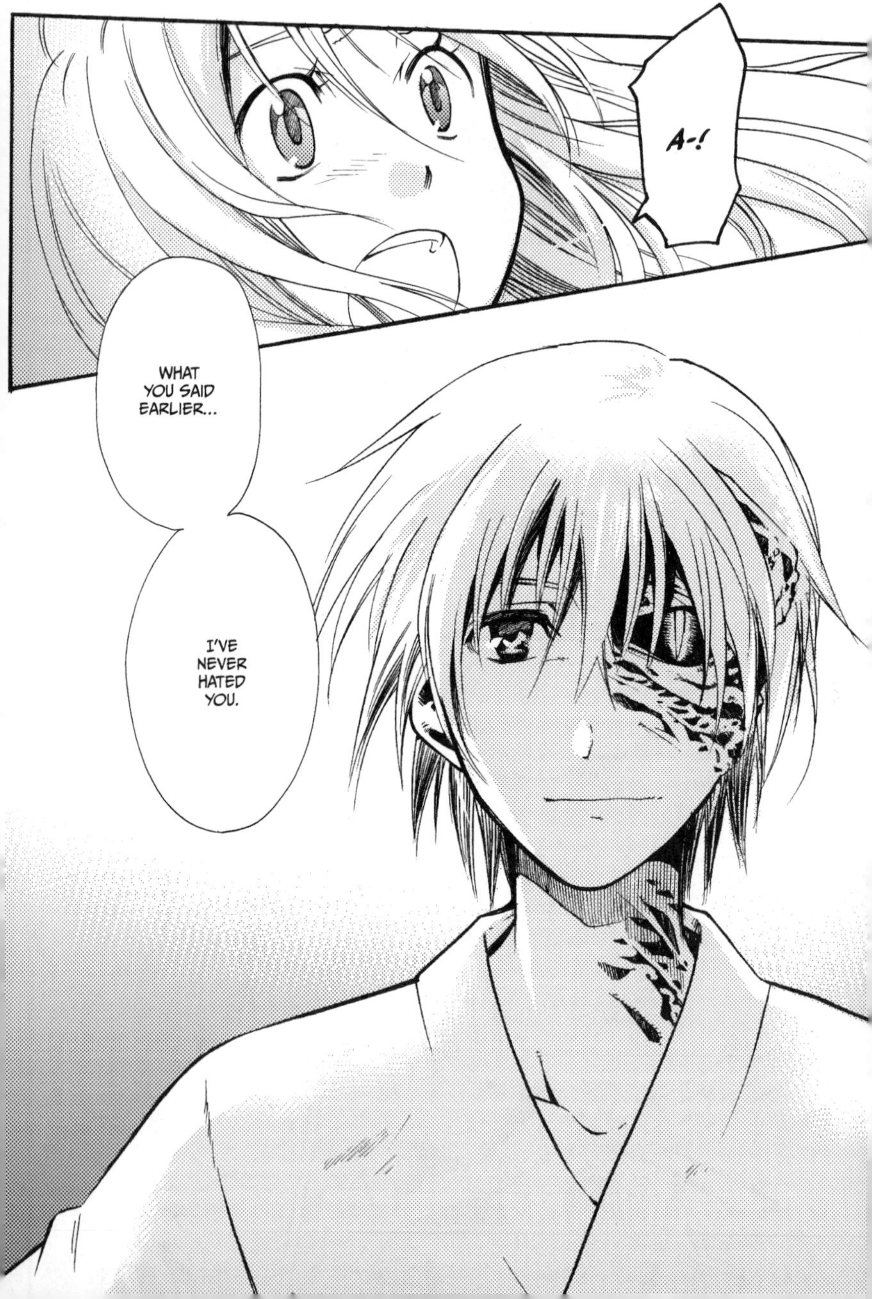
A-!
WHAT YOU SAID EARLIER...
I'VE NEVER HATED YOU.

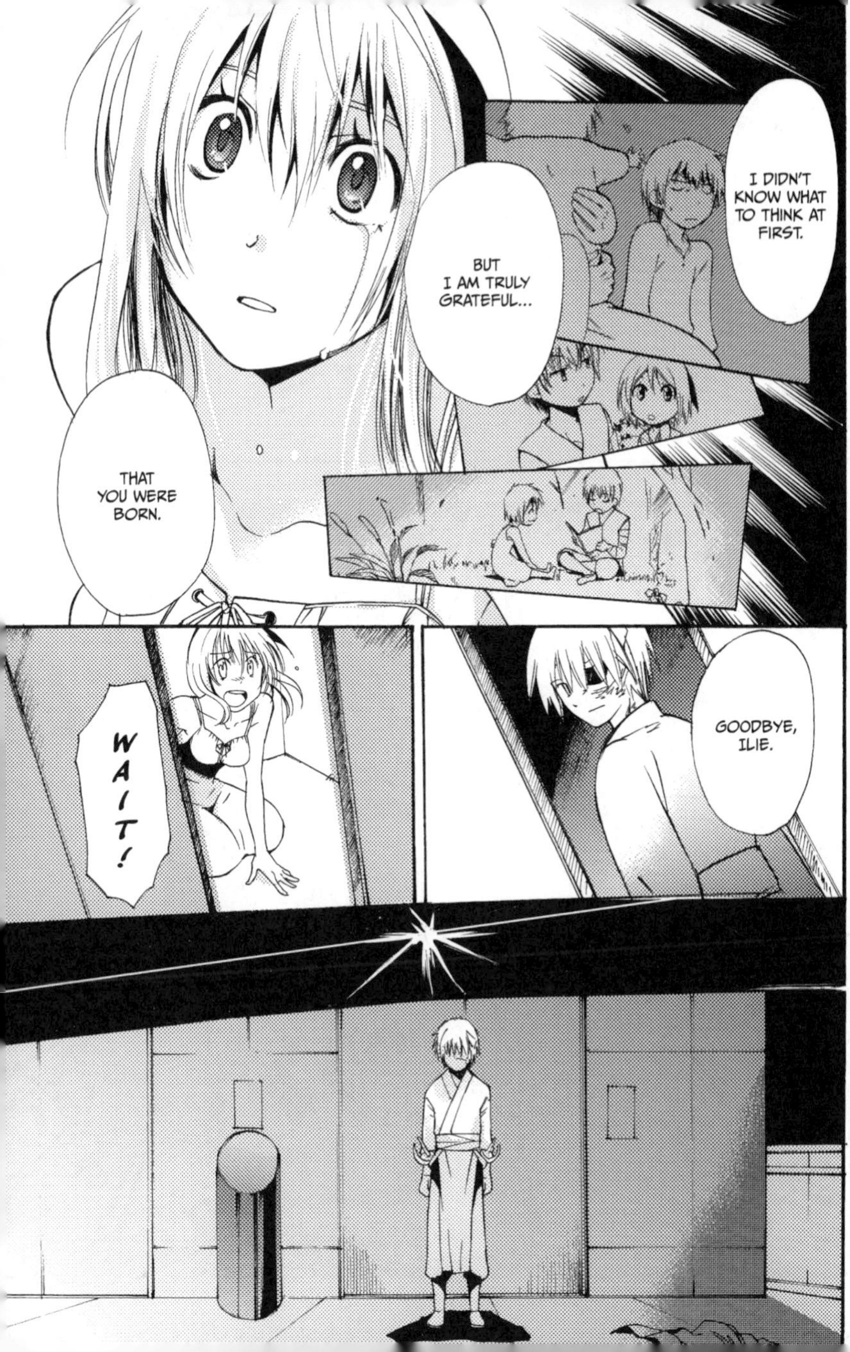
I DIDN'T KNOW WHAT TO THINK AT FIRST.
BUT I AM TRULY GRATEFUL...
THAT YOU WERE BORN.
GOODBYE, ILIE.
WAIT!

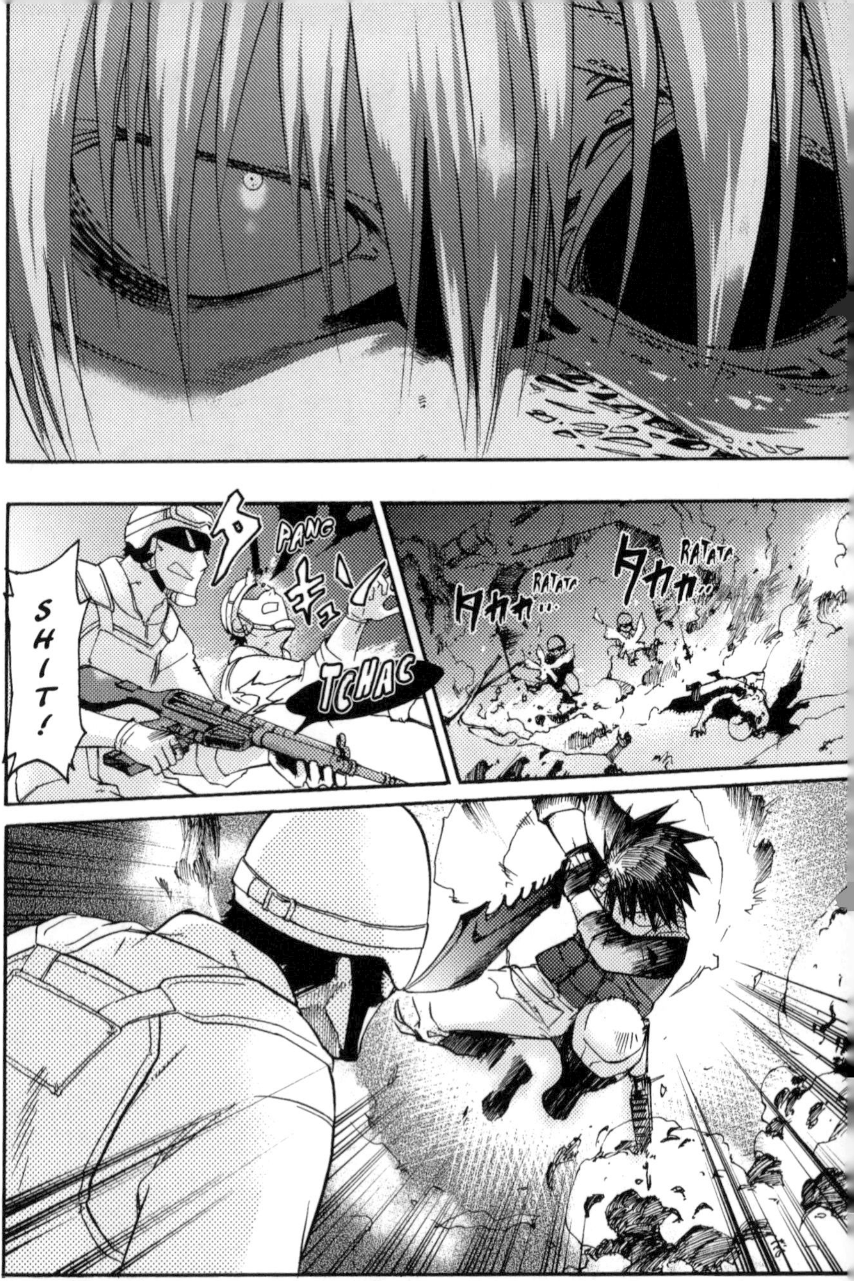
RATATA
タカカ..
RATATA
タカカ..
PANG
キュン
タ
SHIT!
TCHAC

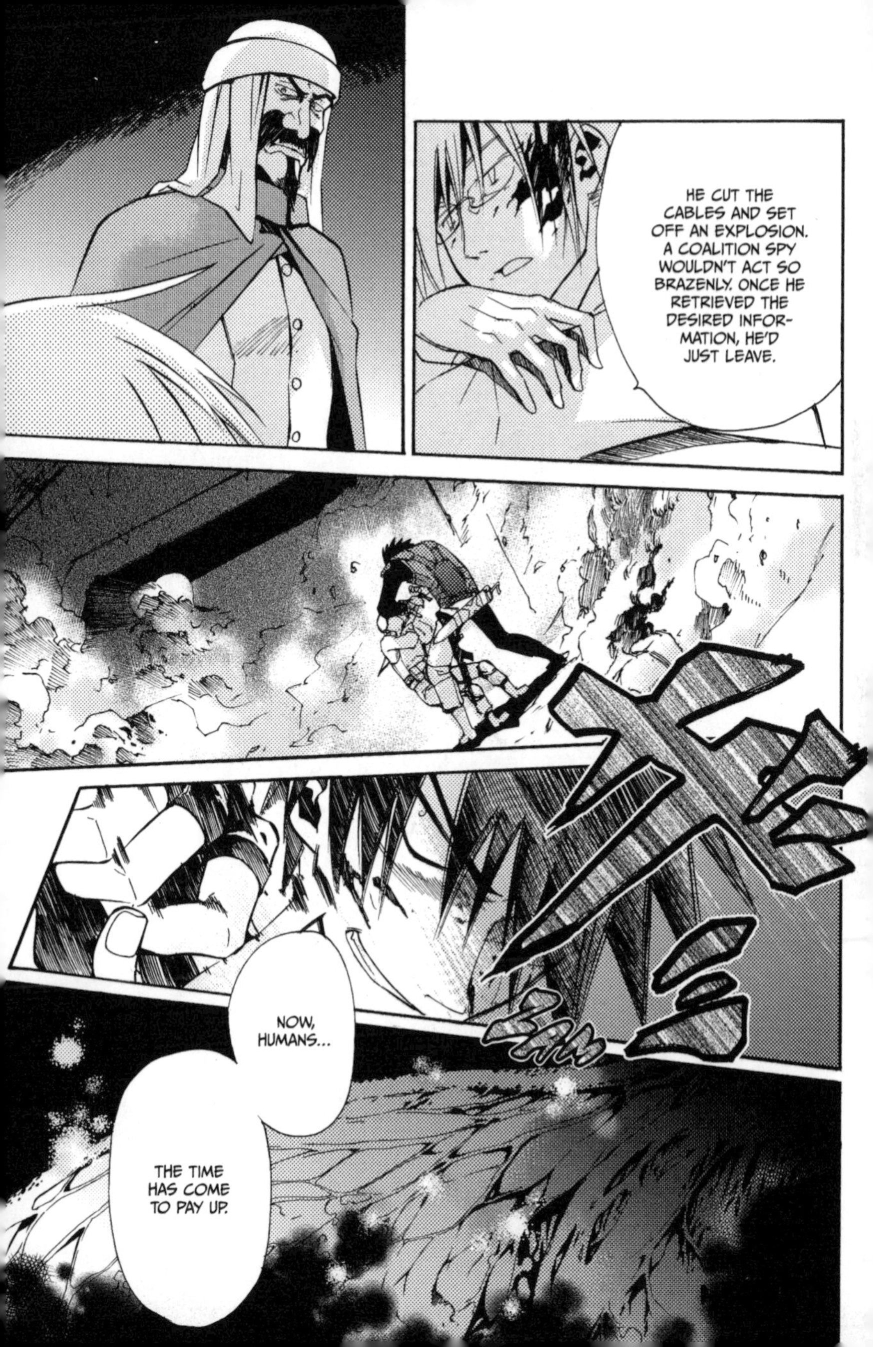
HE CUT THE CABLES AND SET OFF AN EXPLOSION. A COALITION SPY WOULDN'T ACT SO BRAZENLY. ONCE HE RETRIEVED THE DESIRED INFOR-MATION, HE'D JUST LEAVE.
NOW, HUMANS...
THE TIME HAS COME TO PAY UP.

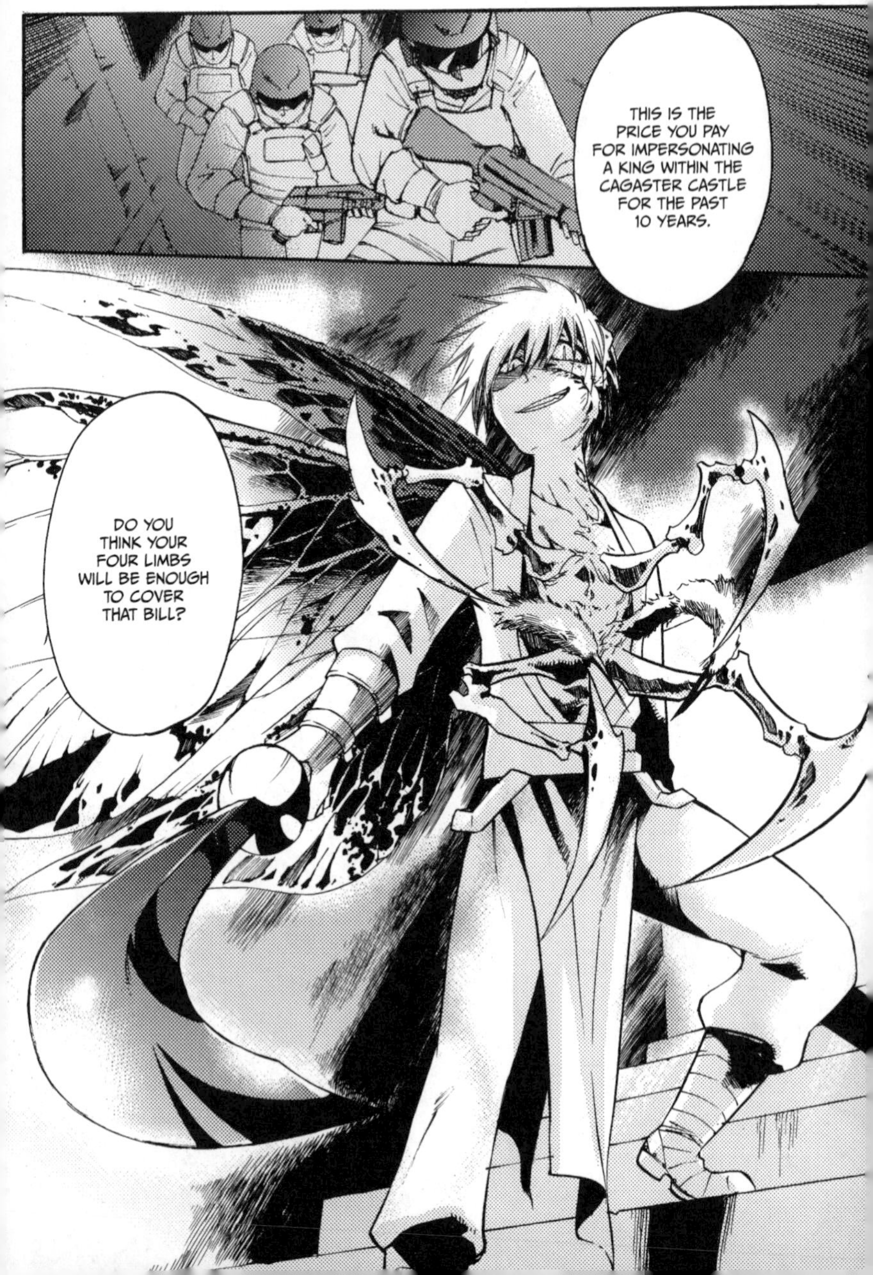
THIS IS THE PRICE YOU PAY FOR IMPERSONATING A KING WITHIN THE CAGASTER CASTLE FOR THE PAST 10 YEARS.
DO YOU THINK YOUR FOUR LIMBS WILL BE ENOUGH TO COVER THAT BILL?

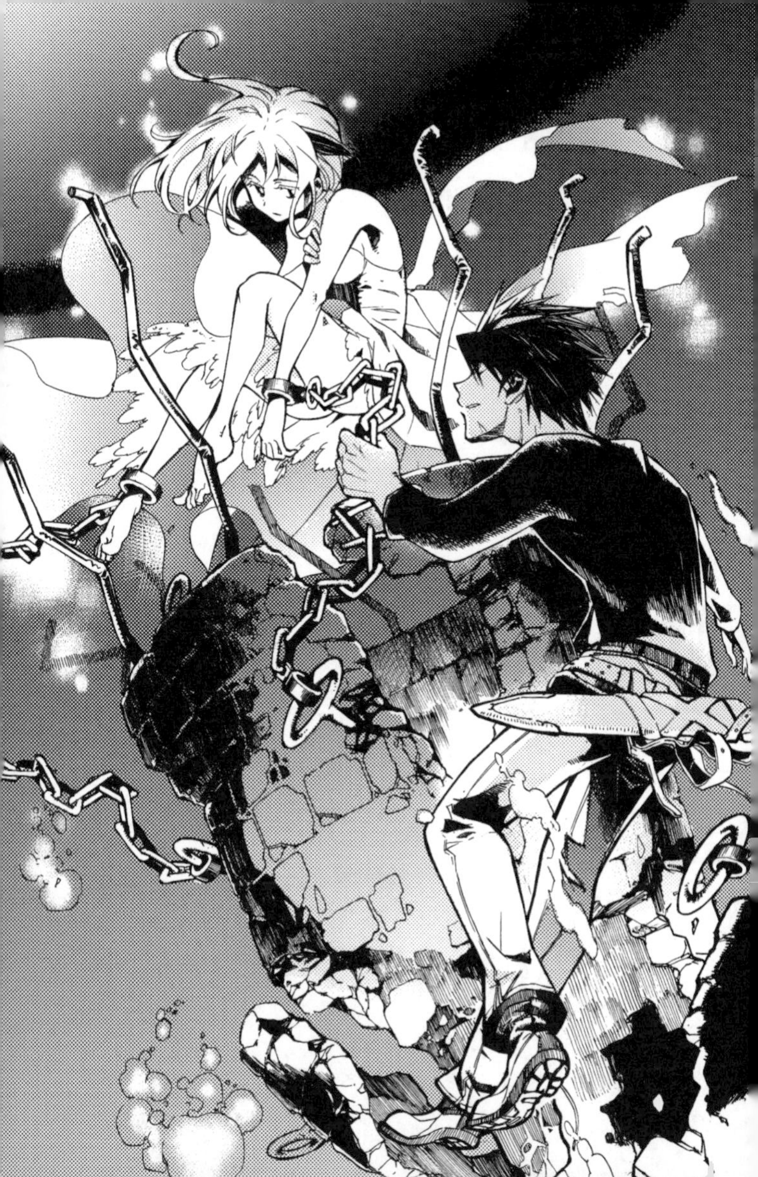

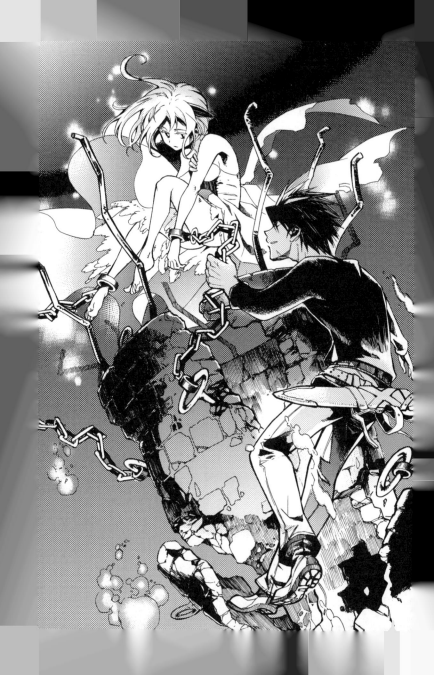

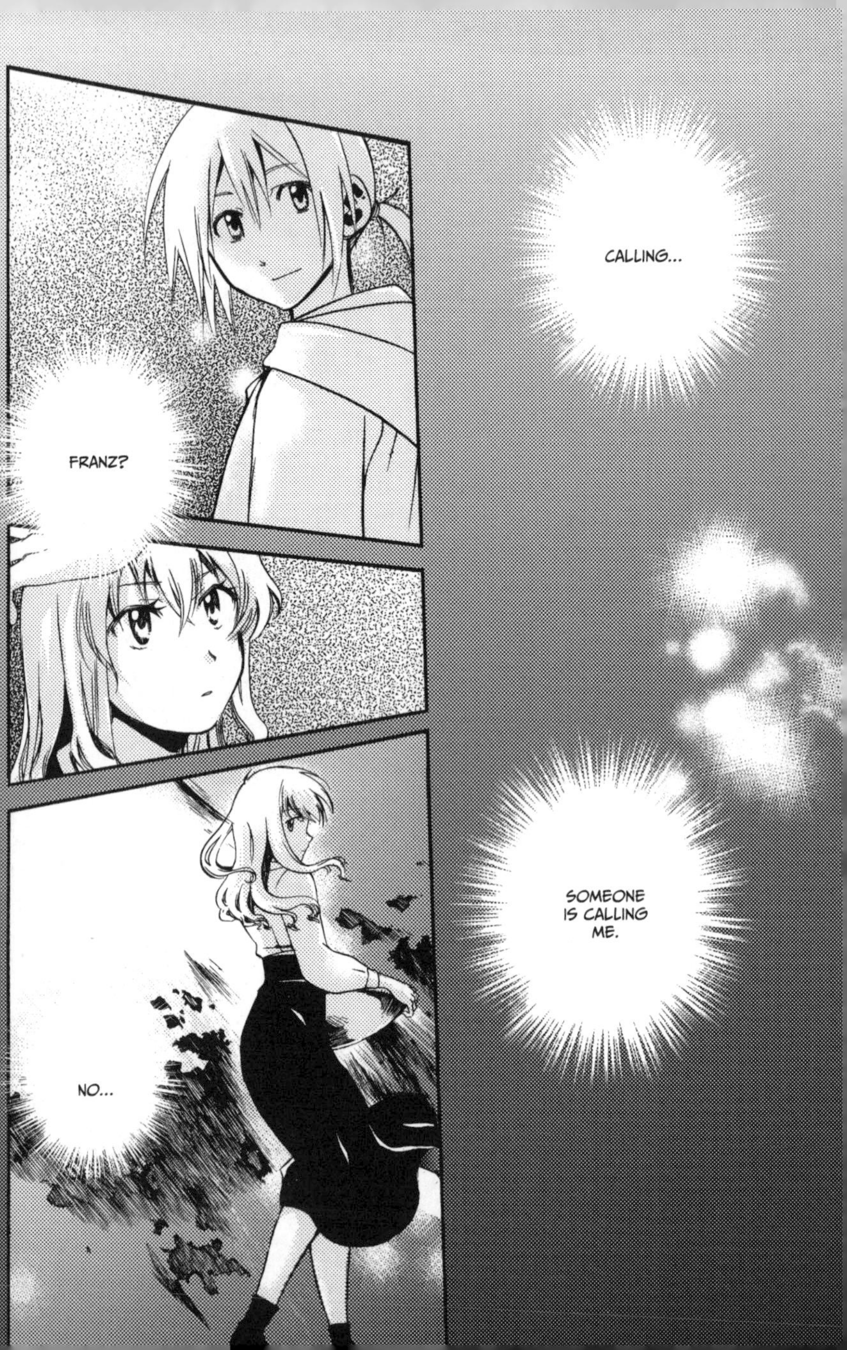
CALLING...
SOMEONE IS CALLING ME.
FRANZ?
NO...

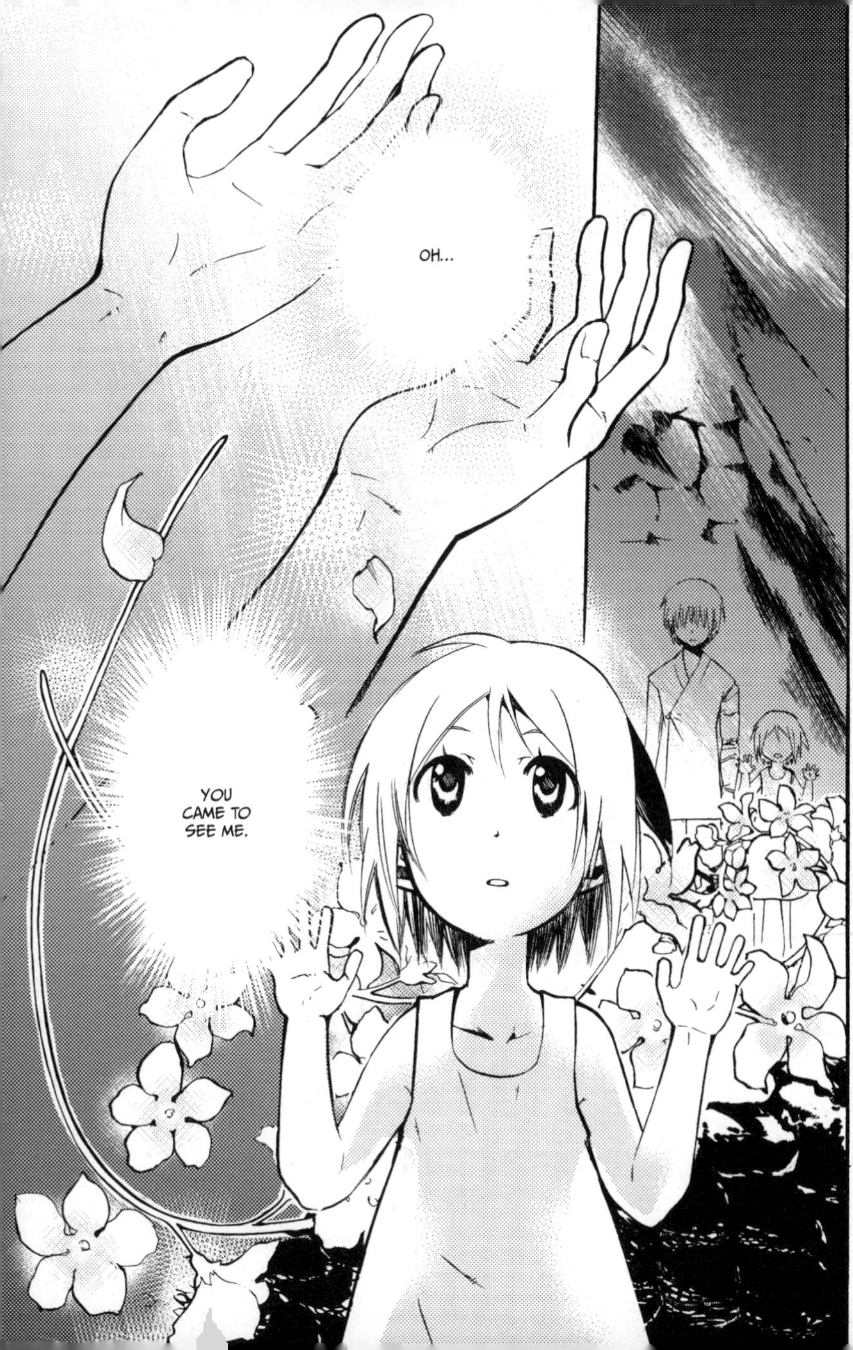
OH...
YOU CAME TO SEE ME.

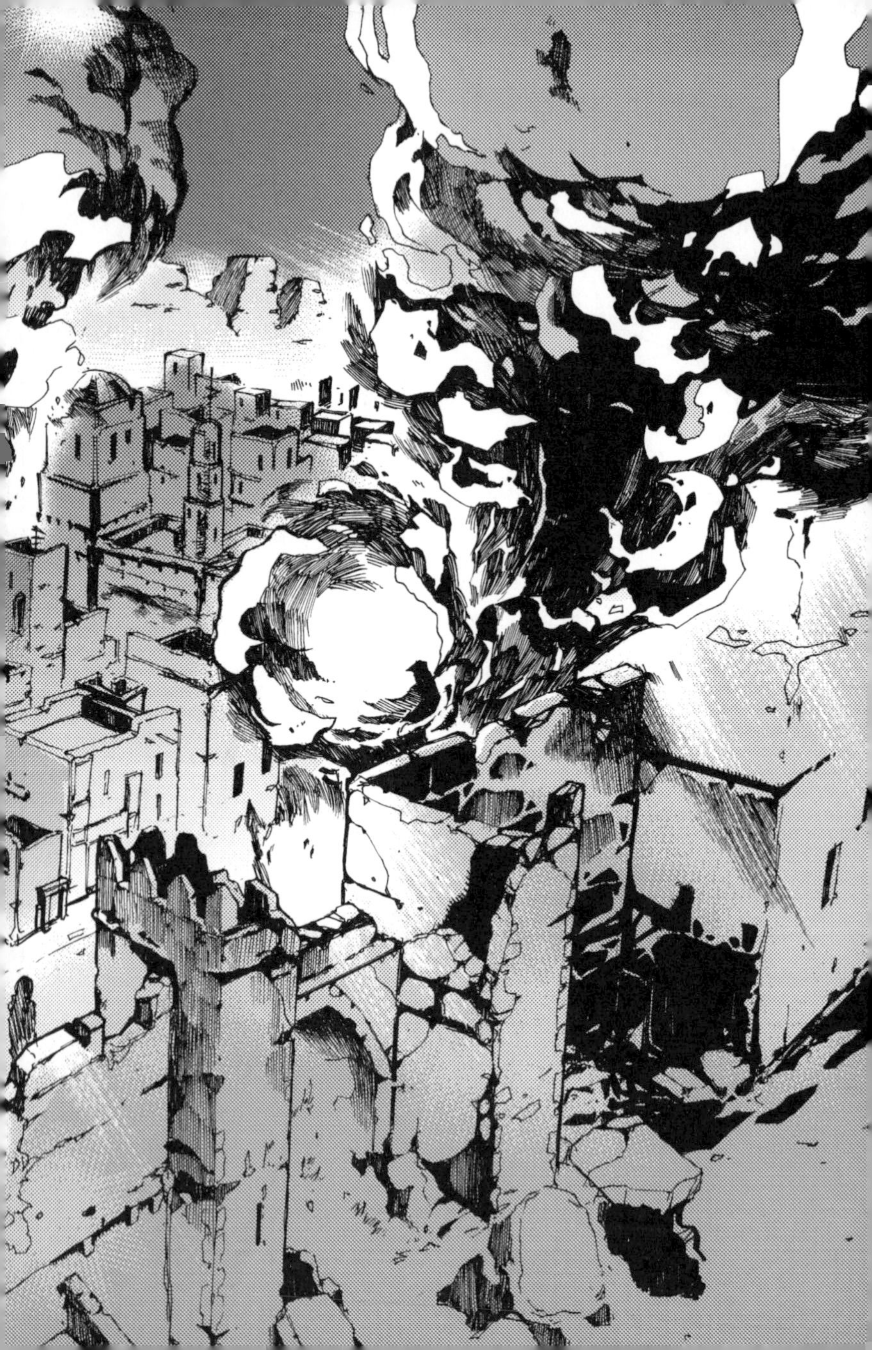

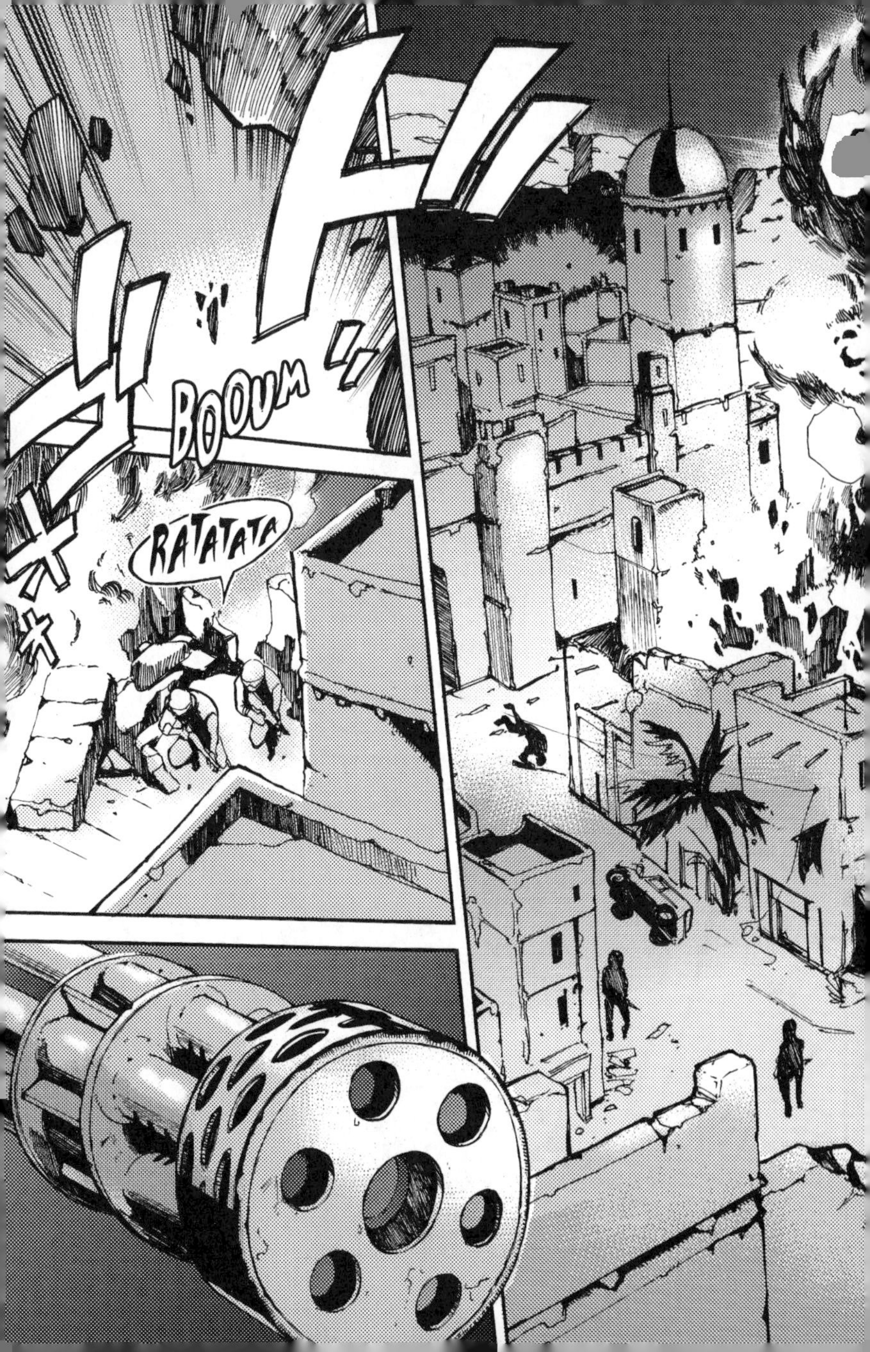
BOOUM
RATATATA

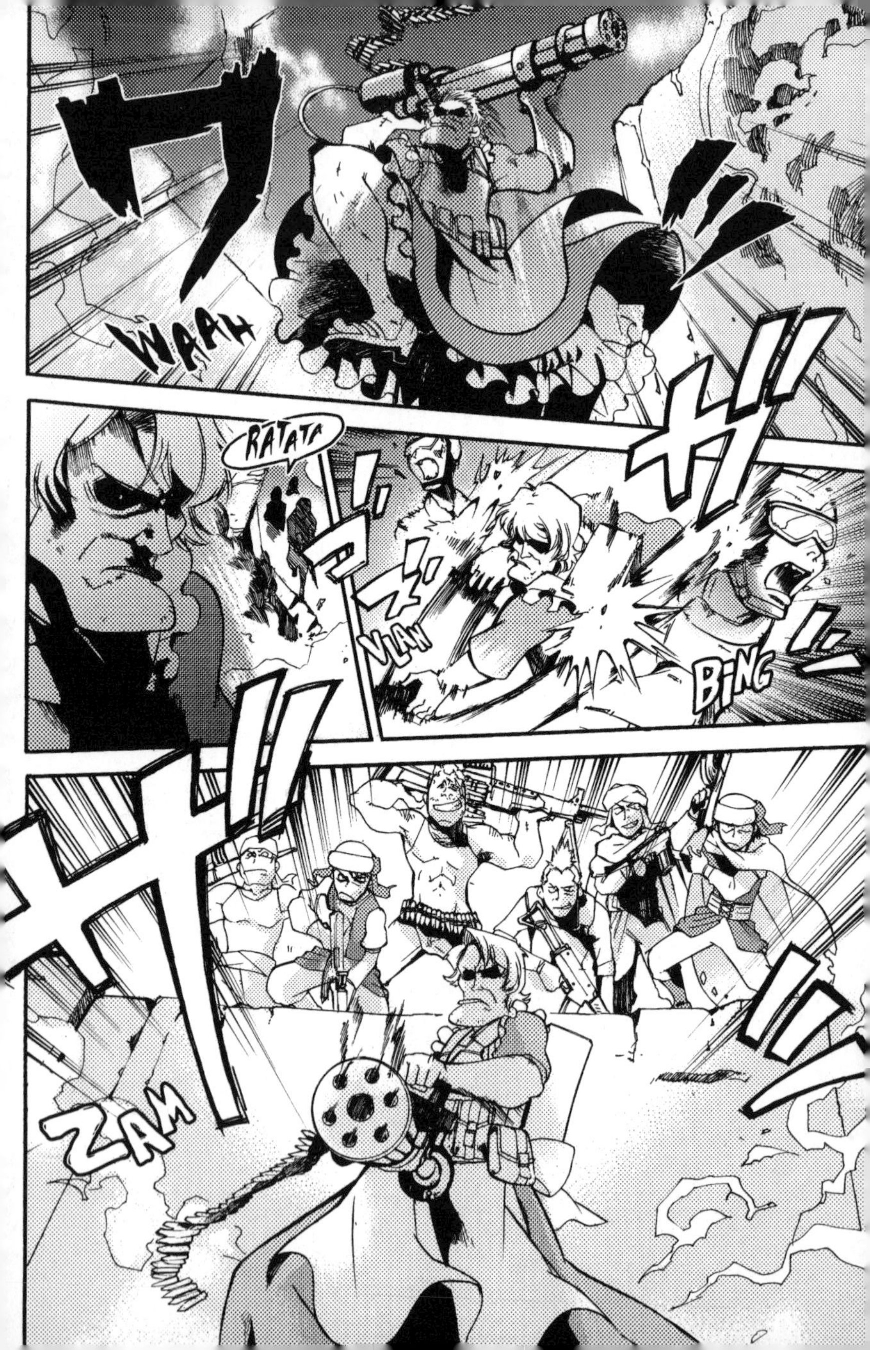
WAAH
BING
VLAN
RATATA
ZAM

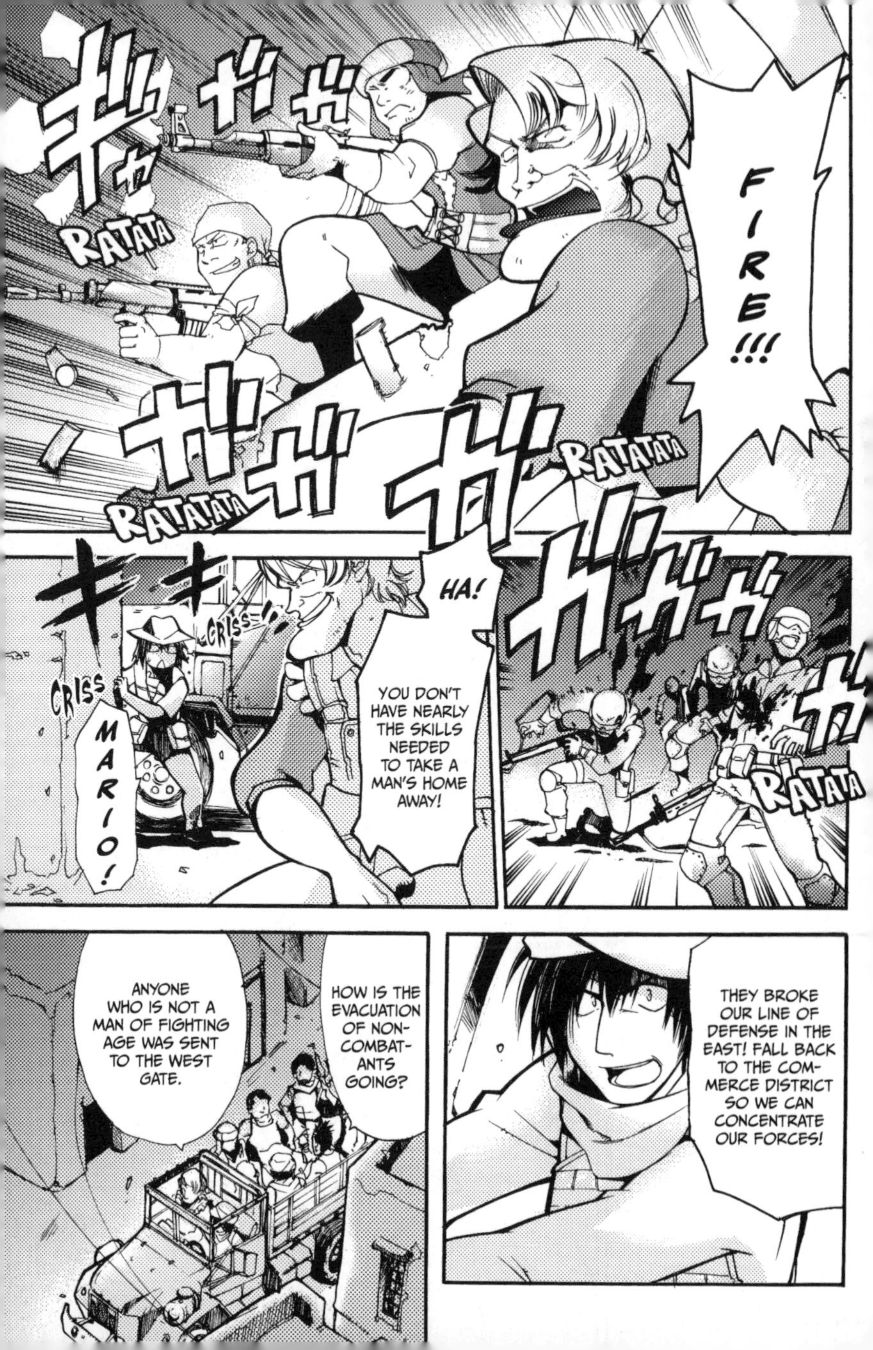
FIRE!!!
RATATATA
RATATA
RATATATA
RATATA
HA!
YOU DON'T HAVE NEARLY THE SKILLS NEEDED TO TAKE A MAN'S HOME AWAY!
CRISS
MARIO!
CRISS
THEY BROKE OUR LINE OF DEFENSE IN THE EAST! FALL BACK TO THE COMMERCE DISTRICT SO WE CAN CONCENTRATE OUR FORCES!
HOW IS THE EVACUATION OF NON-COMBATANTS GOING?
ANYONE WHO IS NOT A MAN OF FIGHTING AGE WAS SENT TO THE WEST GATE.

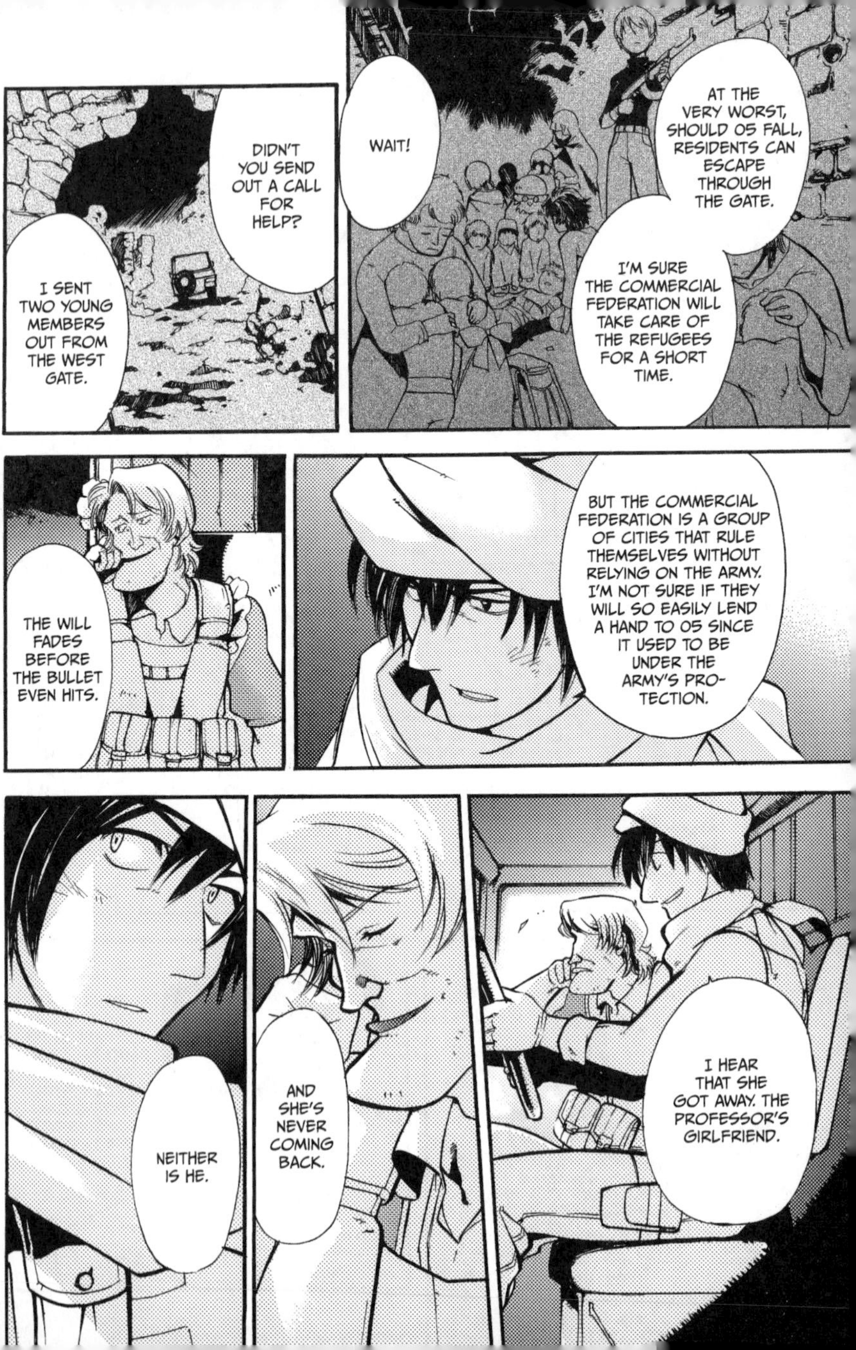
AT THE VERY WORST, SHOULD 05 FALL, RESIDENTS CAN ESCAPE THROUGH THE GATE.
I'M SURE THE COMMERCIAL FEDERATION WILL TAKE CARE OF THE REFUGEES FOR A SHORT TIME.
WAIT!
DIDN'T YOU SEND OUT A CALL FOR HELP?
I SENT TWO YOUNG MEMBERS OUT FROM THE WEST GATE.
BUT THE COMMERCIAL FEDERATION IS A GROUP OF CITIES THAT RULE THEMSELVES WITHOUT RELYING ON THE ARMY. I'M NOT SURE IF THEY WILL SO EASILY LEND A HAND TO 05 SINCE IT USED TO BE UNDER THE ARMY'S PRO-TECTION.
THE WILL FADES BEFORE THE BULLET EVEN HITS.
I HEAR THAT SHE GOT AWAY. THE PROFESSOR'S GIRLFRIEND.
AND SHE'S NEVER COMING BACK.
NEITHER IS HE.

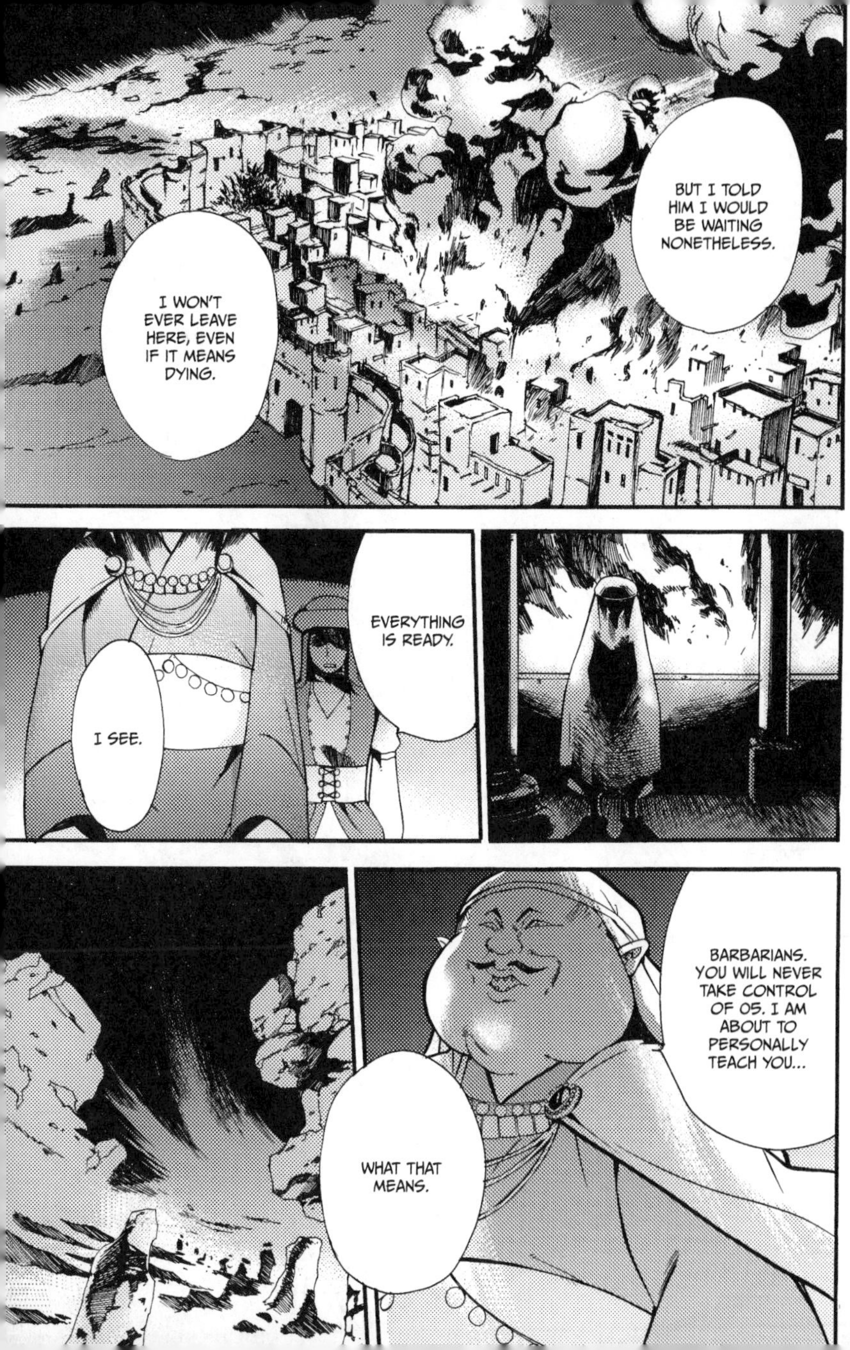
BUT I TOLD HIM I WOULD BE WAITING NONETHELESS.
I WON'T EVER LEAVE HERE, EVEN IF IT MEANS DYING.
EVERYTHING IS READY.
I SEE.
BARBARIANS. YOU WILL NEVER TAKE CONTROL OF 05. I AM ABOUT TO PERSONALLY TEACH YOU...
WHAT THAT MEANS.

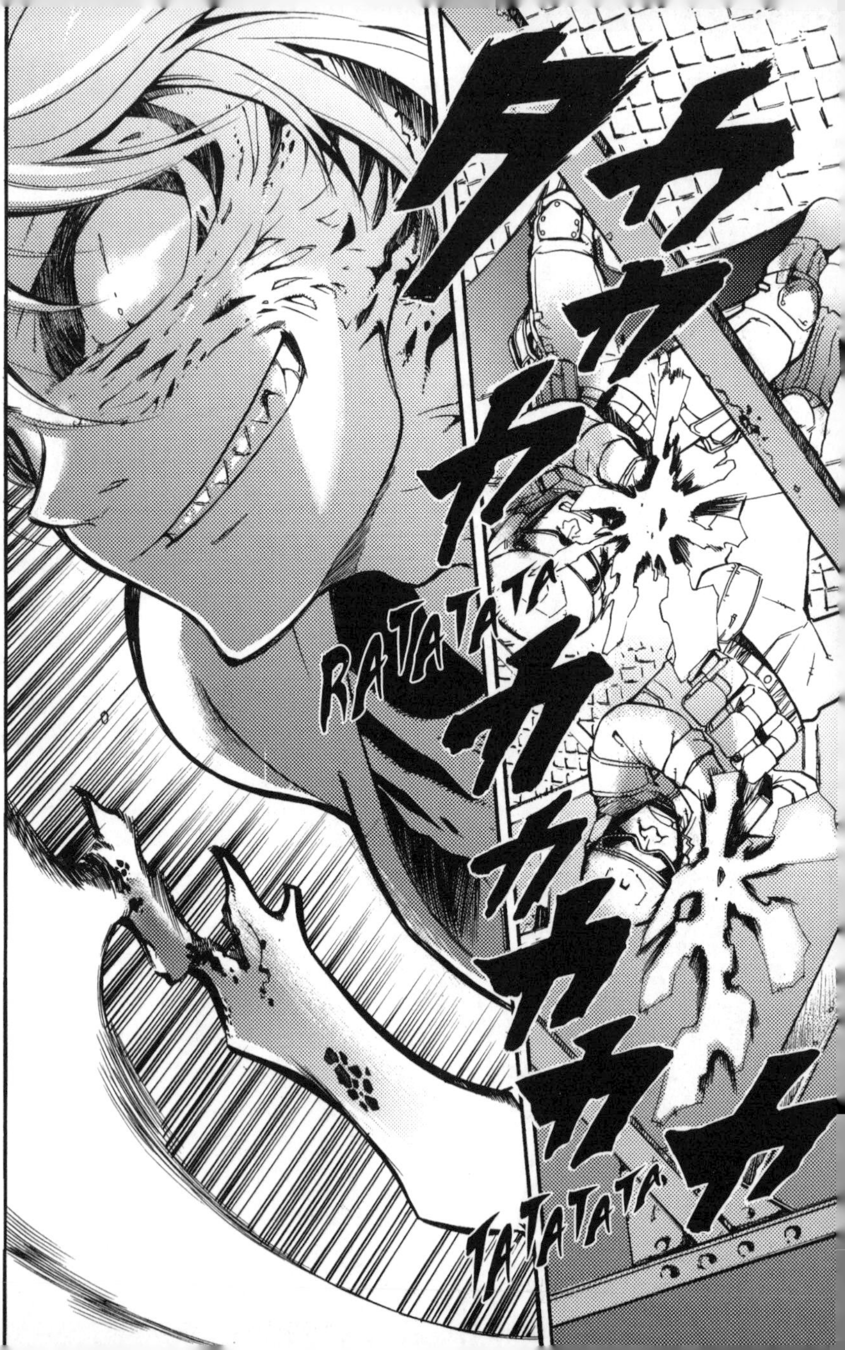
RATATATA
TATATATA

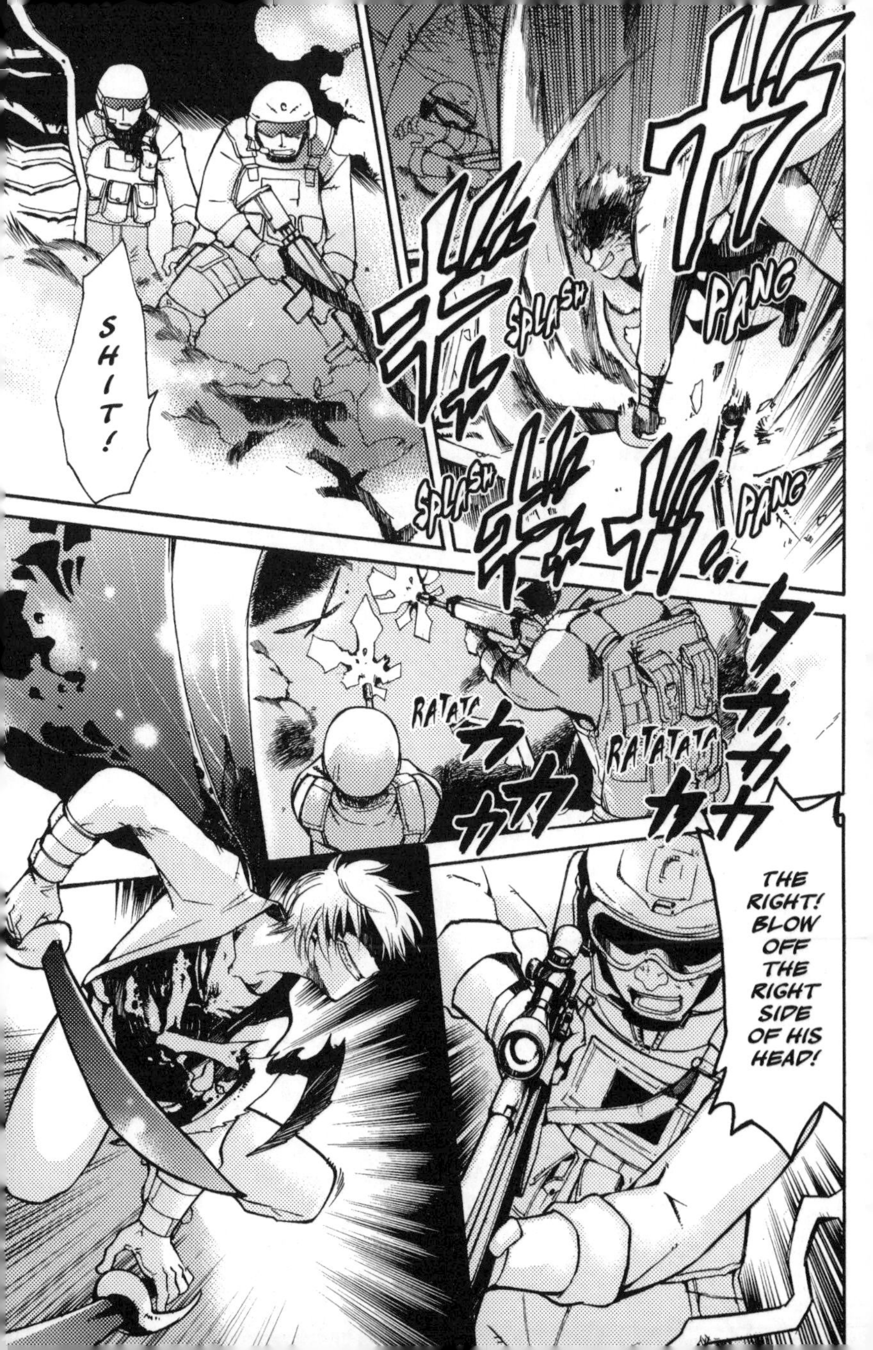
PANG
SPLASH
PANG
SPLASH
SHIT!
RATATATA
RATATA
THE RIGHT! BLOW OFF THE RIGHT SIDE OF HIS HEAD!

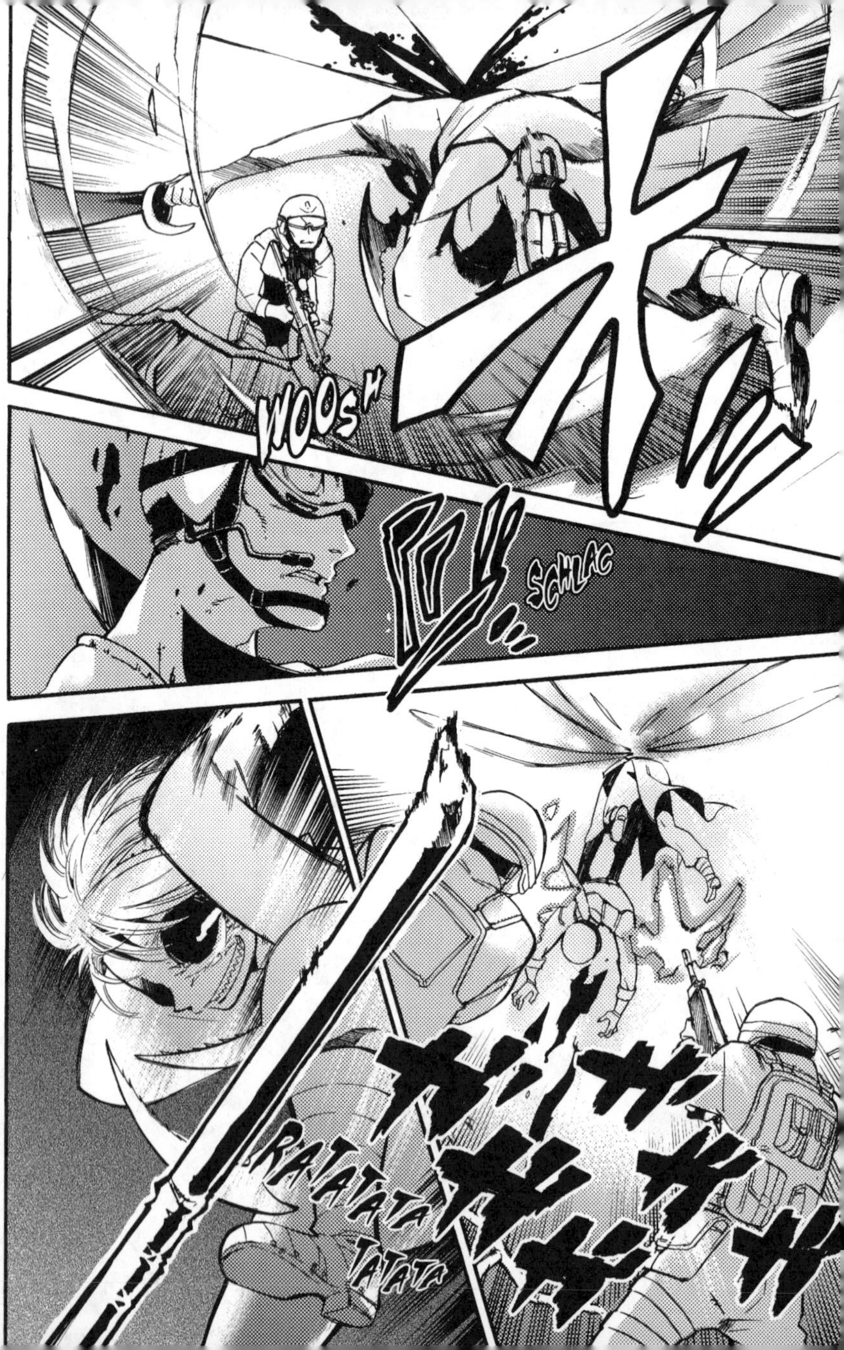
WOOSH
SCHLAC
RATATATA TATATA

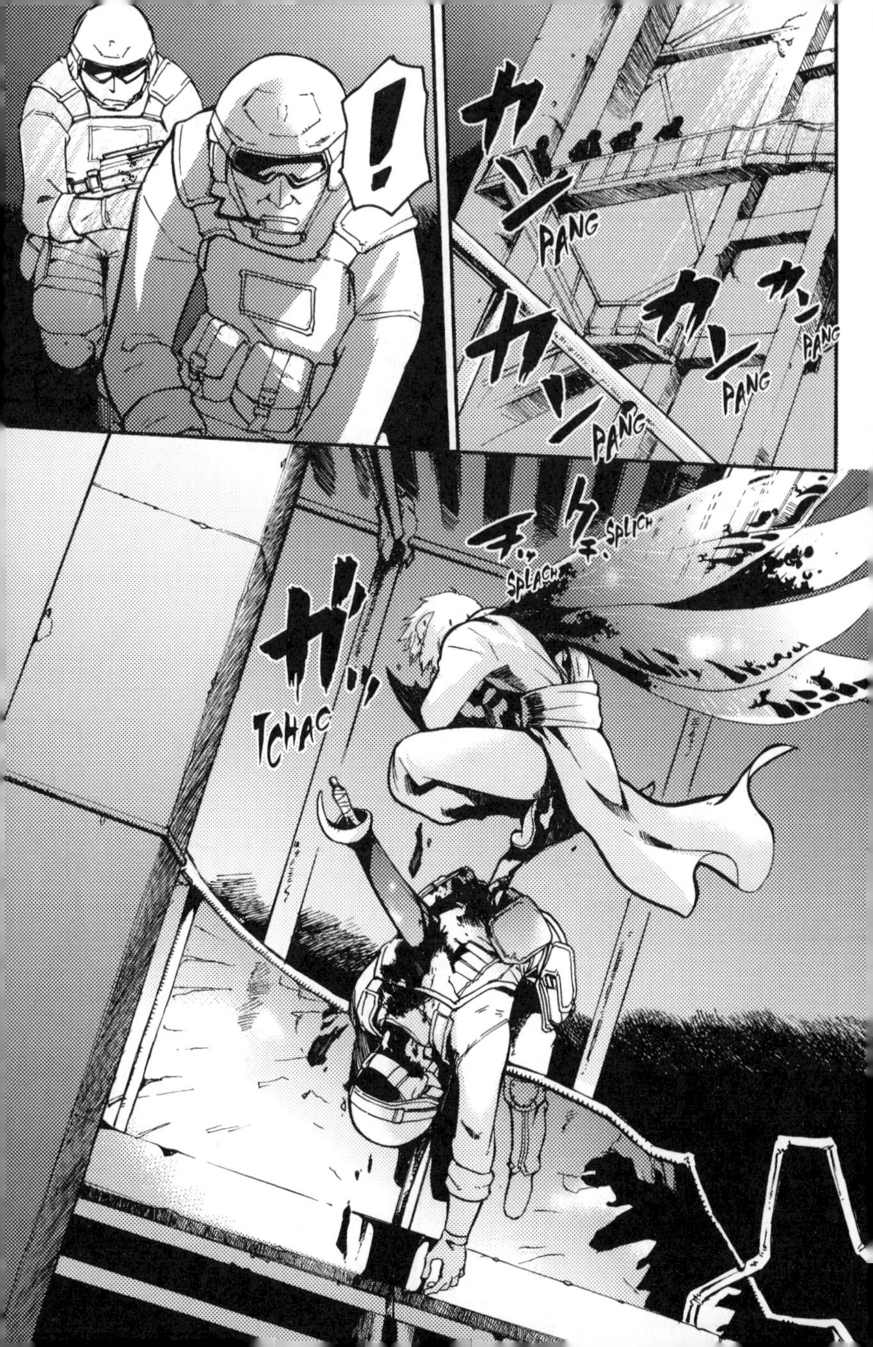

カン
PANG
カン
PANG
カン
PANG
カン
PANG
!
クチ
SPLICH
チ
SPLACH
ガ
TCHAC

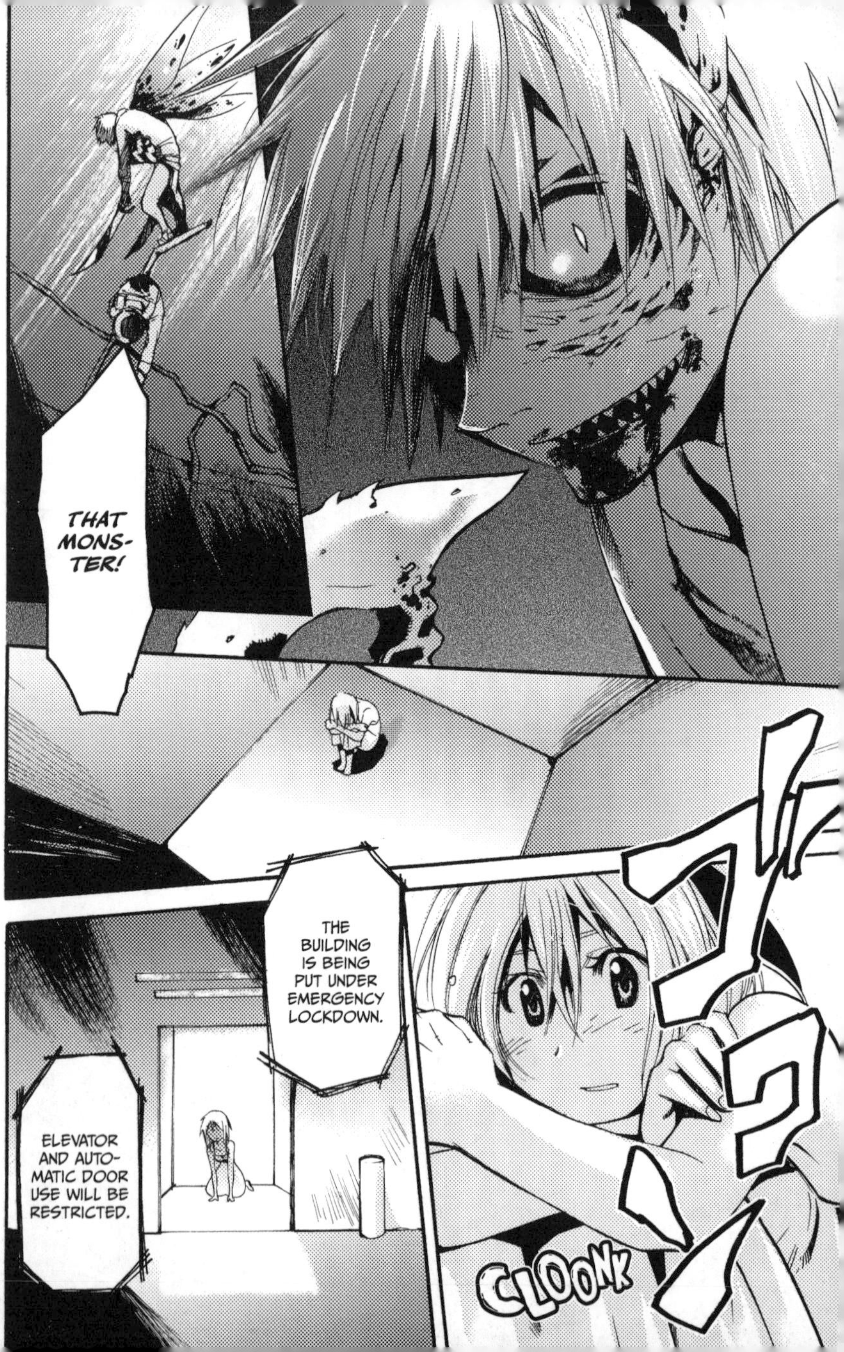
THAT MONSTER!
THE BUILDING IS BEING PUT UNDER EMERGENCY LOCKDOWN.
ELEVATOR AND AUTOMATIC DOOR USE WILL BE RESTRICTED.
CLOONK
?

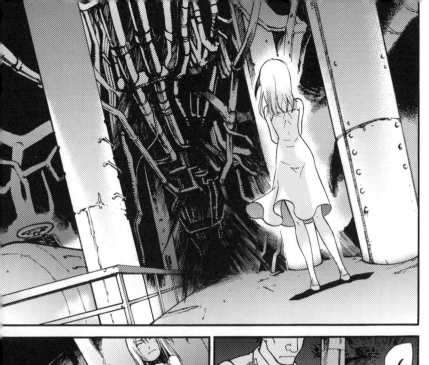

I NEED TO FIND A WAY TO THE TOP FLOOR.

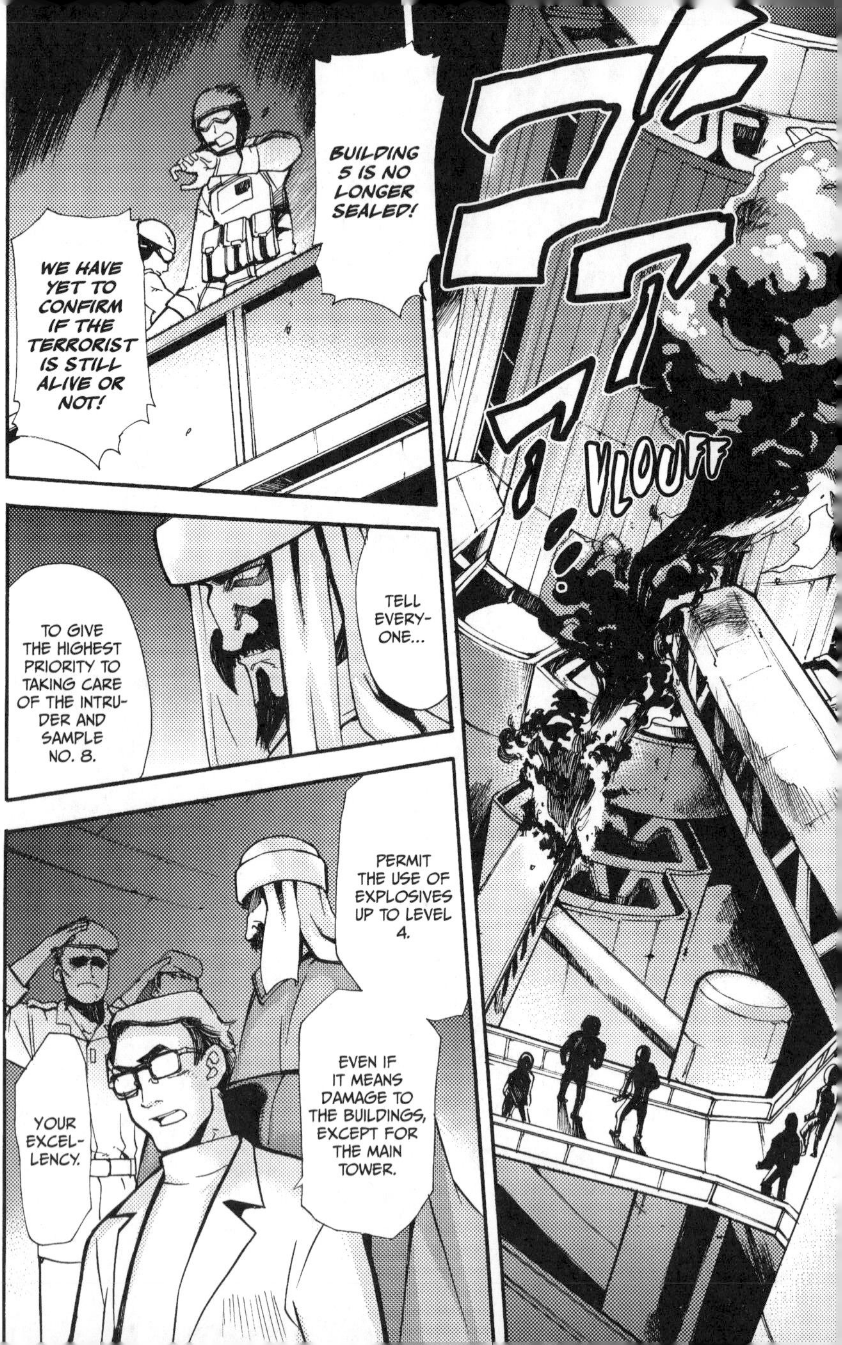
VLOUFF
BUILDING 5 IS NO LONGER SEALED!
WE HAVE YET TO CONFIRM IF THE TERRORIST IS STILL ALIVE OR NOT!
TELL EVERYONE...
TO GIVE THE HIGHEST PRIORITY TO TAKING CARE OF THE INTRUDER AND SAMPLE NO. 8.
PERMIT THE USE OF EXPLOSIVES UP TO LEVEL 4.
EVEN IF IT MEANS DAMAGE TO THE BUILDINGS, EXCEPT FOR THE MAIN TOWER.
YOUR EXCELLENCY.

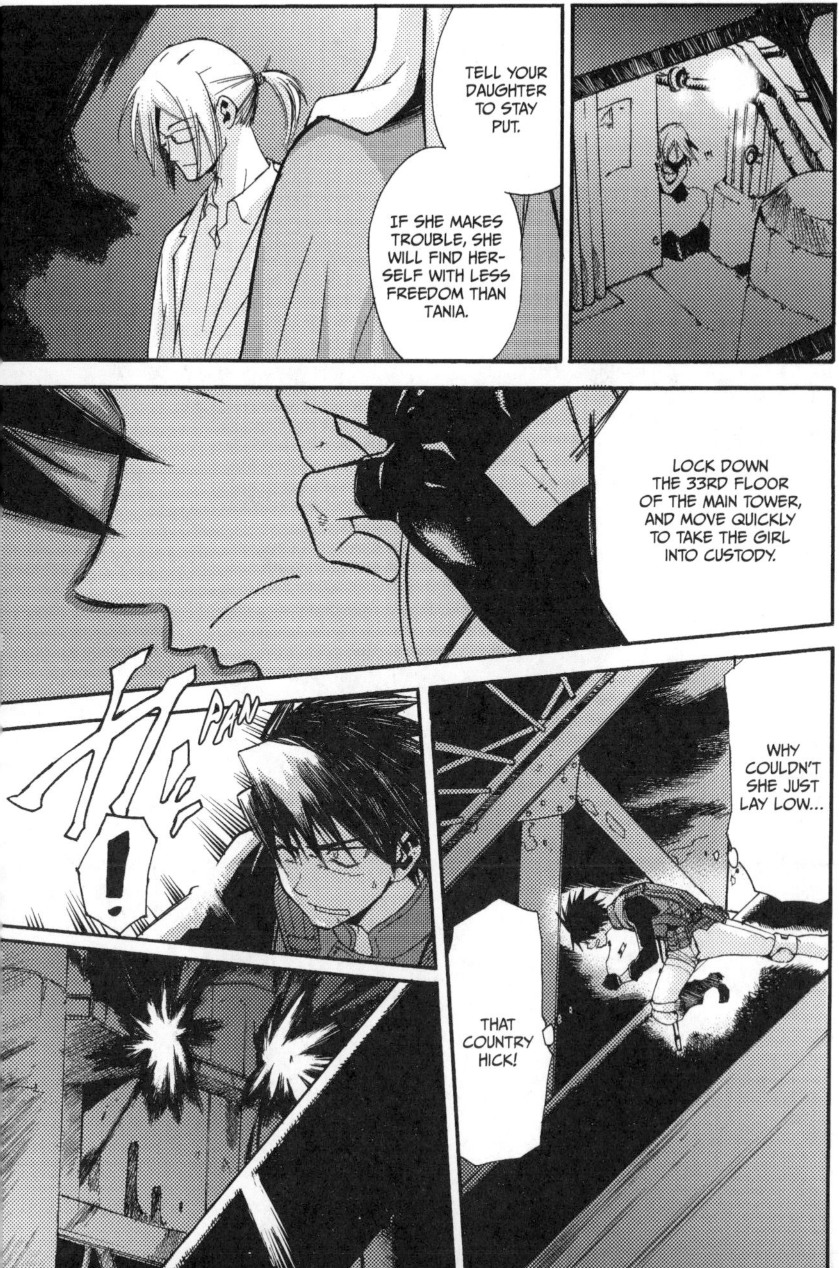
TELL YOUR DAUGHTER TO STAY PUT.
IF SHE MAKES TROUBLE, SHE WILL FIND HER-SELF WITH LESS FREEDOM THAN TANIA.
LOCK DOWN THE 33RD FLOOR OF THE MAIN TOWER, AND MOVE QUICKLY TO TAKE THE GIRL INTO CUSTODY.
WHY COULDN'T SHE JUST LAY LOW...
THAT COUNTRY HICK!
PAN
!

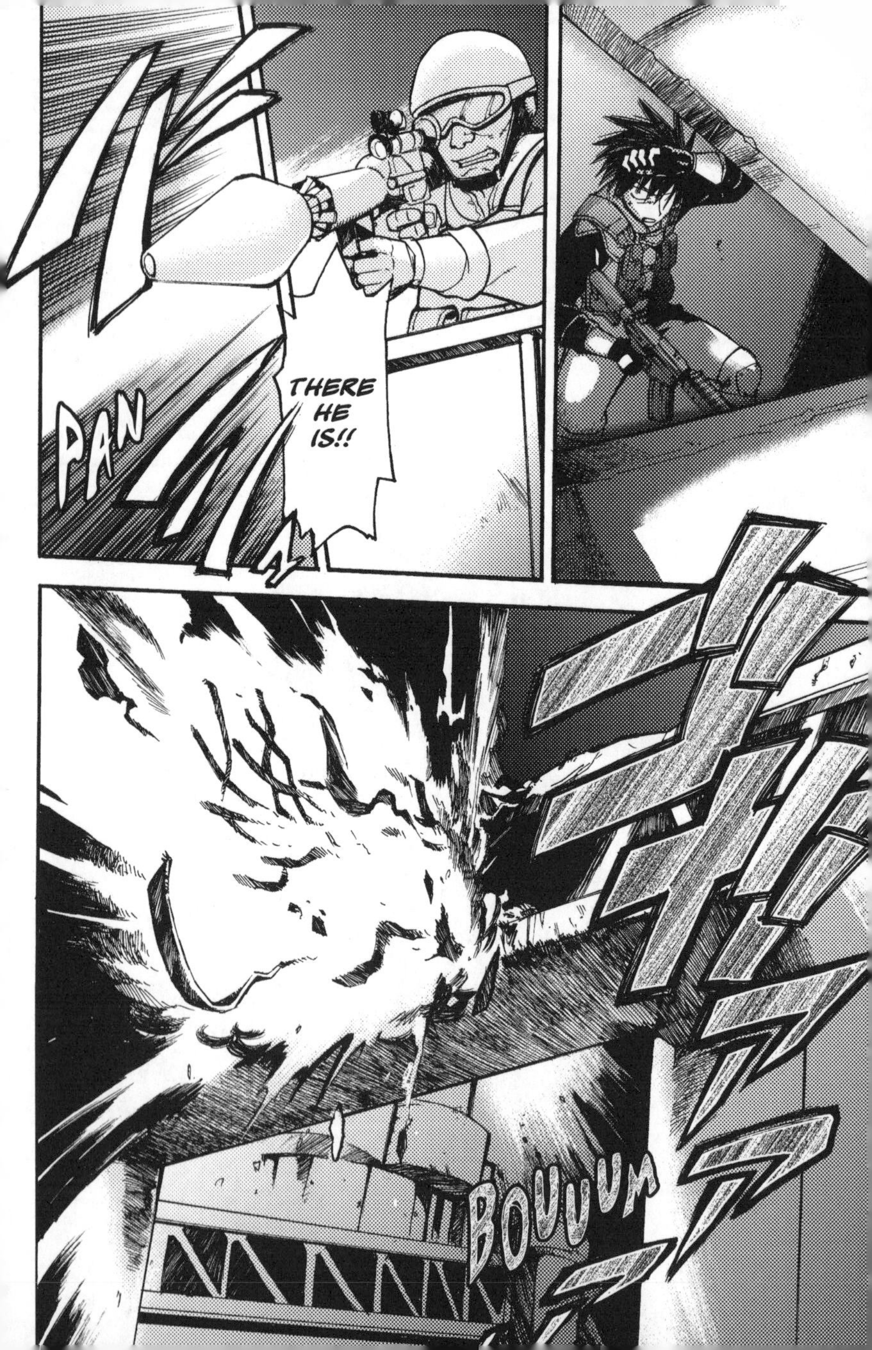
THERE HE IS!!
PAN
BOUUUM

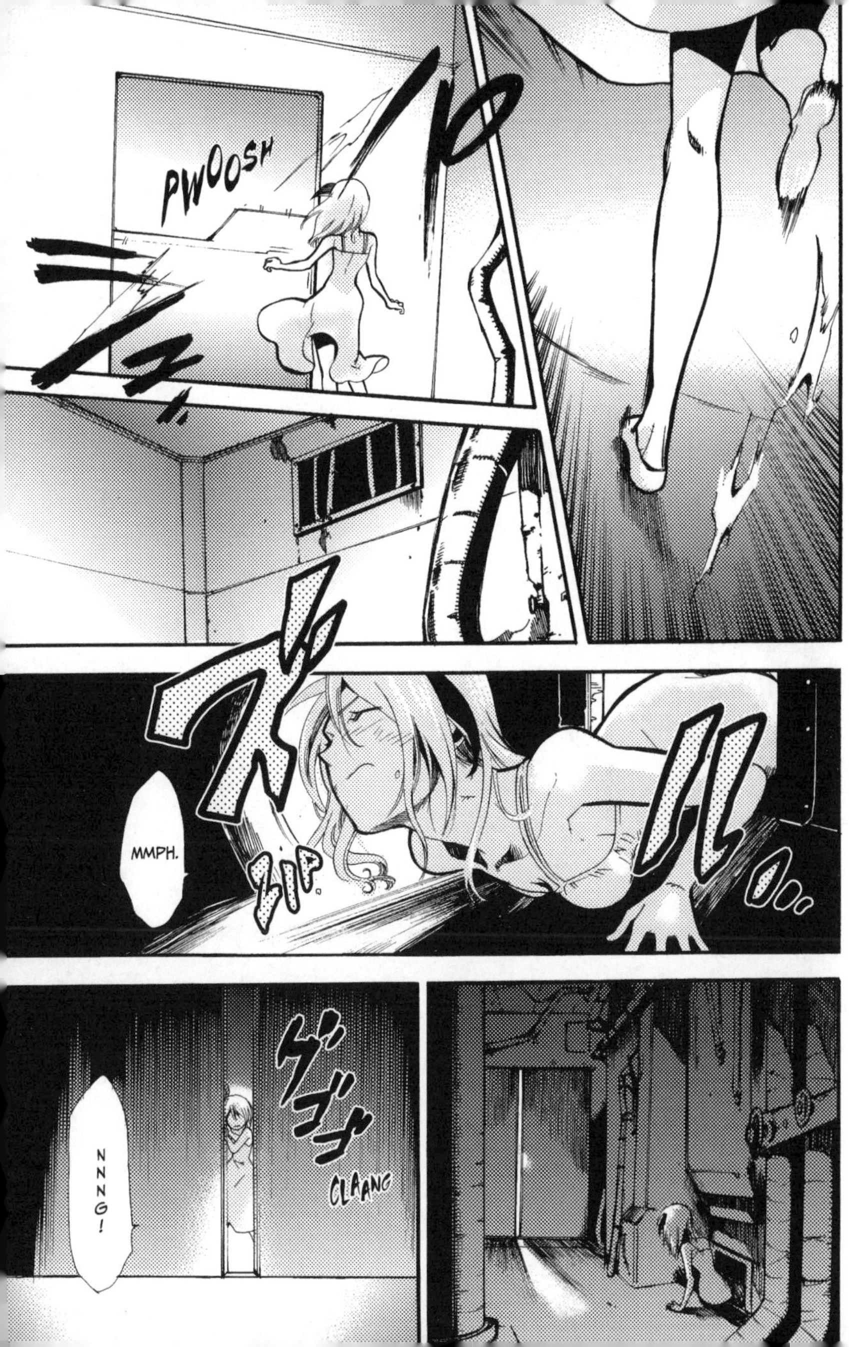
PWOOSH
MMPH.
ZIP.
CLAANG
NNNG!

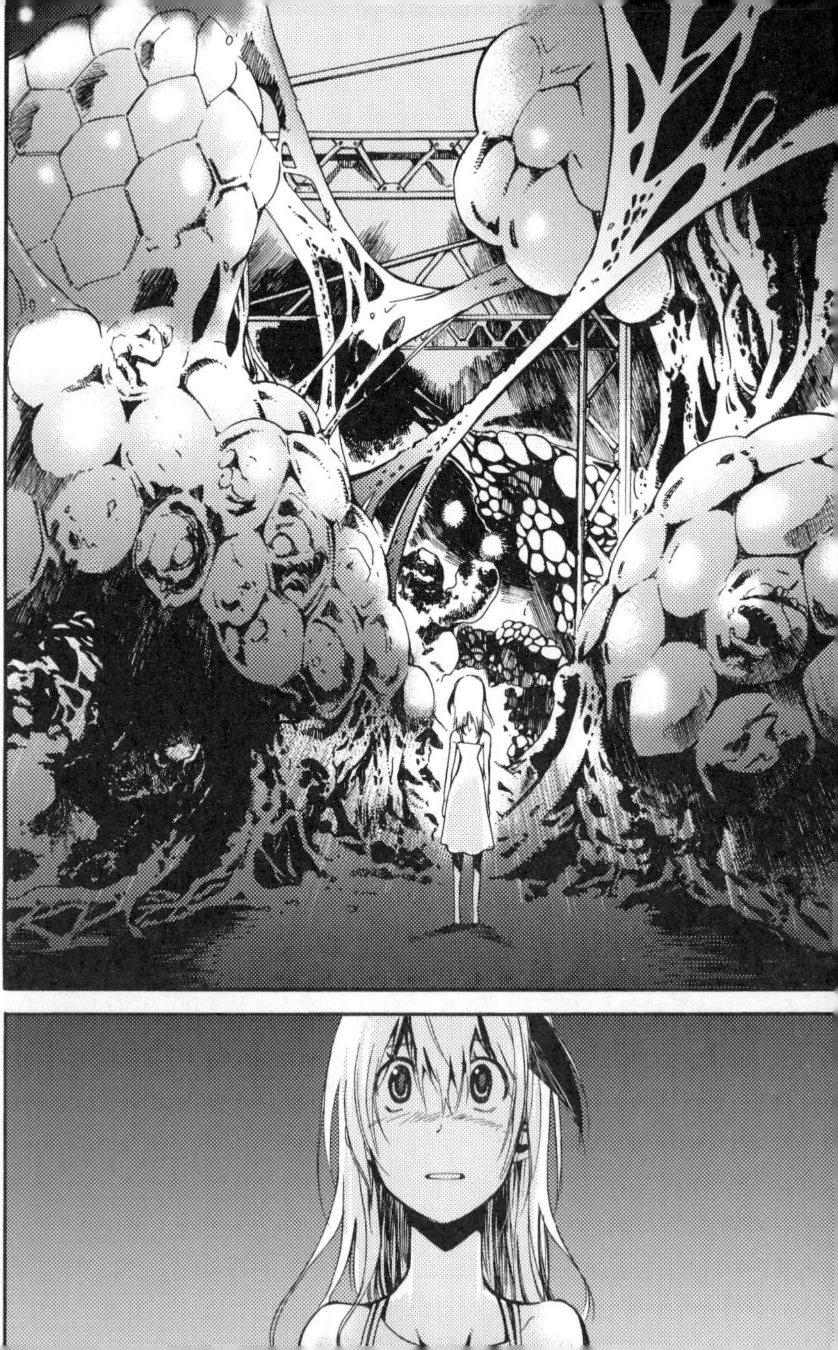

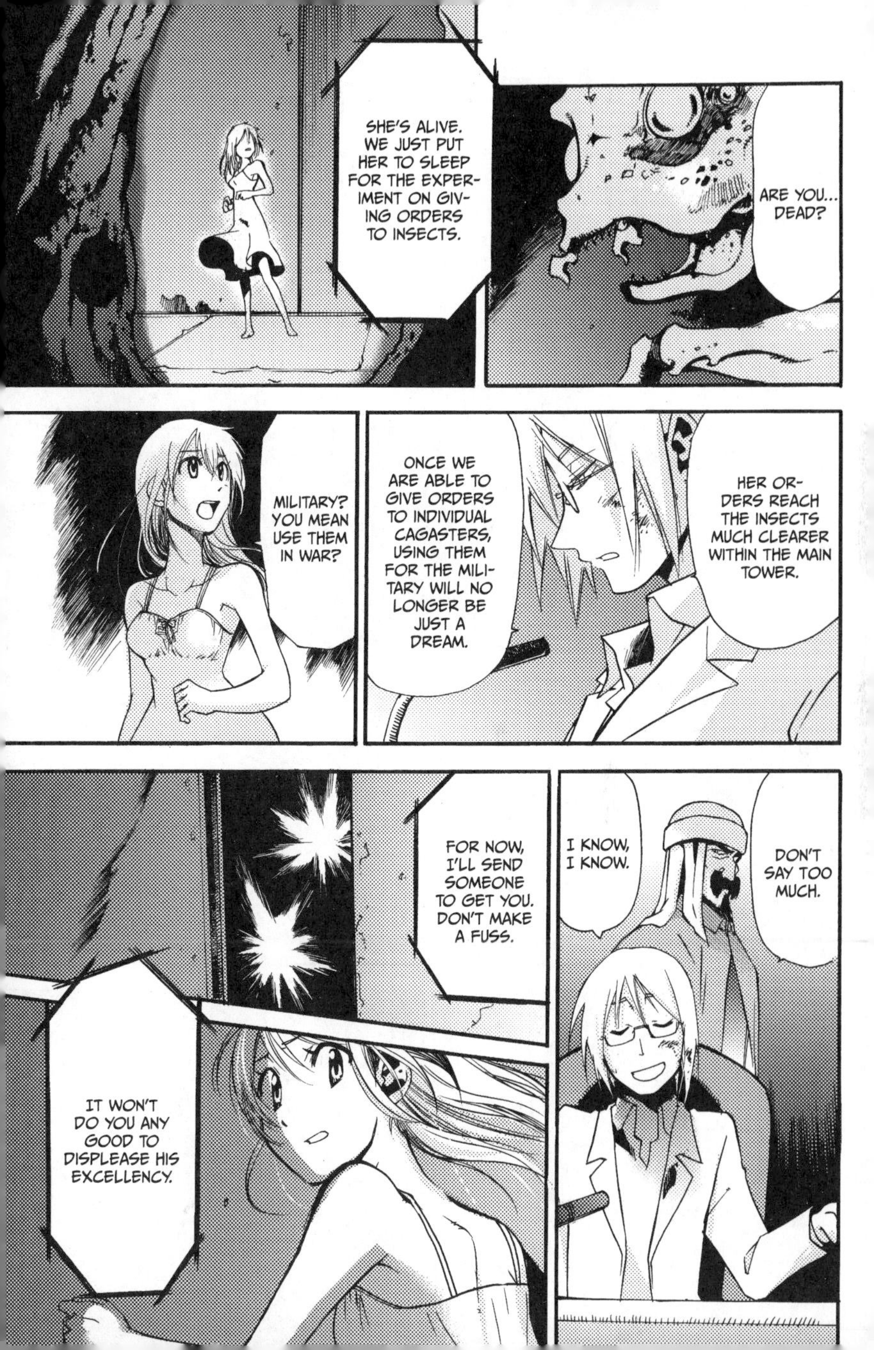
ARE YOU... DEAD?
SHE'S ALIVE. WE JUST PUT HER TO SLEEP FOR THE EXPER-IMENT ON GIV-ING ORDERS TO INSECTS.
HER OR-DERS REACH THE INSECTS MUCH CLEARER WITHIN THE MAIN TOWER.
ONCE WE ARE ABLE TO GIVE ORDERS TO INDIVIDUAL CAGASTERS, USING THEM FOR THE MILI-TARY WILL NO LONGER BE JUST A DREAM.
MILITARY? YOU MEAN USE THEM IN WAR?
DON'T SAY TOO MUCH.
I KNOW, I KNOW.
FOR NOW, I'LL SEND SOMEONE TO GET YOU. DON'T MAKE A FUSS.
IT WON'T DO YOU ANY GOOD TO DISPLEASE HIS EXCELLENCY.

MOTHER...

MOTHER!

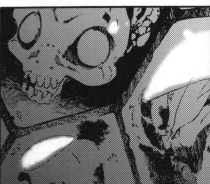

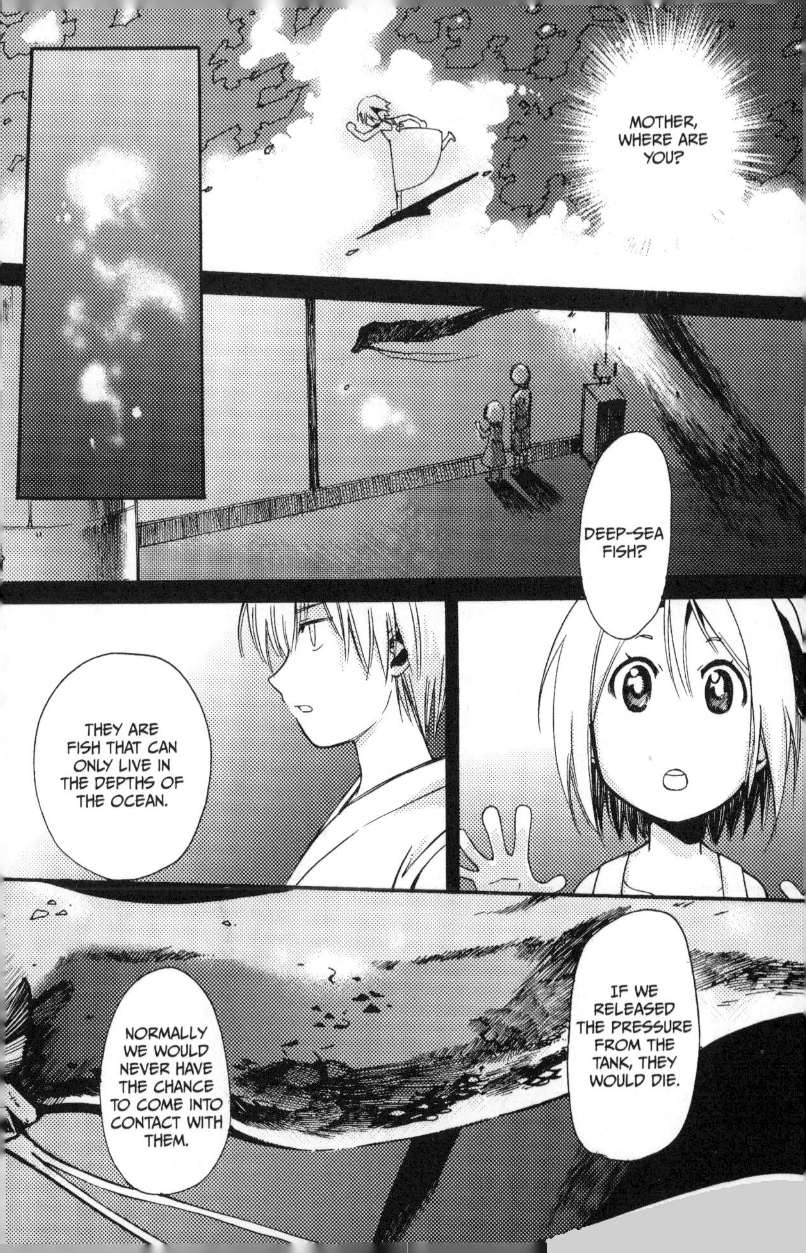
MOTHER, WHERE ARE YOU?
DEEP-SEA FISH?
THEY ARE FISH THAT CAN ONLY LIVE IN THE DEPTHS OF THE OCEAN.
IF WE RELEASED THE PRESSURE FROM THE TANK, THEY WOULD DIE.
NORMALLY WE WOULD NEVER HAVE THE CHANCE TO COME INTO CONTACT WITH THEM.

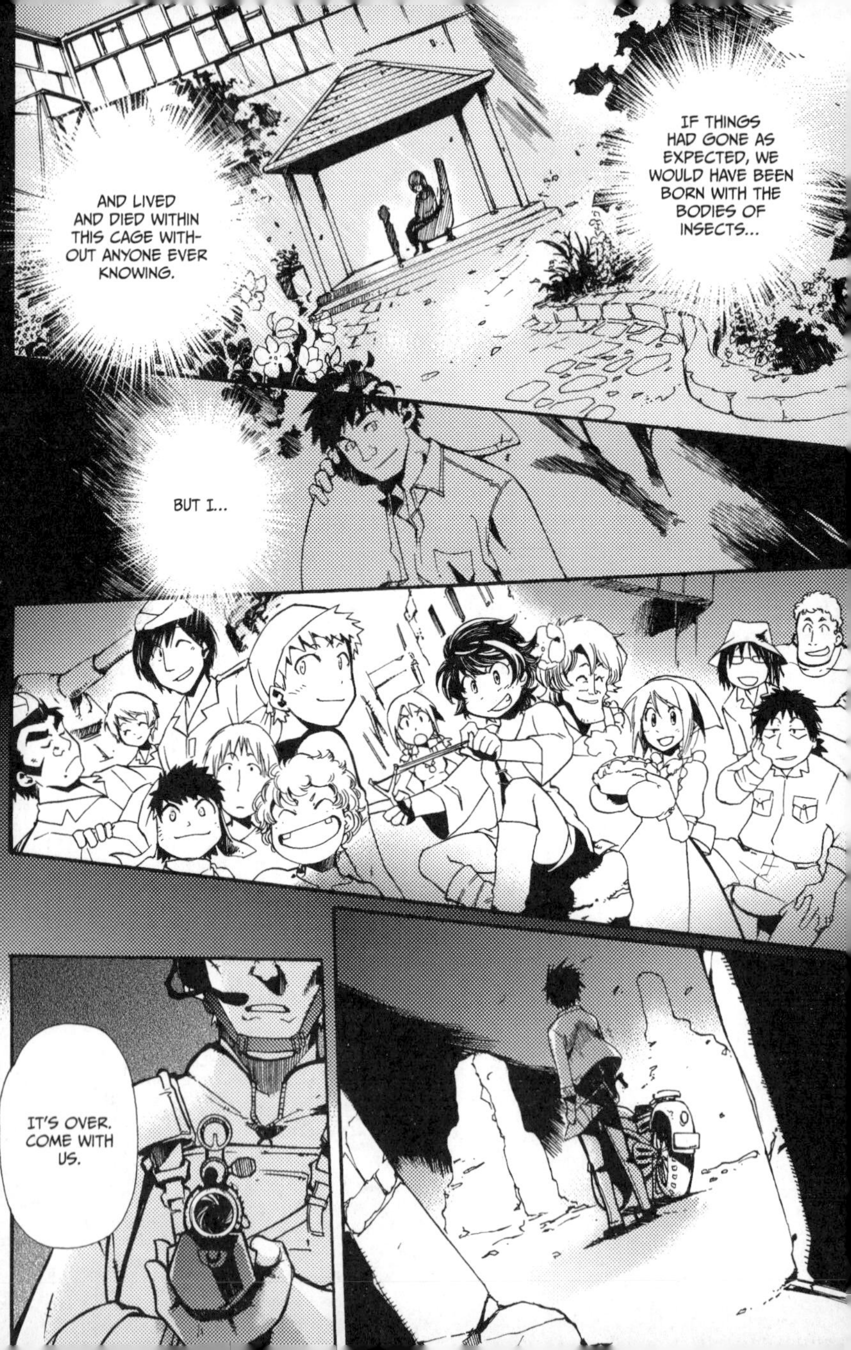
IF THINGS HAD GONE AS EXPECTED, WE WOULD HAVE BEEN BORN WITH THE BODIES OF INSECTS...
AND LIVED AND DIED WITHIN THIS CAGE WITH-OUT ANYONE EVER KNOWING.
BUT I...
IT'S OVER. COME WITH US.

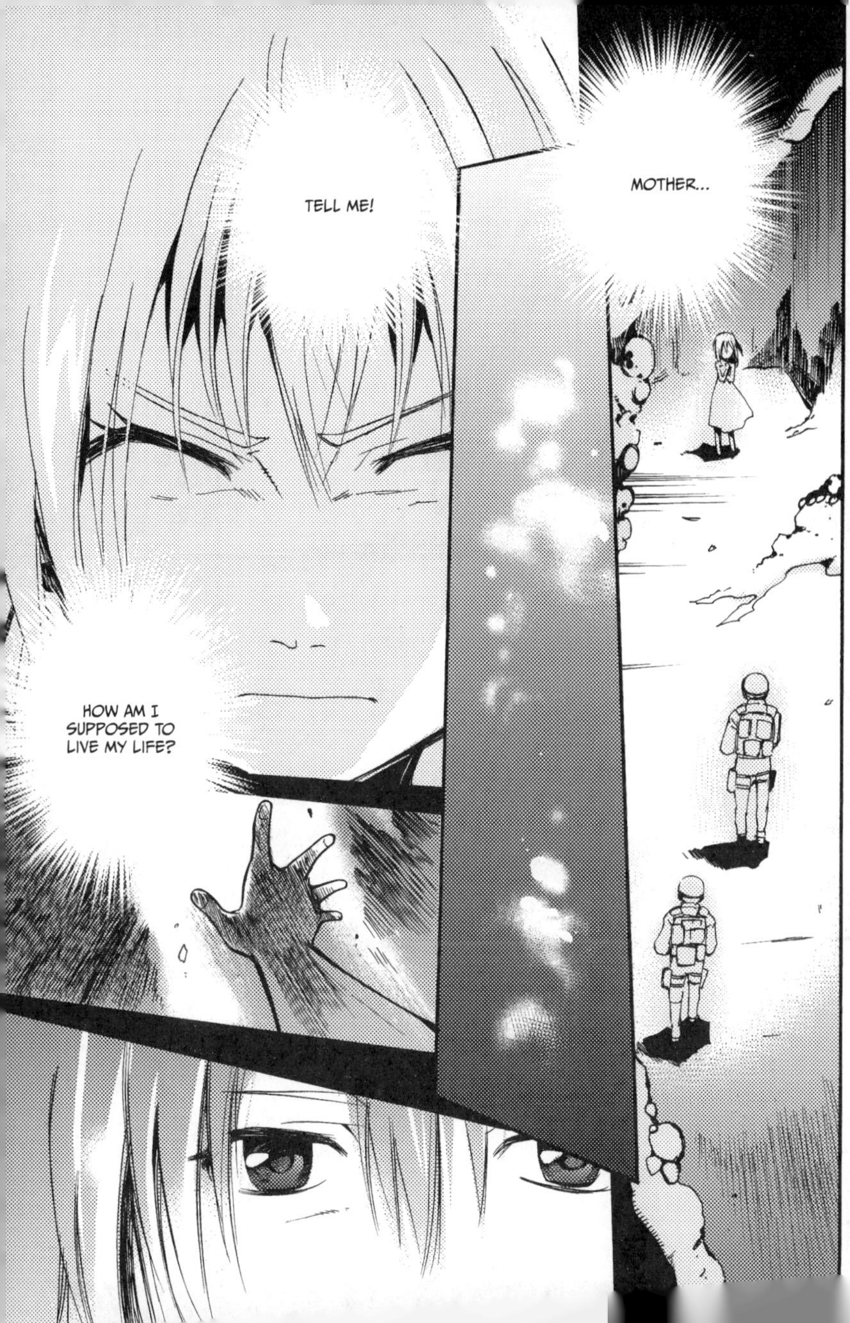
MOTHER...
TELL ME!
HOW AM I SUPPOSED TO LIVE MY LIFE?

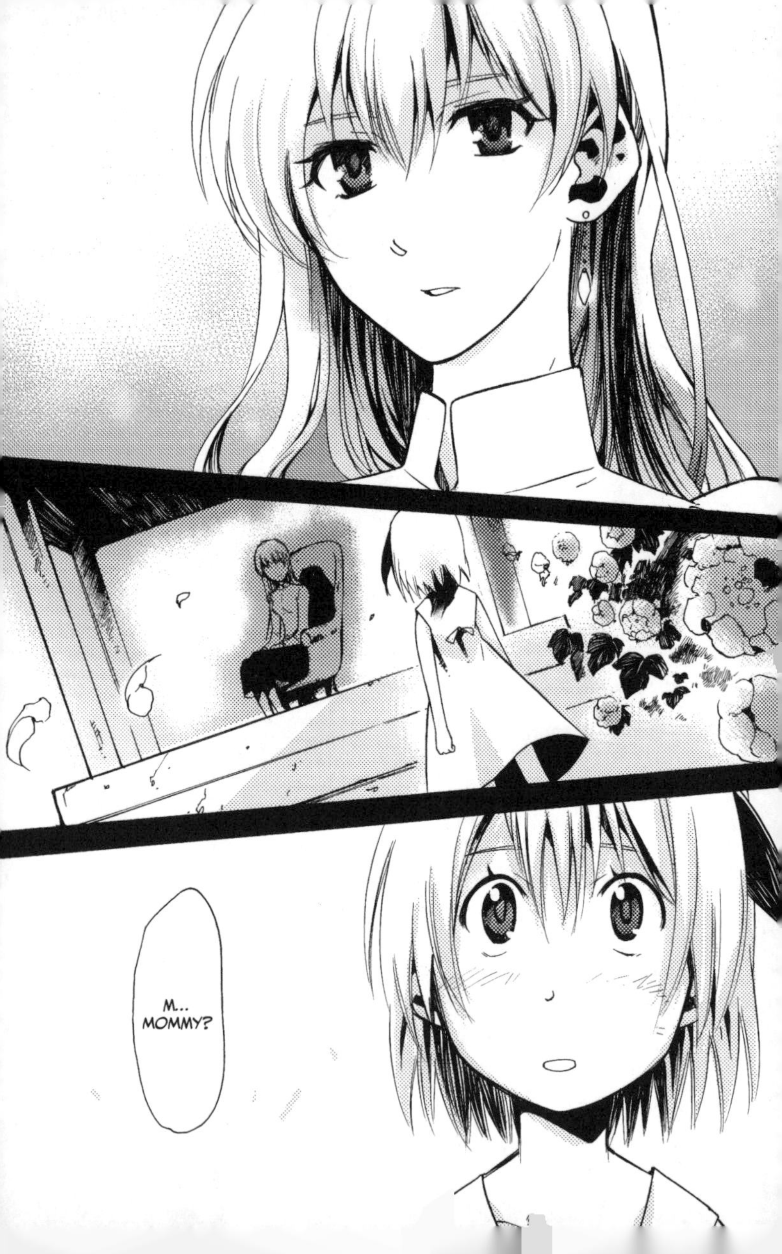
M... MOMMY?

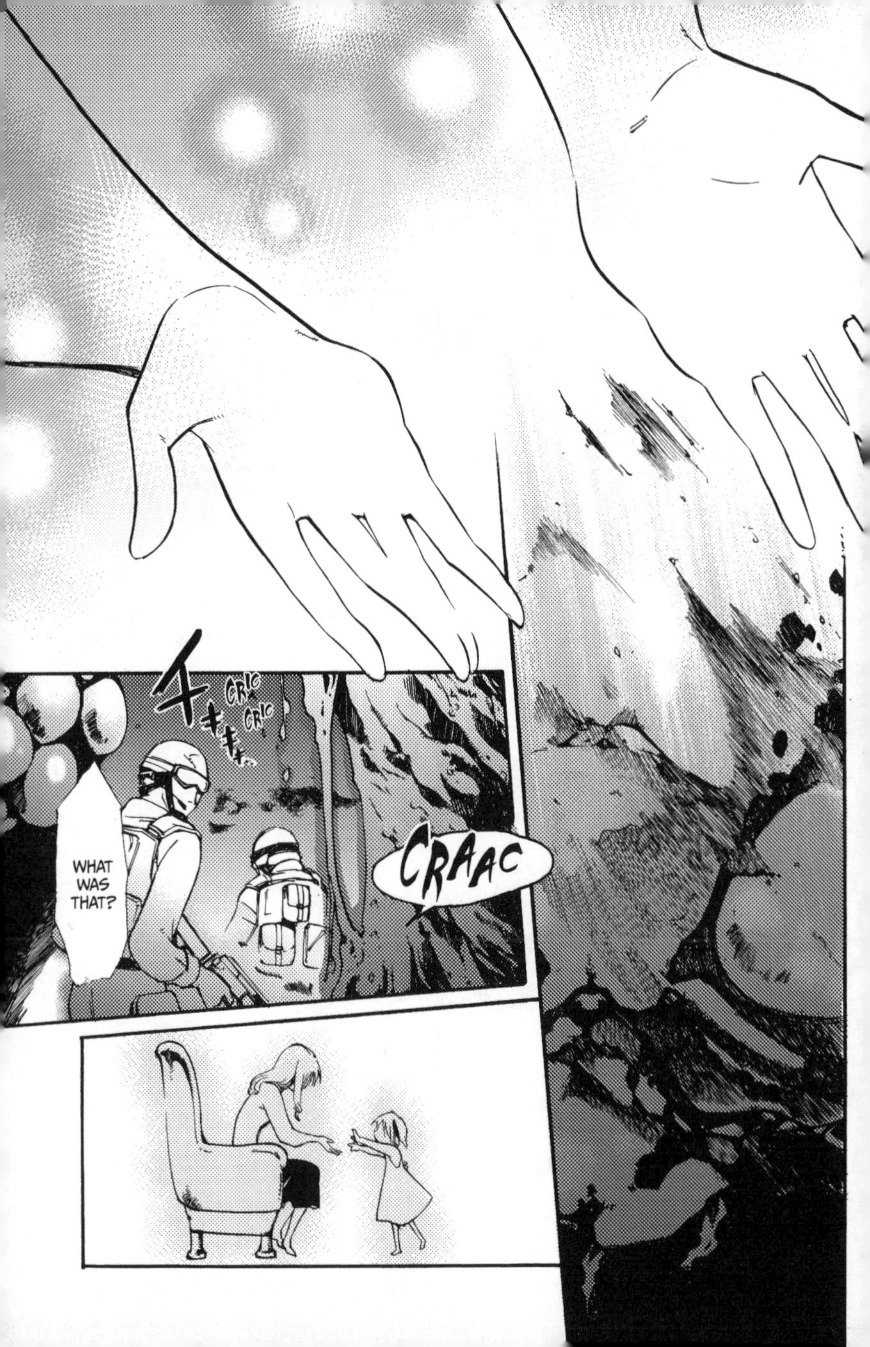
CRIC CRIC
CRAAC
WHAT WAS THAT?

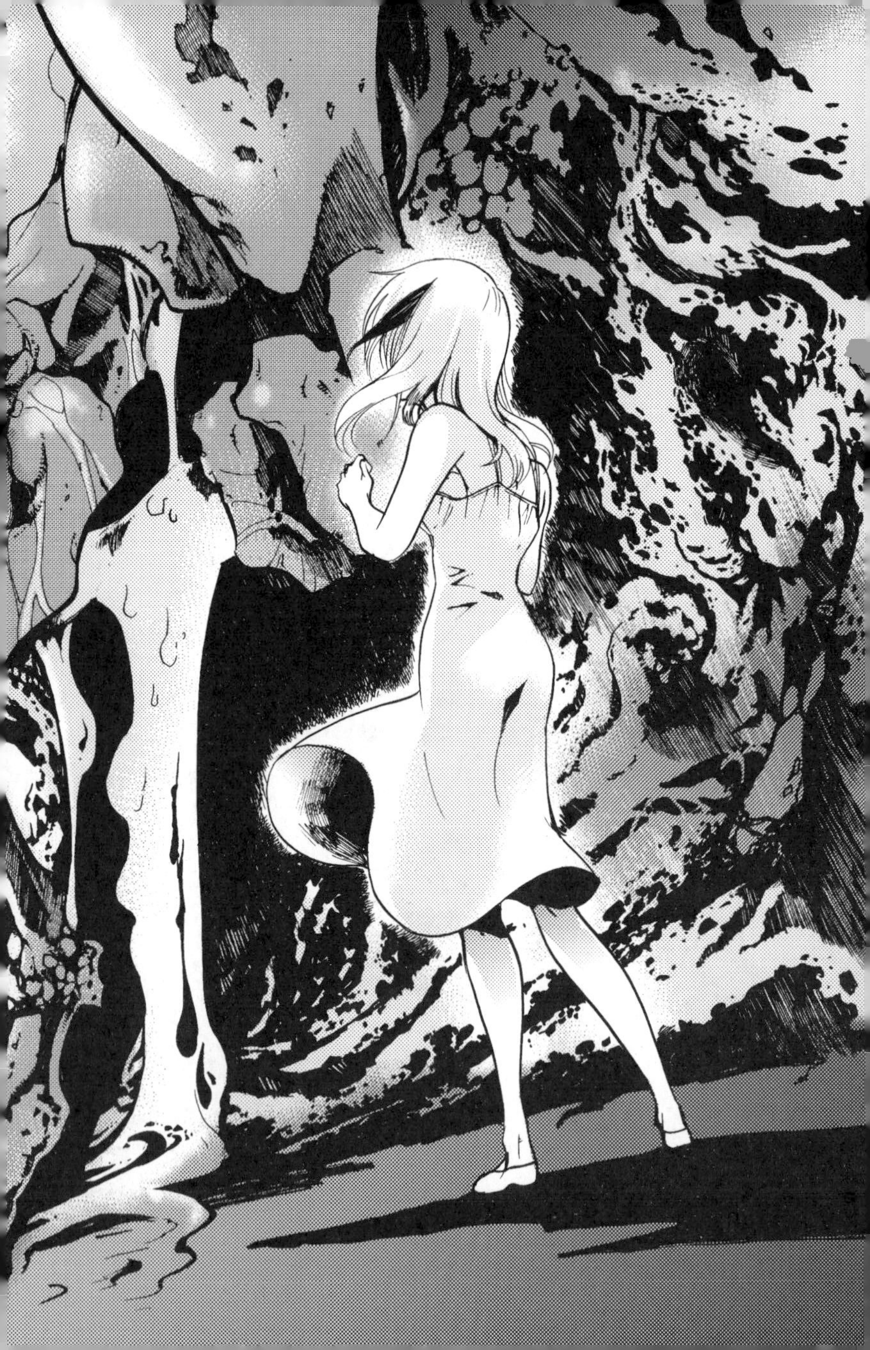

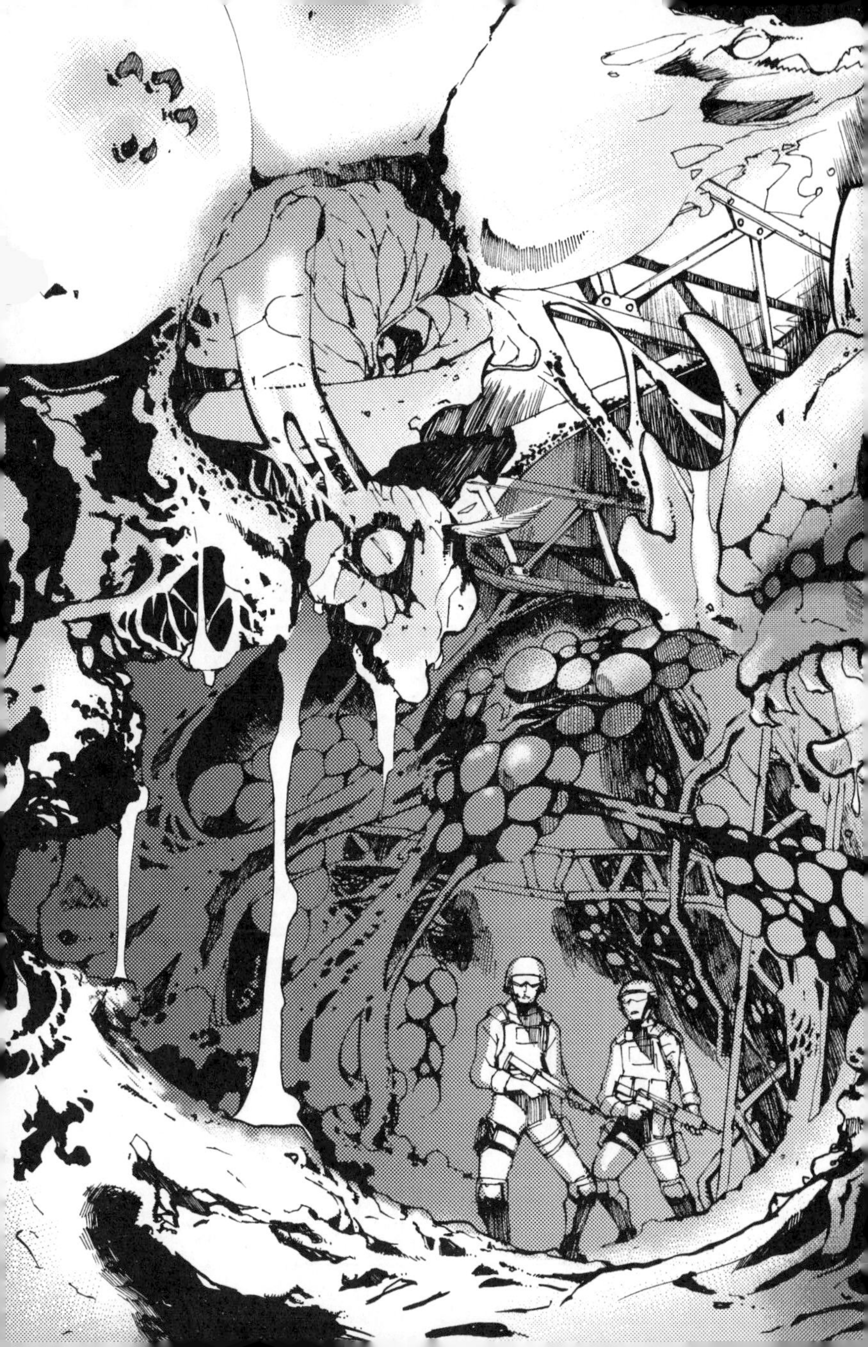

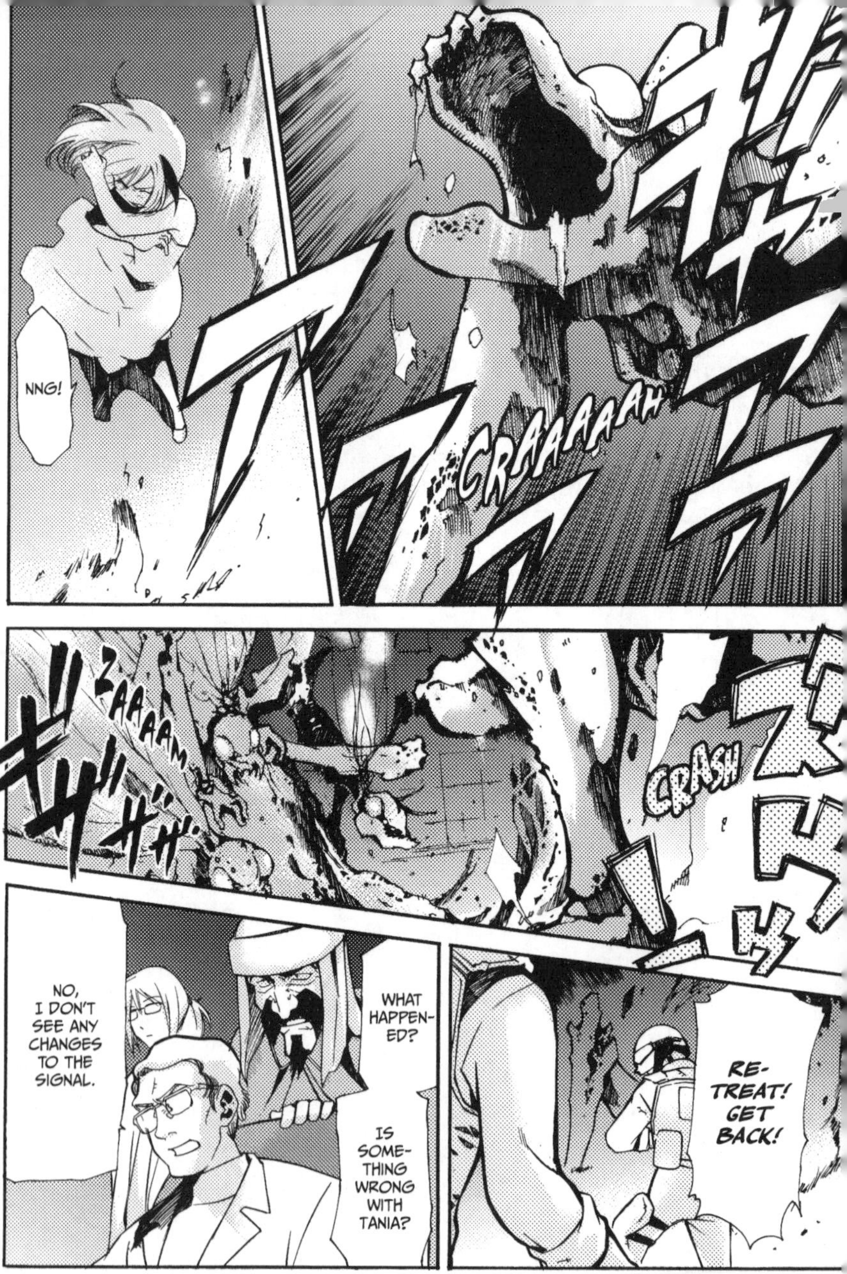
CRAAAAAH
NNG!
CRASH
ZAAAAAM
RE-TREAT! GET BACK!
WHAT HAPPEN-ED?
IS SOME-THING WRONG WITH TANIA?
NO, I DON'T SEE ANY CHANGES TO THE SIGNAL.

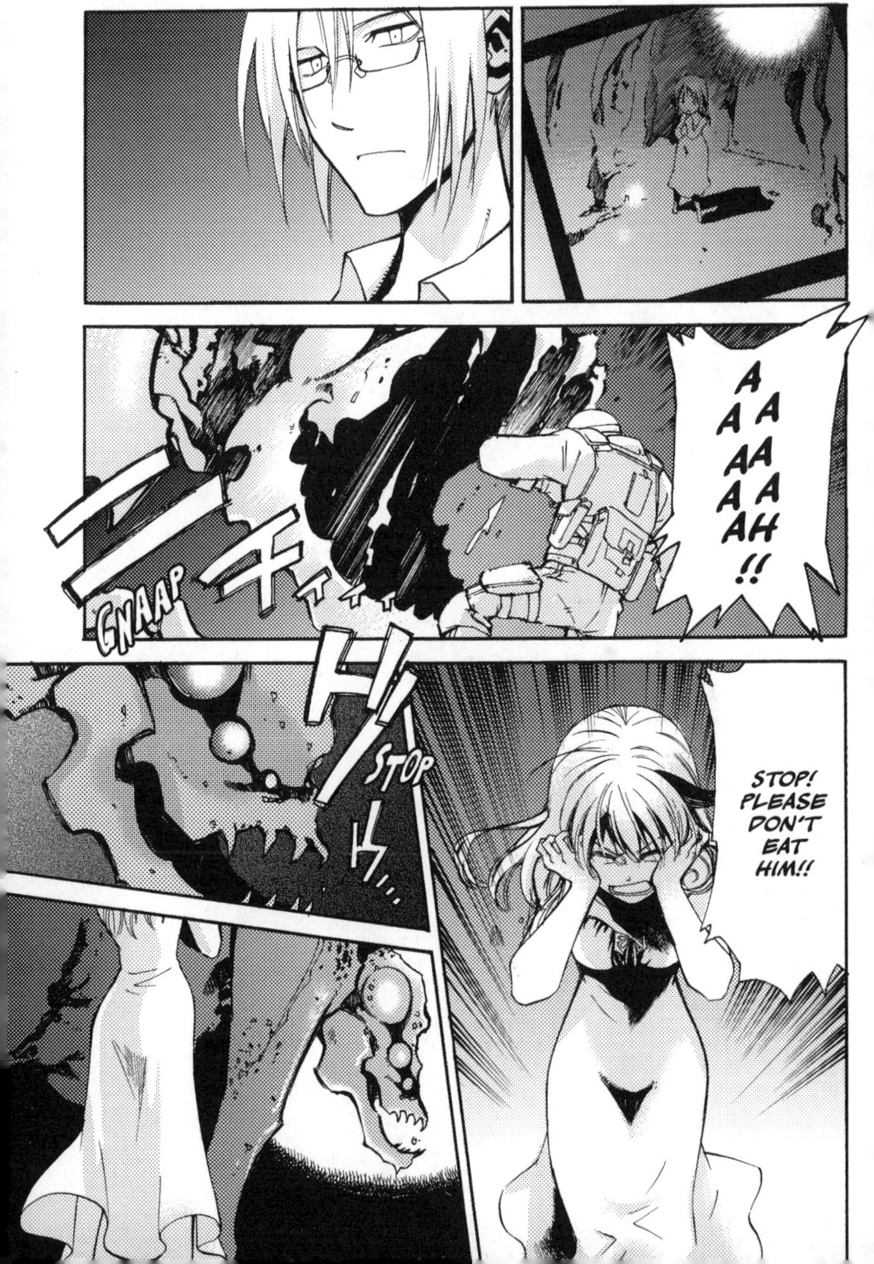
AAAAAAAAH!!
GNAAP
STOP! PLEASE DON'T EAT HIM!!
STOP

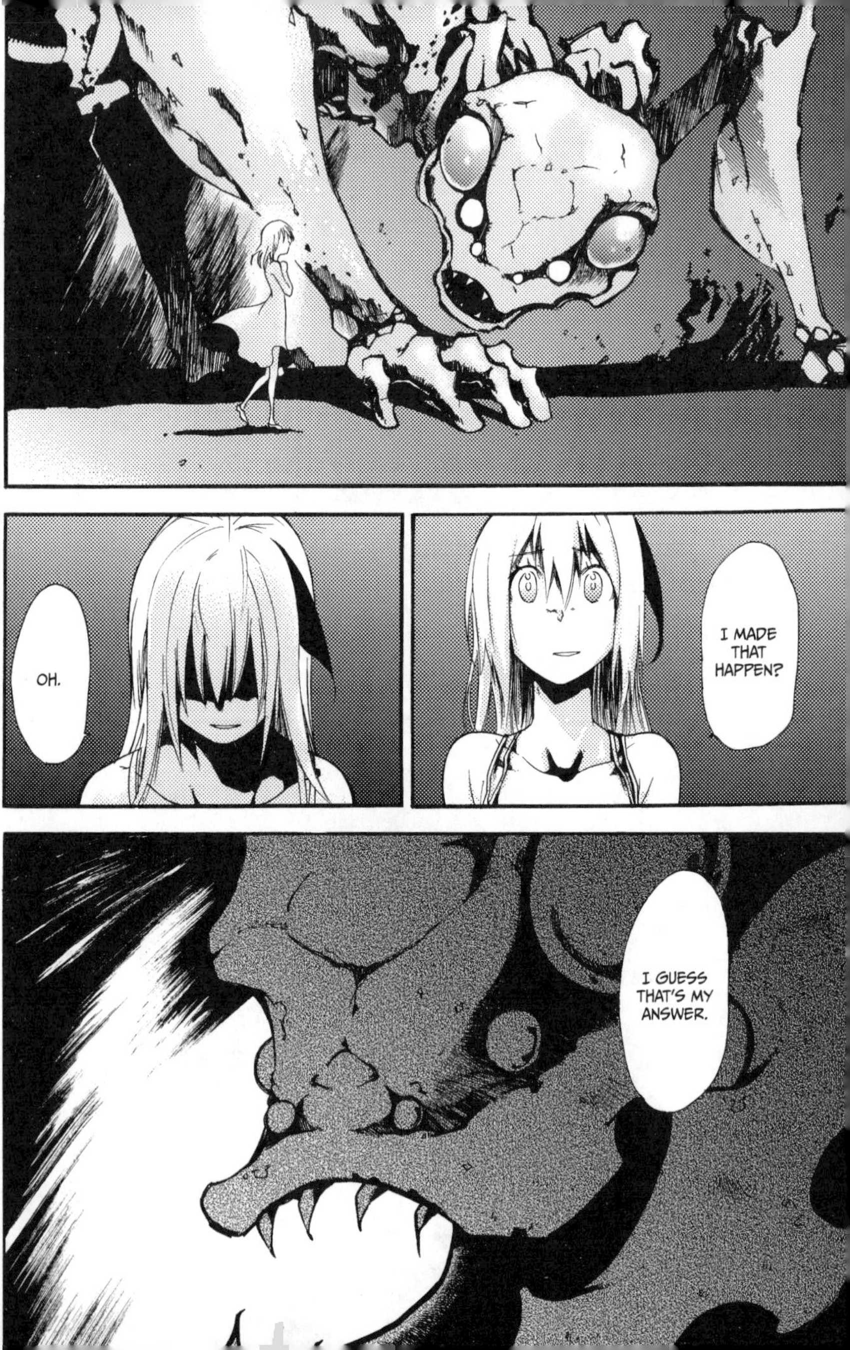
I MADE THAT HAPPEN?
OH.
I GUESS THAT'S MY ANSWER.

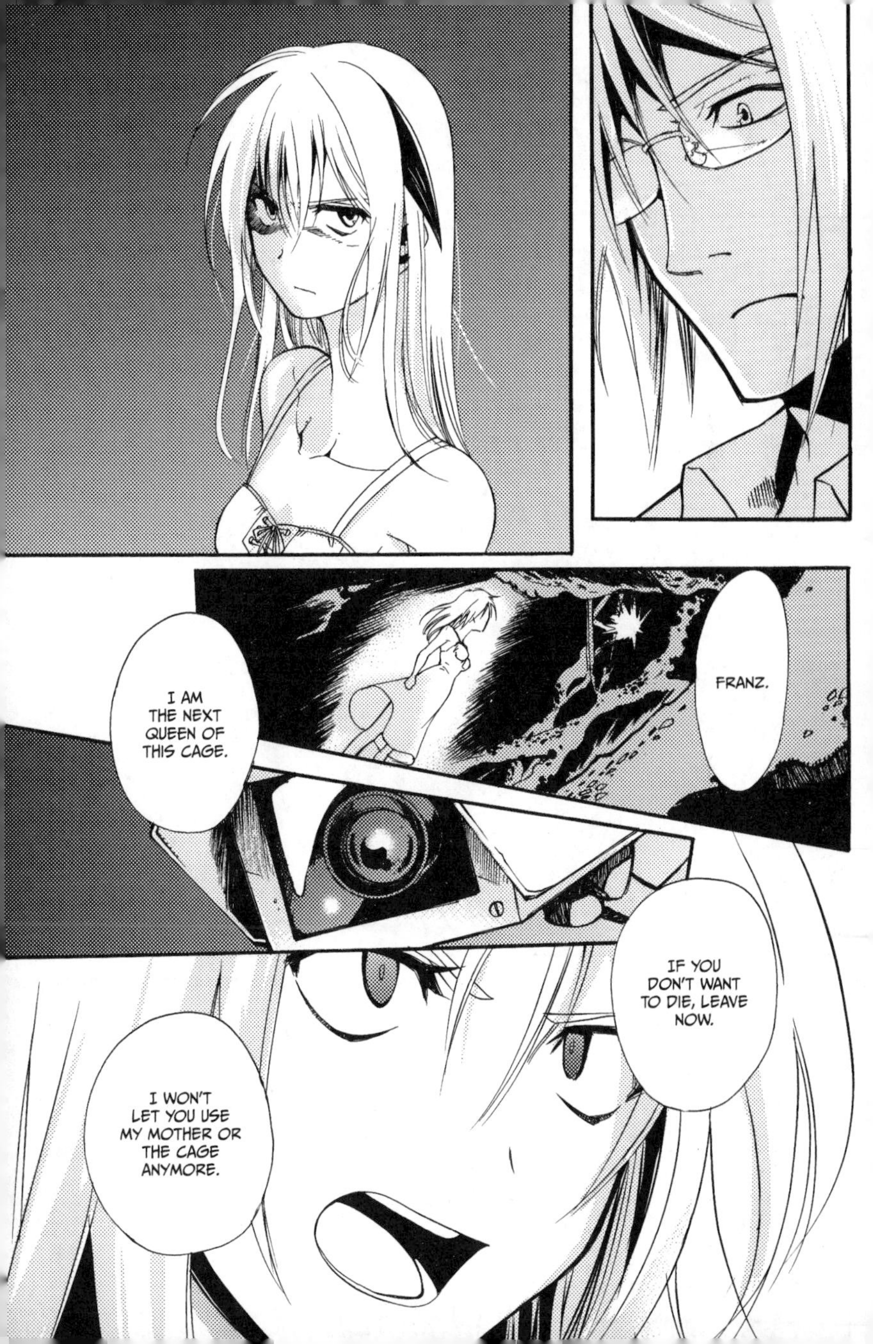
FRANZ.
I AM THE NEXT QUEEN OF THIS CAGE.
IF YOU DON'T WANT TO DIE, LEAVE NOW.
I WON'T LET YOU USE MY MOTHER OR THE CAGE ANYMORE.

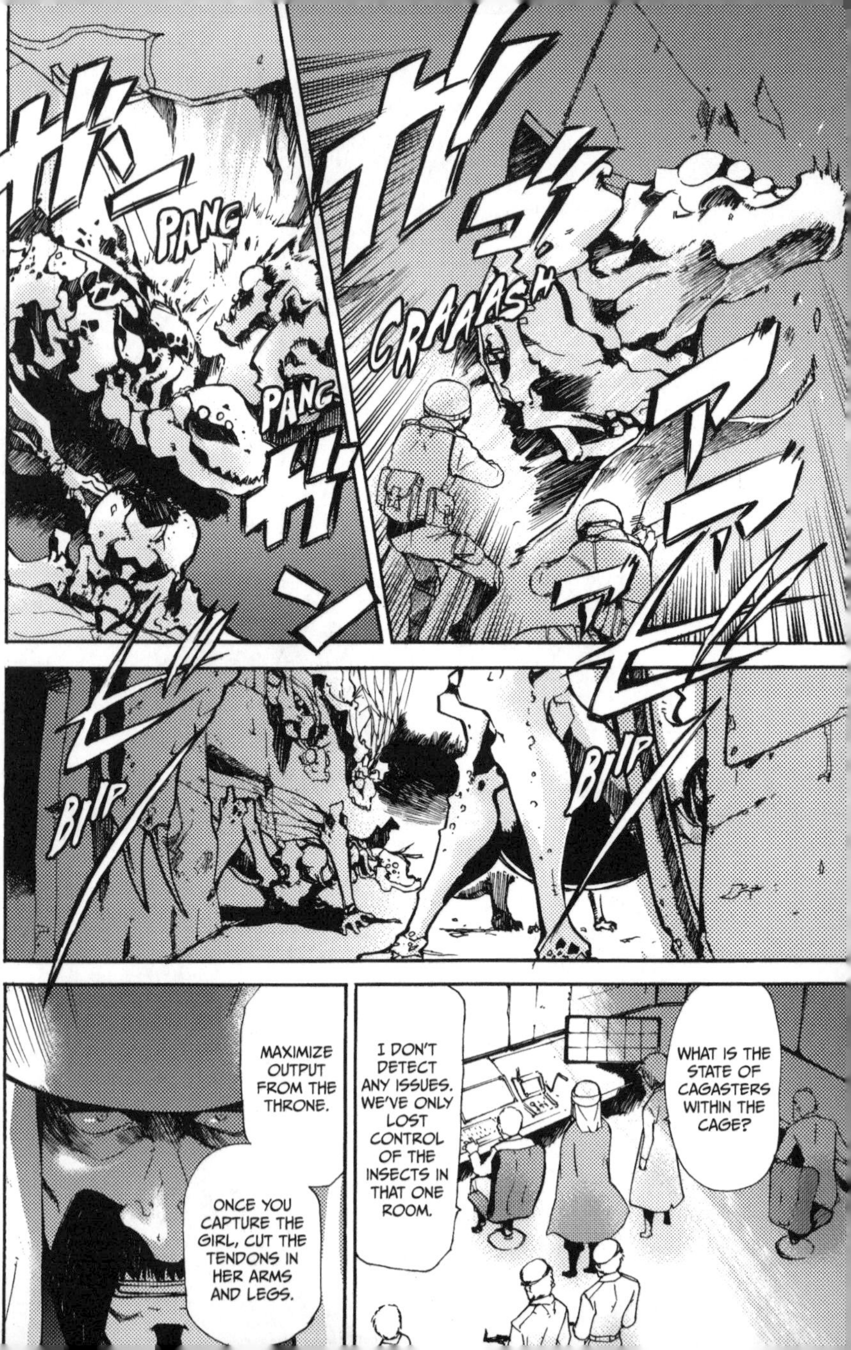
CRAAASH
PANG
PANG
BIIP
BIIP
WHAT IS THE STATE OF CAGASTERS WITHIN THE CAGE?
I DON'T DETECT ANY ISSUES. WE'VE ONLY LOST CONTROL OF THE INSECTS IN THAT ONE ROOM.
MAXIMIZE OUTPUT FROM THE THRONE.
ONCE YOU CAPTURE THE GIRL, CUT THE TENDONS IN HER ARMS AND LEGS.

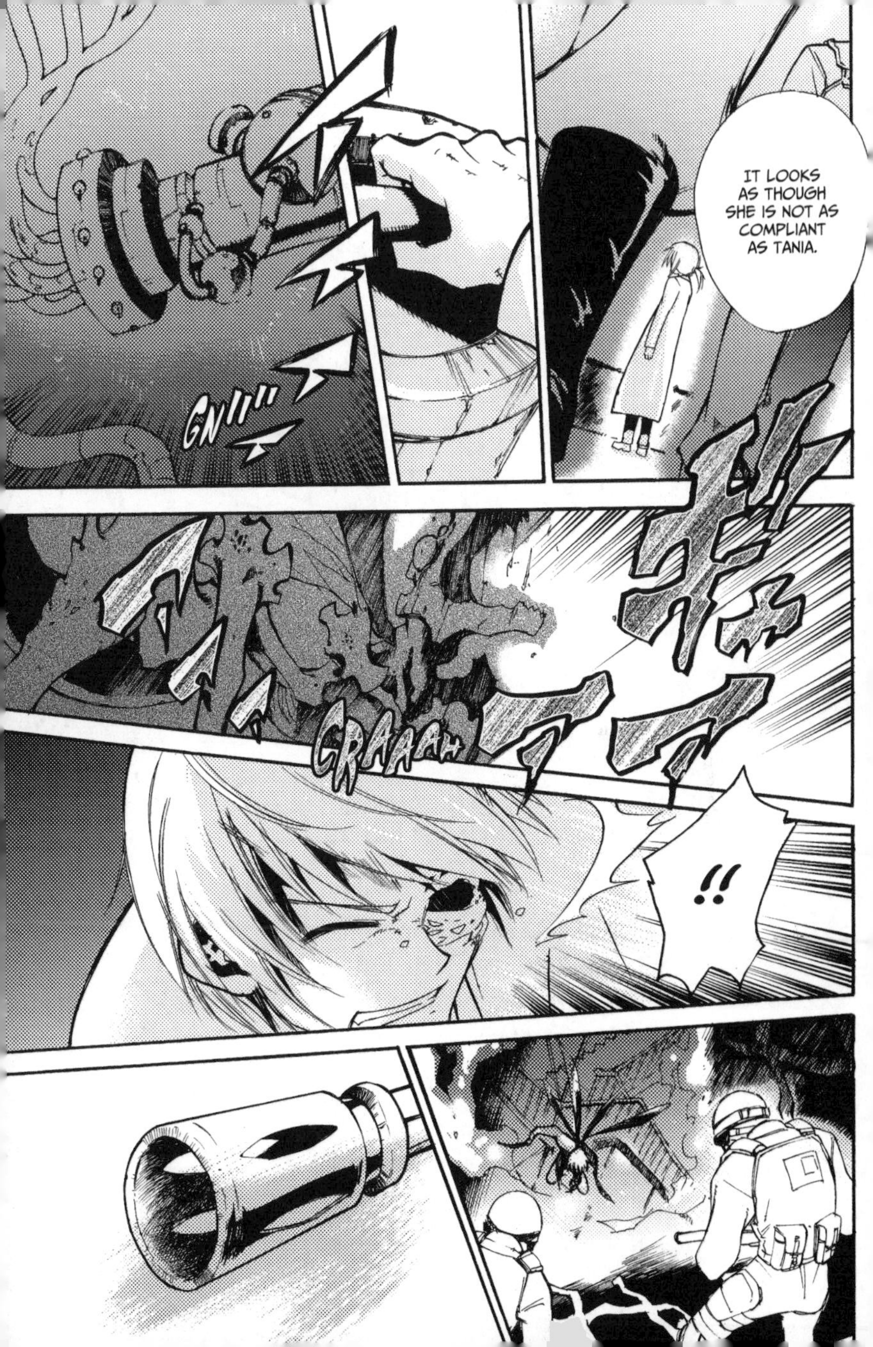
IT LOOKS AS THOUGH SHE IS NOT AS COMPLIANT AS TANIA.
GNII"
CRAAAH
!!

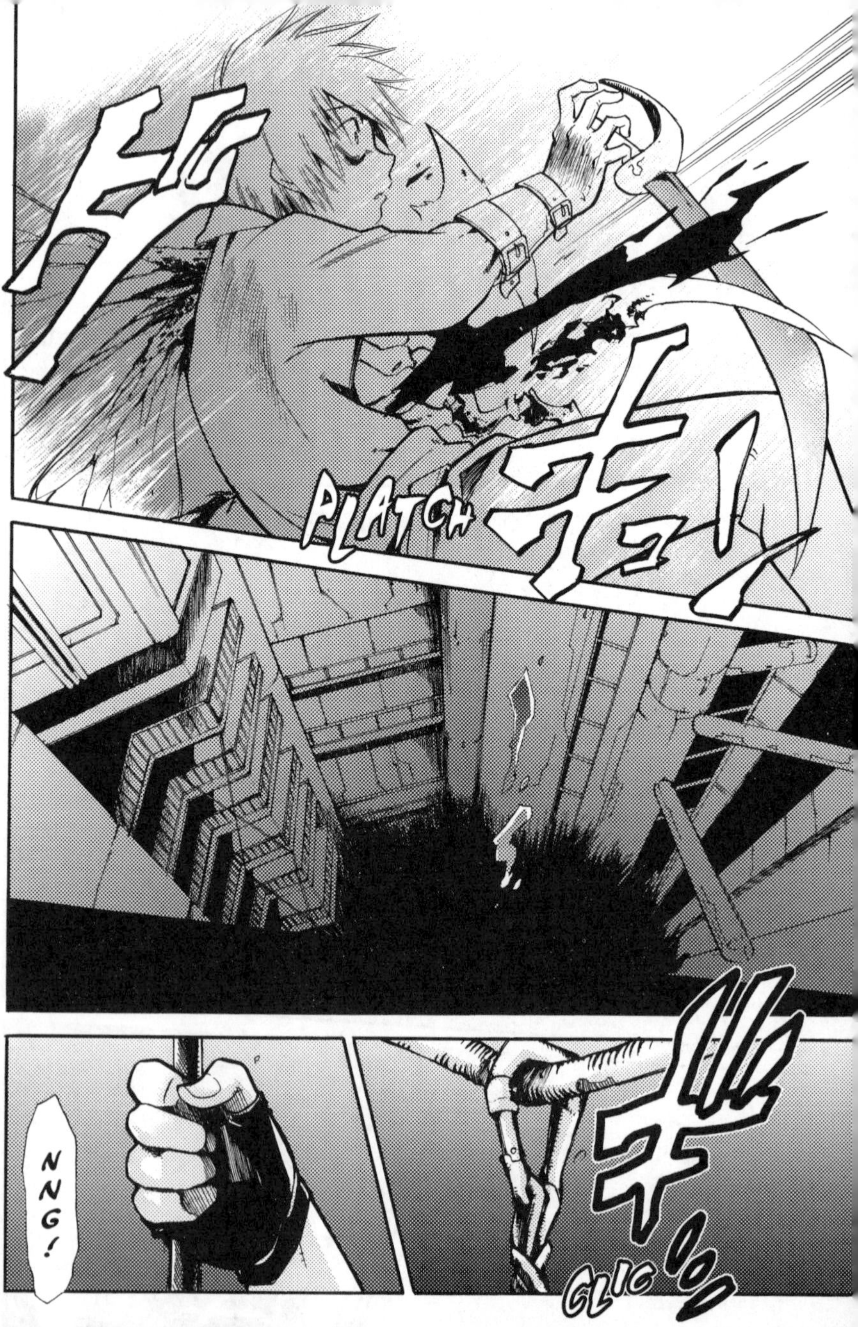
PLATCH
CLIC
NNG!

LOOK AT THE MESS YOU'VE GOTTEN ME INTO!

WHAT'S UP WITH THE CA-GASTERS?

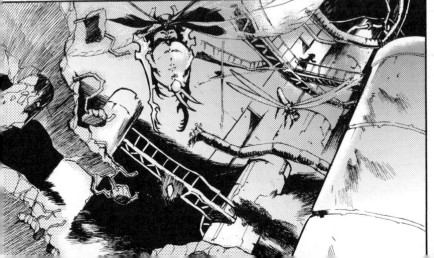

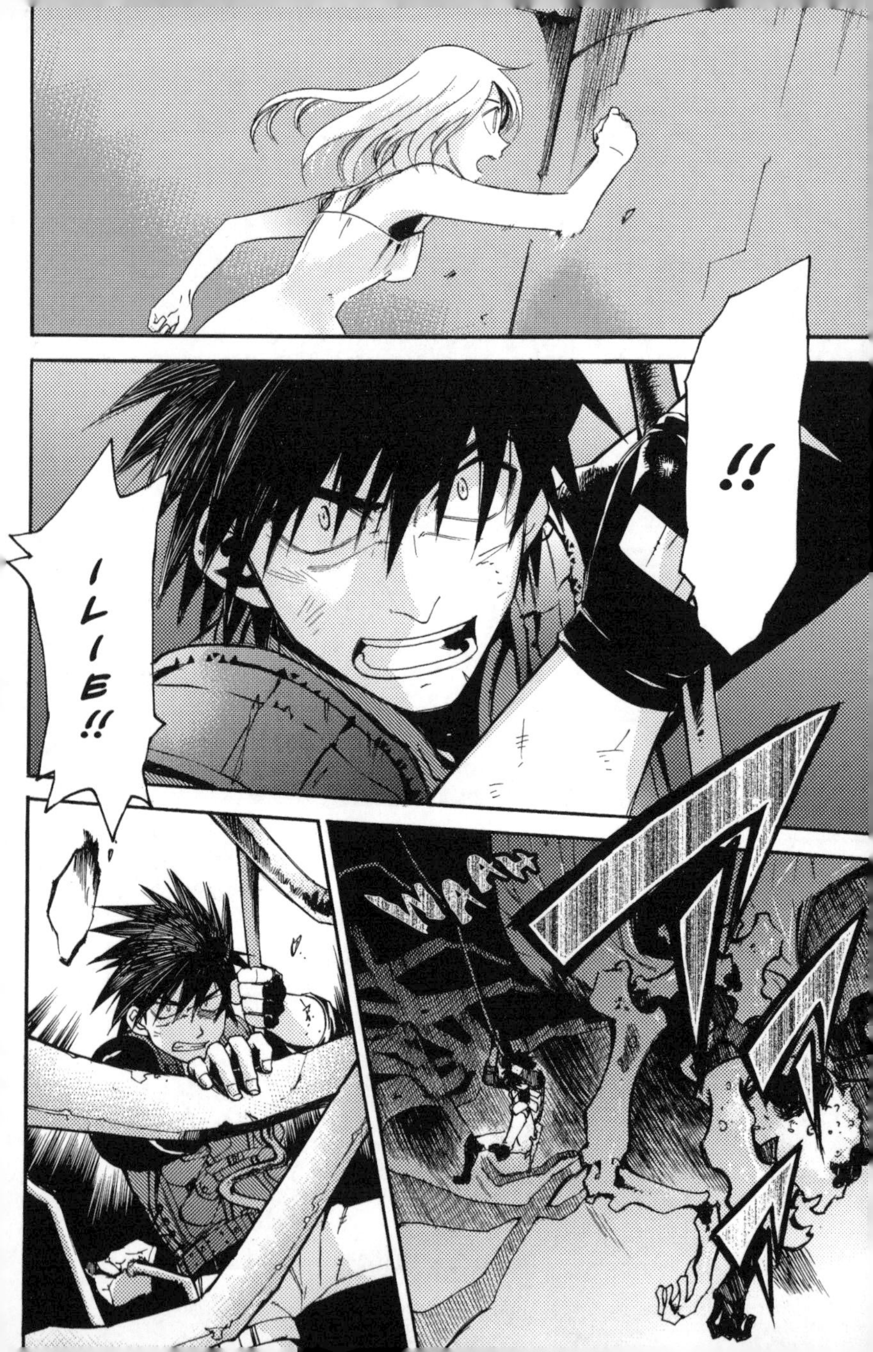
!!
ILLIE!!
WAAH

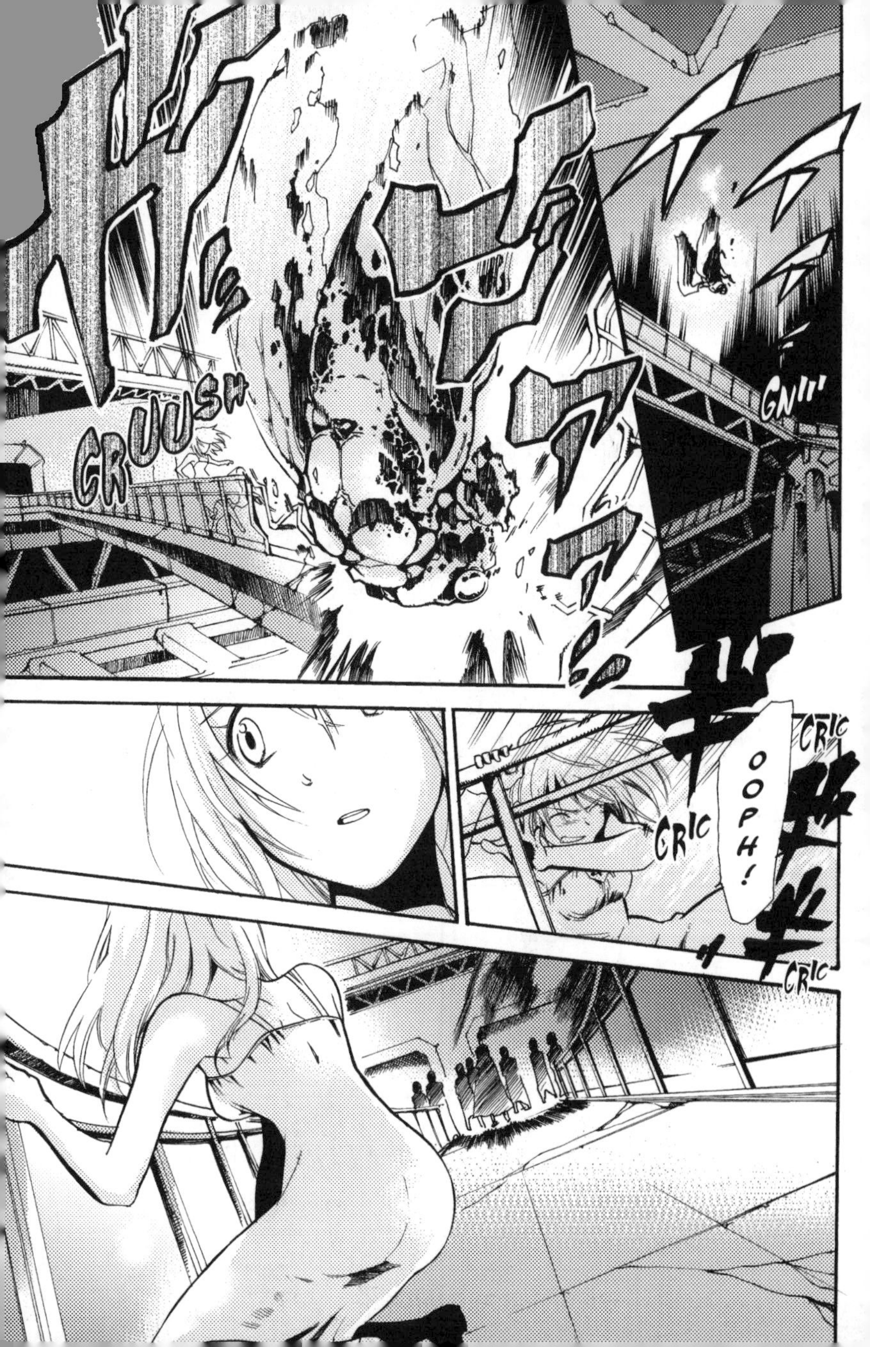
GNII'
CRUUUSH
CRIC
OOPH!
CRIC
CRIC

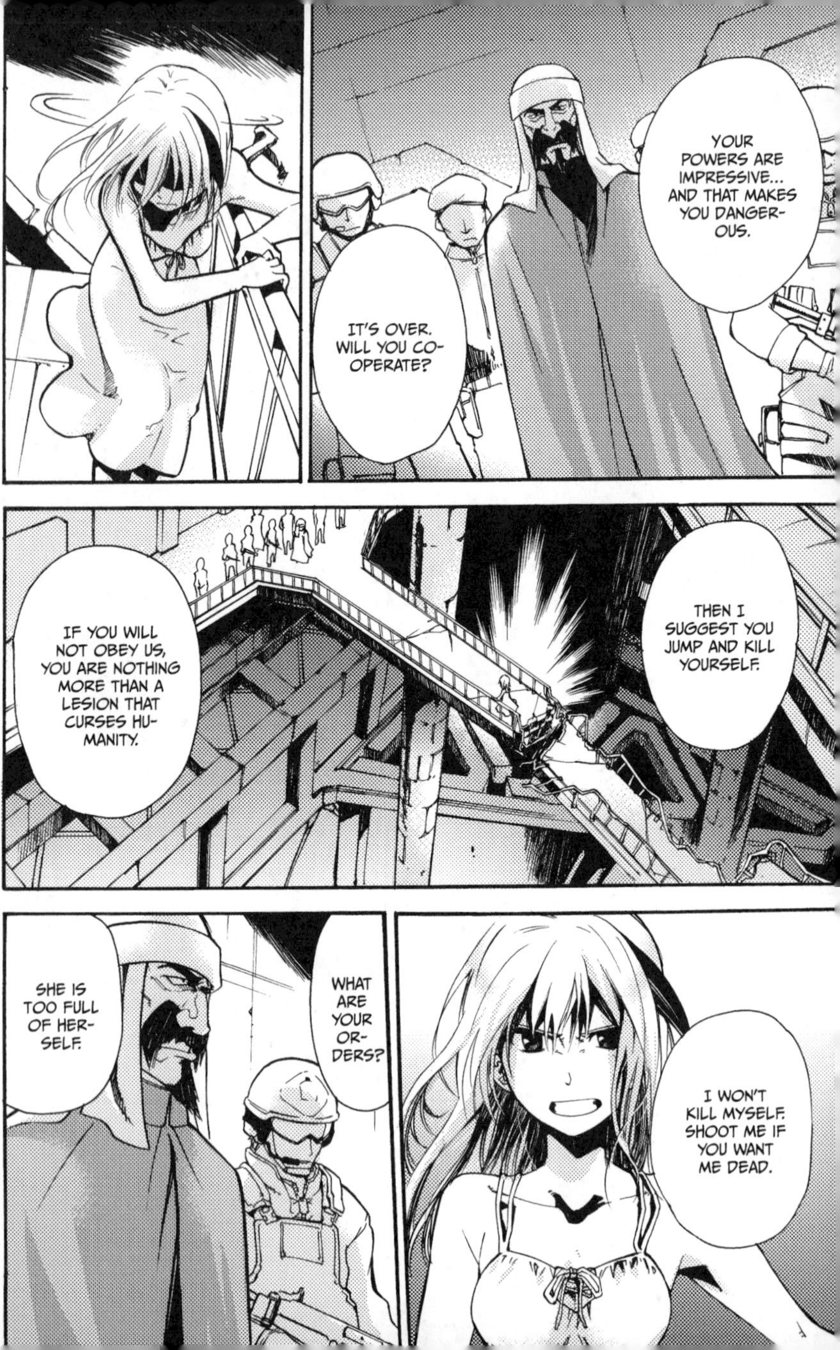
YOUR POWERS ARE IMPRESSIVE... AND THAT MAKES YOU DANGEROUS.
IT'S OVER. WILL YOU CO-OPERATE?
THEN I SUGGEST YOU JUMP AND KILL YOURSELF.
IF YOU WILL NOT OBEY US, YOU ARE NOTHING MORE THAN A LESION THAT CURSES HUMANITY.
I WON'T KILL MYSELF. SHOOT ME IF YOU WANT ME DEAD.
WHAT ARE YOUR ORDERS?
SHE IS TOO FULL OF HERSELF.

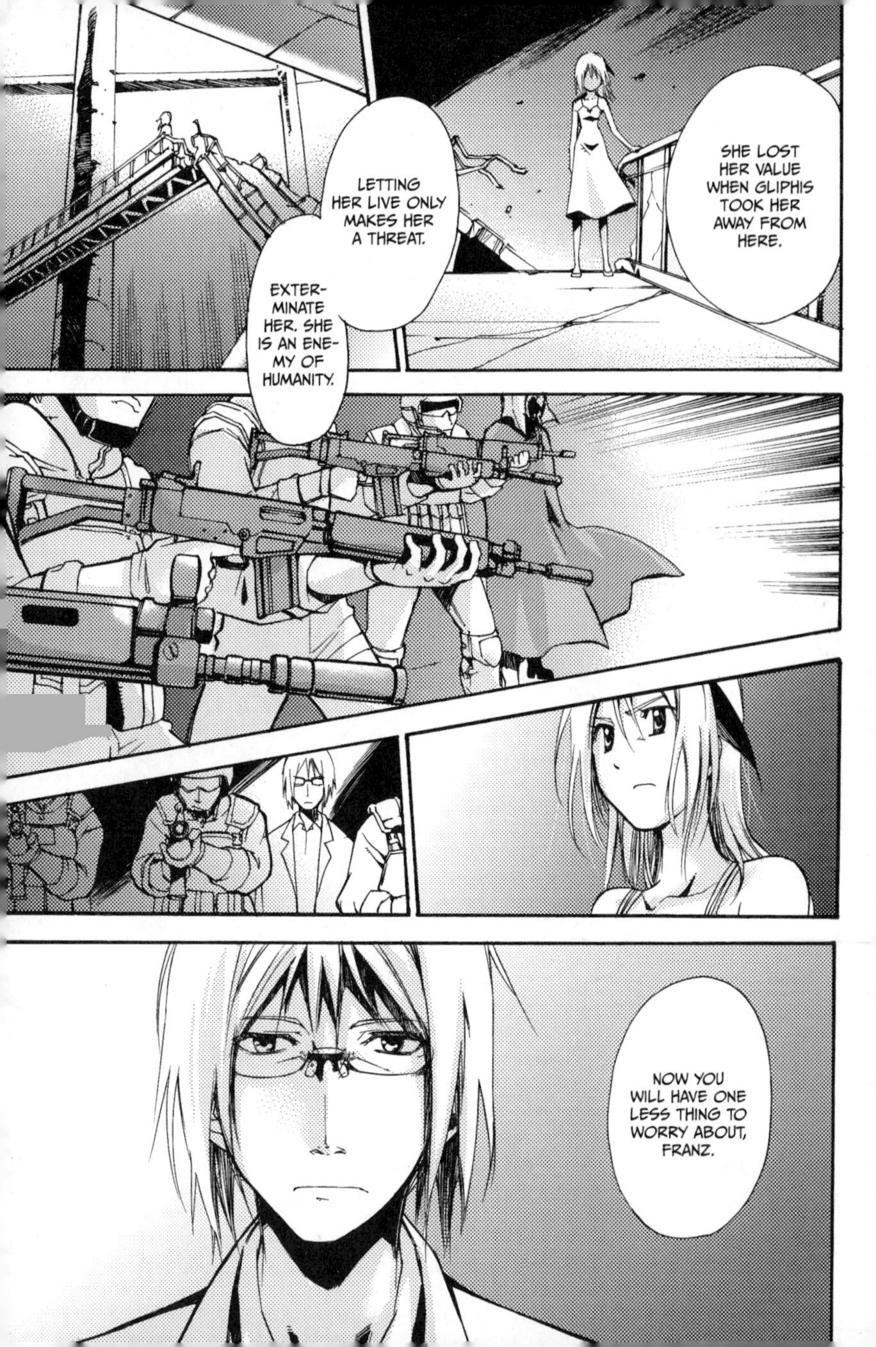
SHE LOST HER VALUE WHEN GLIPHIS TOOK HER AWAY FROM HERE.
LETTING HER LIVE ONLY MAKES HER A THREAT.
EXTER-MINATE HER. SHE IS AN ENE-MY OF HUMANITY.
NOW YOU WILL HAVE ONE LESS THING TO WORRY ABOUT, FRANZ.

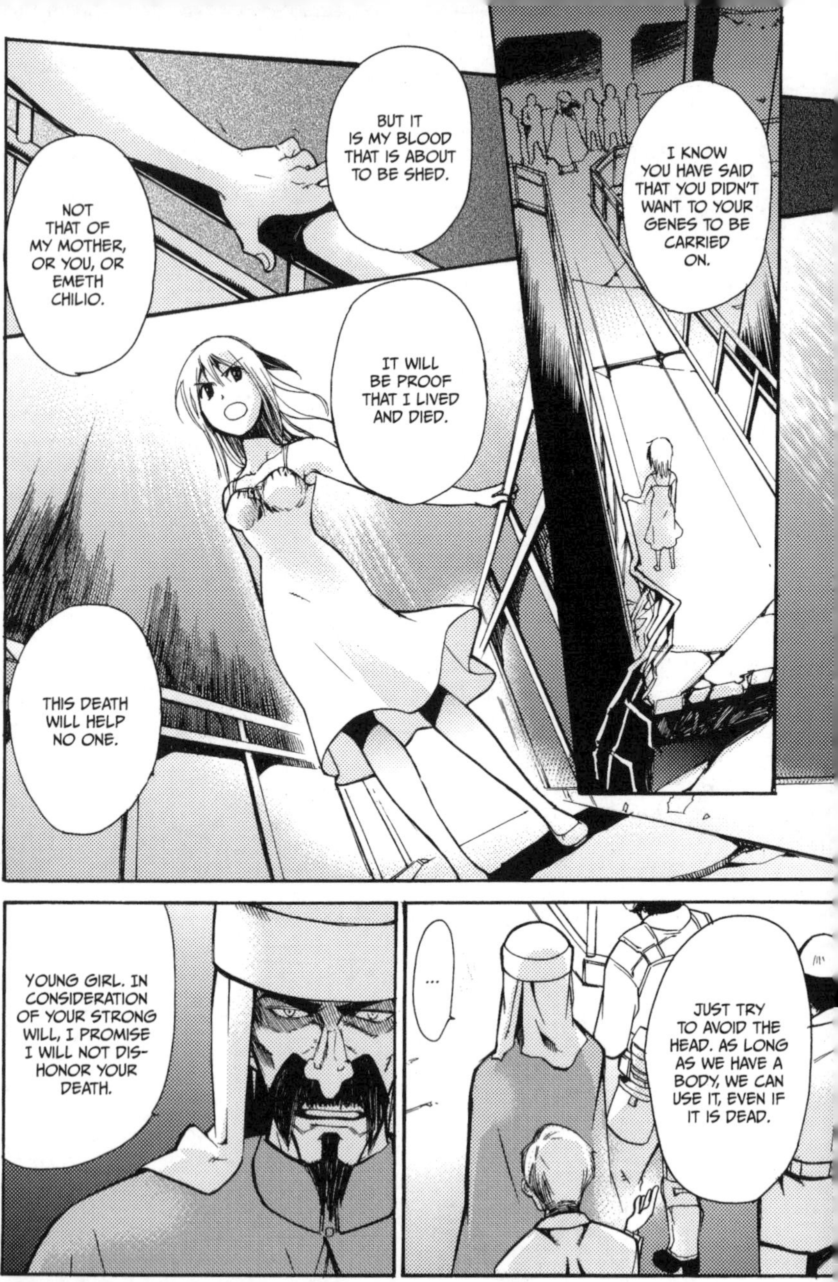
I KNOW YOU HAVE SAID THAT YOU DIDN'T WANT TO YOUR GENES TO BE CARRIED ON.
BUT IT IS MY BLOOD THAT IS ABOUT TO BE SHED.
NOT THAT OF MY MOTHER, OR YOU, OR EMETH CHILIO.
IT WILL BE PROOF THAT I LIVED AND DIED.
THIS DEATH WILL HELP NO ONE.
JUST TRY TO AVOID THE HEAD. AS LONG AS WE HAVE A BODY, WE CAN USE IT, EVEN IF IT IS DEAD.
...
YOUNG GIRL. IN CONSIDERATION OF YOUR STRONG WILL, I PROMISE I WILL NOT DISHONOR YOUR DEATH.

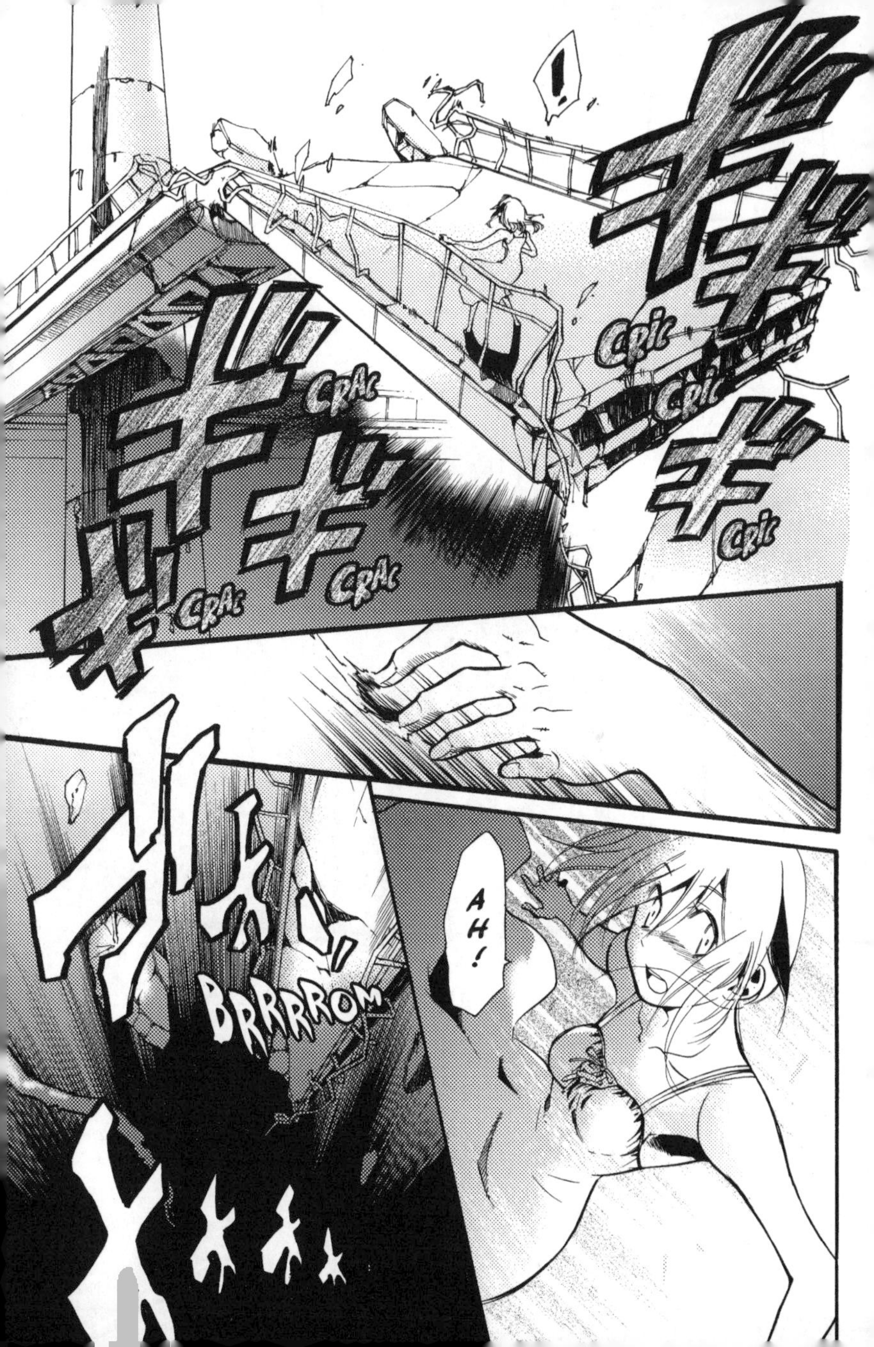
!
ギギギ
CRIC
CRIC
ギギ
CRIC
ギギギ
CRAC
CRAC
CRAC
AH!
!
BRRRROM

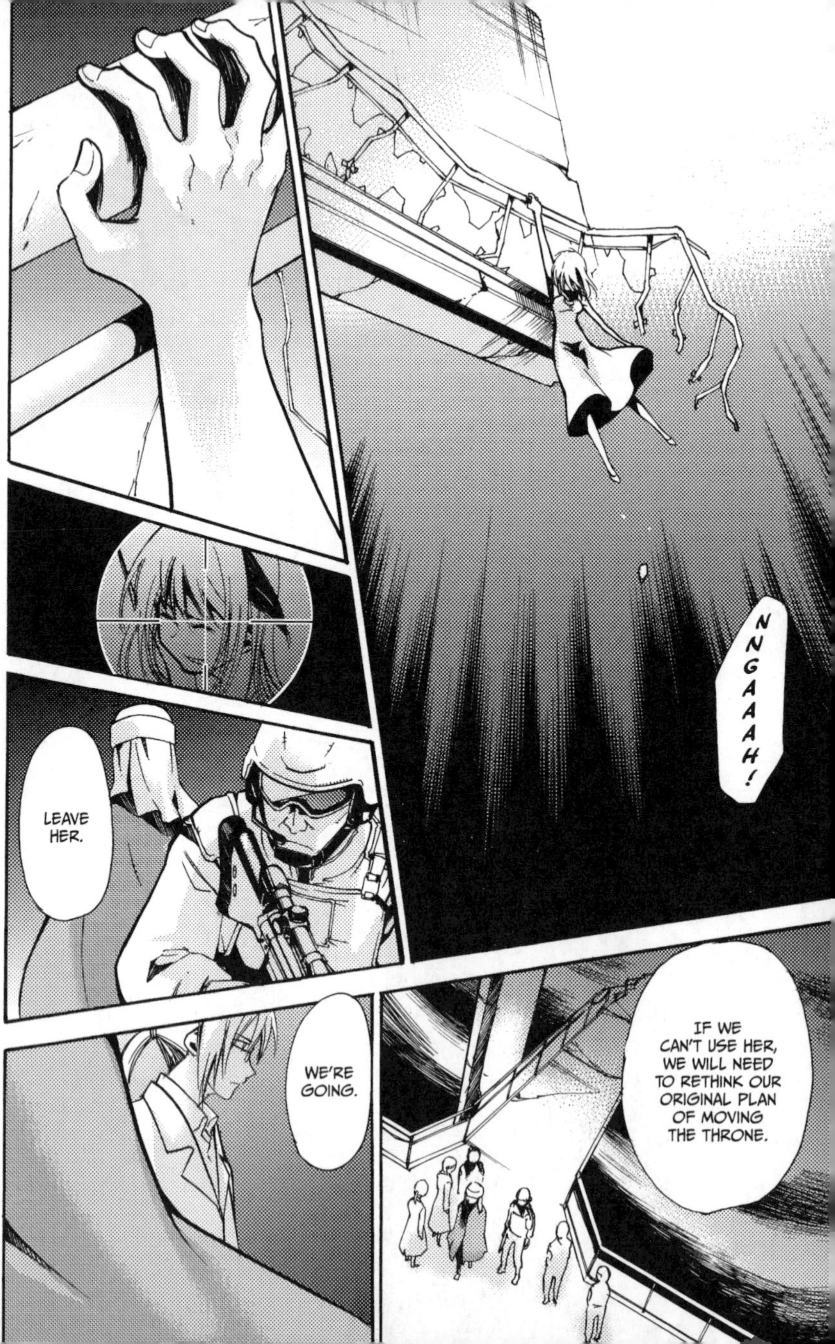
NNGAAAH!
LEAVE HER.
IF WE CAN'T USE HER, WE WILL NEED TO RETHINK OUR ORIGINAL PLAN OF MOVING THE THRONE.
WE'RE GOING.

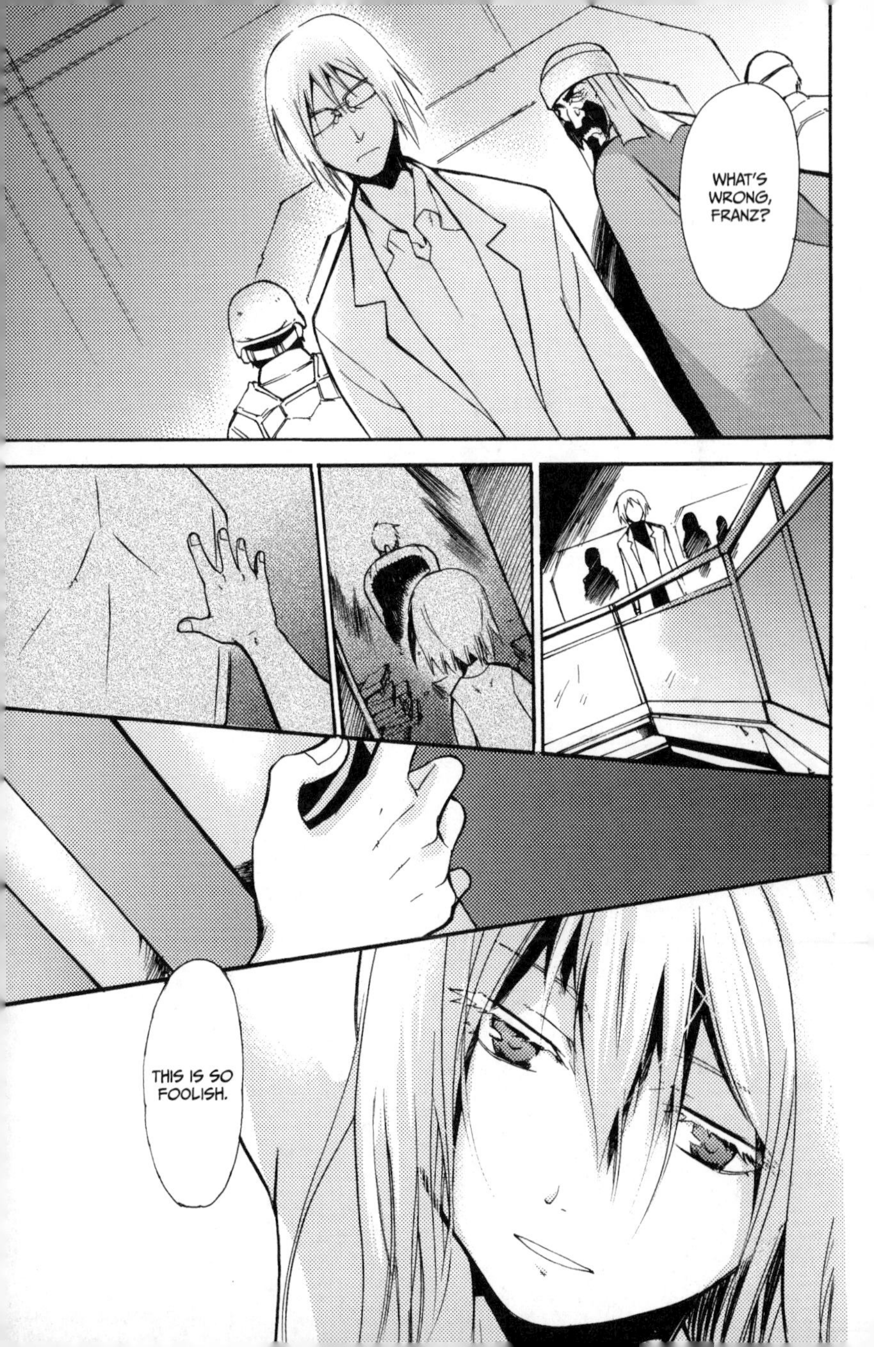
WHAT'S WRONG, FRANZ?
THIS IS SO FOOLISH.

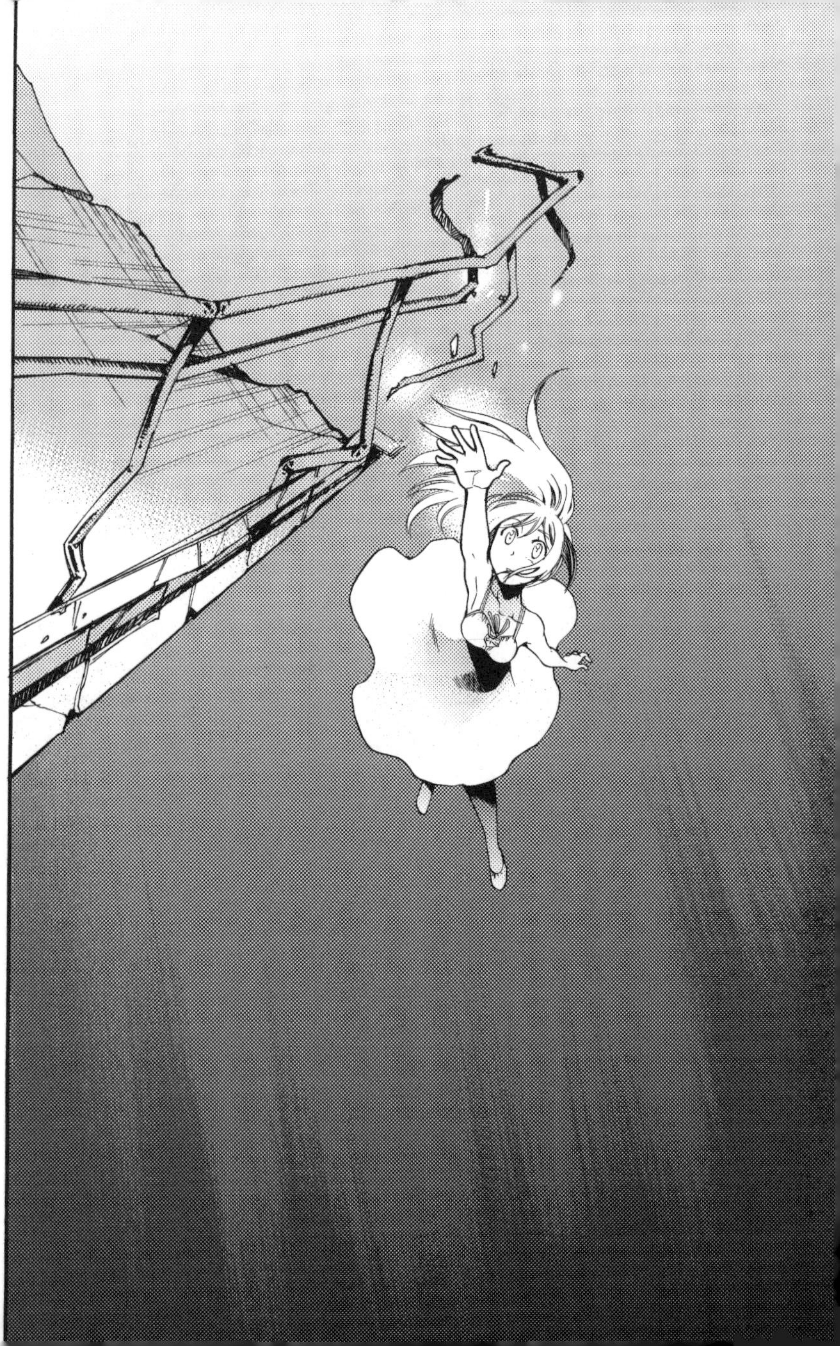

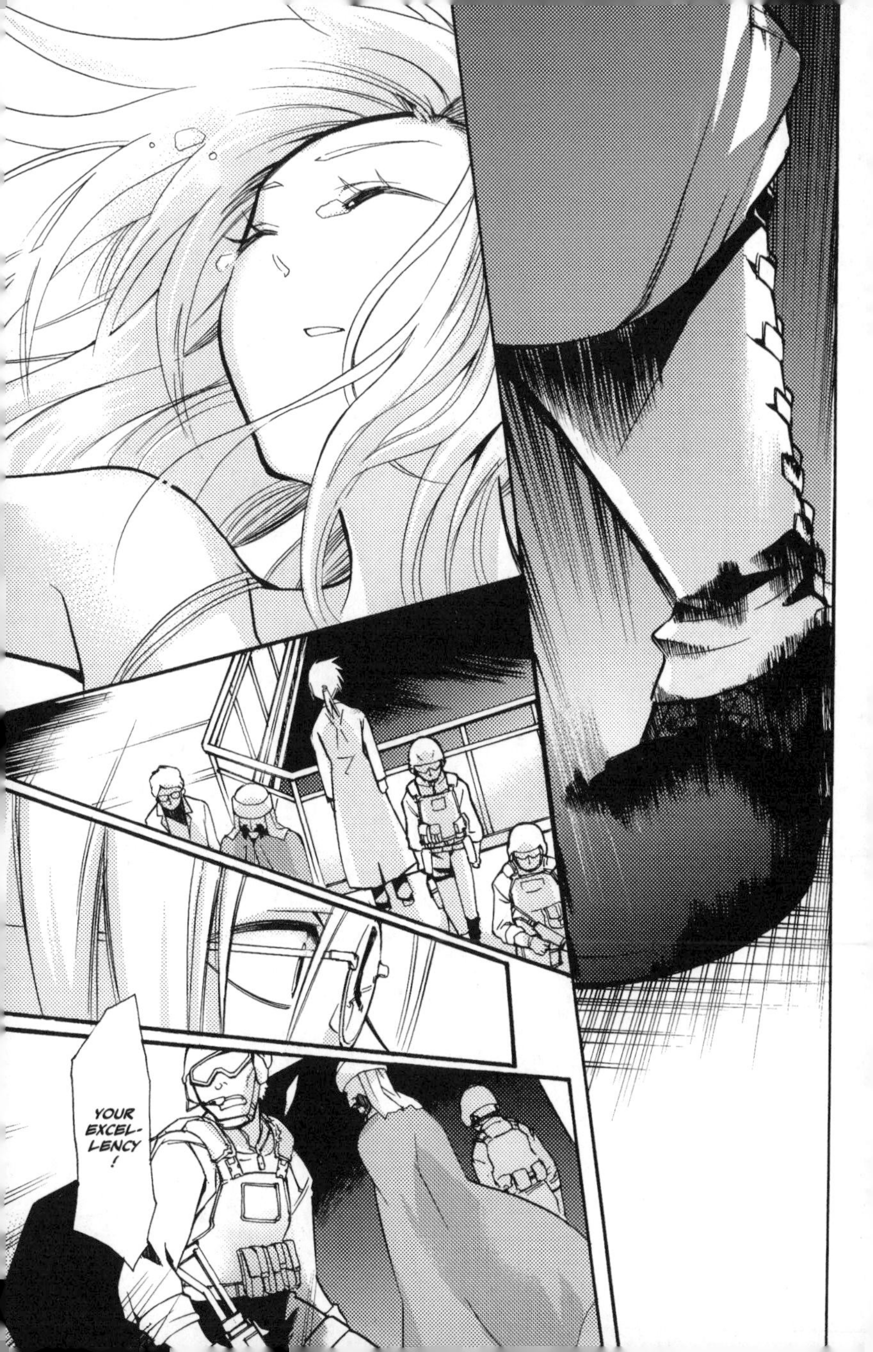
YOUR EXCEL-LENCY!

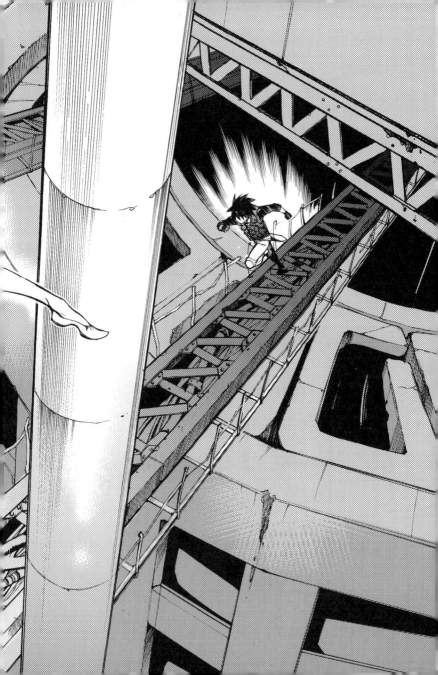

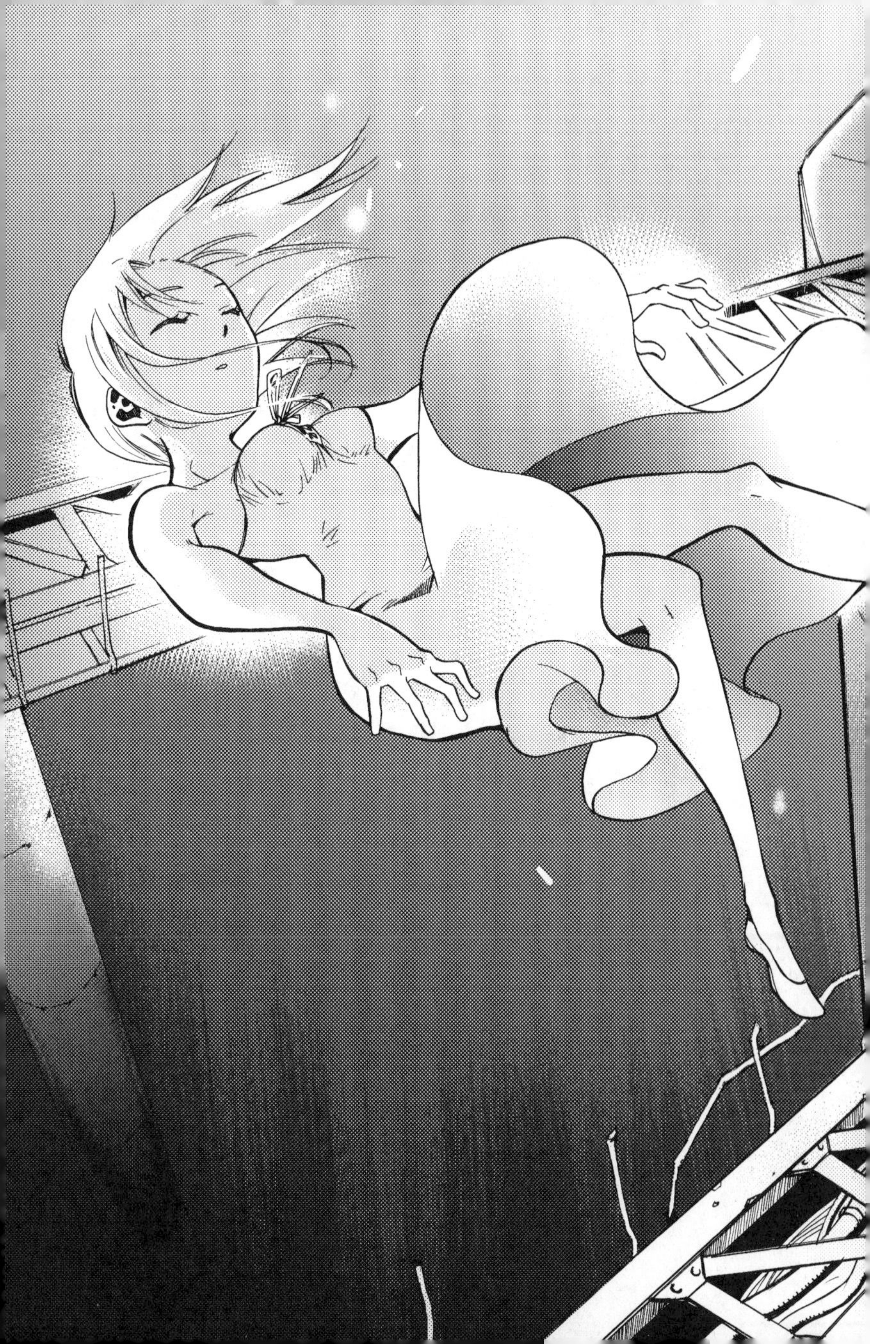

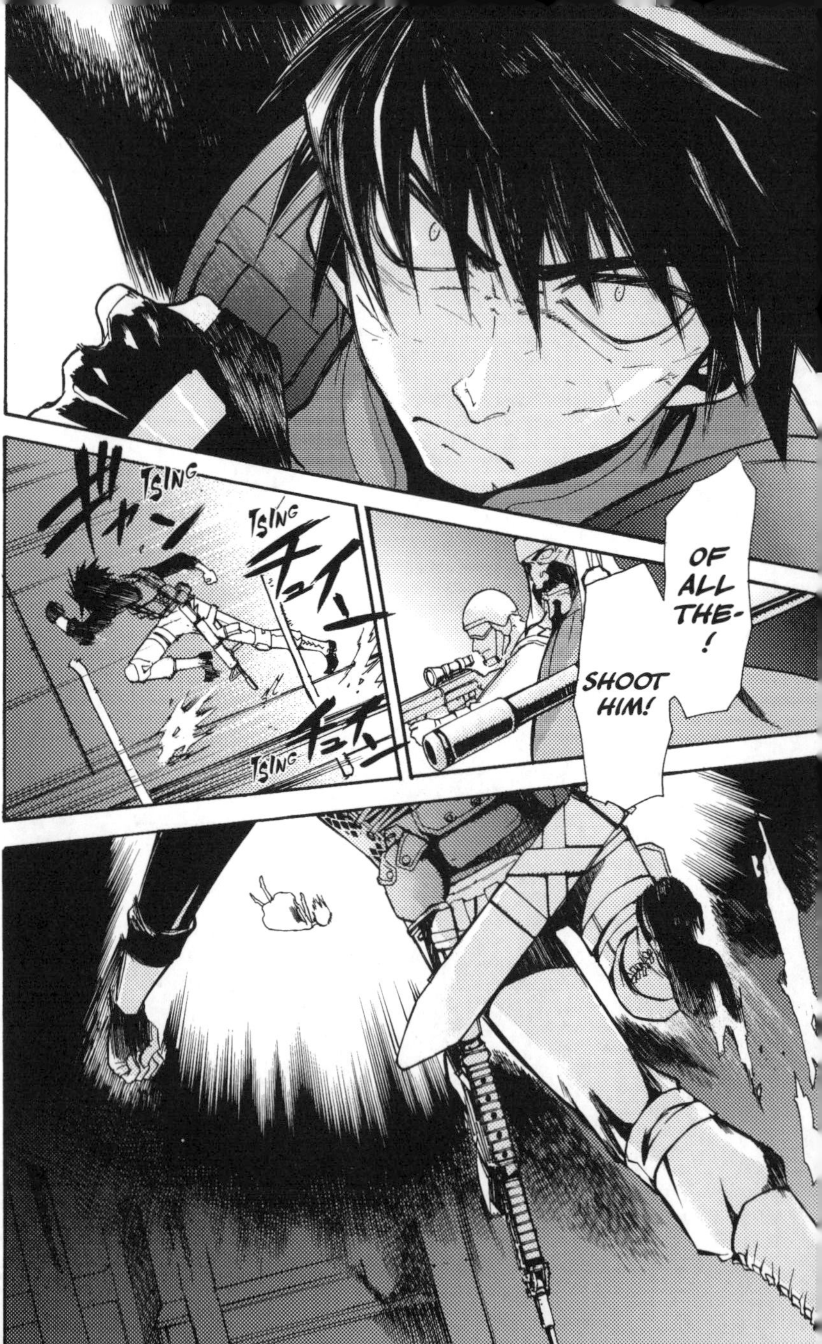
OF ALL THE-!
SHOOT HIM!
TSING
ギャン
TSING
TSING

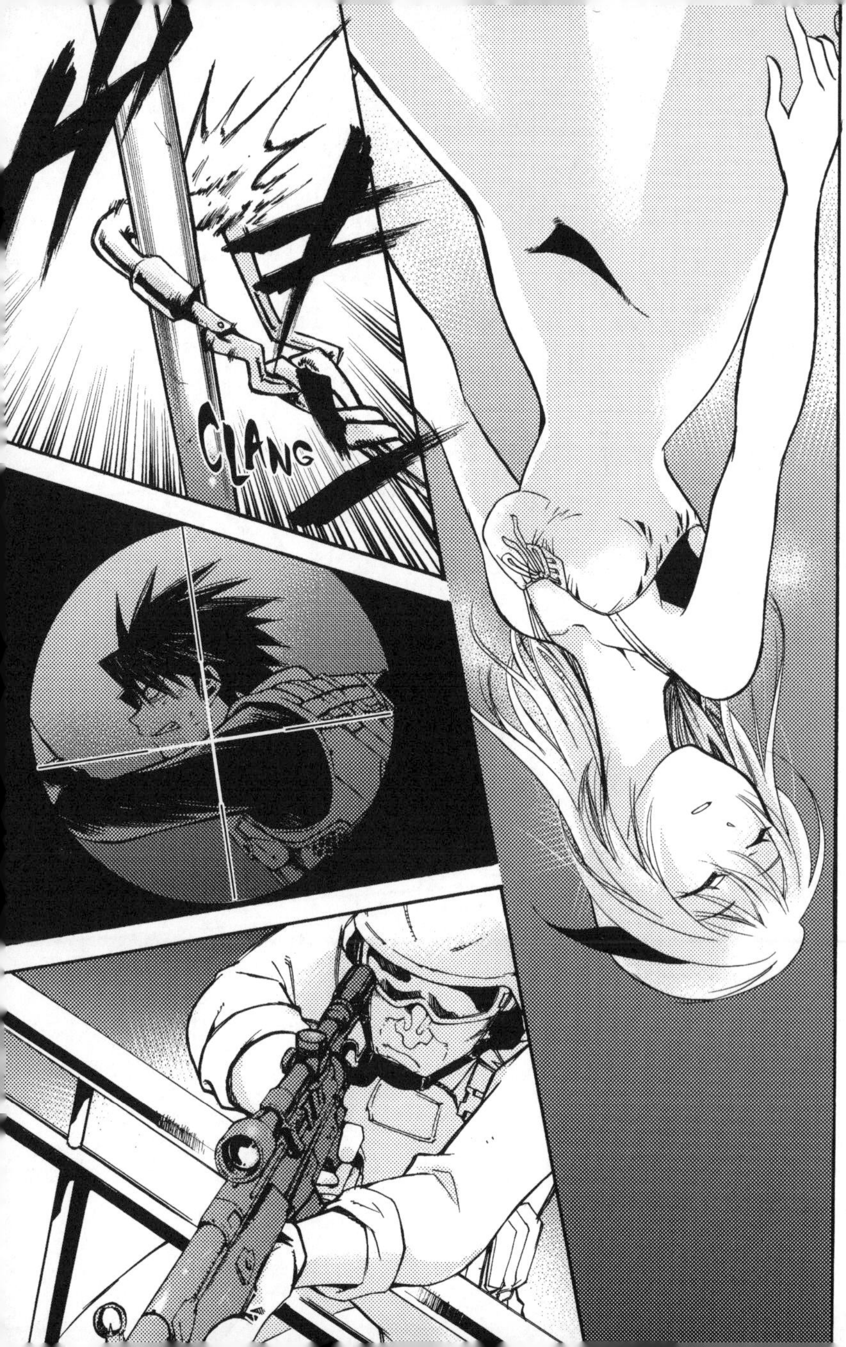
CLANG

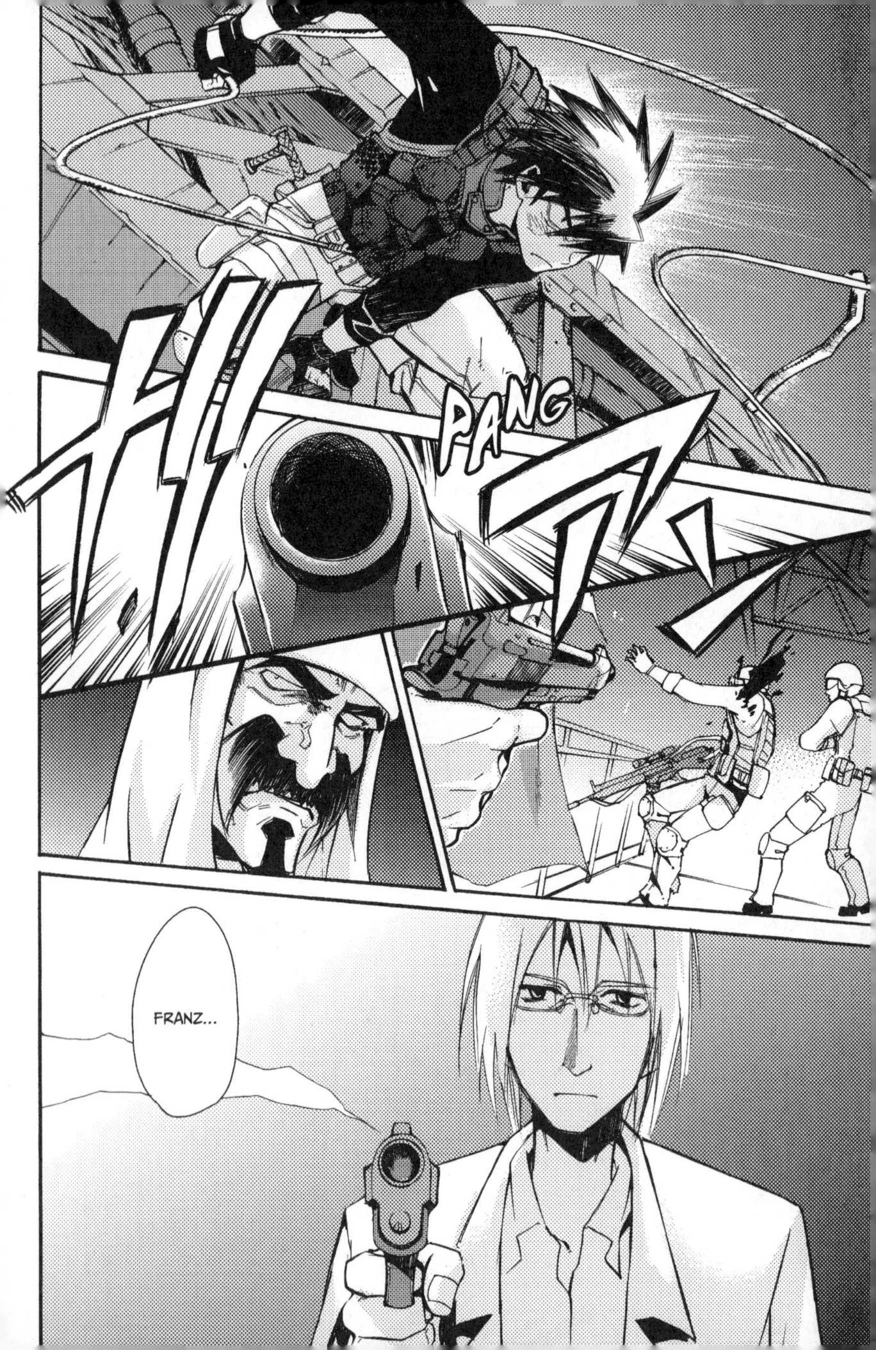
PANG
FRANZ...

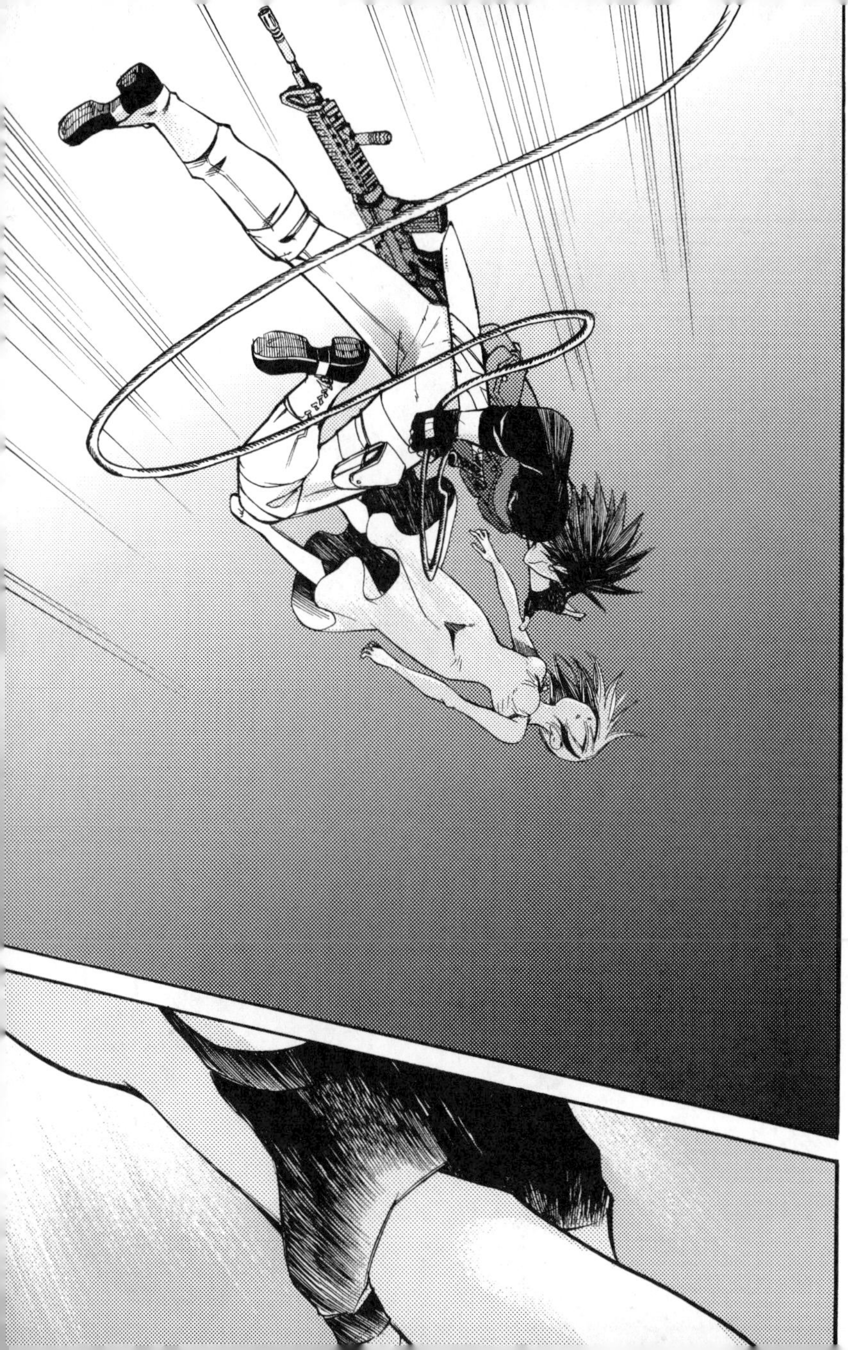

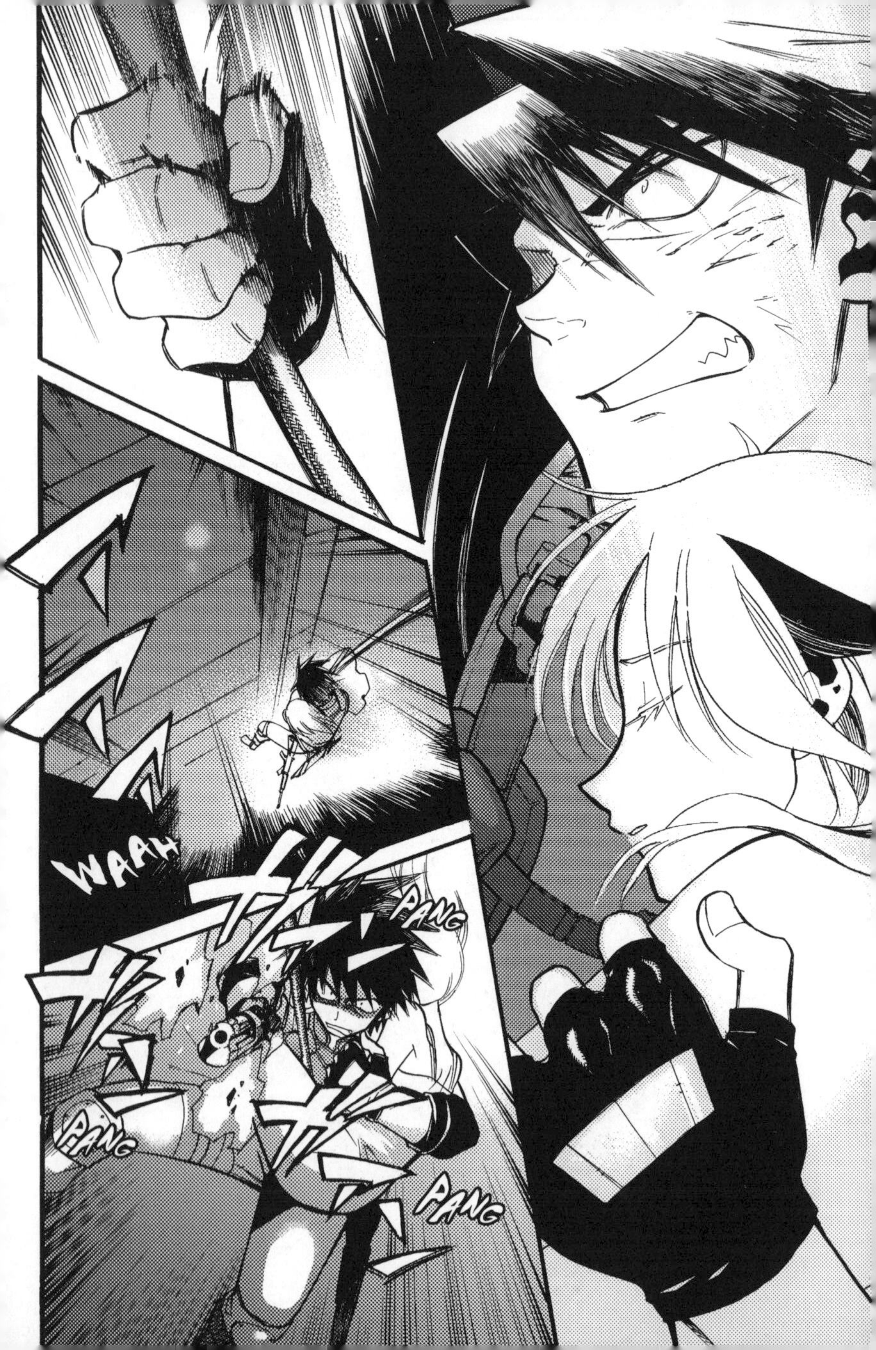
WAAH
PANG
PANG
PANG

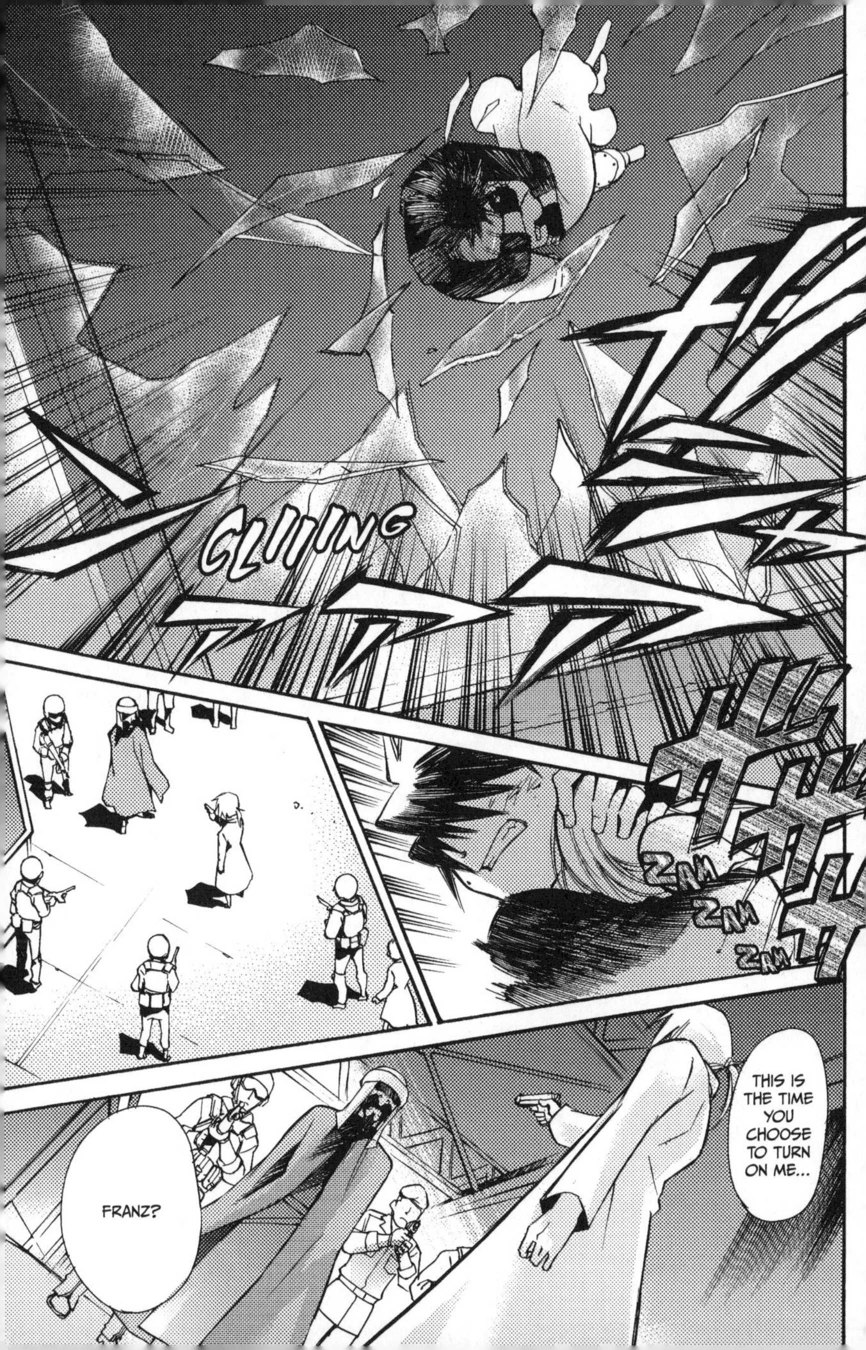
CLIIING
ZAM
ZAM
ZAM
THIS IS THE TIME YOU CHOOSE TO TURN ON ME...
FRANZ?

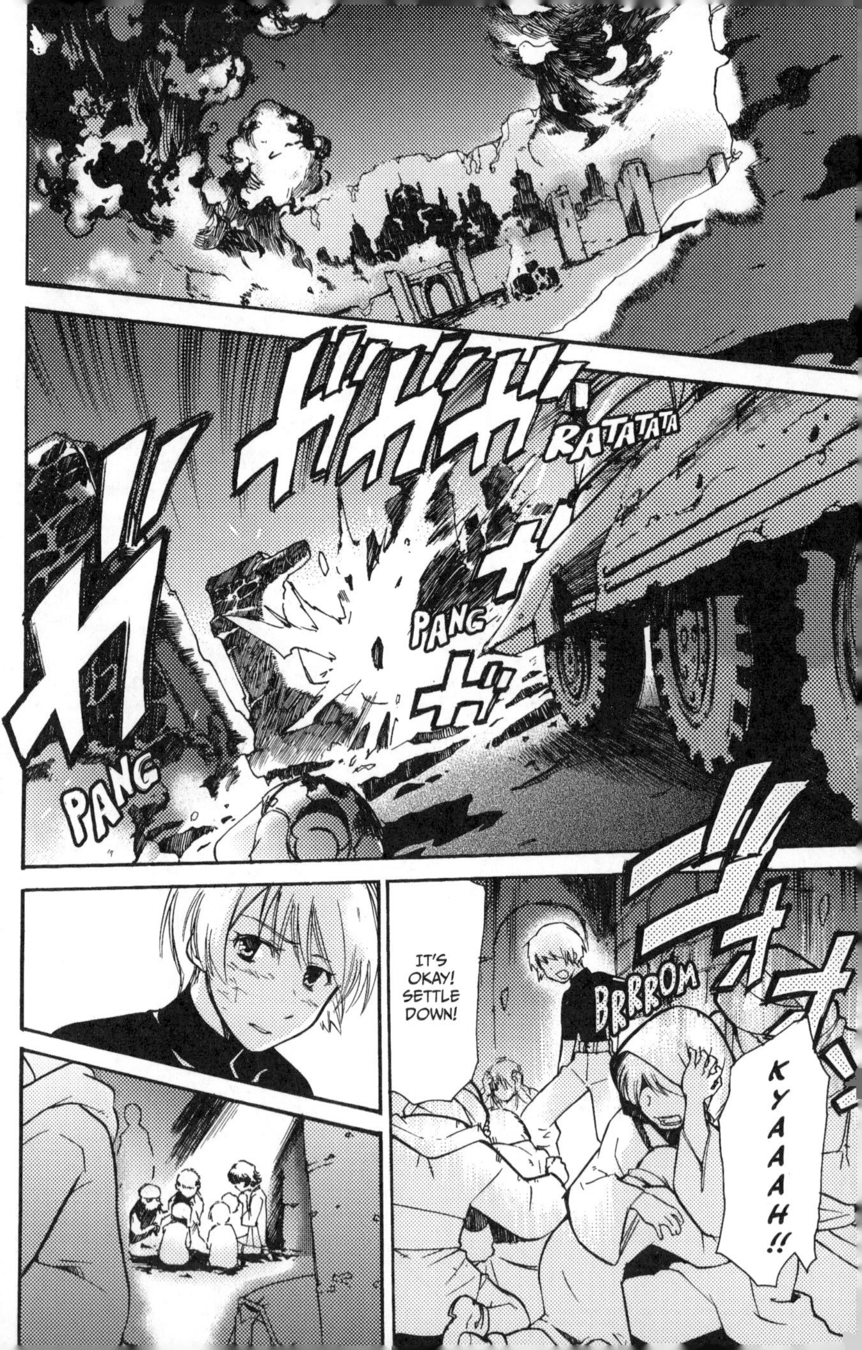
RATATATA
PANG
PANG
BRRROM
KYAAAAH!!
IT'S OKAY! SETTLE DOWN!

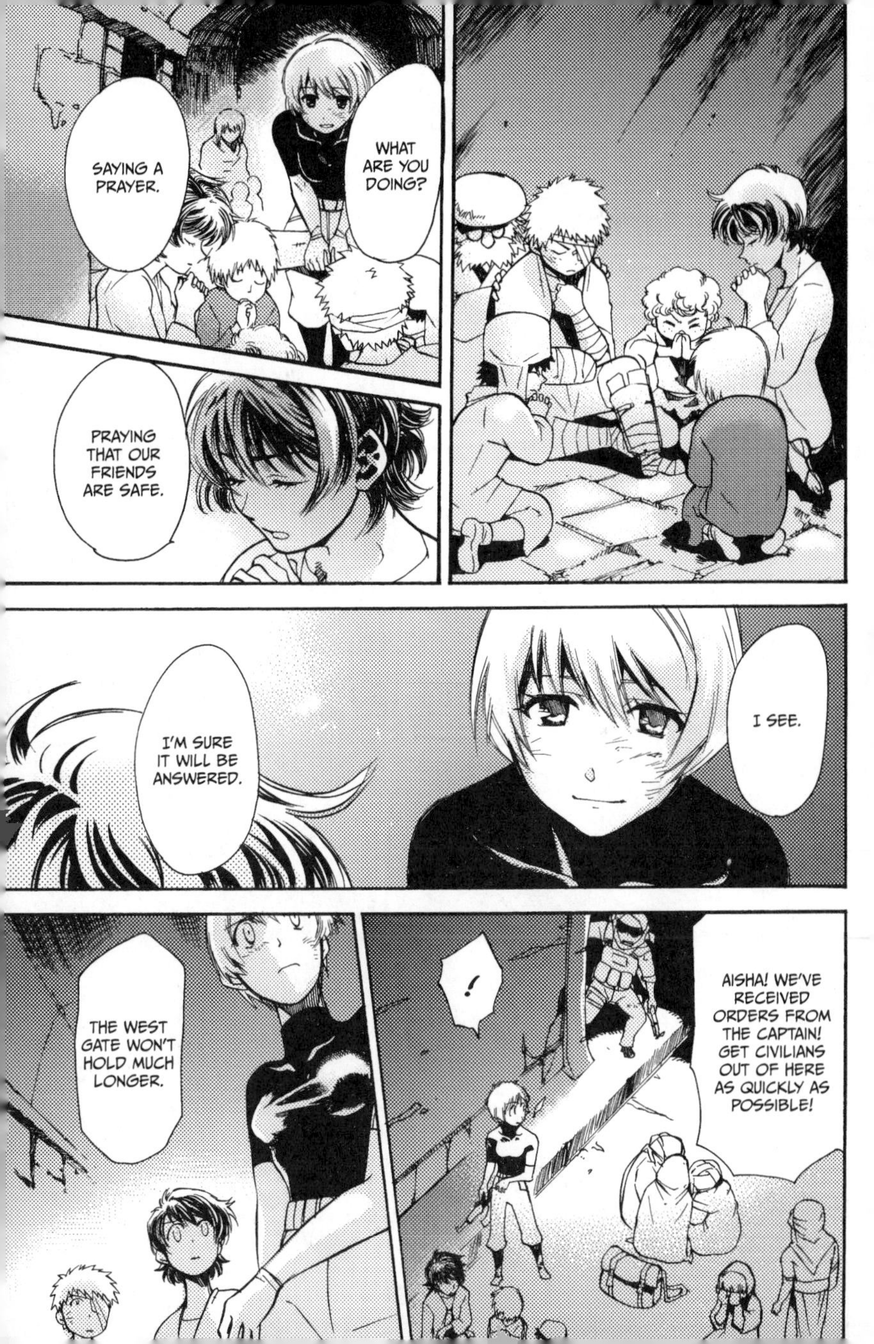
WHAT ARE YOU DOING?
SAYING A PRAYER.
PRAYING THAT OUR FRIENDS ARE SAFE.
I SEE.
I'M SURE IT WILL BE ANSWERED.
AISHA! WE'VE RECEIVED ORDERS FROM THE CAPTAIN! GET CIVILIANS OUT OF HERE AS QUICKLY AS POSSIBLE!
!
THE WEST GATE WON'T HOLD MUCH LONGER.

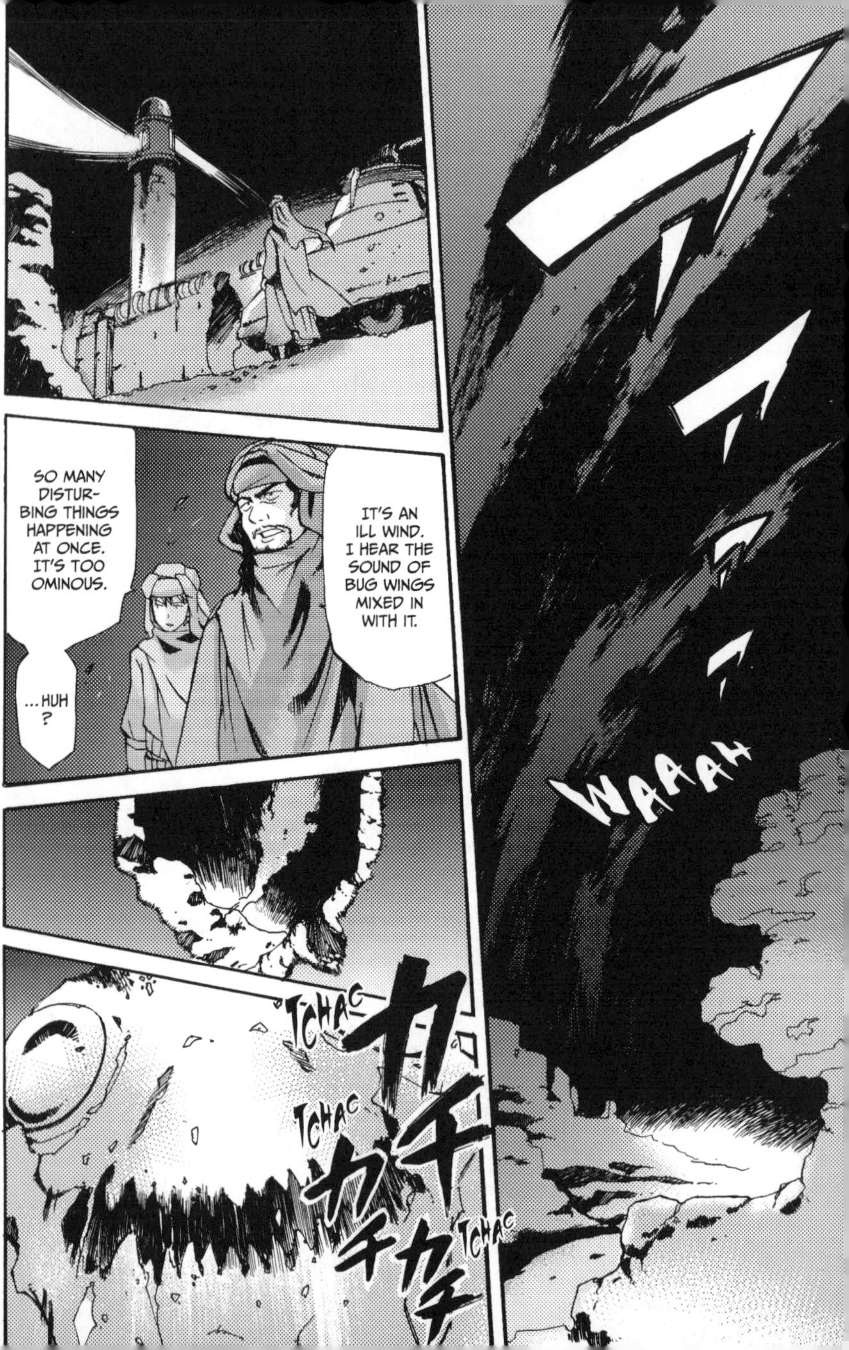
WAAAH
IT'S AN ILL WIND. I HEAR THE SOUND OF BUG WINGS MIXED IN WITH IT.
SO MANY DISTUR-BING THINGS HAPPENING AT ONCE. IT'S TOO OMINOUS.
...HUH ?
TCHAC
カチ
TCHAC
カチ
TCHAC

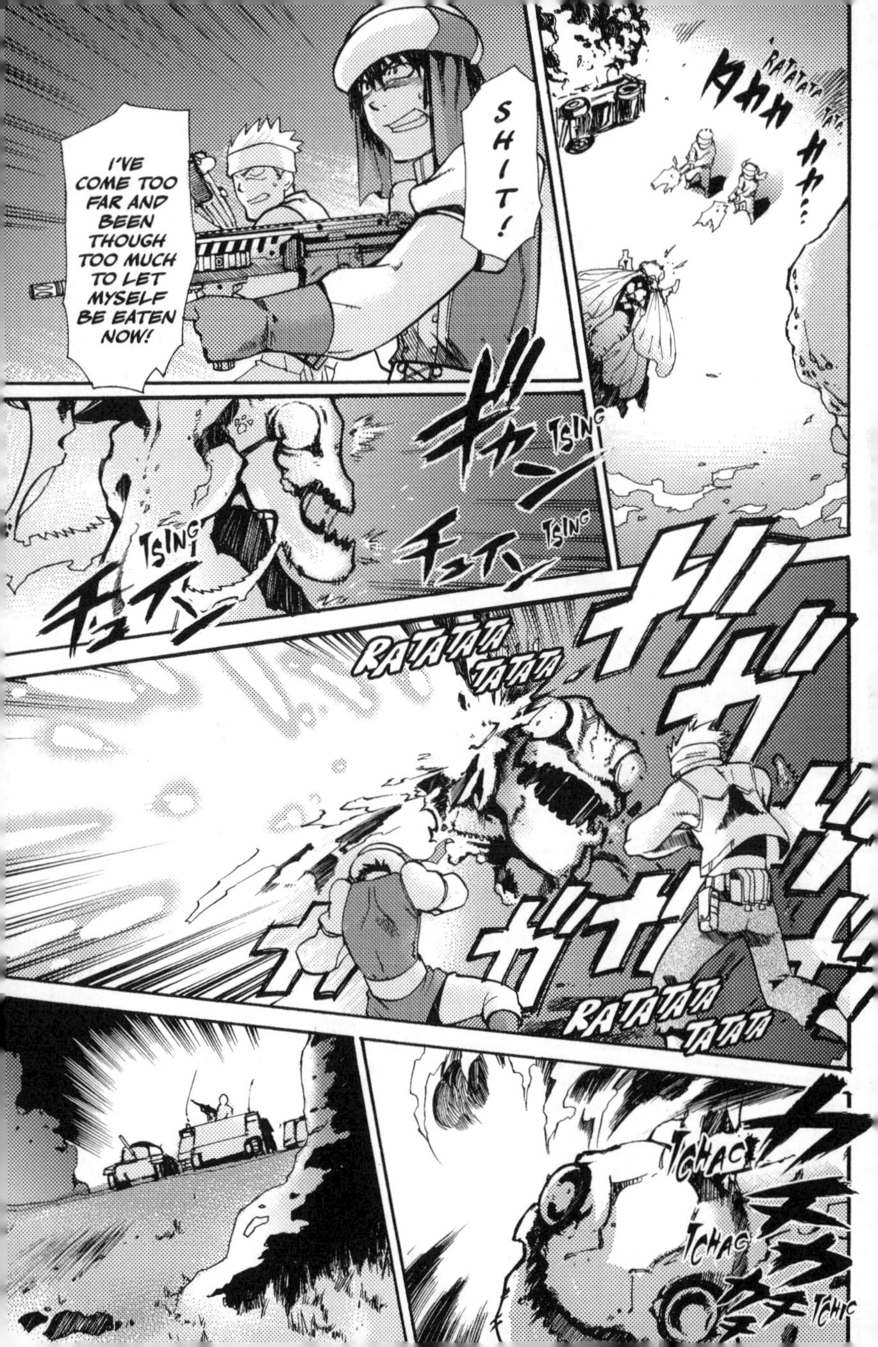
RATATATA TATA
SHIT!
I'VE COME TOO FAR AND BEEN THOUGH TOO MUCH TO LET MYSELF BE EATEN NOW!
TSING
TSING
TSING
RATATATA TATATA
RATATATA TATATA
TCHAC
TCHAC
TCHIC

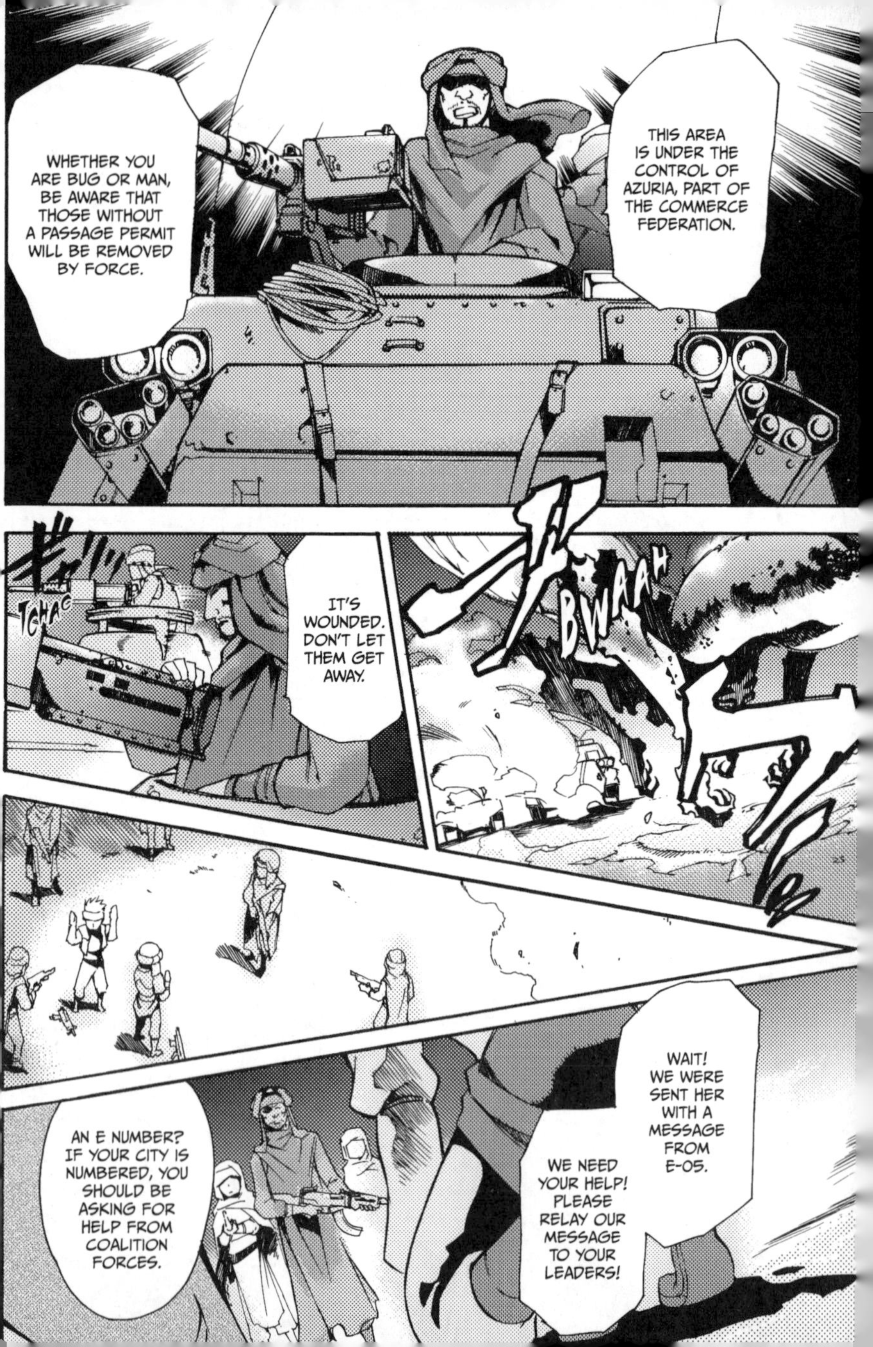
THIS AREA IS UNDER THE CONTROL OF AZURIA, PART OF THE COMMERCE FEDERATION.
WHETHER YOU ARE BUG OR MAN, BE AWARE THAT THOSE WITHOUT A PASSAGE PERMIT WILL BE REMOVED BY FORCE.
BWAAH
IT'S WOUNDED. DON'T LET THEM GET AWAY.
TCHAC
WAIT! WE WERE SENT HER WITH A MESSAGE FROM E-05.
WE NEED YOUR HELP! PLEASE RELAY OUR MESSAGE TO YOUR LEADERS!
AN E NUMBER? IF YOUR CITY IS NUMBERED, YOU SHOULD BE ASKING FOR HELP FROM COALITION FORCES.

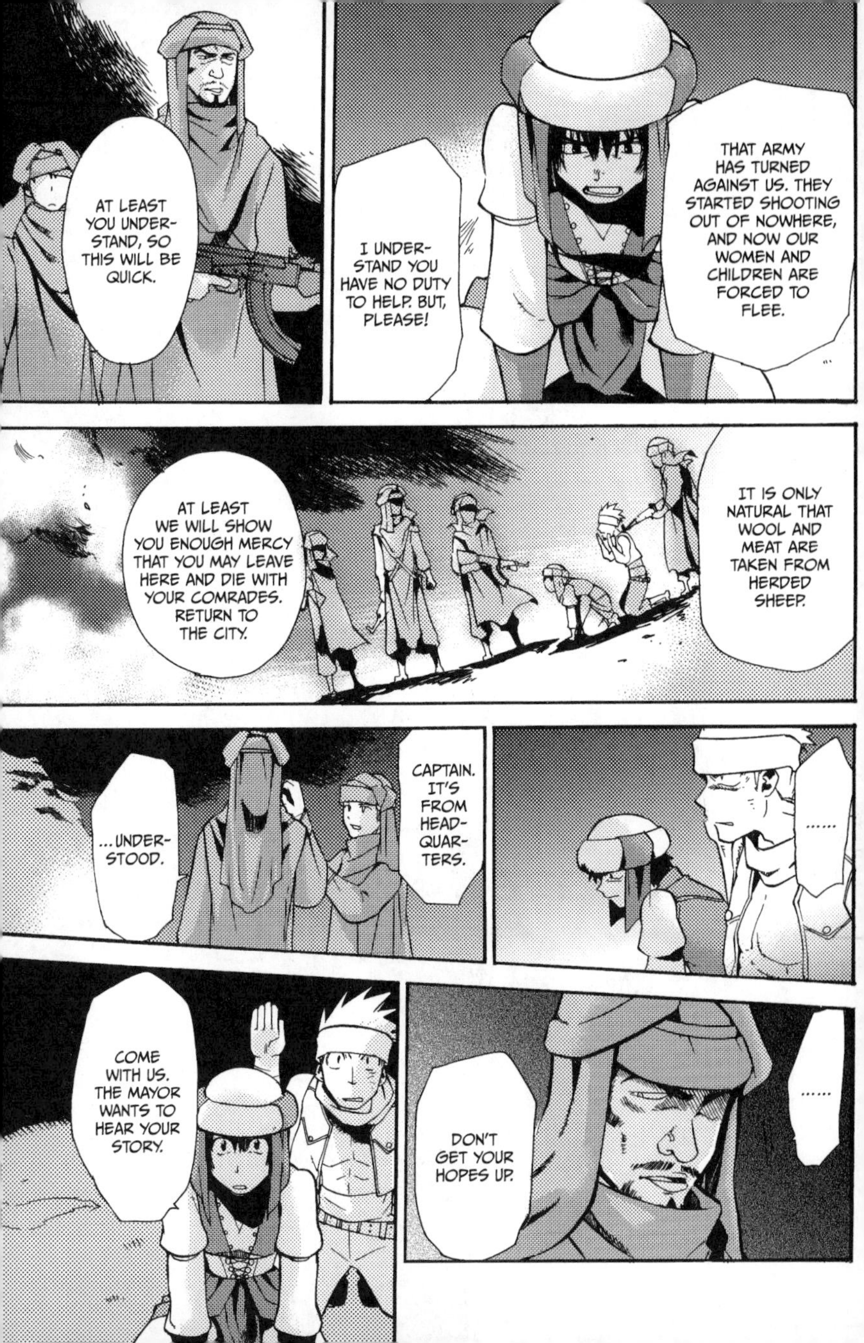
THAT ARMY HAS TURNED AGAINST US. THEY STARTED SHOOTING OUT OF NOWHERE, AND NOW OUR WOMEN AND CHILDREN ARE FORCED TO FLEE.
I UNDER-STAND YOU HAVE NO DUTY TO HELP. BUT, PLEASE!
AT LEAST YOU UNDER-STAND, SO THIS WILL BE QUICK.
IT IS ONLY NATURAL THAT WOOL AND MEAT ARE TAKEN FROM HERDED SHEEP.
AT LEAST WE WILL SHOW YOU ENOUGH MERCY THAT YOU MAY LEAVE HERE AND DIE WITH YOUR COMRADES. RETURN TO THE CITY.
......
CAPTAIN. IT'S FROM HEAD-QUAR-TERS.
...UNDER-STOOD.
......
DON'T GET YOUR HOPES UP.
COME WITH US. THE MAYOR WANTS TO HEAR YOUR STORY.

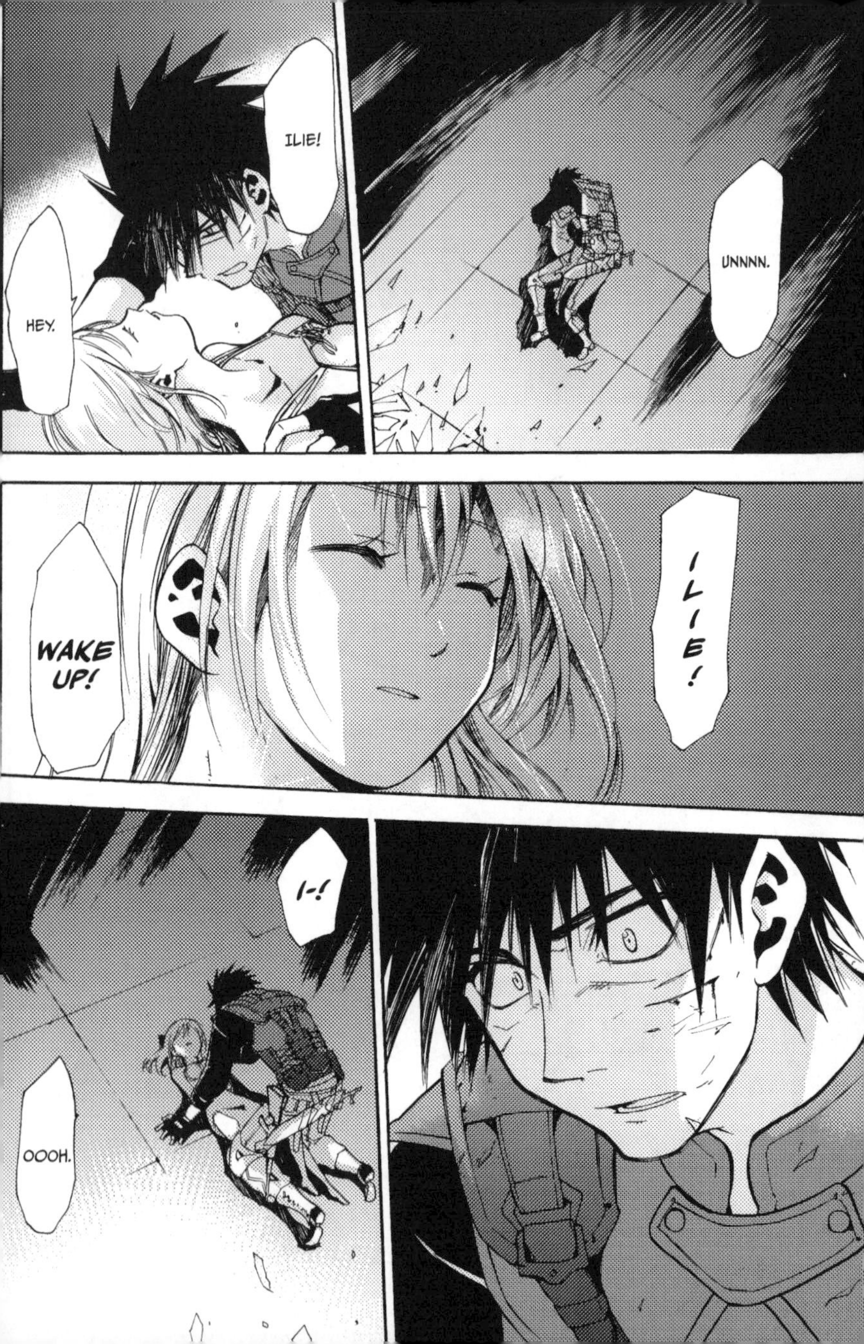
UNNNN.
ILIE!
HEY.
ILIE!
WAKE UP!
I-!
OOOH.

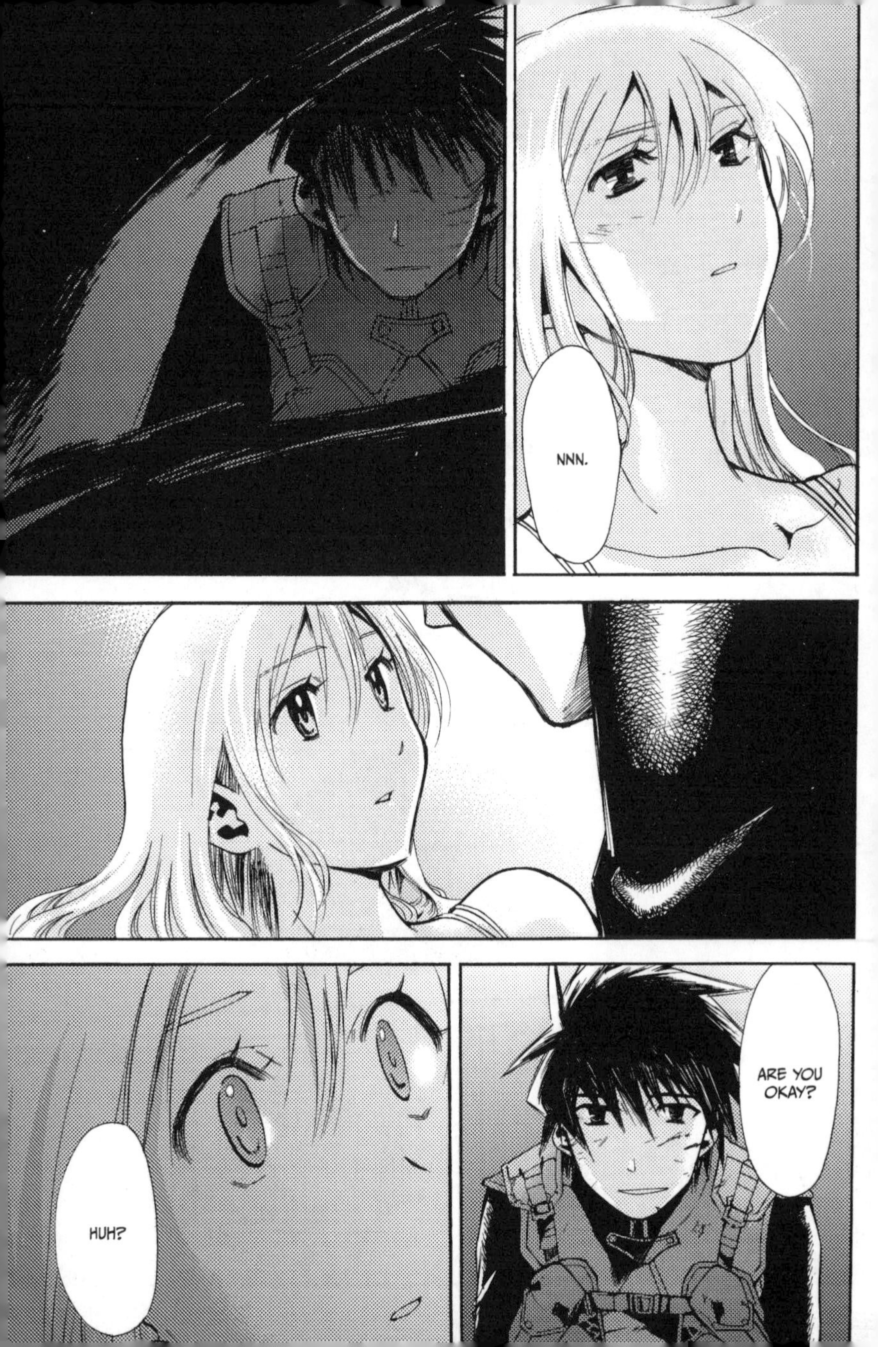
NNN.
ARE YOU OKAY?
HUH?

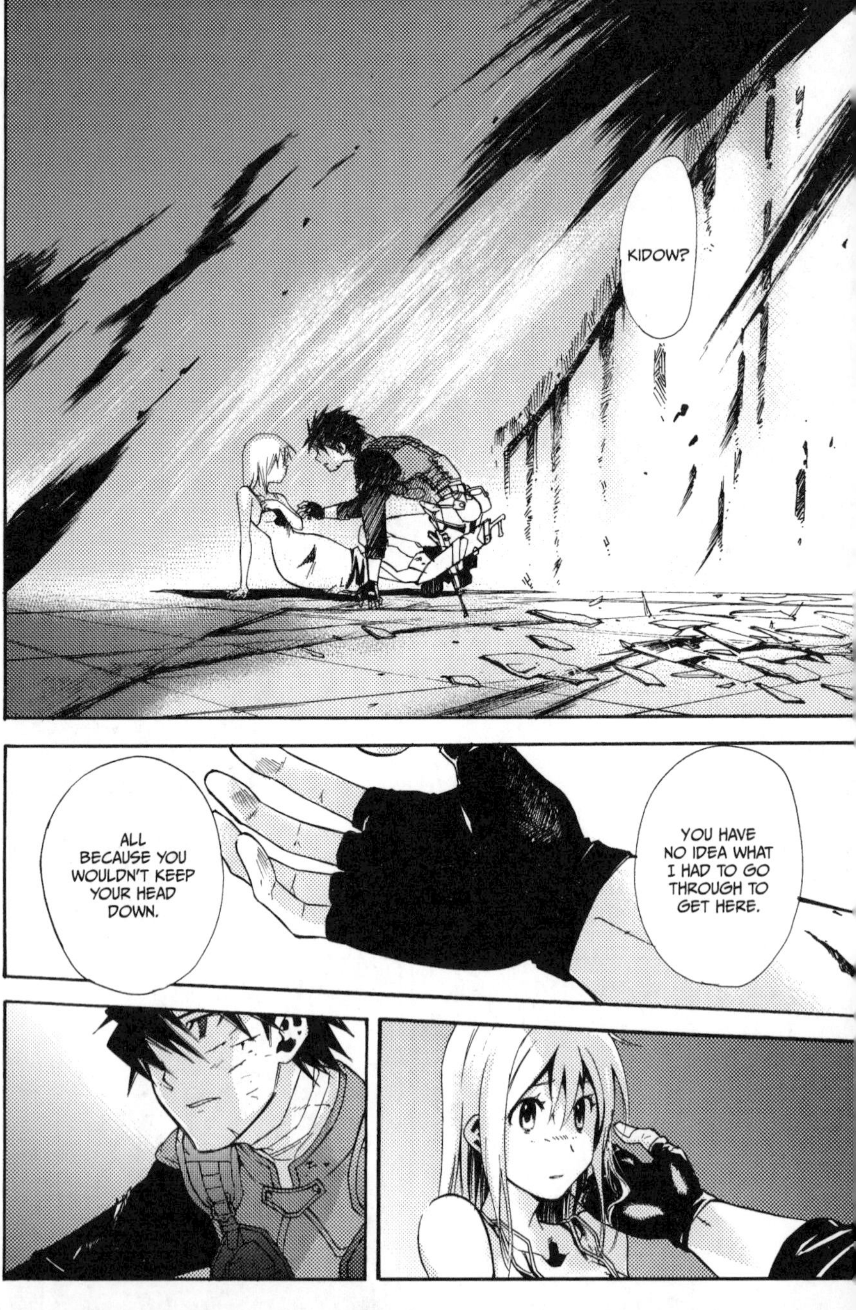
KIDOW?
YOU HAVE NO IDEA WHAT I HAD TO GO THROUGH TO GET HERE.
ALL BECAUSE YOU WOULDN'T KEEP YOUR HEAD DOWN.

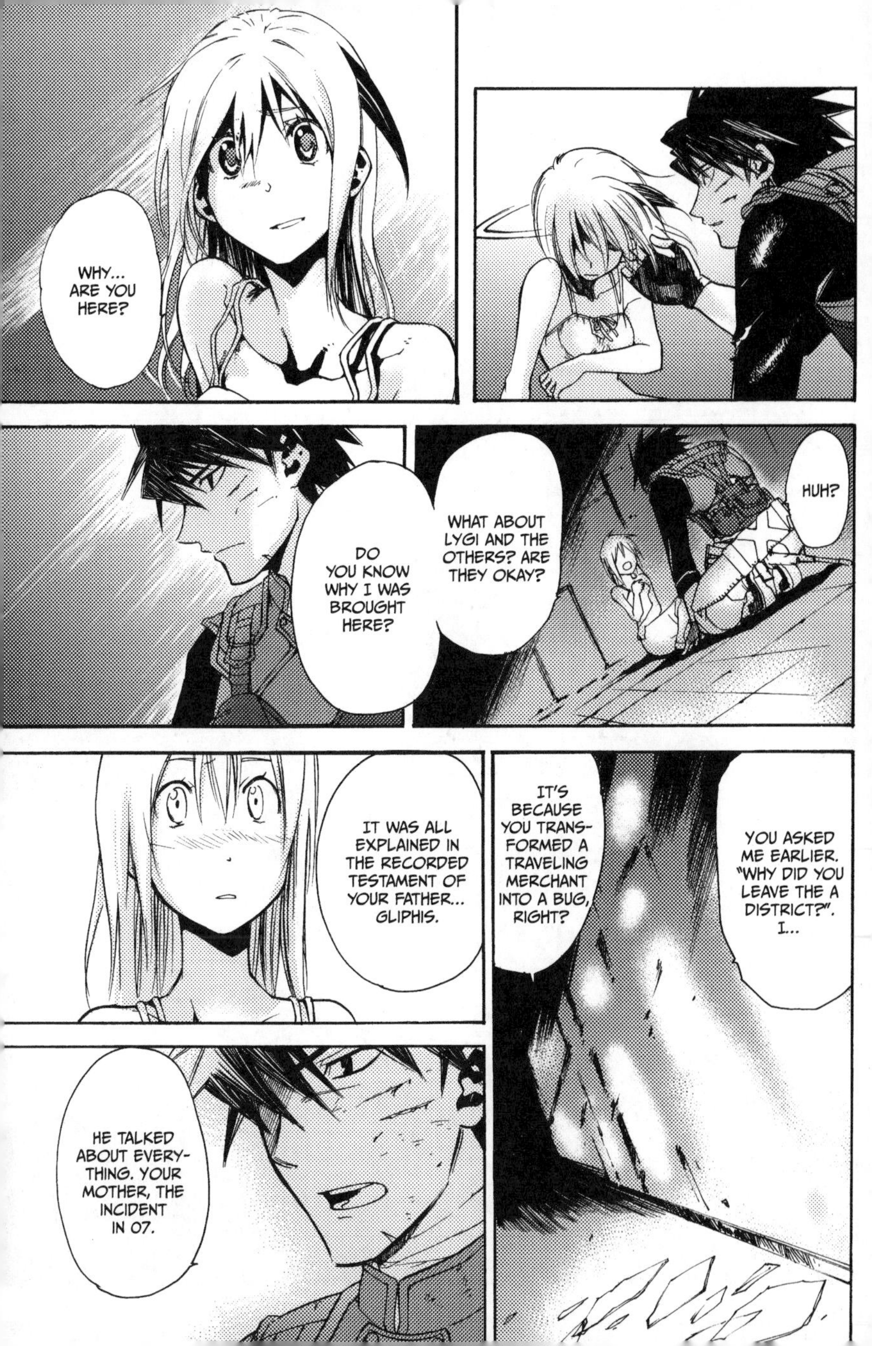
WHY... ARE YOU HERE?
HUH?
WHAT ABOUT LYGI AND THE OTHERS? ARE THEY OKAY?
DO YOU KNOW WHY I WAS BROUGHT HERE?
YOU ASKED ME EARLIER. "WHY DID YOU LEAVE THE A DISTRICT?". I...
IT'S BECAUSE YOU TRANS-FORMED A TRAVELING MERCHANT INTO A BUG, RIGHT?
IT WAS ALL EXPLAINED IN THE RECORDED TESTAMENT OF YOUR FATHER... GLIPHIS.
HE TALKED ABOUT EVERY-THING. YOUR MOTHER, THE INCIDENT IN 07.

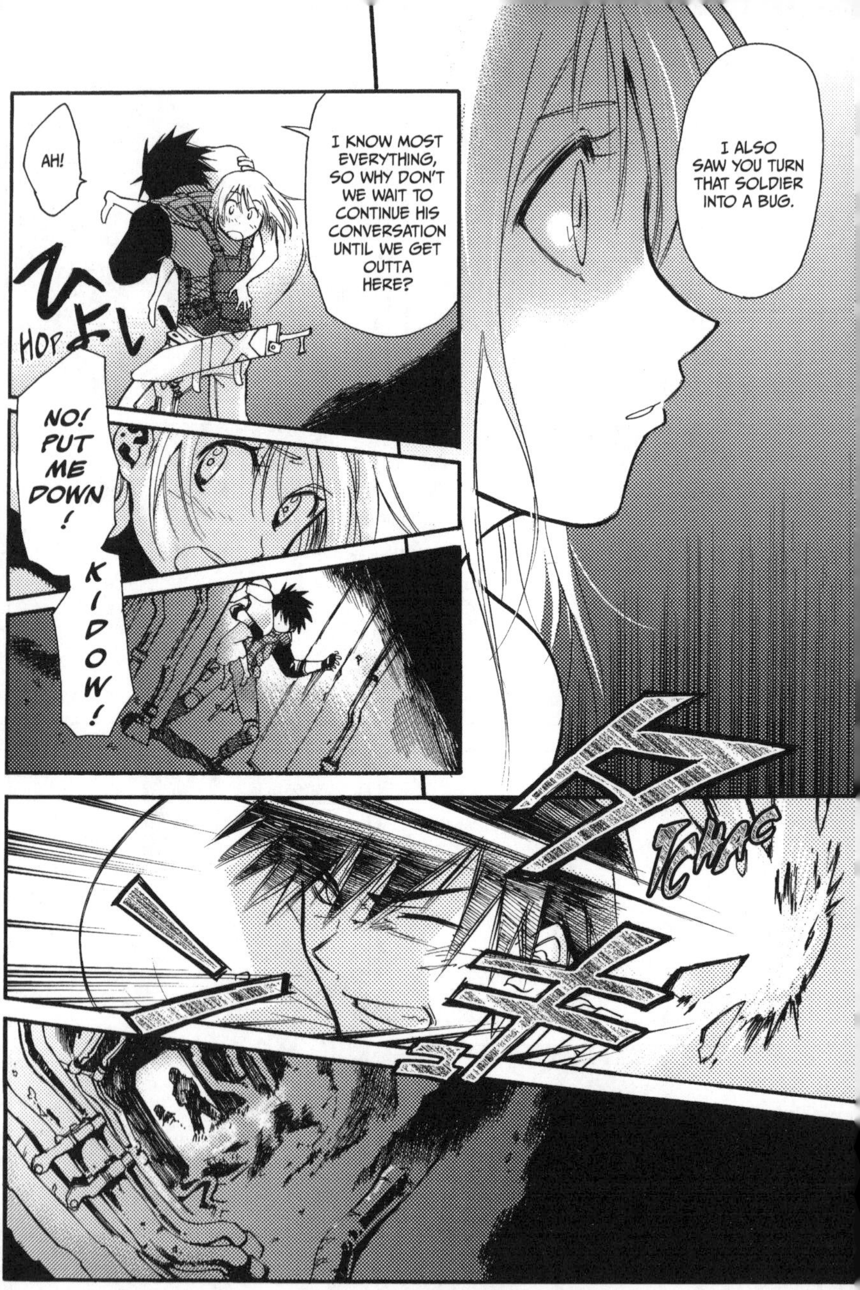
I ALSO SAW YOU TURN THAT SOLDIER INTO A BUG.
I KNOW MOST EVERYTHING, SO WHY DON'T WE WAIT TO CONTINUE HIS CONVERSATION UNTIL WE GET OUTTA HERE?
AH!
ひょい
HOP
NO! PUT ME DOWN!
KIDOW!
TCHAG
!

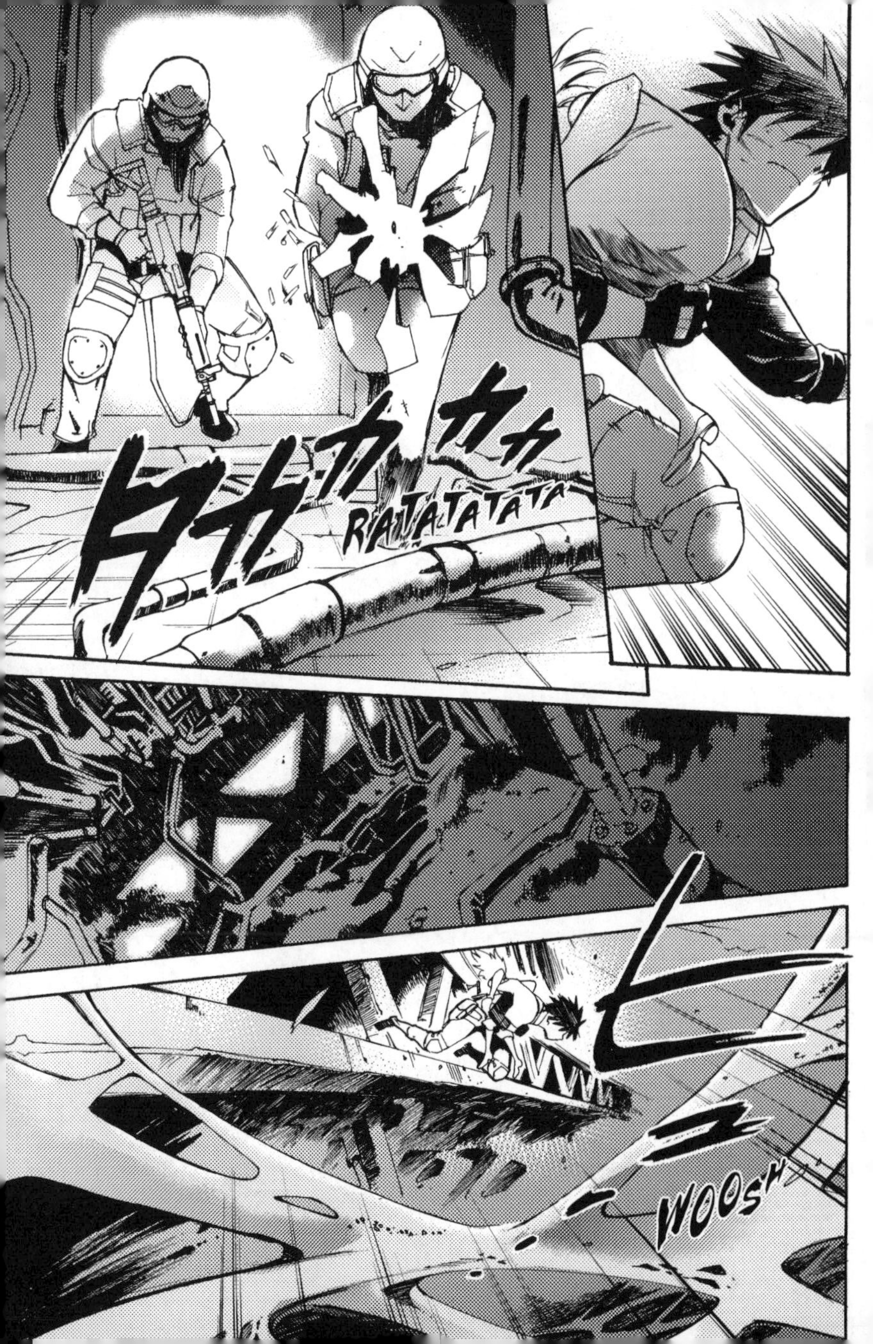

タカカカカ
RATATATATA
WOOSH

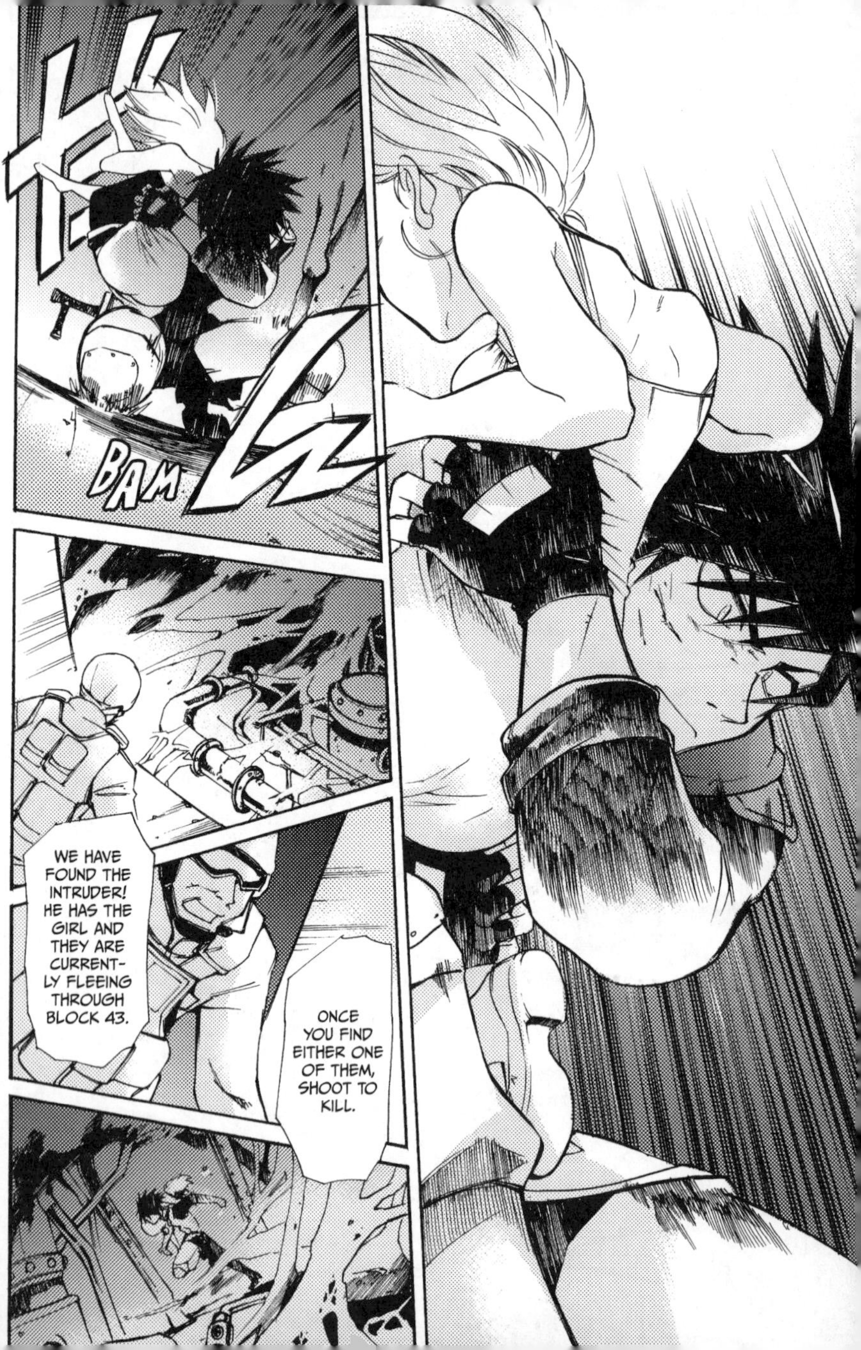
BAM
WE HAVE FOUND THE INTRUDER! HE HAS THE GIRL AND THEY ARE CURRENTLY FLEEING THROUGH BLOCK 43.
ONCE YOU FIND EITHER ONE OF THEM, SHOOT TO KILL.

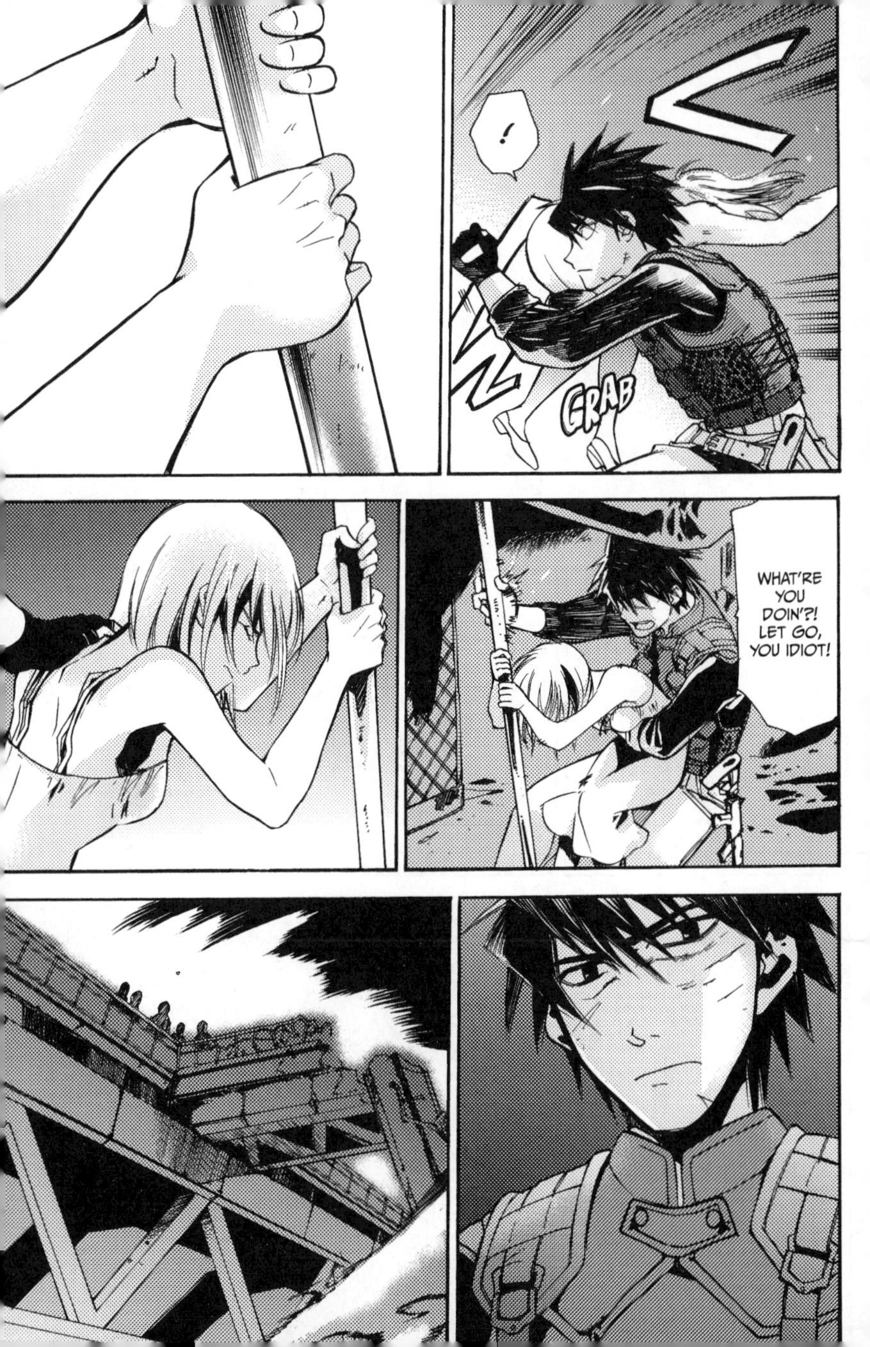
!
GRAB
WHAT'RE YOU DOIN'?! LET GO, YOU IDIOT!

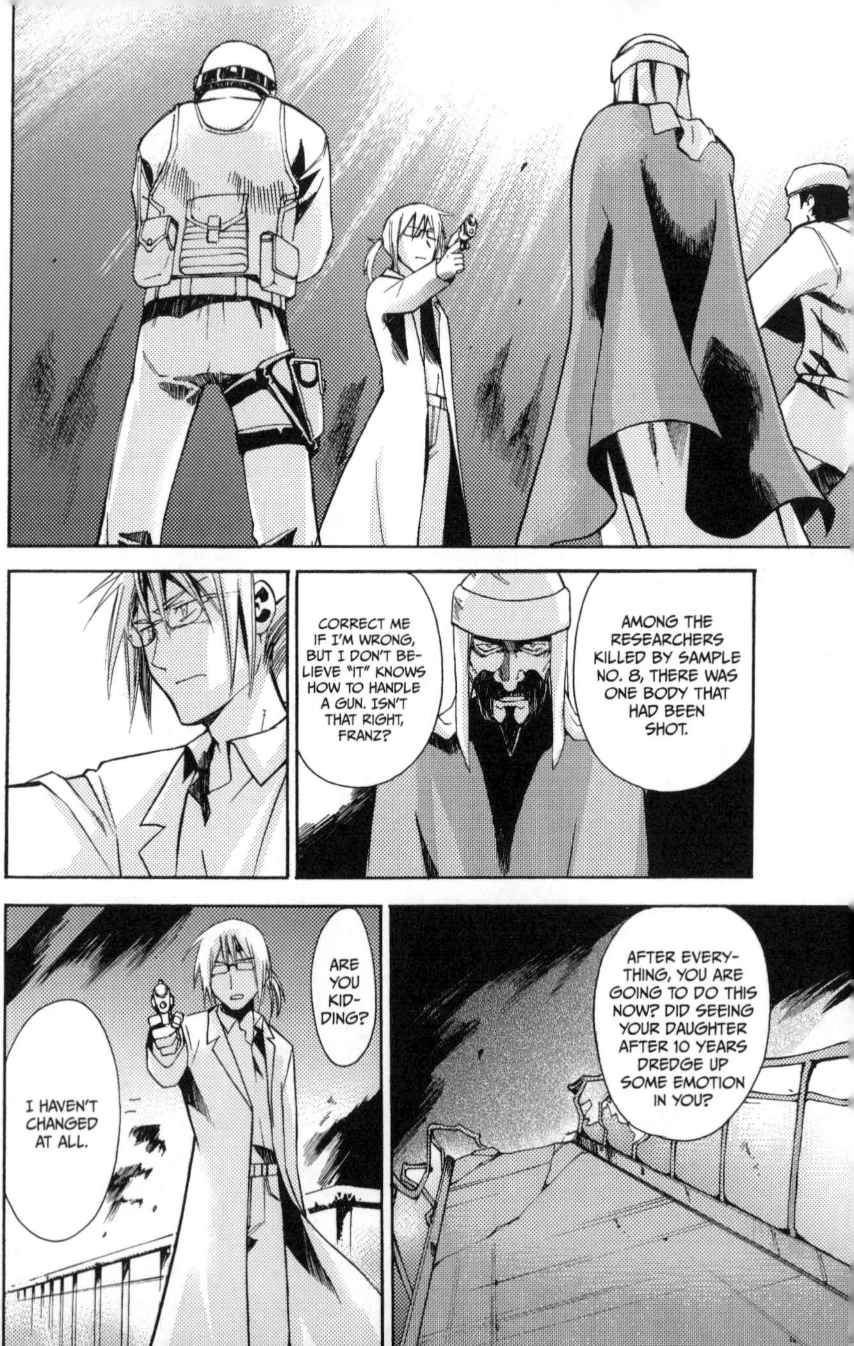
AMONG THE RESEARCHERS KILLED BY SAMPLE NO. 8, THERE WAS ONE BODY THAT HAD BEEN SHOT.
CORRECT ME IF I'M WRONG, BUT I DON'T BE-LIEVE "IT" KNOWS HOW TO HANDLE A GUN. ISN'T THAT RIGHT, FRANZ?
AFTER EVERY-THING, YOU ARE GOING TO DO THIS NOW? DID SEEING YOUR DAUGHTER AFTER 10 YEARS DREDGE UP SOME EMOTION IN YOU?
ARE YOU KID-DING?
I HAVEN'T CHANGED AT ALL.

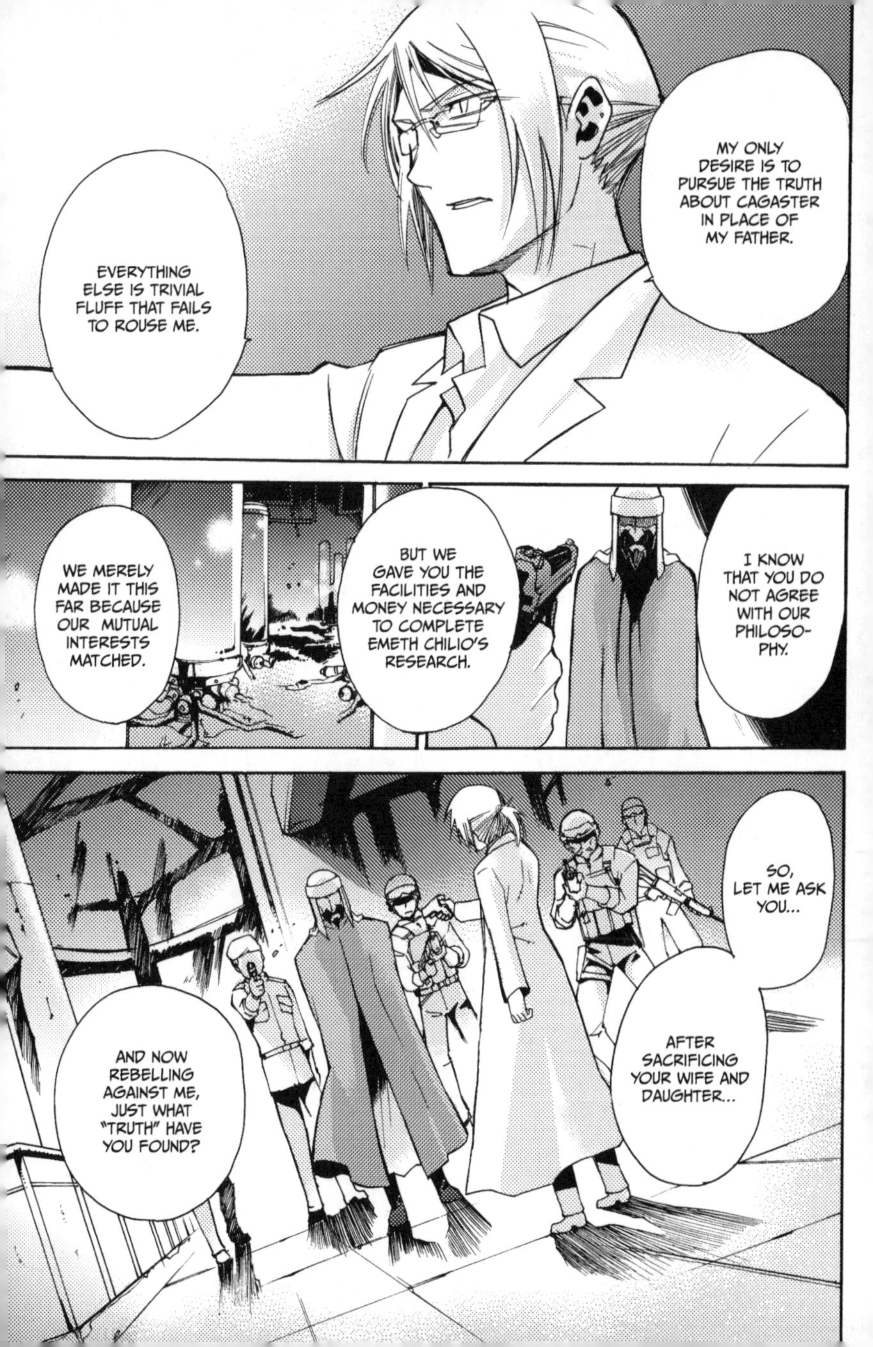
MY ONLY DESIRE IS TO PURSUE THE TRUTH ABOUT CAGASTER IN PLACE OF MY FATHER.
EVERYTHING ELSE IS TRIVIAL FLUFF THAT FAILS TO ROUSE ME.
I KNOW THAT YOU DO NOT AGREE WITH OUR PHILOSO-PHY.
BUT WE GAVE YOU THE FACILITIES AND MONEY NECESSARY TO COMPLETE EMETH CHILIO'S RESEARCH.
WE MERELY MADE IT THIS FAR BECAUSE OUR MUTUAL INTERESTS MATCHED.
SO, LET ME ASK YOU...
AFTER SACRIFICING YOUR WIFE AND DAUGHTER...
AND NOW REBELLING AGAINST ME, JUST WHAT "TRUTH" HAVE YOU FOUND?

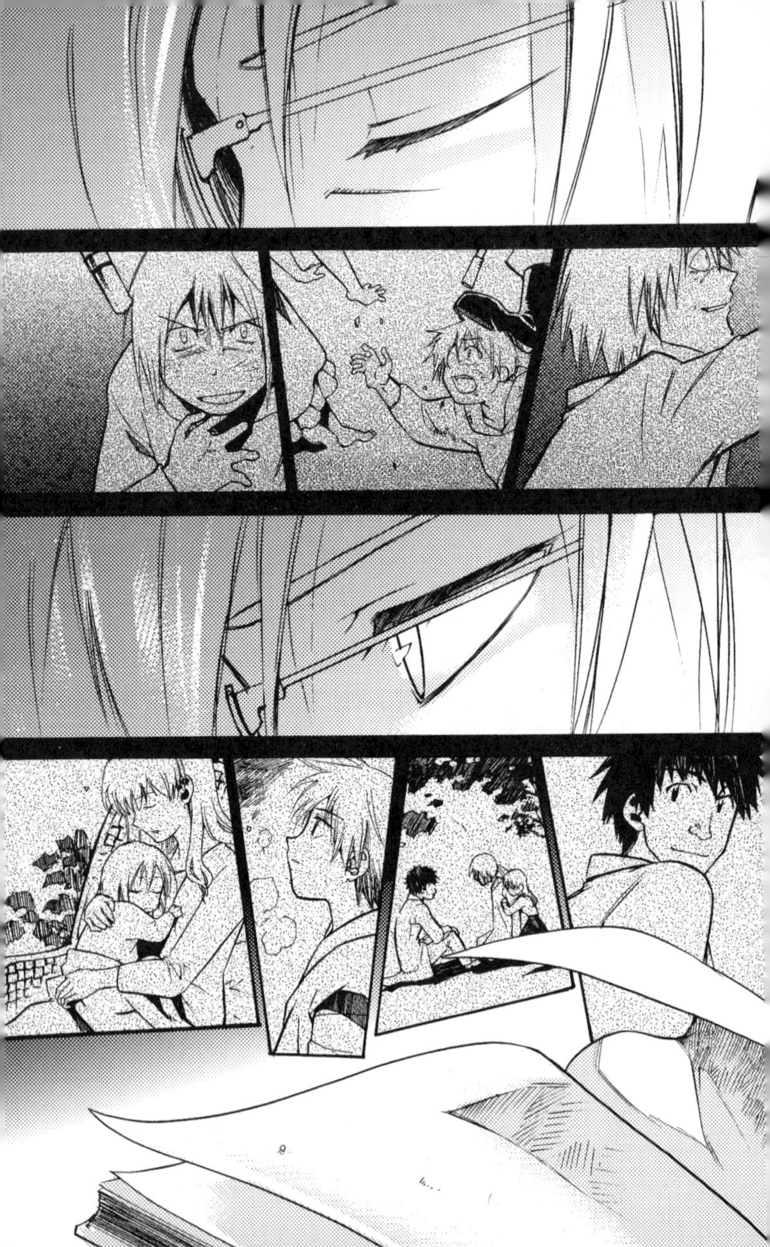

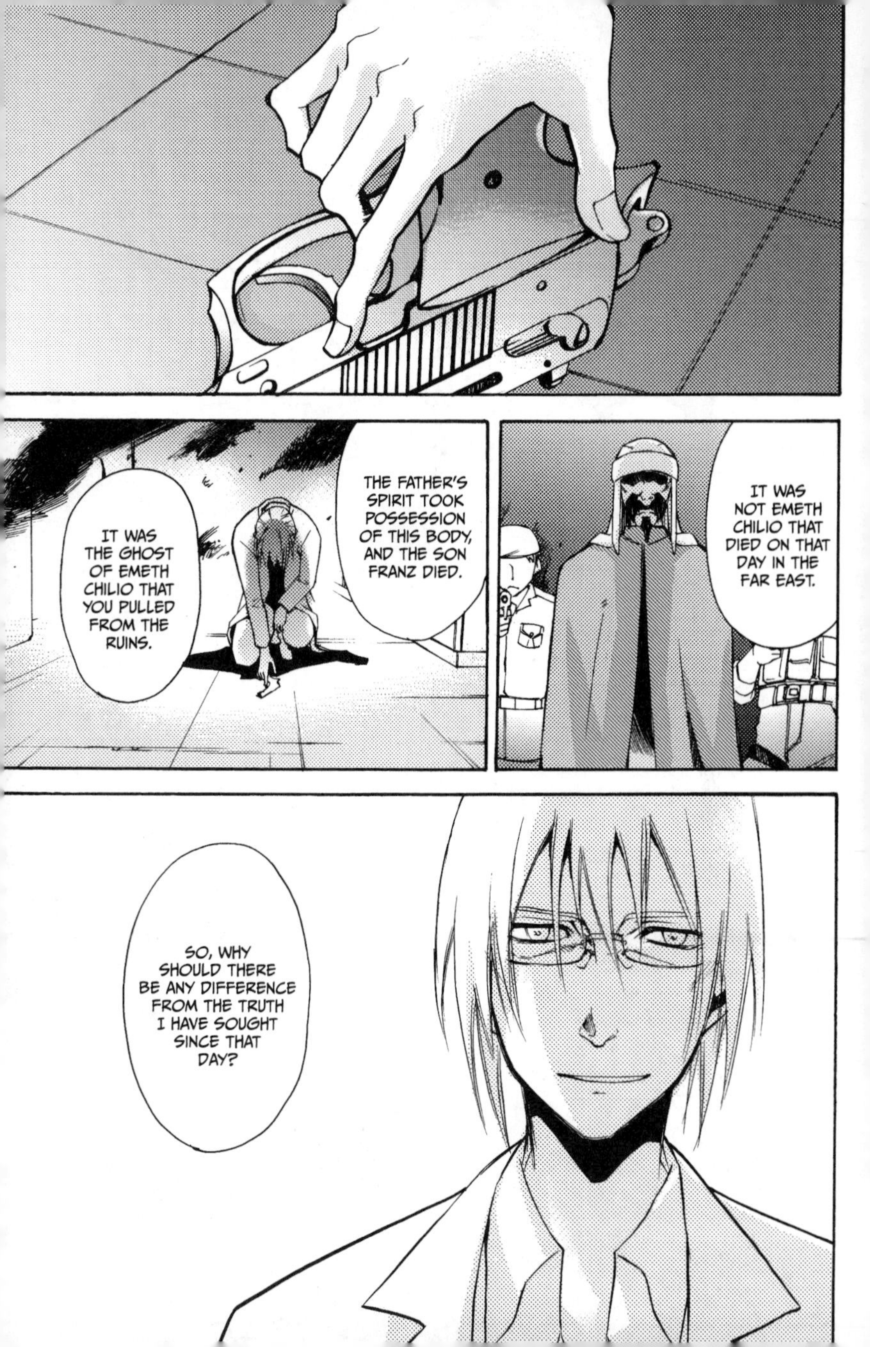
IT WAS NOT EMETH CHILIO THAT DIED ON THAT DAY IN THE FAR EAST.
THE FATHER'S SPIRIT TOOK POSSESSION OF THIS BODY, AND THE SON FRANZ DIED.
IT WAS THE GHOST OF EMETH CHILIO THAT YOU PULLED FROM THE RUINS.
SO, WHY SHOULD THERE BE ANY DIFFERENCE FROM THE TRUTH I HAVE SOUGHT SINCE THAT DAY?

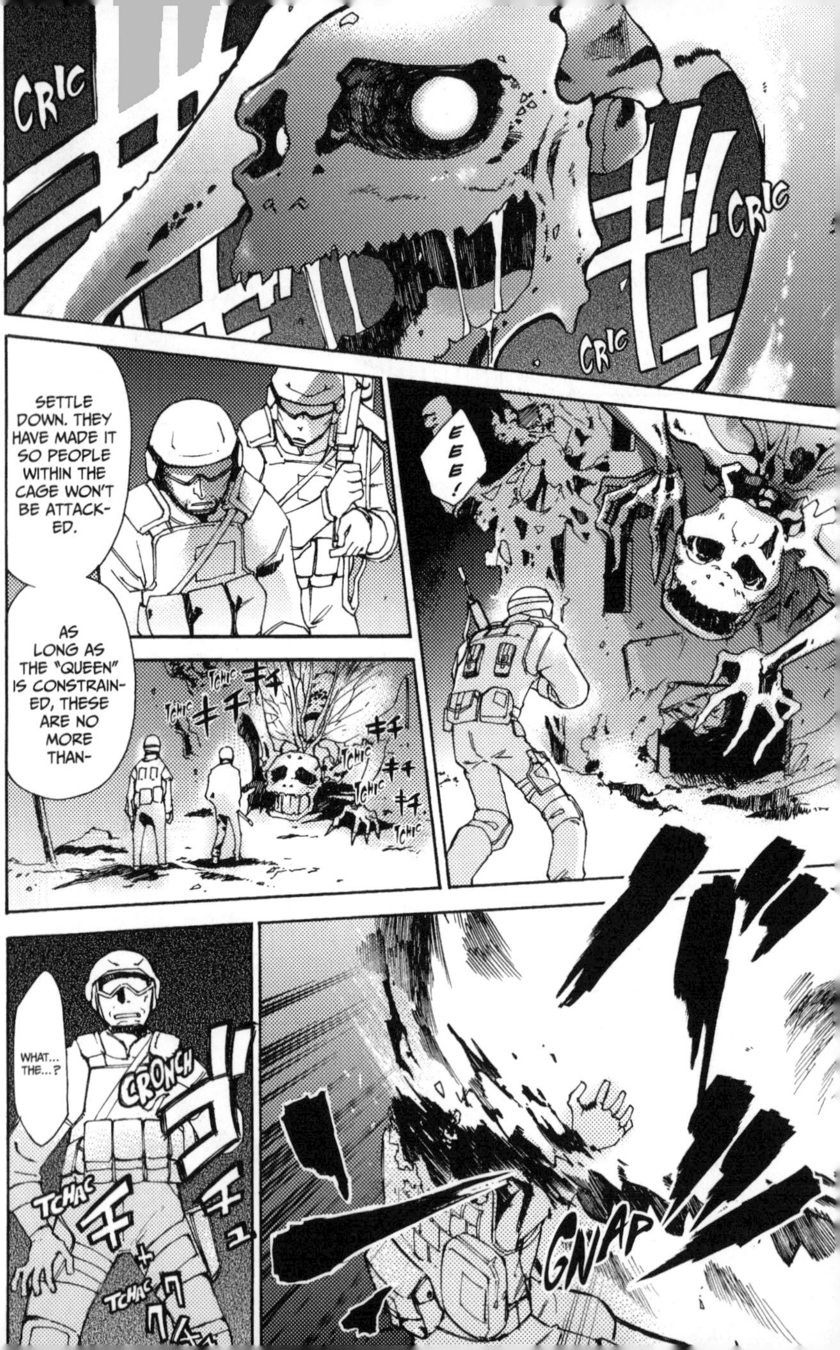
CRIC
CRIC
CRIC
EEE!
SETTLE DOWN. THEY HAVE MADE IT SO PEOPLE WITHIN THE CAGE WON'T BE ATTACK-ED.
AS LONG AS THE "QUEEN" IS CONSTRAIN-ED, THESE ARE NO MORE THAN-
TCHIC
TCHIC
TCHIC
TCHIC
TCHIC
GNAP
WHAT... THE...?
CRONSH
TCHAC
TCHAC

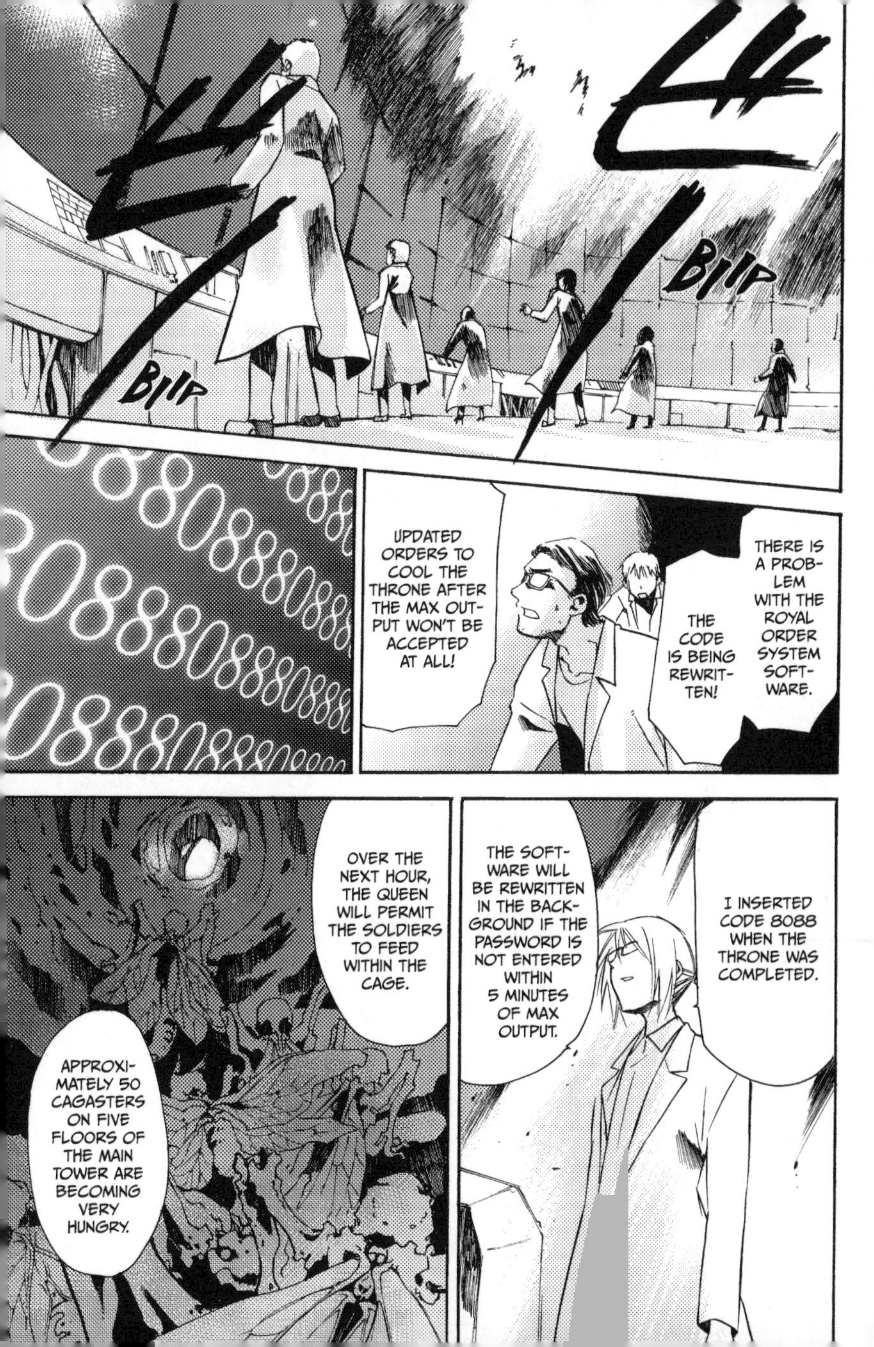
BIIP
BIIP
THERE IS A PROBLEM WITH THE ROYAL ORDER SYSTEM SOFTWARE.
THE CODE IS BEING REWRITTEN!
UPDATED ORDERS TO COOL THE THRONE AFTER THE MAX OUTPUT WON'T BE ACCEPTED AT ALL!
I INSERTED CODE 8088 WHEN THE THRONE WAS COMPLETED.
THE SOFTWARE WILL BE REWRITTEN IN THE BACKGROUND IF THE PASSWORD IS NOT ENTERED WITHIN 5 MINUTES OF MAX OUTPUT.
OVER THE NEXT HOUR, THE QUEEN WILL PERMIT THE SOLDIERS TO FEED WITHIN THE CAGE.
APPROXIMATELY 50 CAGASTERS ON FIVE FLOORS OF THE MAIN TOWER ARE BECOMING VERY HUNGRY.

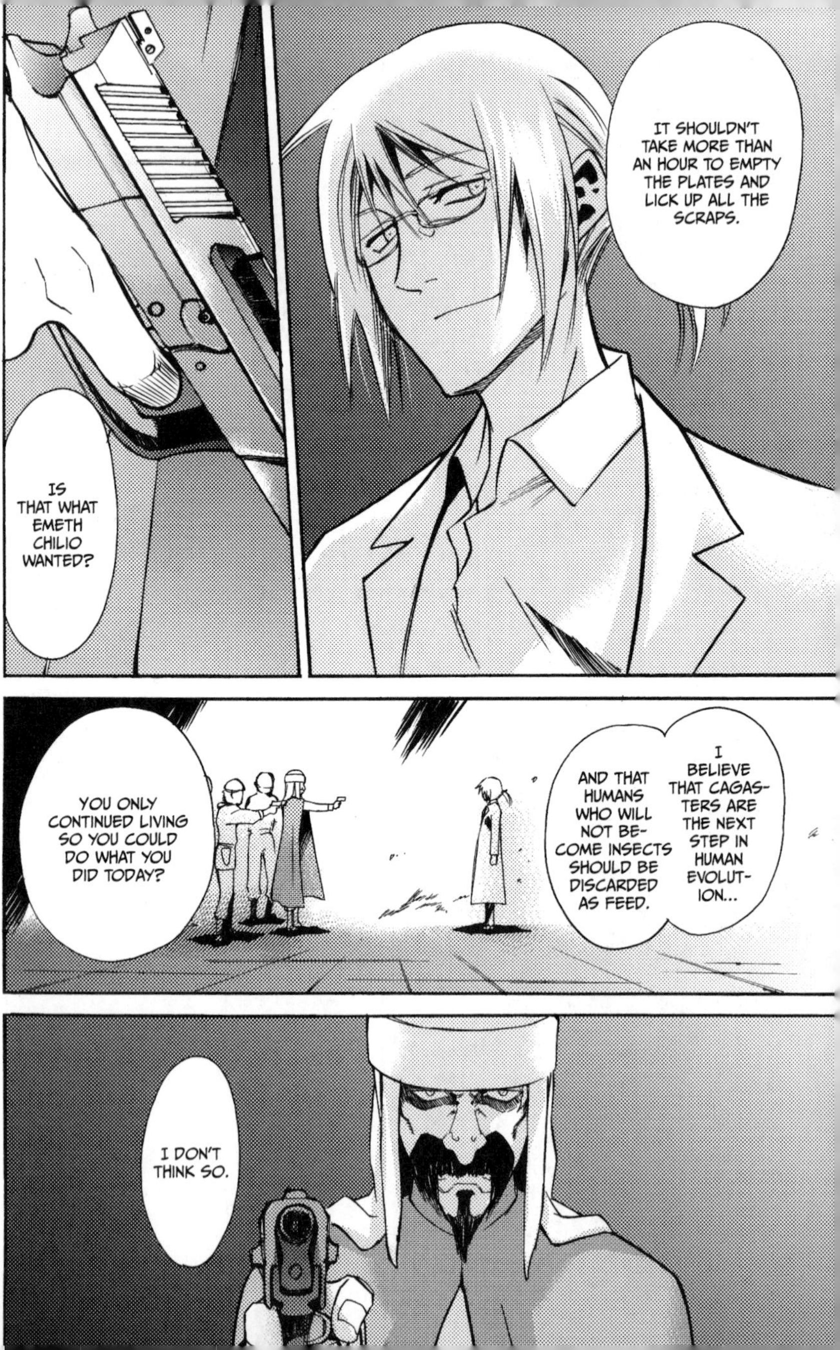
IT SHOULDN'T TAKE MORE THAN AN HOUR TO EMPTY THE PLATES AND LICK UP ALL THE SCRAPS.
IS THAT WHAT EMETH CHILIO WANTED?
I BELIEVE THAT CAGASTERS ARE THE NEXT STEP IN HUMAN EVOLUTION...
AND THAT HUMANS WHO WILL NOT BECOME INSECTS SHOULD BE DISCARDED AS FEED.
YOU ONLY CONTINUED LIVING SO YOU COULD DO WHAT YOU DID TODAY?
I DON'T THINK SO.

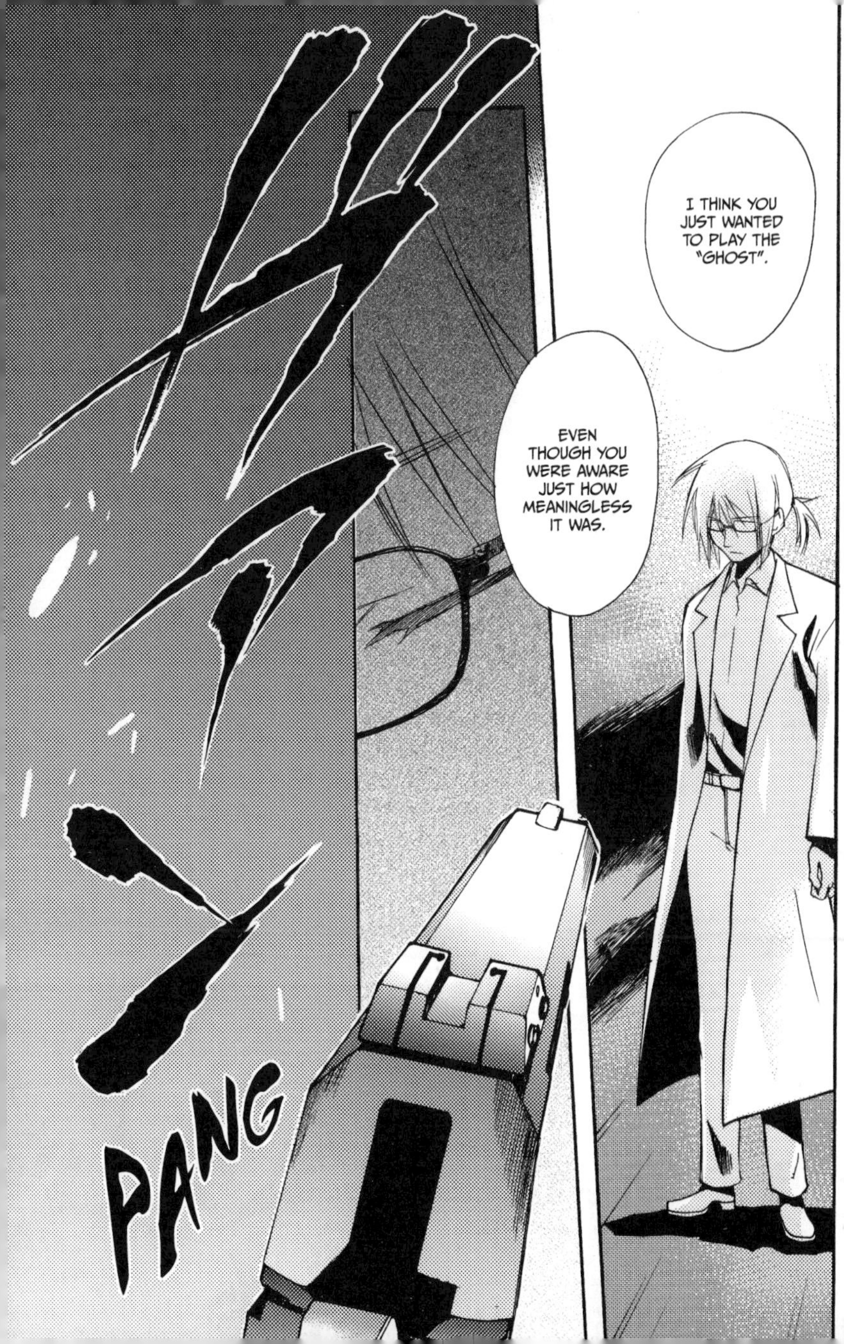
I THINK YOU JUST WANTED TO PLAY THE "GHOST".
EVEN THOUGH YOU WERE AWARE JUST HOW MEANINGLESS IT WAS.
PANG

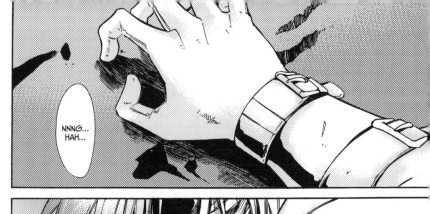

NNNG...
HAH...

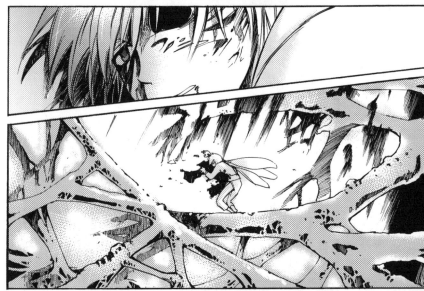

-:COUGH:-

I'M
ALIVE.

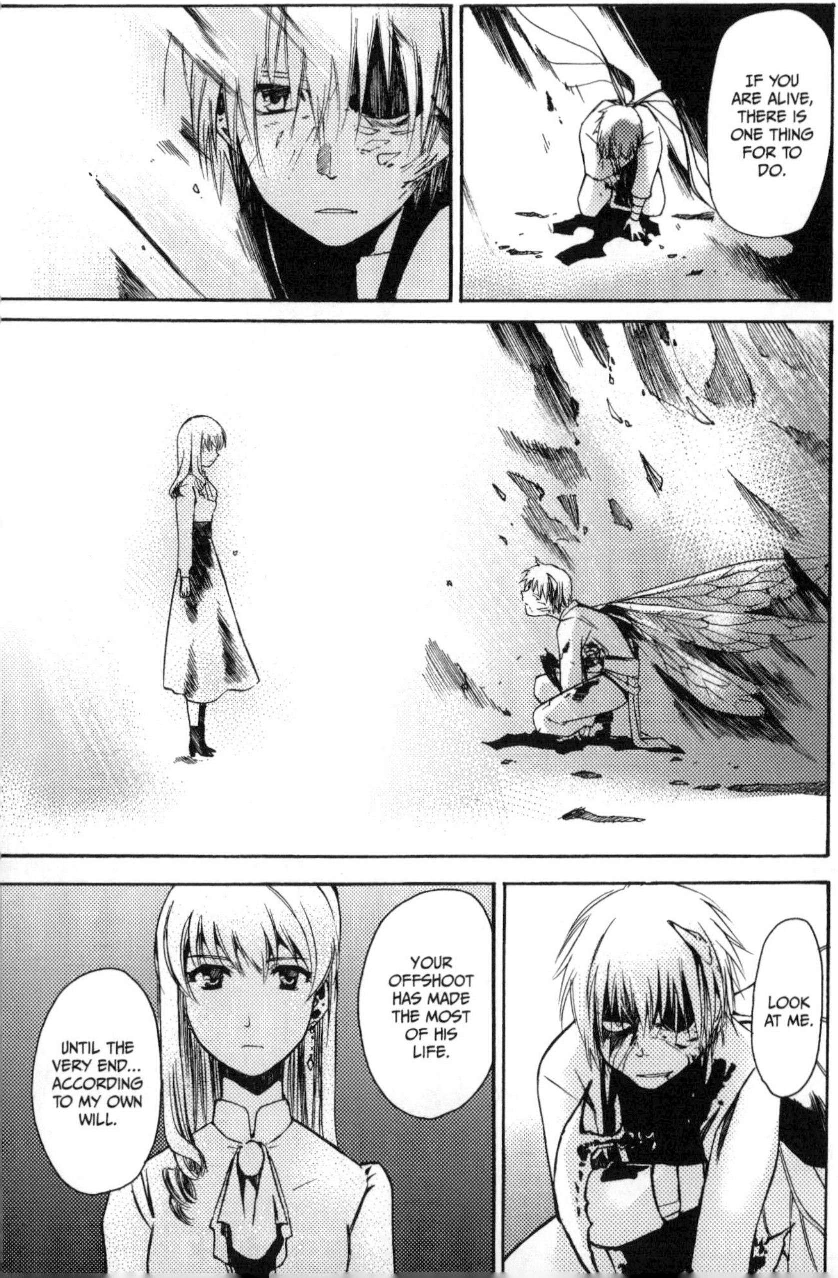
IF YOU ARE ALIVE, THERE IS ONE THING FOR TO DO.
LOOK AT ME.
YOUR OFFSHOOT HAS MADE THE MOST OF HIS LIFE.
UNTIL THE VERY END... ACCORDING TO MY OWN WILL.

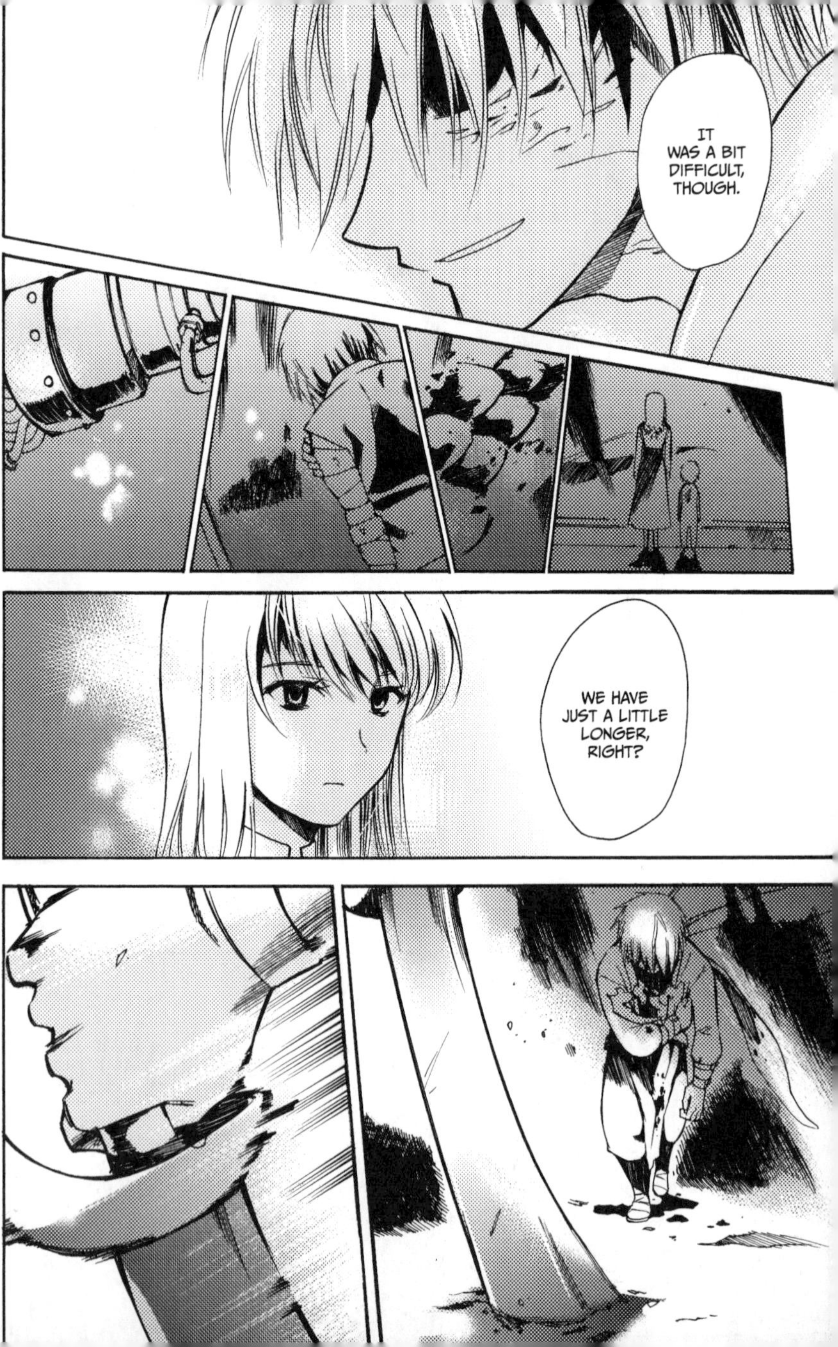
IT WAS A BIT DIFFICULT, THOUGH.
WE HAVE JUST A LITTLE LONGER, RIGHT?

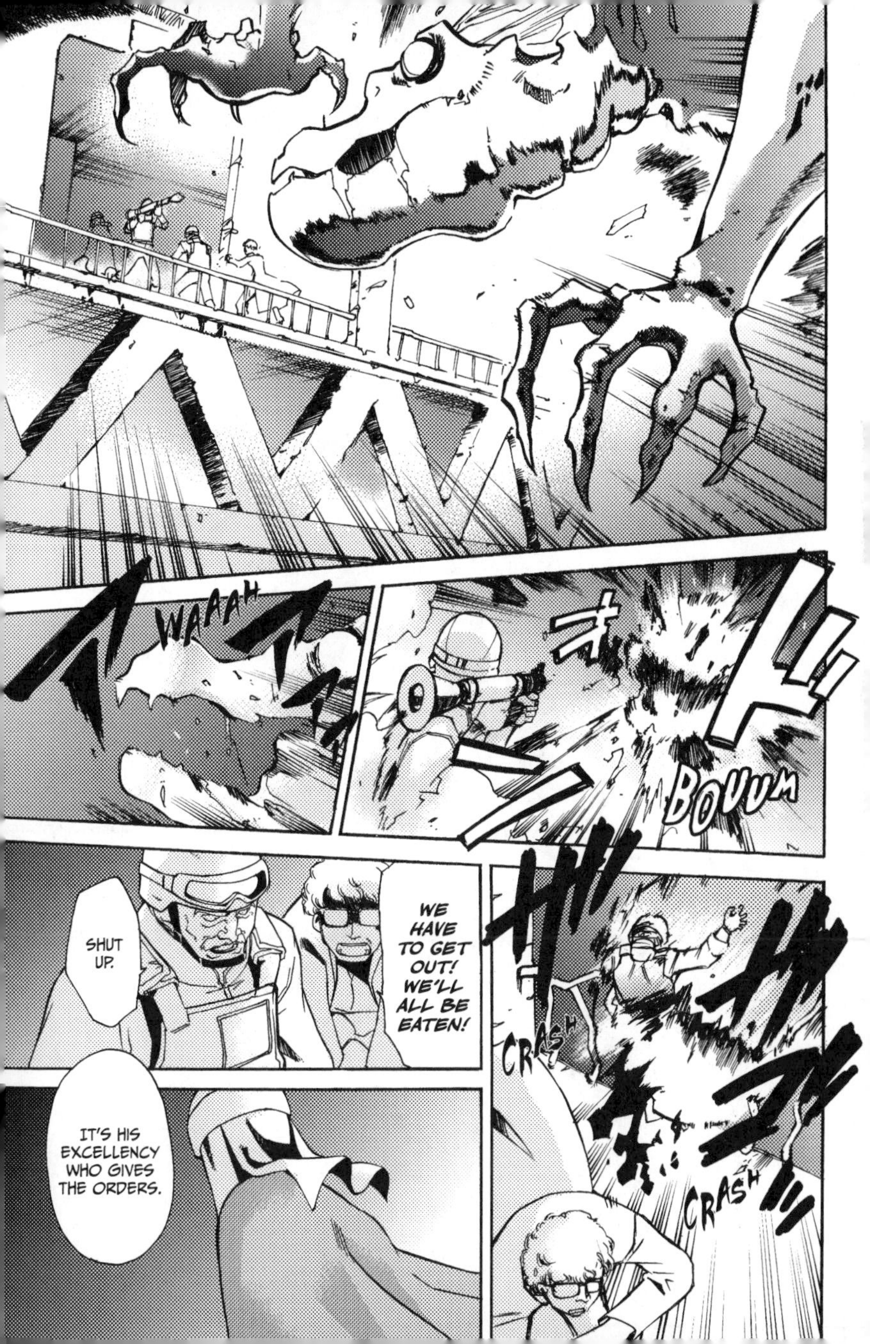
BOUUM
WAAAH
CRASH
CRASH
WE HAVE TO GET OUT! WE'LL ALL BE EATEN!
SHUT UP.
IT'S HIS EXCELLENCY WHO GIVES THE ORDERS.

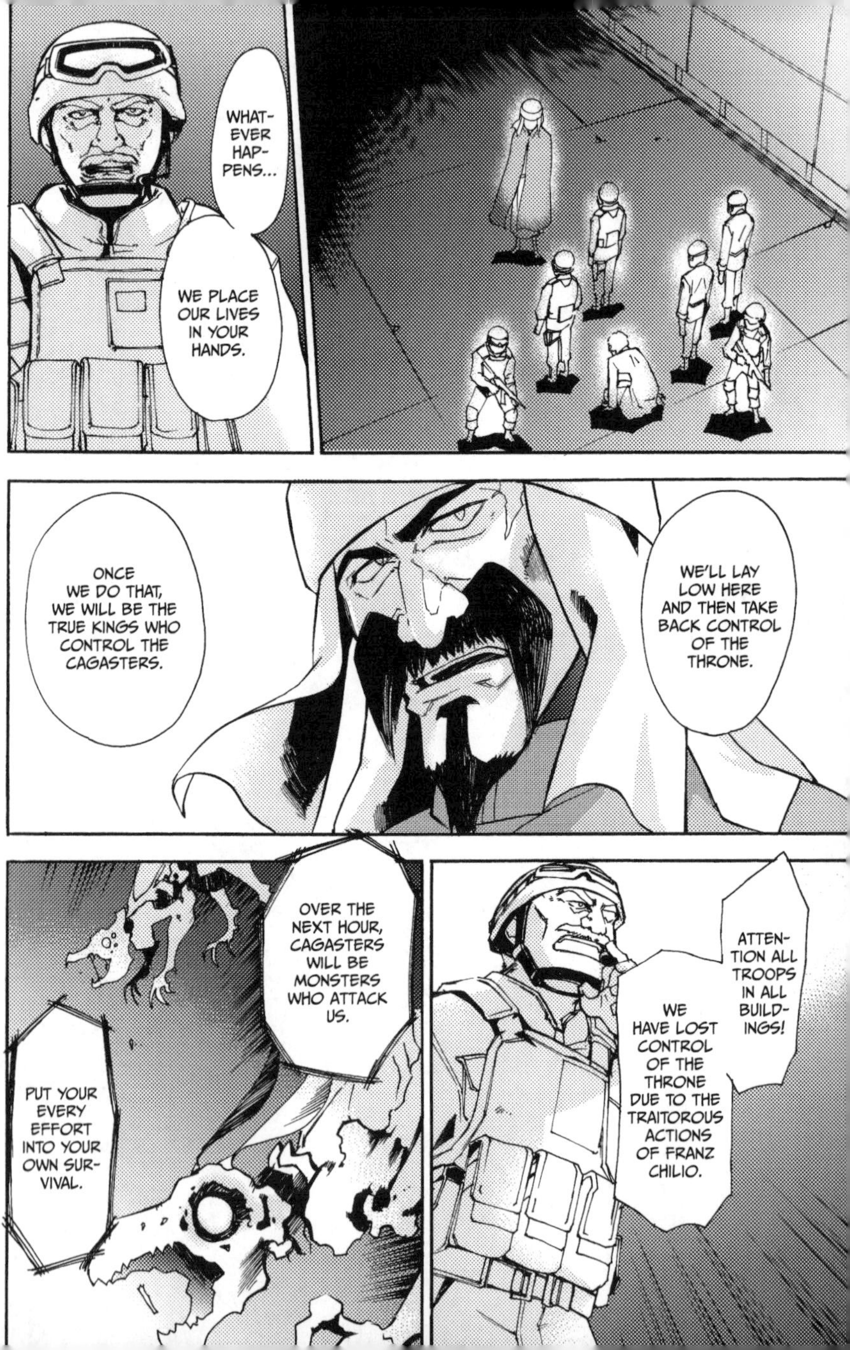
WHATEVER HAPPENS...
WE PLACE OUR LIVES IN YOUR HANDS.
WE'LL LAY LOW HERE AND THEN TAKE BACK CONTROL OF THE THRONE.
ONCE WE DO THAT, WE WILL BE THE TRUE KINGS WHO CONTROL THE CAGASTERS.
ATTENTION ALL TROOPS IN ALL BUILDINGS!
WE HAVE LOST CONTROL OF THE THRONE DUE TO THE TRAITOROUS ACTIONS OF FRANZ CHILIO.
OVER THE NEXT HOUR, CAGASTERS WILL BE MONSTERS WHO ATTACK US.
PUT YOUR EVERY EFFORT INTO YOUR OWN SURVIVAL.

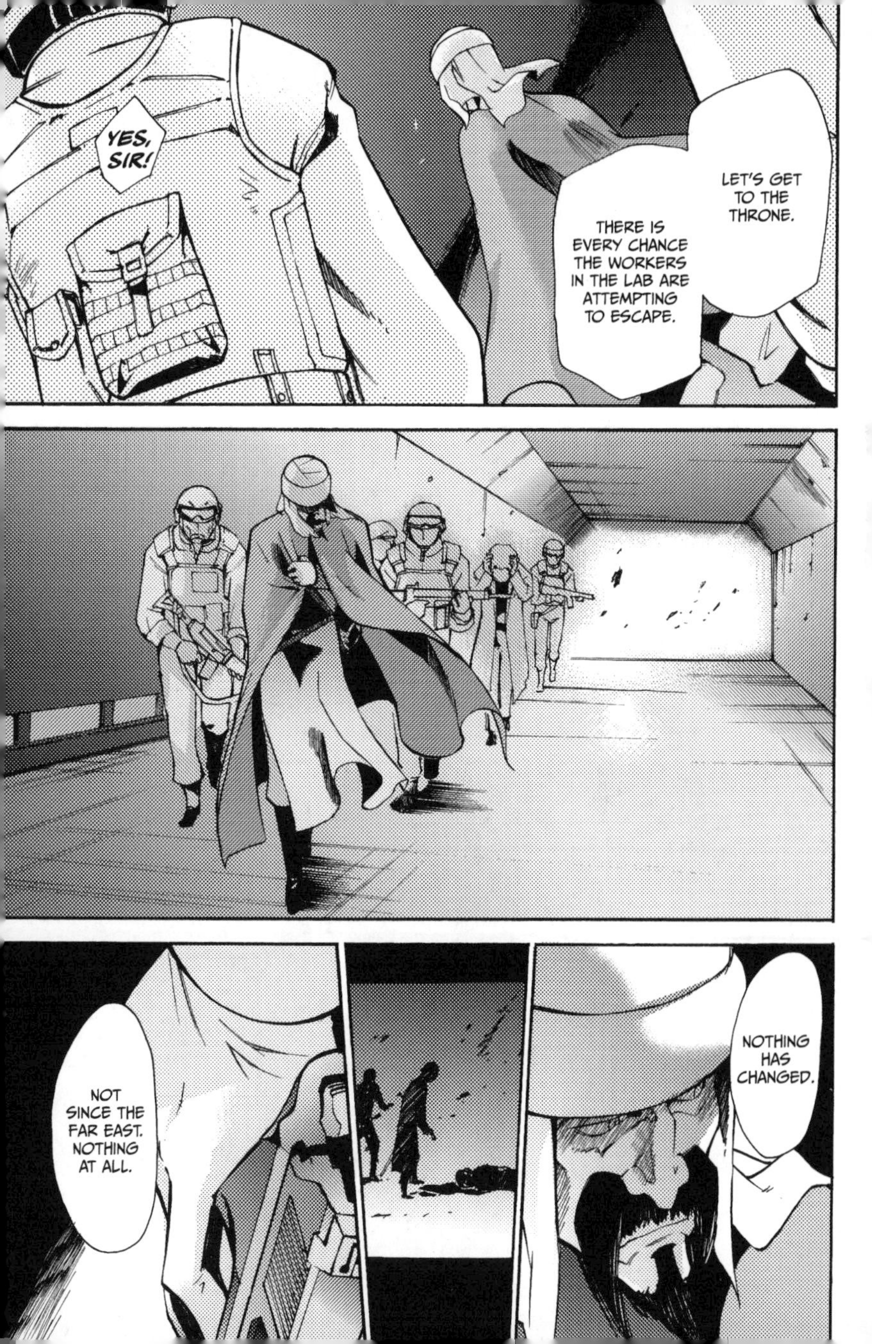
LET'S GET TO THE THRONE.
THERE IS EVERY CHANCE THE WORKERS IN THE LAB ARE ATTEMPTING TO ESCAPE.
YES, SIR!
NOTHING HAS CHANGED.
NOT SINCE THE FAR EAST. NOTHING AT ALL.

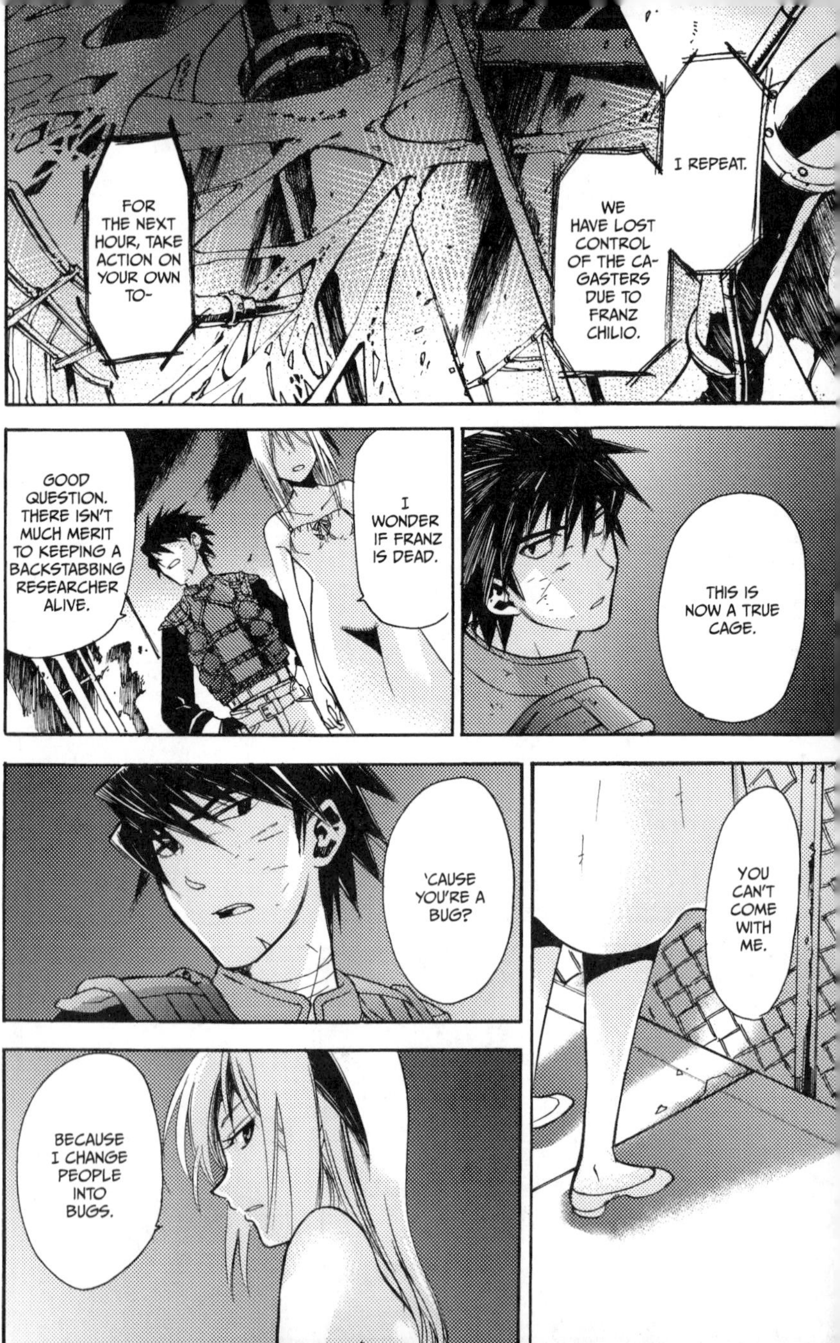
I REPEAT.
WE HAVE LOST CONTROL OF THE CA-GASTERS DUE TO FRANZ CHILIO.
FOR THE NEXT HOUR, TAKE ACTION ON YOUR OWN TO-
THIS IS NOW A TRUE CAGE.
I WONDER IF FRANZ IS DEAD.
GOOD QUESTION. THERE ISN'T MUCH MERIT TO KEEPING A BACKSTABBING RESEARCHER ALIVE.
YOU CAN'T COME WITH ME.
'CAUSE YOU'RE A BUG?
BECAUSE I CHANGE PEOPLE INTO BUGS.

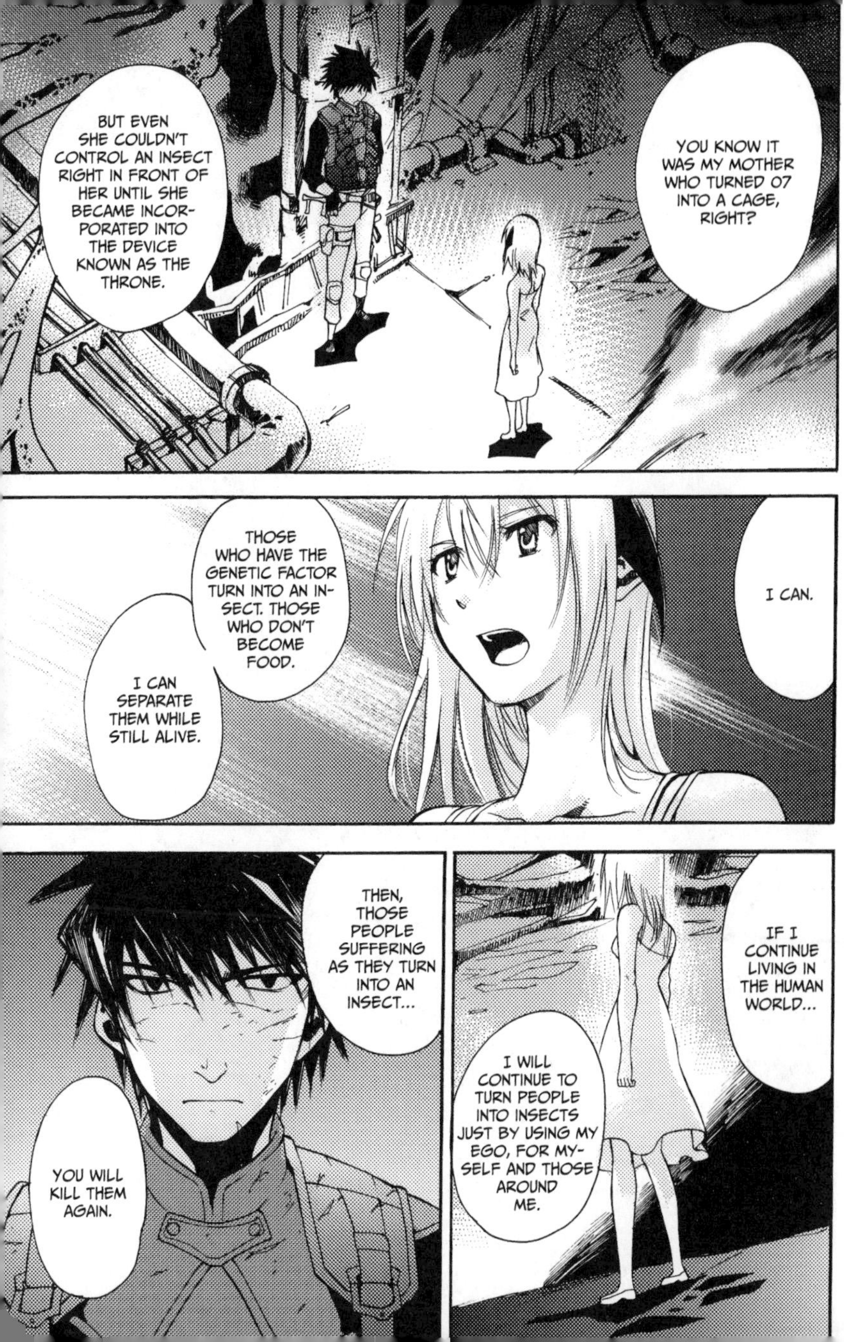
YOU KNOW IT WAS MY MOTHER WHO TURNED 07 INTO A CAGE, RIGHT?
BUT EVEN SHE COULDN'T CONTROL AN INSECT RIGHT IN FRONT OF HER UNTIL SHE BECAME INCORPORATED INTO THE DEVICE KNOWN AS THE THRONE.
I CAN.
THOSE WHO HAVE THE GENETIC FACTOR TURN INTO AN INSECT. THOSE WHO DON'T BECOME FOOD.
I CAN SEPARATE THEM WHILE STILL ALIVE.
IF I CONTINUE LIVING IN THE HUMAN WORLD...
I WILL CONTINUE TO TURN PEOPLE INTO INSECTS JUST BY USING MY EGO, FOR MYSELF AND THOSE AROUND ME.
THEN, THOSE PEOPLE SUFFERING AS THEY TURN INTO AN INSECT...
YOU WILL KILL THEM AGAIN.

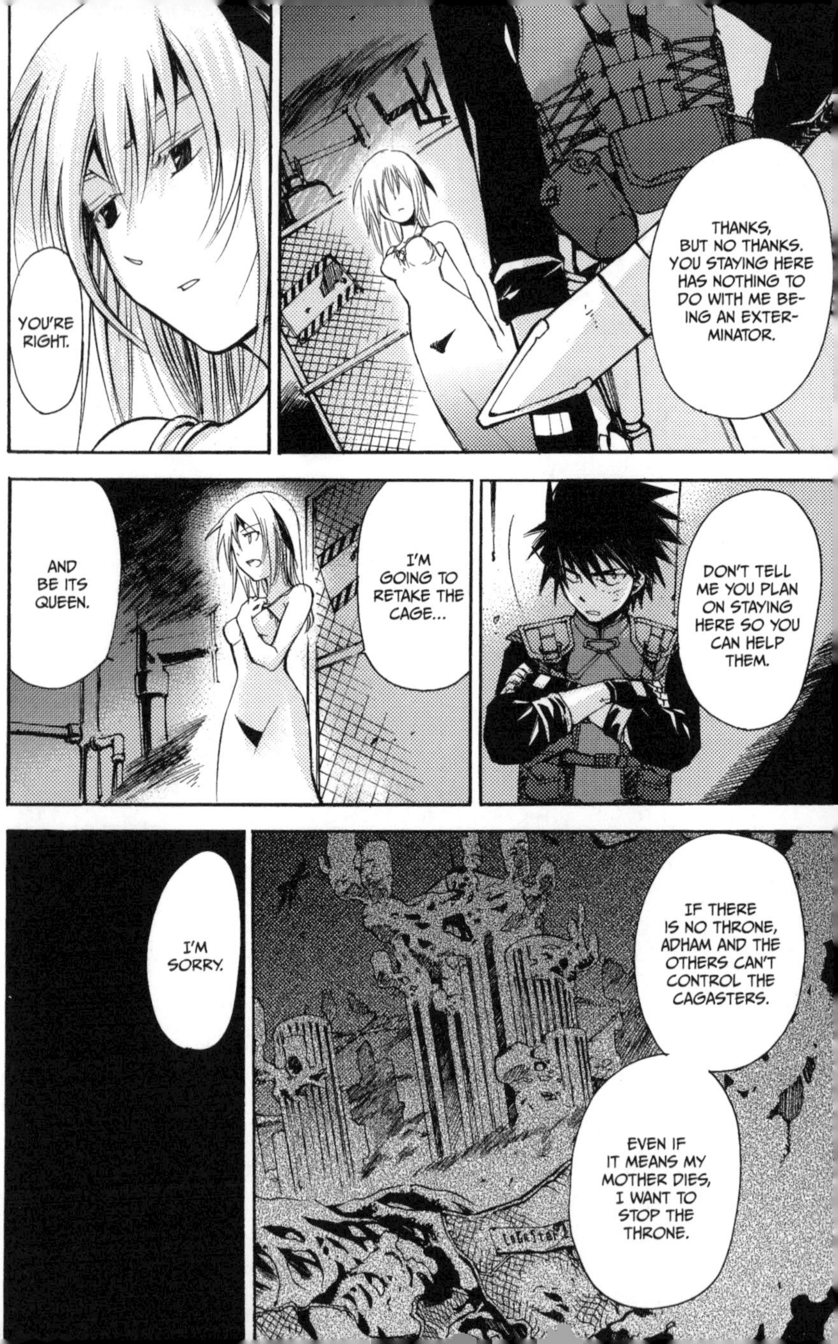
THANKS, BUT NO THANKS. YOU STAYING HERE HAS NOTHING TO DO WITH ME BEING AN EXTERMINATOR.
YOU'RE RIGHT.
DON'T TELL ME YOU PLAN ON STAYING HERE SO YOU CAN HELP THEM.
I'M GOING TO RETAKE THE CAGE...
AND BE ITS QUEEN.
IF THERE IS NO THRONE, ADHAM AND THE OTHERS CAN'T CONTROL THE CAGASTERS.
EVEN IF IT MEANS MY MOTHER DIES, I WANT TO STOP THE THRONE.
I'M SORRY.

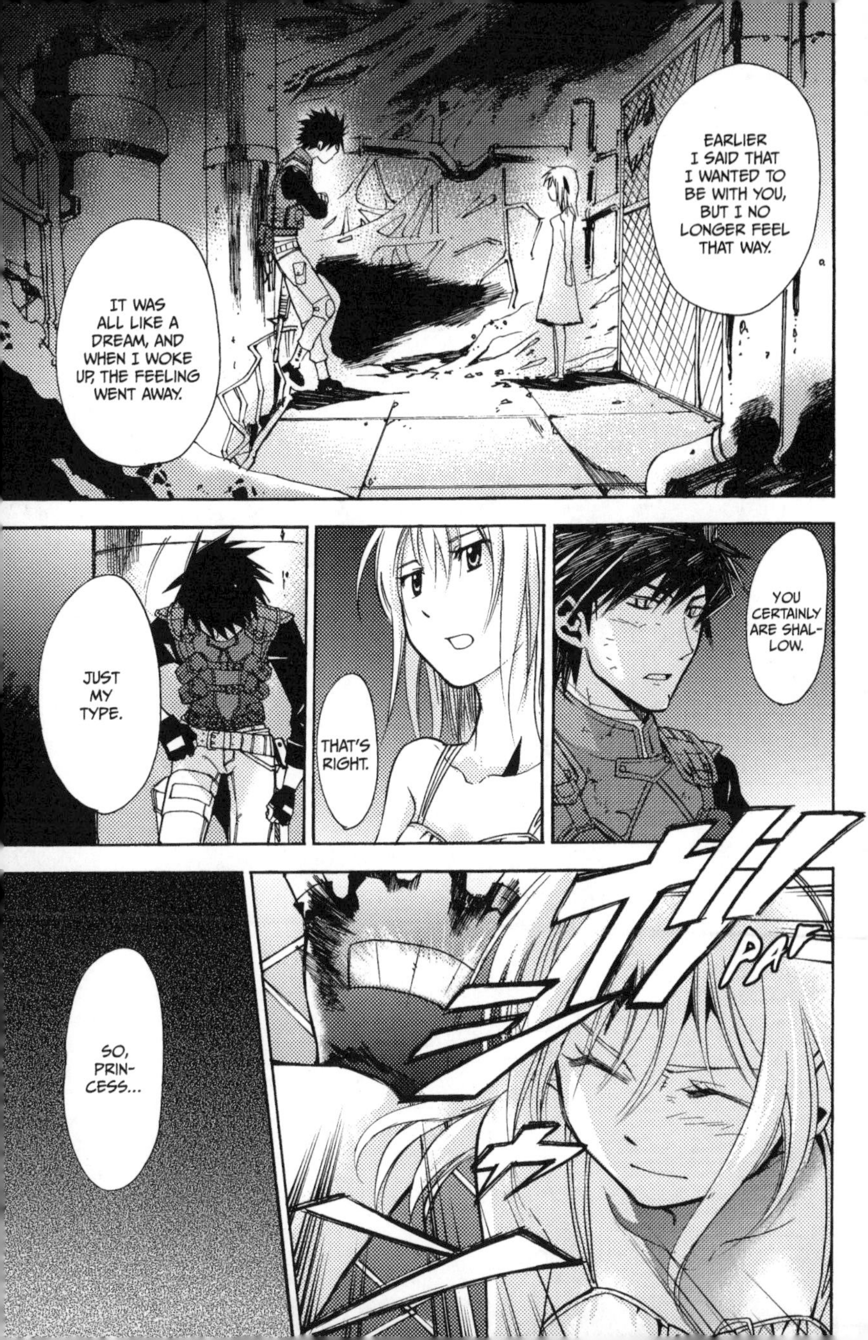
EARLIER I SAID THAT I WANTED TO BE WITH YOU, BUT I NO LONGER FEEL THAT WAY.
IT WAS ALL LIKE A DREAM, AND WHEN I WOKE UP, THE FEELING WENT AWAY.
YOU CERTAINLY ARE SHAL-LOW.
THAT'S RIGHT.
JUST MY TYPE.
PAF
SO, PRIN-CESS...

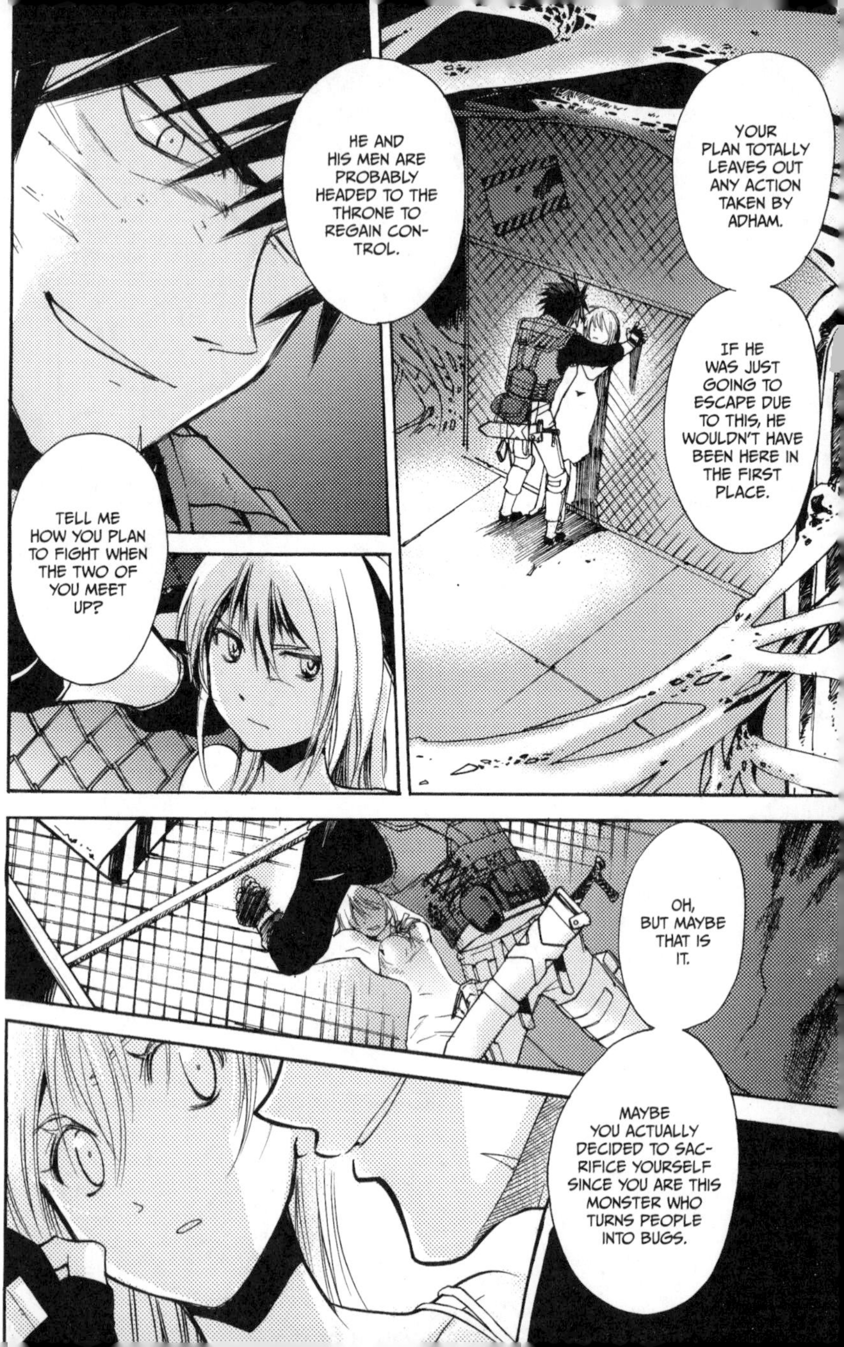
YOUR PLAN TOTALLY LEAVES OUT ANY ACTION TAKEN BY ADHAM.
IF HE WAS JUST GOING TO ESCAPE DUE TO THIS, HE WOULDN'T HAVE BEEN HERE IN THE FIRST PLACE.
HE AND HIS MEN ARE PROBABLY HEADED TO THE THRONE TO REGAIN CON-TROL.
TELL ME HOW YOU PLAN TO FIGHT WHEN THE TWO OF YOU MEET UP?
OH, BUT MAYBE THAT IS IT.
MAYBE YOU ACTUALLY DECIDED TO SAC-RIFICE YOURSELF SINCE YOU ARE THIS MONSTER WHO TURNS PEOPLE INTO BUGS.

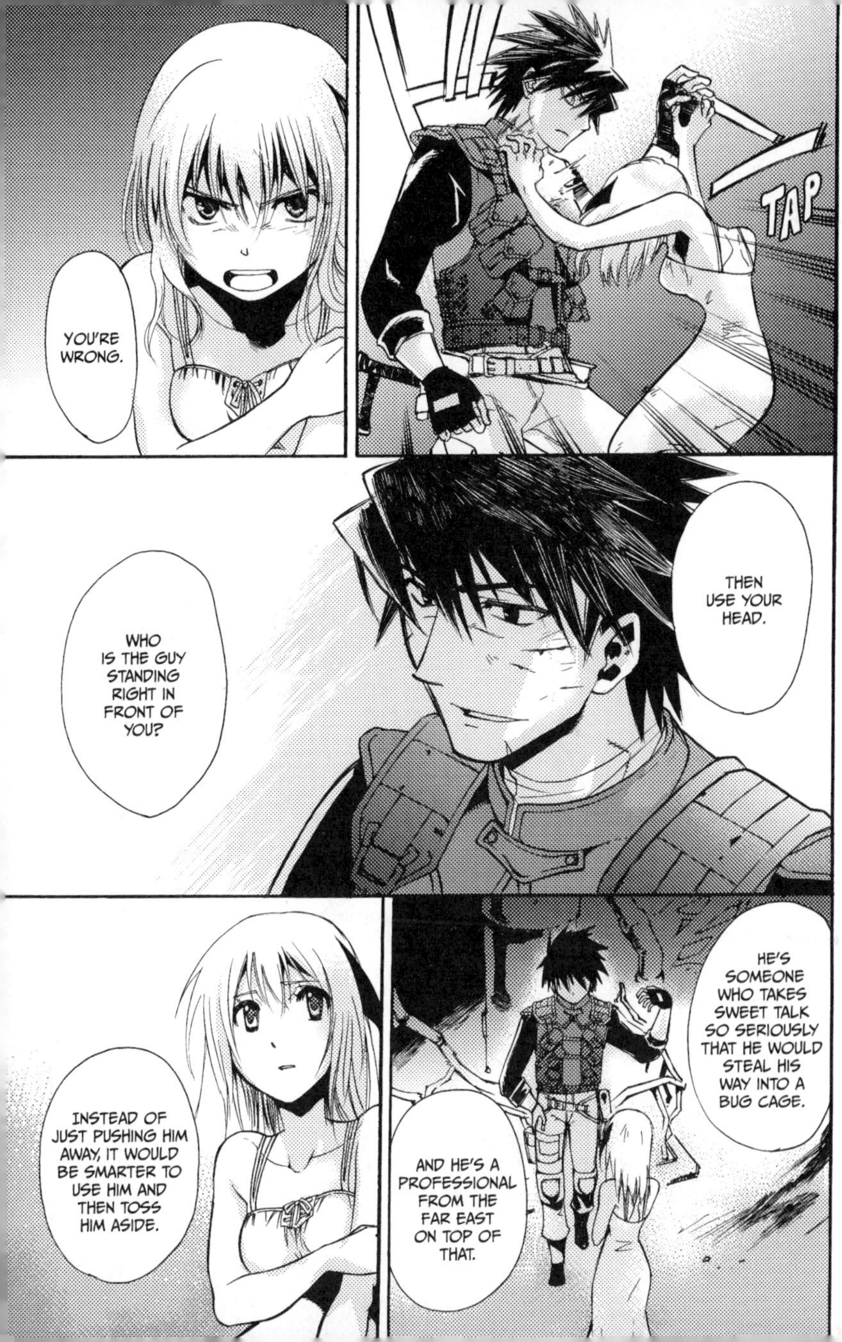
TAP
YOU'RE WRONG.
THEN USE YOUR HEAD.
WHO IS THE GUY STANDING RIGHT IN FRONT OF YOU?
HE'S SOMEONE WHO TAKES SWEET TALK SO SERIOUSLY THAT HE WOULD STEAL HIS WAY INTO A BUG CAGE.
AND HE'S A PROFESSIONAL FROM THE FAR EAST ON TOP OF THAT.
INSTEAD OF JUST PUSHING HIM AWAY, IT WOULD BE SMARTER TO USE HIM AND THEN TOSS HIM ASIDE.

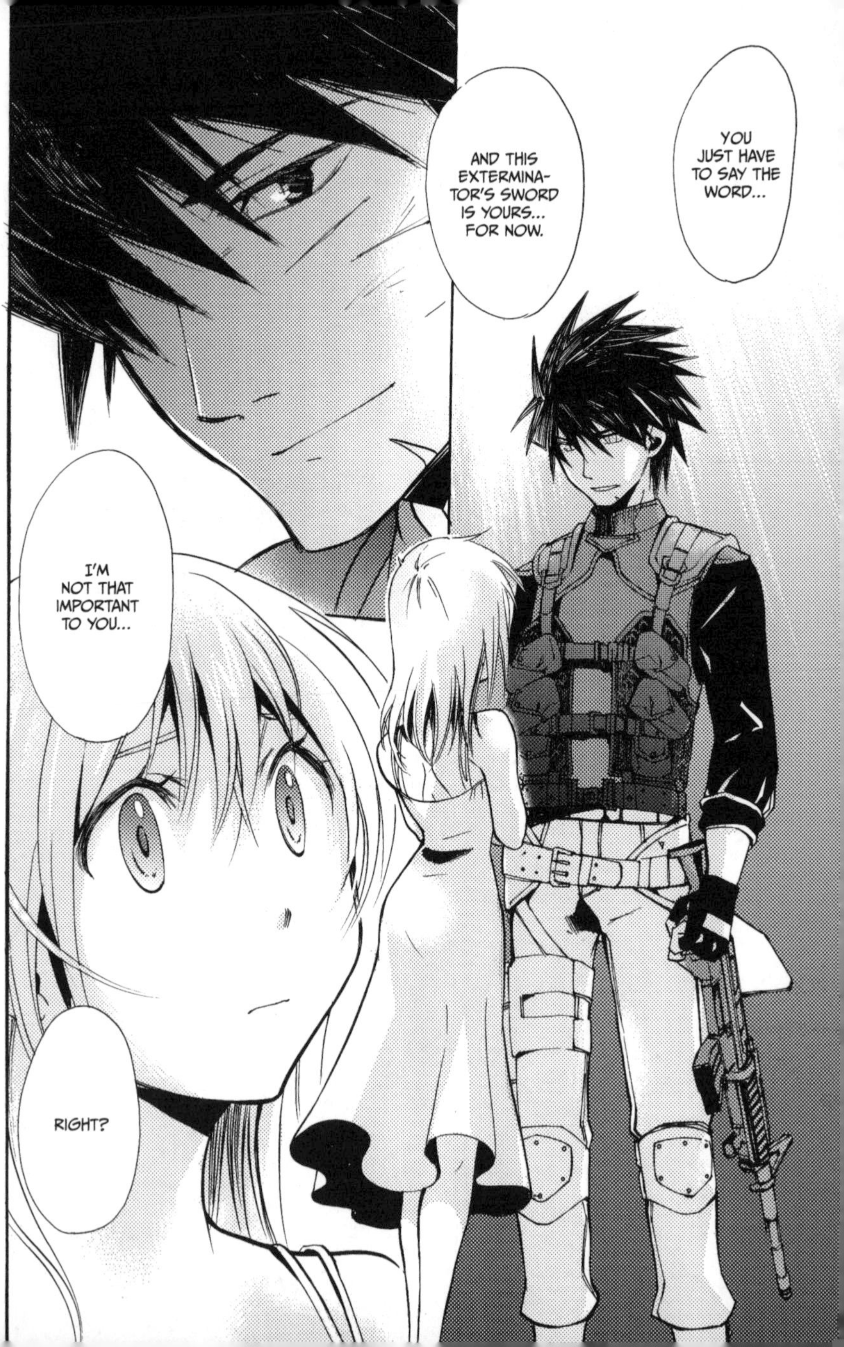
YOU JUST HAVE TO SAY THE WORD...
AND THIS EXTERMINA-TOR'S SWORD IS YOURS... FOR NOW.
I'M NOT THAT IMPORTANT TO YOU...
RIGHT?

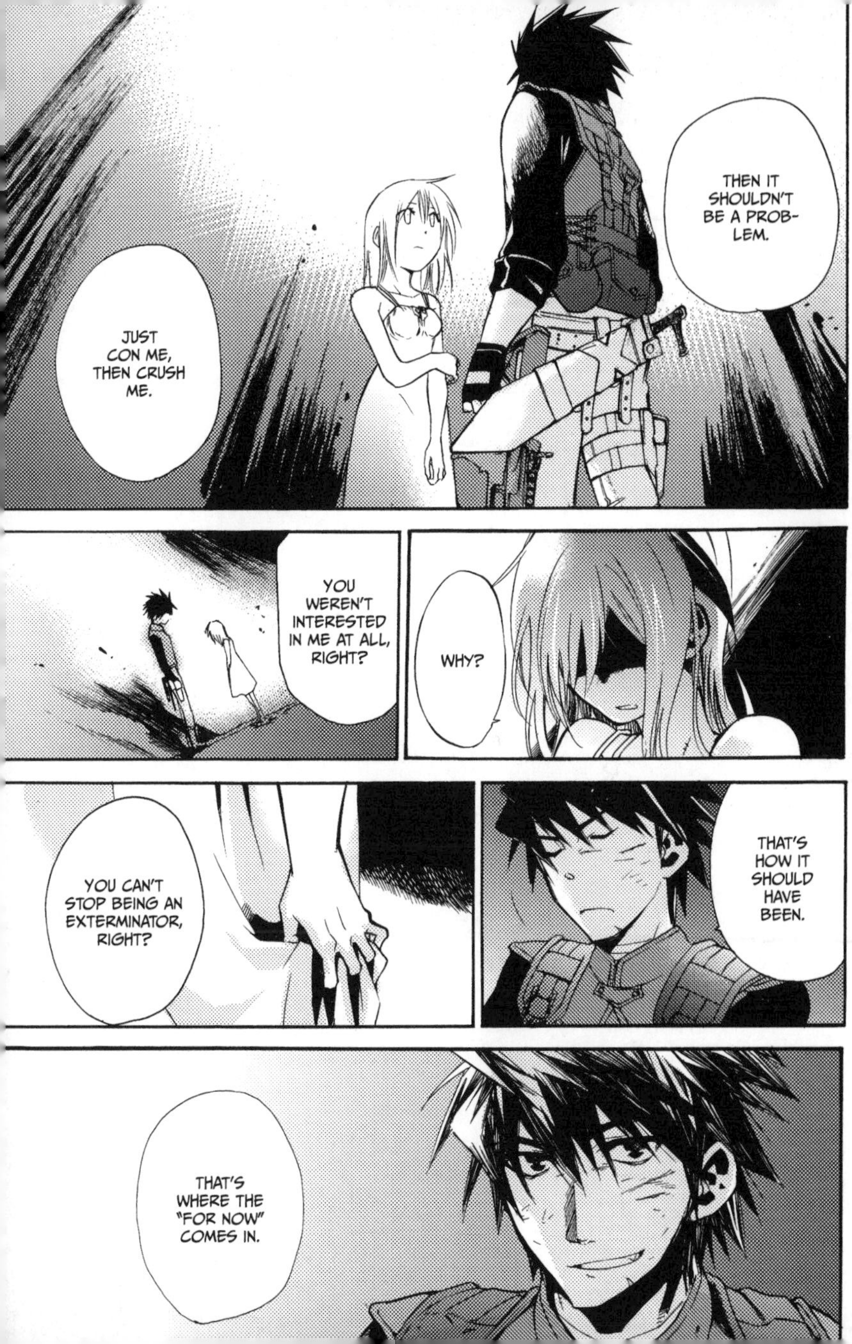
THEN IT SHOULDN'T BE A PROB-LEM.
JUST CON ME, THEN CRUSH ME.
WHY?
YOU WEREN'T INTERESTED IN ME AT ALL, RIGHT?
THAT'S HOW IT SHOULD HAVE BEEN.
YOU CAN'T STOP BEING AN EXTERMINATOR, RIGHT?
THAT'S WHERE THE "FOR NOW" COMES IN.

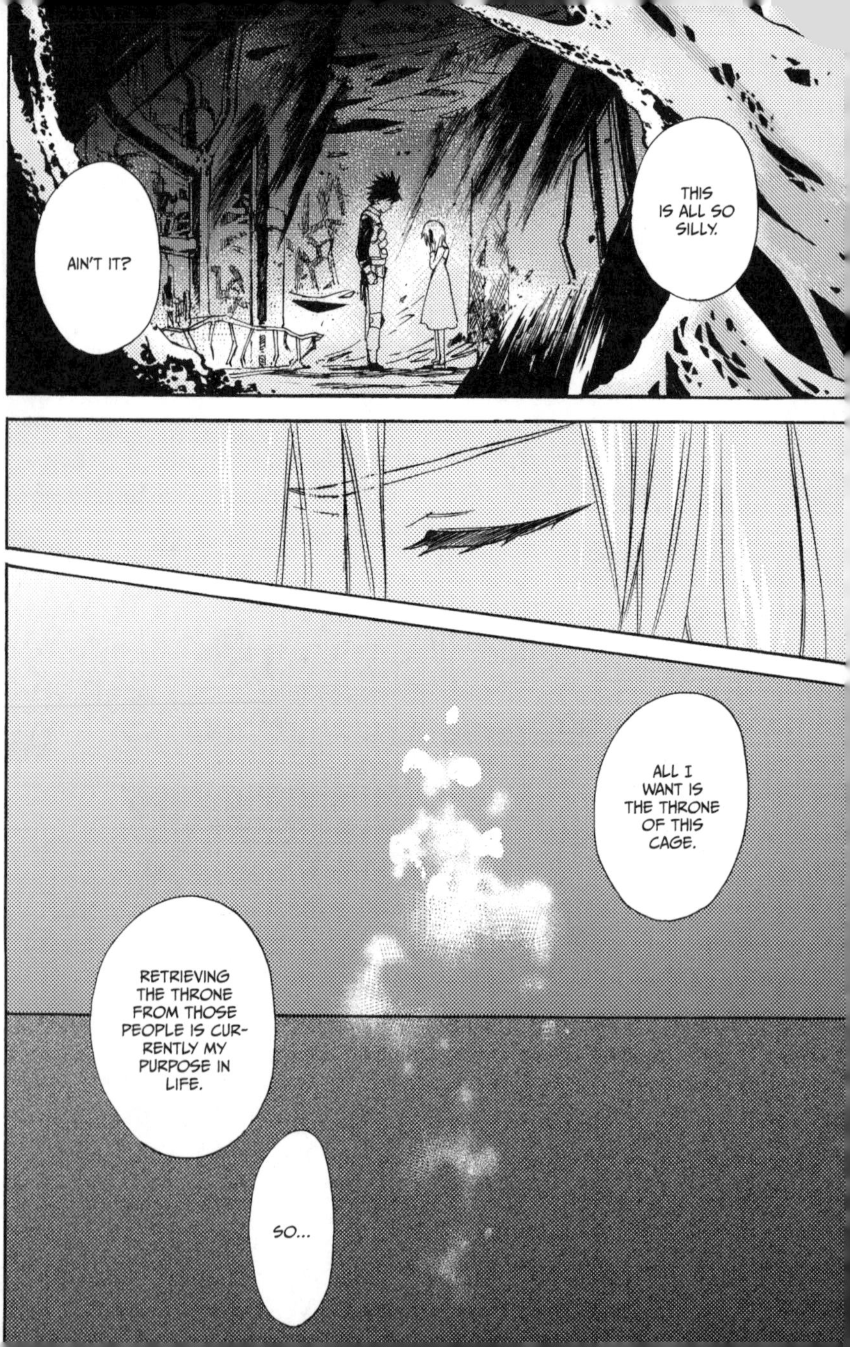
THIS IS ALL SO SILLY.
AIN'T IT?
ALL I WANT IS THE THRONE OF THIS CAGE.
RETRIEVING THE THRONE FROM THOSE PEOPLE IS CUR-RENTLY MY PURPOSE IN LIFE.
SO...

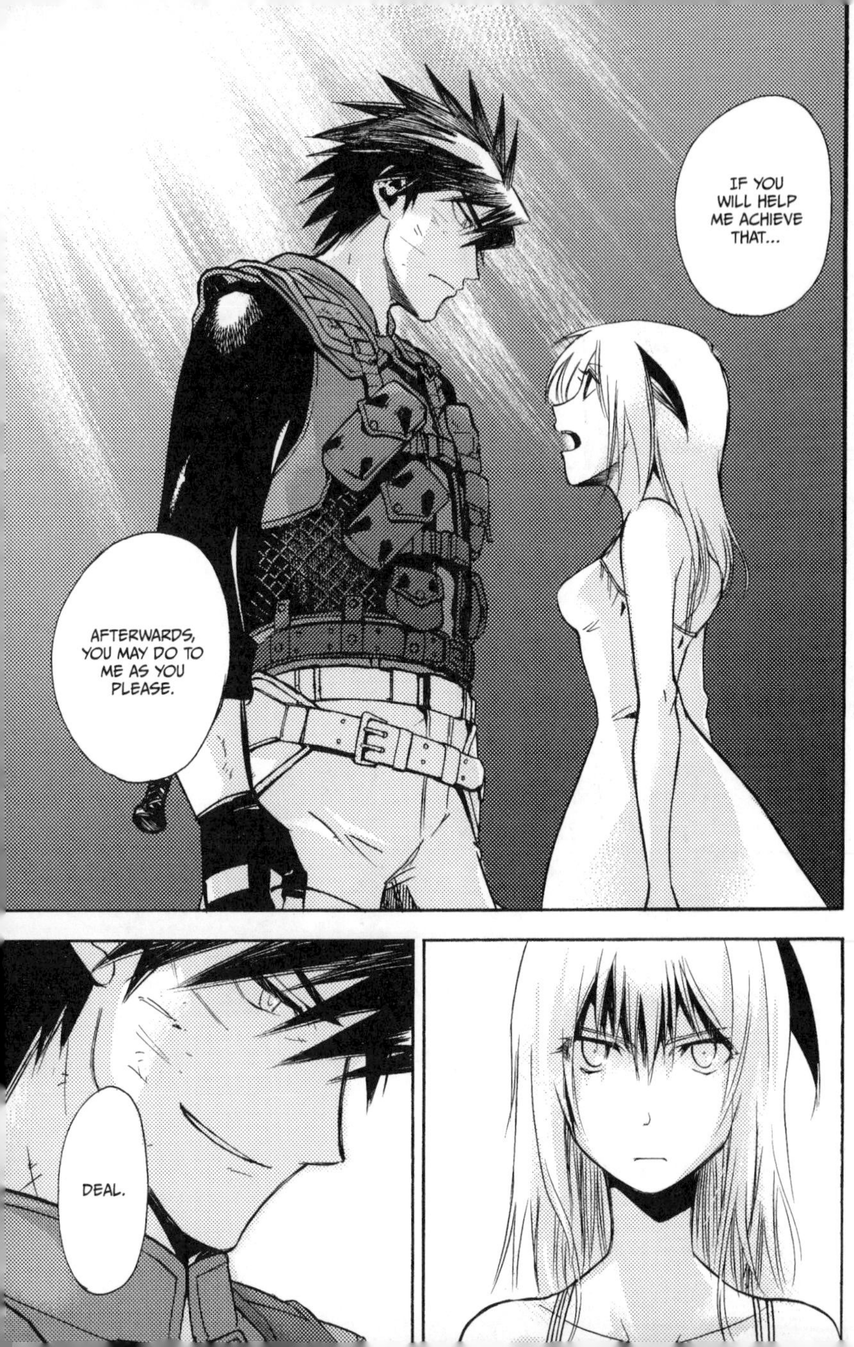
IF YOU WILL HELP ME ACHIEVE THAT...
AFTERWARDS, YOU MAY DO TO ME AS YOU PLEASE.
DEAL.

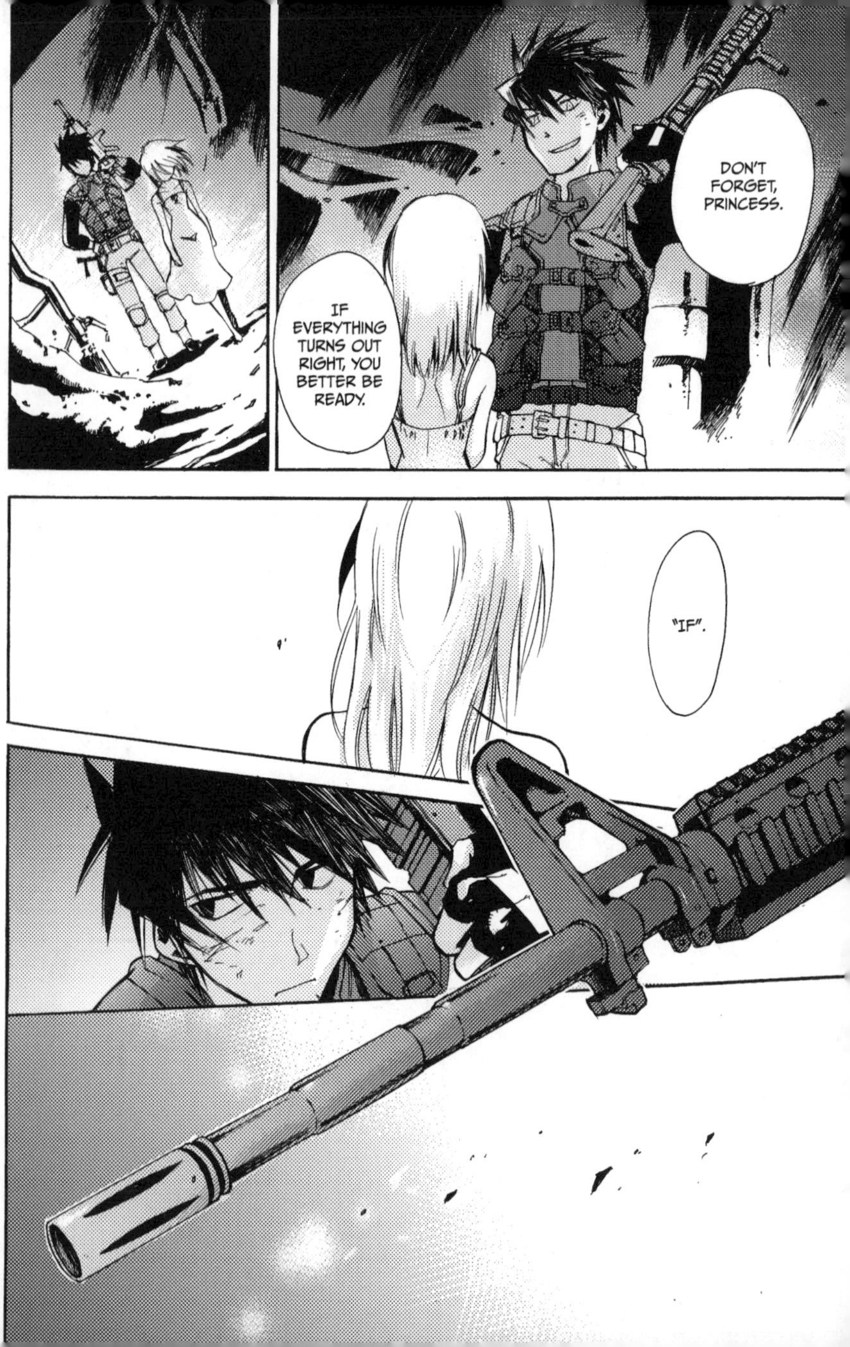
DON'T FORGET, PRINCESS.
IF EVERYTHING TURNS OUT RIGHT, YOU BETTER BE READY.
"IF".

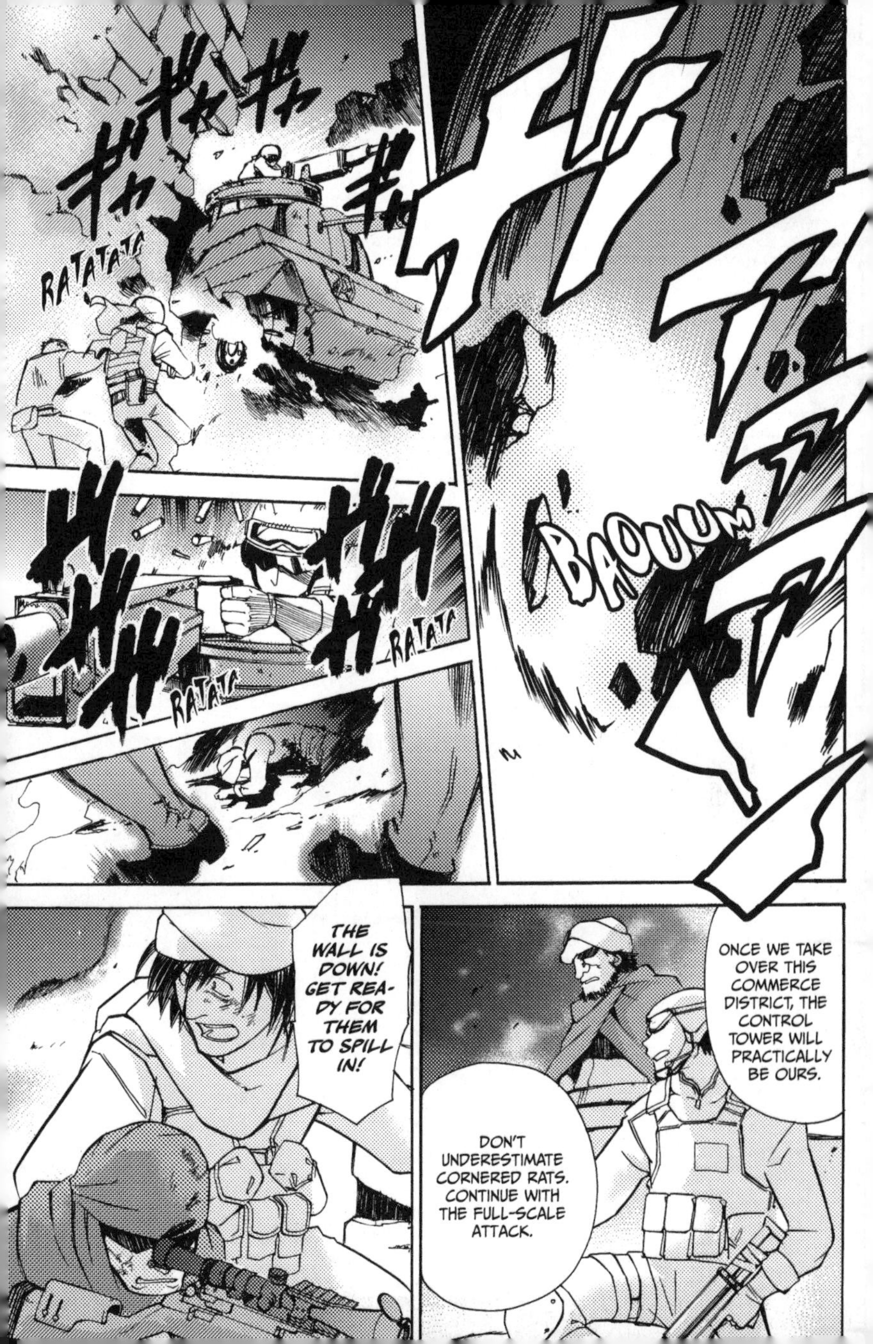

BAOUUM
RATATATA
RATATA
RATATA
ONCE WE TAKE OVER THIS COMMERCE DISTRICT, THE CONTROL TOWER WILL PRACTICALLY BE OURS.
DON'T UNDERESTIMATE CORNERED RATS. CONTINUE WITH THE FULL-SCALE ATTACK.
THE WALL IS DOWN! GET REA-DY FOR THEM TO SPILL IN!

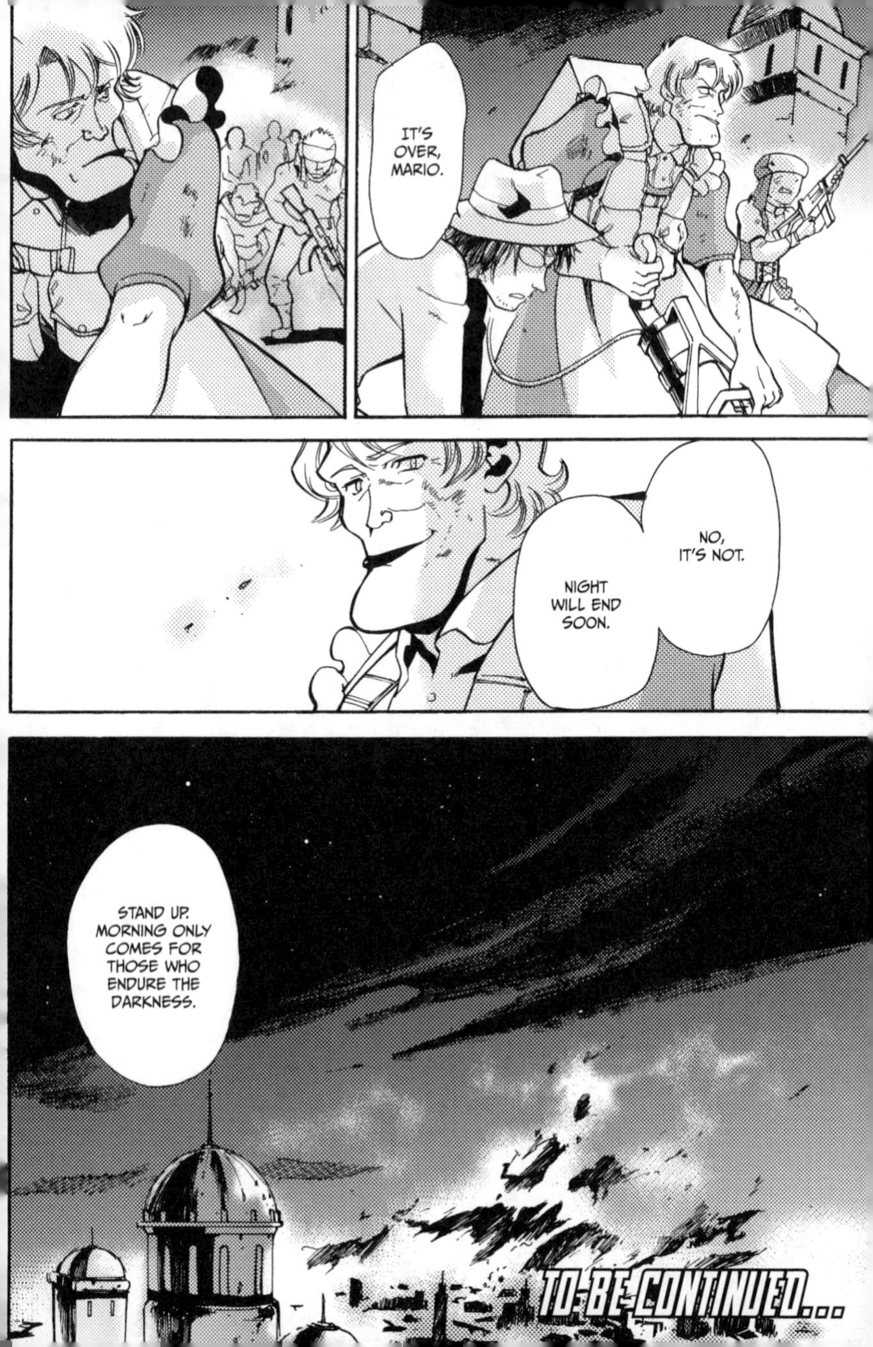
IT'S OVER, MARIO.
NO, IT'S NOT.
NIGHT WILL END SOON.
STAND UP. MORNING ONLY COMES FOR THOSE WHO ENDURE THE DARKNESS.
TO BE CONTINUED...

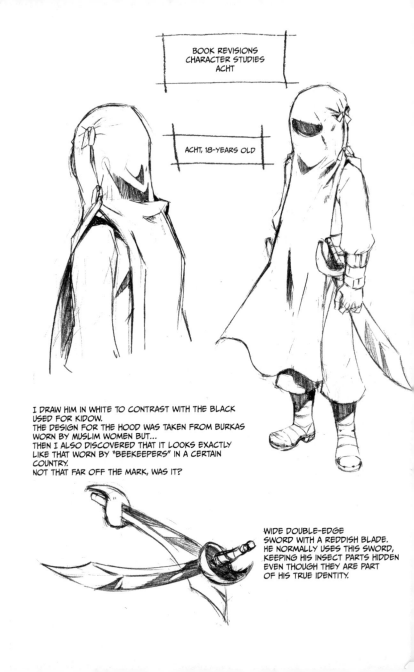

BOOK REVISIONS
CHARACTER STUDIES
ACHT

ACHT, 18-YEARS OLD

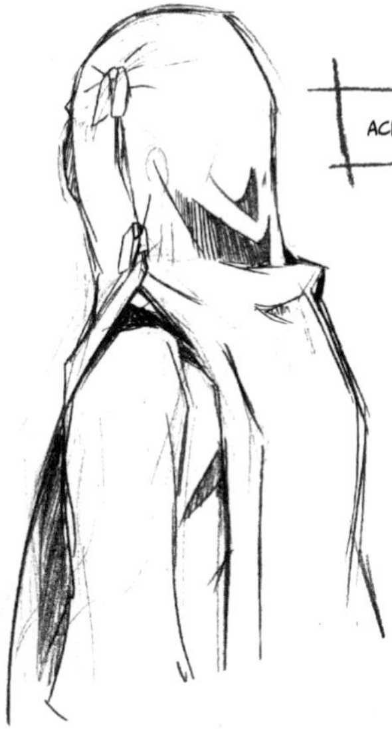

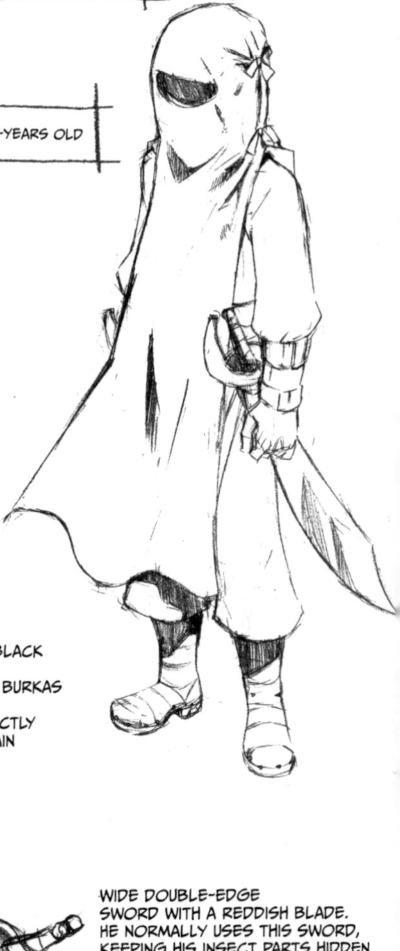

I DRAW HIM IN WHITE TO CONTRAST WITH THE BLACK USED FOR KIDOW.
THE DESIGN FOR THE HOOD WAS TAKEN FROM BURKAS WORN BY MUSLIM WOMEN BUT...
THEN I ALSO DISCOVERED THAT IT LOOKS EXACTLY LIKE THAT WORN BY "BEEKEEPERS" IN A CERTAIN COUNTRY.
NOT THAT FAR OFF THE MARK, WAS IT?

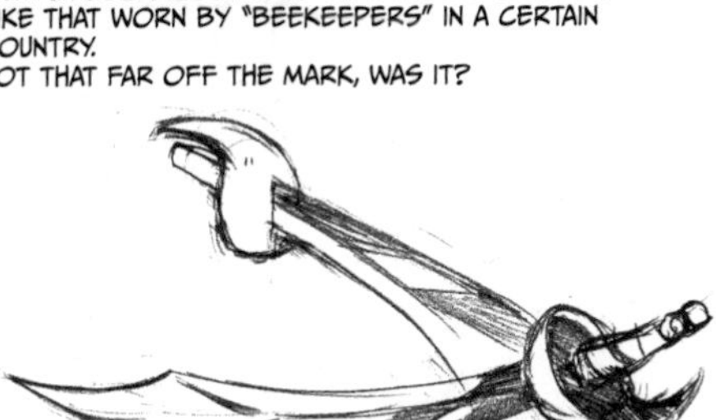

WIDE DOUBLE-EDGE SWORD WITH A REDDISH BLADE.
HE NORMALLY USES THIS SWORD, KEEPING HIS INSECT PARTS HIDDEN EVEN THOUGH THEY ARE PART OF HIS TRUE IDENTITY.

FROM EARLY ON, ACHT WAS DESIGNED
AS "KIDOW'S RIVAL".
HOWEVER, ALL I HAD DECIDED IS THAT HE
WOULD BE HALF-HUMAN, HALF-INSECT,
AND I DIDN'T EVEN KNOW WHAT HIS FACE
WOULD LOOK LIKE. THEN I DECIDED THAT
HE WOULD BE THE OFFSHOOT OF TANIA,
SO THAT MEANT ONE HALF WOULD
BE HANDSOME.

HIS HAIR IS SILVER WITH TOUCHES OF LIGHT PURPLE.
THE RIGHT EYE IS BLUE, WHILE THE LEFT ONE,
WHICH IS TURNING INTO THAT OF AN INSECT, IS RED.

SINCE I IMAGINE HIM AS A LIGHTLY-ARMED,
AGILE SOLDIER, I MADE HIM A LITTLE
SHORTER WHEN THE TIME CAME FOR
BOOK REVISIONS.

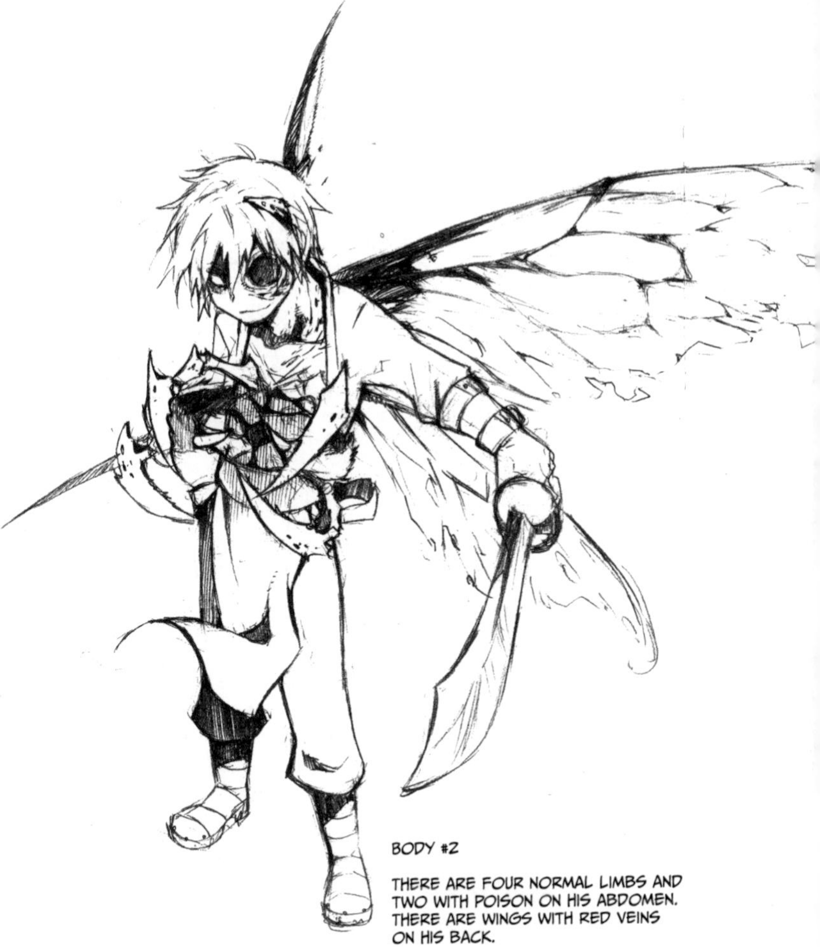

BODY #2

THERE ARE FOUR NORMAL LIMBS AND TWO WITH POISON ON HIS ABDOMEN. THERE ARE WINGS WITH RED VEINS ON HIS BACK.

HE CANNOT FLY FOR LONG PERIODS, BUT AS SHOWN AT THE BEGINNING OF CHAPTER 14, THEY ARE USEFUL FOR GETTING SOME ELEVATION.

THOUGH IT ISN'T SHOWN IN THE STORY, HE ALSO HAS HEAT SENSOR ABILITIES FOR DETECTING HUMANS.
IT LOOKS LIKE HIDING IS NO HELP FOR "FOOD".

THERE ARE SLITS WHERE THE WINGS COME OUT ON THE BACK. IF IT WASN'T THIS WAY, HE WOULD RUIN HIS CLOTHES EVERY TIME THE WINGS WERE EXPOSED. THE LAB CAME UP WITH THIS INNOVATION TO STOP WASTEFUL SPENDING.
THAT'S NICE, BUT IT IS NOT THE ONLY THING THAT IS GOING TO KEEP THESE NICE, WHITE CLOTHES FROM REUSE CONSIDERING HIS VARIOUS ACTIONS.

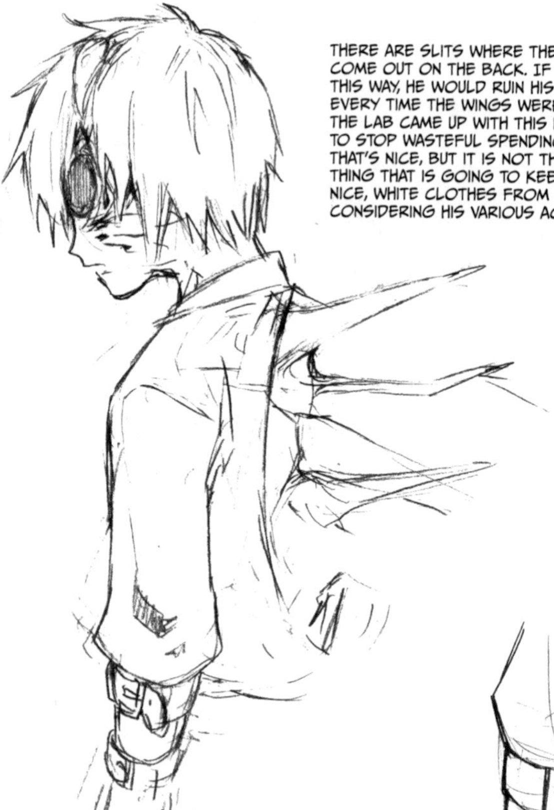

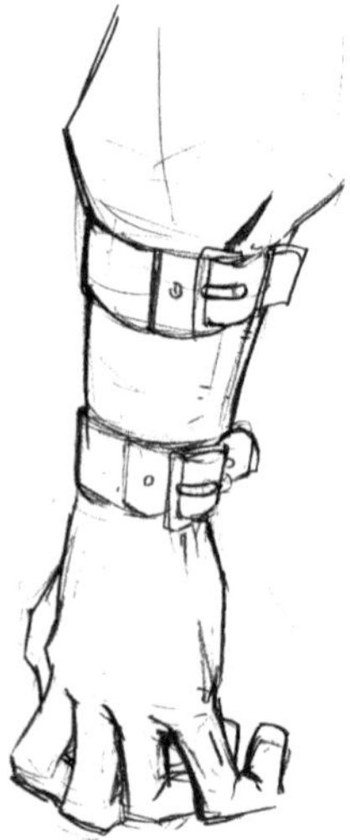

THE GLOVES ARE NOT THE ONLY PART OF HIS COSTUME THAT ARE STOCKY AND THICK IN ORDER TO HIDE THE TRUE FORM UNDERNEATH.

CAGASTER
by Kachou Hashimoto

Translation: Matthew Johnson
Lettering: Studio Makma
Editor: Rich Young
Designer: Rodolfo Muraguchi

For advertising and licensing email: info@ablazepublishing.com

---

Publisher's Cataloging-in-Publication Data
Names: Hashimoto, Kachou, author.
Title: Cagaster, Volume 4 / Kachou Hashimoto.
Series: Cagaster
Description: Portland, OR: Ablaze Publishing, 2020.
Identifiers: ISBN 978-1-950912-10-0
LCSH Mutation (Biology)–Fiction. | Cannibalism–Fiction. | Dystopias. | Fantasy fiction. | Science fiction. | Adventure and adventurers– Fiction. | Graphic novels. | BISAC COMICS & GRAPHIC NOVELS / Manga / Dystopian | COMICS & GRAPHIC NOVELS / Manga / Fantasy | COMICS & GRAPHIC NOVELS / Manga / Science Fiction
Classification: LCC PN6790.J33 .H372 v. 4 2020 | DDC 741.5–dc23

 /ablazepub  @AblazePub @AblazePub
ablazepublishing.com

To find a comics shop in your area go to:
www.comicshoplocator.com

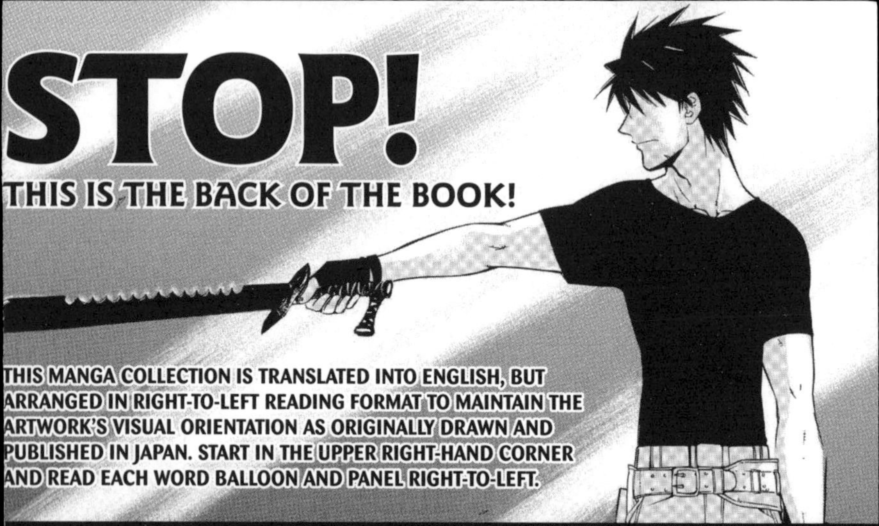

STOP!

THIS IS THE BACK OF THE BOOK!

THIS MANGA COLLECTION IS TRANSLATED INTO ENGLISH, BUT ARRANGED IN RIGHT-TO-LEFT READING FORMAT TO MAINTAIN THE ARTWORK'S VISUAL ORIENTATION AS ORIGINALLY DRAWN AND PUBLISHED IN JAPAN. START IN THE UPPER RIGHT-HAND CORNER AND READ EACH WORD BALLOON AND PANEL RIGHT-TO-LEFT.

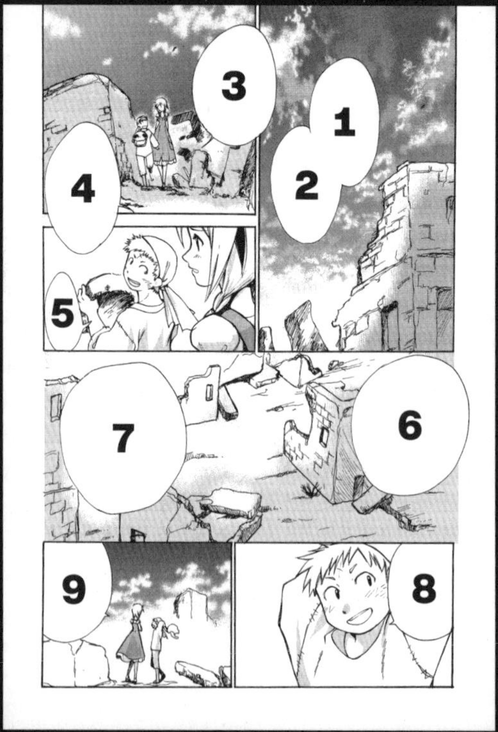
1
2
3
4
5
6
7
8
9